Finding Me, Penelope

by

J.M. Davis

The Wild Rose Press, Inc.
PO Box 708
Adams Basin, NY 14410-0708
Visit us at www.thewildrosepress.com

Publishing History
First Edition, 2024
Trade Paperback ISBN 978-1-5092-5728-7
Digital ISBN 978-1-5092-5729-4

Published in the United States of America

Dedication

To Shannon
The most deserving of a happily-ever after.

Chapter 1

"Just sign here and it's done," Mr. Douglas says, stabbing a fat finger at the paper. I stare at his hairy knuckles, the dark patches reminding me of fuzzy tarantulas. I gulp as I picture them skittering off his fingers and down to the polished mahogany desk that's splayed before me.

"Go ahead, Penelope," Mom urges from beside me. She tries to draw closer, but as she does, the legs of her chair snag on the carpet.

Mr. Douglas quickly comes to her rescue. "I told Lisa to get chairs with wheels," he grumbles, pushing in Mom's chair with a little too much force. She's pinned tightly against the desk. She winces but doesn't say anything. She just frees the long chain hanging from her neck, setting the silver heart pendant on the desktop. *He just crushed your lungs! Say something!*

Mom flashes Mr. Douglas a small smile. "Thank you."

In my head, I groan. *Not that!* What did I expect, though? Mom is being typical Mom. She won't say anything to Mr. Douglas—or Frank—as she calls him. He's a friend the family, so she's going to be respectful and keep to her usual course: being overly kind. What am I saying? It doesn't matter whether he's a friend of the family or not. Mom is nice to *everyone.*

"Of course," Mr. Douglas says. He presses a finger

1

to the bridge of his glasses, pushing them back into his face. His tiny eyes move to me. "Ready to make it official?" He reaches across me, his cheap cologne wafting heavily through the air. He picks up the pen lying lifeless before him. All of this seems to happen in slow motion, even though I know it's not. Like a movie scene where the audience is shouting, *don't do it* at the screen. He holds the pen out to me, urging me to take it. I don't.

I glance over at Mom. She is all smiles; her pretty face lit up with a happiness I wish I shared. She leans closer, her sweet perfume coming with her, contrasting with Mr. Douglas' musky odor. It invades my space, and suddenly I hate it. It used to be a comforting scent when I was younger. But things have changed. Now the sickening sweet smell turns my stomach. I turn back to the paperwork in front of me. With one simple stroke of the pen, I will officially be Penelope Jackson.

"Honey?" Mom touches my arm. "Are you okay?"

I don't answer her because I can't. The words are stuck in my throat. *Am I okay?* Judging by my dry mouth and trembling hands, I'd say no. A stab of betrayal stings in my heart. *You want me to give up the only thing I have left?*

I glare down at the paperwork. The typed words on the page, all legal jargon and formality, swim before my eyes. If I sign it, my last name will change forever. Erasing Penelope Reza. Erasing who I was—who I *still* am. Eight years ago I would have scribbled my signature with a crayon and never looked back. But I was just a little kid then. A kid thrilled to have finally found a foster family who wanted me.

What did I know back then? *Nothing,* I think with a

frown. Recalling my past, I clearly remembered being eight years old, and craving a sitcom-type family. Parents who spat out pearls of wisdom as easily and as often as they hurled funny one-liners. A couple of siblings to play with, and at times, fight with, cause that's what I saw them do on TV. And a dog to tie everything together in a pretty package. The perfect family unit.

The temperature in the room warms to an unbearable degree. I feel stifled. Mom is too close. Mr. Douglas is too close. I sink into my palms, trying to gather my thoughts. *Come on, Penelope. Get yourself together.* I clamp my eyes tight. The maddening tick from the clock on the wall is too loud. The pounding from my heart is too loud.

I have to get out of here. I lurch to my feet, surprising Mom with a gasp. I don't apologize, though the tug at my heart tells me to. I grab my phone off the desk and slip it into my pocket. Mr. Douglas takes a startled step back, his eyes wide from behind his wire-rimmed glasses.

"I need air," I manage as I shove the chair away. Stumbling over weighted feet, I somehow make it to the door and yank it open. *I need to be alone.* I nearly scoff at the absurdity of the idea. *Since when do you want to be alone?* the snarky voice within my head whispers. I shake my head to rid the voice and I nearly run out of Mr. Douglas' office, not caring how I look as I speed past his secretary. She whirls around in her chair, watching me with a "*what the hell?*" look on her face as I burst out of the double glass doors of the law firm.

I spill out into the parking lot, dragging in deep breaths of the fresh, autumn-crisp air. *The voice is right. When have I ever wanted to be alone?* I sink down to the asphalt and wrap my arms around my knees, drawing myself into a tight ball. I lay my forehead against my wrists. *You knew this day was coming,* I scold myself. *Hell, at one time you were even excited for it.* With a clenched chest, I recall the day Mom made the appointment with Mr. Douglas.

I bounced on the balls of my feet, anxious as she spoke on the phone. I could only hear her side of the conversation, but I connected the dots easily. October seventh. Four o'clock. *That's the day my life will change.* Mom thanked the person on the other end and hung up. "Well. That's that. We sign the documents in one month."

I clasped my hands together and gave a squeal. *Finally!* I had been waiting for this since I was nine years old. Mom dropped her phone in her purse and opened her arms wide, inviting me to a celebratory hug. I step into her embrace and rest my head on her shoulder. Though we are the same height now, I still find comfort in her arms. She squeezed me and touched a hand to the back of my head. "Penelope Jackson. Has a nice ring to it, don't you think?"

I murmured an affirmation and inhaled her rosy perfume. We stayed that way for a long while. It felt good to be hugged. To be wanted. Mom broke the embrace first, leaning back to look me in the eye. "It's been a long time coming, but we finally did it." Her lips threatened a tremble, but she pursed them into a smile instead.

The memory eats at me. How could things change so quickly? Just one month ago, I was walking on cloud nine, ready to forget my old life. Ready to change my name to match Mom's. I don't notice I'm crying until my wet lashes sweep across my skin. I lift my head and wipe my eyes, blankly staring out at the parking lot in front of me. A few parked cars are sprinkled here and there, but other than that, I see no one. *What the hell happened? Why am I hesitating?* I frown at myself. *Jenna. She's the reason I'm hesitating. The reason I'm overthinking all of this.*

I pull the sleeve of my Reedmont High hoodie over my fingers and furiously scrub my face. I hate her for making me think. For making me question the idea of legally changing my last name. I think of Jenna with her sleek auburn hair and apple-like cheeks. I almost smile when I think of her impish laugh and weird obsession with narwhals. Of course, I don't really hate her. Jenna's been my best friend for the past three years. We've been inseparable ever since I started at Reedmont High. I just hate her for dredging up things I wish to forget. For stirring up long-forgotten feelings and resentment. For making me want to remain Penelope Reza.

"Pen?" Mom says softly. I didn't hear her walk up. I smooth my long hair over my face, trying to shield myself from her penetrating gaze. I feel her eyes boring into me, questioning why I'm not over the moon with happiness right now. Why we're not out celebrating like we had planned, each with our own thick slices of delicious cheesecake oozing with cherry topping.

Cheesecake is our go-to celebratory meal. From birthdays to straight-A report cards, Mom and I always enjoy the high-calorie wedge of goodness with zero regrets. I stare at her grey ankle boots, her long, flowy skirt skimming the toes as she moves. Right now, I'd rather down an entire fish bowl, fish and all, then eat a slice of *celebratory* cheesecake.

"Pen?" she tries again. "What's wrong?"

"Nothing." I shift, putting my back to her. My ass is starting to go numb from sitting on the cold pavement for so long, but I remain planted. "I just…"

"Just what?" Her hand touches my shoulder. "Tell me."

My phone beeps with a new text message. I take it from my pocket and glimpse the screen. *Jenna.* Her message is one word. —*Done?*—

I quickly punch out a response. —*No.*— Then I add a sad emoji and press SEND. I wait for her to text back.

"Penelope?" Mom says. Oops. I forgot about her.

"Just a second, Mom. Jenna's texting me."

Mom huffs, but says nothing. I didn't expect her to. Mom never fusses at me. Or anyone, for that matter.

—*What happened?*— Jenna asks.

My cheeks burn as a sliver of anger tears through me. *Seriously? You should know.*

As if on cue, my screen lights up with another message.

—*Was it me?*—

I roll my eyes. *Duh.* My fingers hover over the phone keys. I decide to send her an emoji to match how I feel. *Where is that stupid eye-rolling emoji?* I rarely ever use that one. My favorite emojis are the heart-eyed kitten, the blushing face, and the thumbs-up. I find the eye-rolling emoji and tap the tiny yellow face, hitting SEND with satisfaction.

Jenna texts right back. —*Don't be mad at me. I just want you to be sure about this. It's a big step.*—

I glance over my shoulder at Mom. She's pretending to busy herself with fixing her bun, sweeping the fading blonde strands back from her face. Her face is still pretty after all the years of stress she's endured. Her phone rings and she drops what she's doing to answer it. Her smile is genuine when she greets, "Trip. Hi."

What does he want? I arch my brow, listening.

Mom stutters something. I climb to my feet, ready to rip the phone from her hand if need be. Her eyes meet mine, and she takes a step back, putting distance between us, but I can still hear Trip cussing at her from the other end of the line.

"Just hang up on him," I demand. She doesn't-of course. She just stands there, taking whatever punishment he's dealing out. "Mom," I say again. "Hang up on him or I will." I advance on her, grabbing for her phone. Like a graceful ballerina, she spins away, just out of reach.

"Well, Trip. I'm sorry," she says. "I didn't read the label. I didn't realize it was dry-cleaner only. I'll buy you a new shirt, all right?"

I put my hands on my hips, watching Mom's cheeks blush as she tries to put out yet another fire. A blazing, blow-hard, chauvinistic fire named Trip Jackson.

Looking down at my cellphone, Jenna's last message almost screams at me. —*It's a big step.*— I sigh and stare at her words. A big step. *Jenna's right. Changing my name is a big step.* I lift my face just in time to see Mom hang up, catching the slight shake in her hands. My stomach twists.

But is it the step in the right direction?

Chapter 2

"What was that all about?" I ask her. My hand fists my phone, as it normally does whenever she explains Trip's behavior.

She waves me off. "Oh. I accidentally ruined one of his shirts. I...I should have read the tag before I washed it." She tucks her phone back into her purse.

"Or. He can get off his lazy ass and wash his own clothes." My neck flushes hot. Trip has a way of doing that. He's biologically Mom's child, whereas I am not...and he likes to remind me of that fact nearly every day. Trip moved out last year (thank God) but he's constantly coming to the house. Raiding our refrigerator and dropping off dirty laundry for Mom to either wash or mend. Mom happily coddles him. I can't stand it, but I can't stop her.

"Penelope," Mom scolds. "Language."

I lower my gaze. "Sorry."

"Now. What's going on with you?" she asks gently. "I thought you wanted this?"

I pull my sleeves over my fingers and cross my arms. "I did."

"Did?" She sounds surprised.

Our eyes meet, and my heart sinks. Her brows are scrunched up tight, and her face has gone pale.

"Do," I correct. "I do." I grow frustrated with myself, heaving a sigh as I roll my eyes up at the sky. "I think."

Mom crosses the space between us. A plane flies overhead, its engine thundering in my ears. For a moment I wish I were on it, heading to anyplace but here. Mom waits until it passes before saying, "Penelope." Her touch is light on my elbow. "We don't have to do this today. We can wait. It looks like you need more time to think it over."

I don't respond.

"Come on. Let's go talk to Frank. Maybe he'll let us take the paperwork home." She gives me a gentle pull. "You can sign it with the uni-pen," she says in a sing-song voice. She gives me a wink.

I try to offer her a smile, but it comes across strained. The uni-pen she's referring to is a sparkly white pen that stays in a glass jar in the kitchen. We use it to jot down phone messages and grocery lists. It writes in electric pink ink and has a unicorn with a flowing mane as a cap. It's silly, but it was worth every penny each time I see Mom use it.

Mom is a bit of stiff, really. I love her dearly, but her sense of humor stinks. She spends most of her time with her nose in a book or working extra shifts at the hospital. She's a medical biller, so I guess processing health insurance all day zaps your funny bone.

Mom squeezes my arm and together, we go back inside to find Mr. Douglas. He's standing at the front desk, chatting with his secretary. She takes a folder from him, and stores it away. When he notices us, he sweeps his gaze across us, his brows pinched tight.

"Everything okay?" He adjusts his necktie, smoothing it over his protruding belly. The buttons on his starched shirt strain so hard I fear one might break loose at any moment, fly across the room, and poke my eye out.

"Yes," Mom says, "Sorry to keep you waiting." Her eyes flick to me. "Penelope just needs a little more time, if that's all right."

Mr. Douglas eyes me. "You having second thoughts? I thought you were ready to be a Jackson."

I hug myself tighter, wishing to wall myself away from him and his condescending tone.

Mom pats my arm. "She just needs to sleep on it, that's all."

Mr. Douglas grunts. "Jackson is a fine name. Wesley made sure of that. You should be proud to take it as your own."

I dig my nails into my skin. Mr. Douglas knew my adoptive father as a business associate only. He doesn't know what he was like outside of the office. Outside of the handshakes and scribbled signatures. Wesley didn't want me. Trip certainly didn't want me either.

Miranda Jackson was the only one who wanted little Penelope Reza. And even then, she had a hard time showing it because of Wesley. Wesley only agreed to the adoption to make Mom happy. I was like a porcelain doll to be given. A porcelain doll to be seen. And not heard.

Mr. Douglas' eyes probe me, as if trying to see my thoughts. He must think I'm crazy to not snap up the chance to be a Jackson. Or stupid. Or maybe both. Mom only considers Mr. Douglas a family friend because of how long he and Wesley had done business together. He personally handled all the fine print for the homes Wesley purchased and flipped. His law firm also finalized my adoption and…executed Wesley's will.

Mr. Douglas scoops up some loose paperwork and

tucks it under his arm. "Lisa." He turns to his secretary. "Make up an envelope for them to take with them." She stands, adjusting her black pencil skirt before she scurries off. He faces us again, addressing Mom more than me. "Once you've signed it, drop it off here and I'll submit it." He starts to walk away, then thinks better of it. He's not done. *Great.*

"Think long and hard about this, Penelope. You have an opportunity to rid yourself of the name Reza. You may not see it now, but one day, you'll be glad you did." He gives a curt nod and leaves, his shiny oxfords swiftly sweeping him out of the room and down the corridor on the left.

I drop my arms, whirling on my mother. "What does that mean?" I hold her in a hard stare, willing her to speak. She opens her mouth and just when I think she might actually say something, she clamps her chin, stealing away whatever is on the tip of her tongue. "Mom!" My fists ball. "What is he talking about? Tell me!"

Lisa, the secretary, floats back into the room. "Here we are," she says cheerily, clearly oblivious to the tension between me and Mom. "Everything is in here." She presses the large envelope into my mother's hand. "Give me a call if you have any questions."

"I will, thanks."

Lisa smiles, then returns to her desk.

Mom tries to pretend everything is normal and takes my sleeve to leave, but I pull away. *Oh, no you don't. Not this time.* I stomp ahead of her, angry all over again. The same damn question pops back into my mind. *What happened? Today was supposed to be a good day. A happy day.* I shove the office doors open and I make my way to Mom's white sedan.

Mom unlocks the car before I reach it, so I yank the passenger door open and sink inside. I slam the door shut. *Once she's trapped in here with me, she will have to talk. Nowhere to run, Mom...sorry.* Mom gets in a second later. She doesn't put her seat belt on. She just sits. Staring ahead, she stays quiet for a long time. I grow impatient.

"Well?"

"Frank didn't mean anything by that." She sets her hands on the steering wheel. She clamps them firmly as if needing support.

Bullshit. I know what he meant. I just want to hear her say it out loud.

"He is just looking out for you." She finally looks at me. Her brown eyes are strangely misty. "There's nothing wrong with that, is there?"

Aw hell. She's going to cry. "No," I find myself saying. "I appreciate that, but..." *Don't back down. Don't let a few tears stop you.* I steel myself, not ready to surrender just yet. "But it's my life we're talking about. It's my name, so it's my choice."

"I thought you wanted to change your name." She blinks back tears. "What changed?"

I sigh and turn to look out the window. I lean my forehead on the cool glass, letting it soothe my flushed skin. "I don't know," I whisper. "I just...don't think I'm ready to lose the one thing that's really mine."

My name is all I have. It's all I had going into foster care all those years ago, and it's all I had leaving it. I let out a long breath, watching it fog up the window glass. I lift my finger and begin drawing swirls in it.

"I understand," Mom says, her tone choked up with

emotion. "Really, I do."

My finger stops mid-swirl, and I snap my head to glare at Mom. "Then why did you let Mr. Douglas drag my name through the dirt like that? I know what he meant by that little comment, by the way. I'm not an idiot." I let out a harsh laugh. "He thinks I'd be better off without an *Arabian* last name. Like Jackson is the holy grail of surnames and the cure for God-damn cancer, or something."

"Penelope," she says quietly. I'm burning her ears today with my colorful language. Mom hates swearing. The worst I've ever heard her say is "Oh foot," and "son of a birch tree." To be fair, this is probably the most back-talk I've ever given her. We generally get along well.

Our personalities are so similar, we rarely find reasons to argue. Mom is soft-spoken and I'm pretty shy myself. At school, I have a few close friends, but I'm far from being popular. I prefer it that way, actually. I like to fly under the radar. The less eyes upon you, the less chances to make a fool of yourself.

When Mom isn't working or reading, she's busy running errands for the Bowers, our next-door neighbors. They're an elderly couple who no longer can drive at night. If something comes up, and they need a lift after dusk, Mom volunteers to drive them wherever they need to go. The grocery store, the pharmacy, their bingo game each Friday night at Gigi's Bingo Shack.

Of course, Mom is also busy washing Trip's clothes, making extra meals and freezing them for Trip, picking up Trip's suits at the dry cleaners, and mailing packages for Trip. *What does Trip do on his own,* I wonder? *Oh right. I remember .Work, gamble online, and boss Mom around.*

I apologize to her. I shouldn't treat her this way. She doesn't deserve it. I'm just completely turned upside down right now. Being adopted by the Jacksons was a dream come true. After being in foster care for four years and being shuttled between three different families in that time frame really took a toll on me. I felt worthless. Like an old doll being handed down from generation to generation, growing weary and ragged with each handoff.

When the Jacksons came into my life, I thought I'd won the lottery. Miranda, Wesley, and their eleven-year-old son, Trip, welcomed me into their home with kind, open arms. Well, Miranda did anyway. Wesley was successful in real estate, flipping old houses and selling them for double what he paid. Miranda was a stay-at-home mom back then. She made delicious southern style dinners and fawned over her young son.

She once told me that the reason she and Wesley adopted me was because she needed another person to love. That she had so much love in her heart, she needed to share it before it burst. I smiled when she told me that. I remember my first Christmas in the Jackson home. Wesley had dragged in a huge artificial tree. He set it up in the living room, right in front of the window so everyone in the neighborhood could see.

We listened to Christmas music and sipped hot chocolate while we decorated. Trip and I hung shiny ornaments while Mom strung blinking white lights. When we were through, Wesley topped the tree with a huge golden star. The night was magical. I don't remember what I got that year because the gifts didn't matter. I had all that I needed. A family.

Mom suddenly starts the engine. "Let's get home. I have dinner waiting in the crock pot." She backs out of the parking spot and points the car toward home. I pull the seat belt over me and click it into place. I'm exhausted. I settle back into the seat, and stare unseeing out the window.

I was supposed to walk away from Penelope Reza today. But surprisingly, I didn't do that. I kept a grip on that girl, and I didn't back down. I didn't let Mr. Douglas sway me and didn't allow Mom to influence me. *I* decided what was best for *me*. Something inside me flickers. It's an emotion I've never felt before. *Is it pride?* Whatever it is, it feels good. Unfortunately, the feeling is fleeting.

Chapter 3

Last night's sleep was just awful. After tossing and turning most of it, I decide to just give up and get ready for school. I slip into a pair of jeans and pull a soft grey sweater over my head. I drag myself to the bathroom to splash water on my face. I peer into the mirror. I look terrible. Dark circles rim my eyes. My lips are dry and cracking. *No way am I walking into school looking like this. I look like a zombie.* I shake out my hair. *A zombie with bedhead.*

My morning routine is pretty simple. I brush my teeth. I smooth on some chap stick and swipe a little mascara on my lashes. Done. As for my hair, well, that's another story. Thanks to the Arabian heritage on my biological father's side, my hair is super-thick and has to be handled like a wild animal. It needs taming, or it will curl and frizz out of control. Each morning I slather on conditioners and other products and then blast them with a diffuser. This leaves my hair in pretty waves and has become my signature style.

I walk into school and head straight for the cafeteria. Jenna waits for me there each morning. While I snack on bagels or pop-tarts from home, Jenna eats breakfast at school for some reason. Cafeteria lunch is bad enough. Why would you willingly eat two meals here?

When I push through the cafeteria doors, the smell of grease slams into me and I'm suddenly relieved to have the protein bar in my book bag. I'd much rather eat it than the mystery meal being served this morning. A quick survey of the room gives me an estimate of time. With just a few kids grabbing trays and heading for the food line, it must mean the breakfast bar is close to shutting down. Breakfast at Reedmont ends at eight-fifteen on the dot. Most of the kids are already seated, eating what looks like razor-thin flapjacks.

I find Jenna easily. She's at our usual table. She has a plate of the flatter than flat pancakes in front of her. She's talking in her usual animated way to Carlos Rivera, a mutual friend of ours who seems to favor Jenna over me. Secretly, I think he has a thing for her, but so far, he hasn't admitted to it. Carlos is sitting *on* the table, rather than at it. His feet are planted on the chair to Jenna's right, his sneakers a flash of bright white.

Carlos takes pride in his shoes. He can be found constantly fussing over them, polishing them on the school bus, spit-shining them between classes. He's quick to snap at anyone who dares to get too close, for fear of being accidentally stepped on. A scuff will ruin his entire week. Today, Jenna is wearing dark blue skinny jeans and a plaid button-up shirt. Her coppery hair is pulled into a sleek ponytail. She forks a piece of pancake and stuffs it into her mouth, laughing at something Carlos said. Her eye catches me, and she waves. Carlos notices and acknowledges me with a nod.

I take a seat next to Jenna. "Hey."

"Hey," she says back. "Want some?" She offers me her plate. The pancakes are smothered with clumps of butter and so much syrup my sweet tooth starts to ache.

"No, thanks."

"How did things go yesterday?" She sets her fork

down.

I shrug, not sure where to begin.

"Well? Did you sign it?" Carlos prods.

Jenna waits expectedly, her knee bouncing beneath the table. Carlos takes a long swig from his milk carton. He wipes his face with the back of his hand when he's through.

I look at my clasped hands in my lap. "No," I whisper to them.

"What? You didn't sign it?" Carlos says. "Why not?" I look up at him, his eyes wide with questions. Carlos has big brown eyes naturally, but when he's surprised, they nearly bug out of his head.

"I just didn't, okay?" I take a section of my hair and twirl it through my fingers, a nervous habit I can't seem to break.

Jenna pushes away her plate of unfinished pancakes. She's quiet for a moment, probably deciding how she should approach this. After all, she is the one who started all of this. If it wasn't for her, I'd be a Jackson right now. And things wouldn't be as complicated as they are.

"Are you upset that you didn't?" She says it slowly, as if unsure she should ask.

"No. Yes. A little." I wrap the hair tight around my index finger, allowing the discomfort to ground me before my head starts to swim again. I haven't had a clear head in two days. Not since Jenna asked me that one life-changing question. I close my eyes for a beat, remembering our phone conversation.

"I am so excited for tomorrow," I say to Jenna, tossing myself backward onto my bed. I stare up at the ceiling, my heart giddy within my chest. "Finally, things will be as they should be." Jenna is silent. I don't notice

at first because I'm talking enough for the both of us. "Mom and I plan on hitting up Ragamuffins for cheesecake and chocolate shakes afterward. You should meet us there."

Nothing.

"Or not," I say. What's her problem? I roll onto my stomach, drawing my favorite down-pillow underneath my chin. "Hello? Earth to Jenna."

Her voice is small, but she answers, "I'm here."

"So? You wanna meet up tomorrow? I can call you when we leave the law firm."

"Are you sure you want to do this, Pen?"

The excitement within me fades. "What do you mean?"

"Are you sure you want to change your name? It's so final, you know what I mean? Do you really want to erase who you are?"

"It won't erase who I am," I counter sharply. "Changing my name will give me a fresh start. I want my name to match my family."

"But Reza is a part of who you are, Penelope. Are you ready to let that part go?"

I open my mouth to tell her yes, but nothing comes out. Am I? I thought I was. I mean, it's not like I have fond memories of my parents or anything. I've never met my biological father and I don't remember my biological mother at all. She abandoned me when I was eleven months old. Just gave me to her sister, like I was nothing more than a hand-me-down jacket.

I lived with Auntie Lola until she died in a car accident. I was only four. With no next of kin, I was placed in the care of the child protection services of Charlotte. From the stories I've heard, my parent's relationship went something like this. Boy with a work visa from Egypt meets girl. Girl falls for boy. Boy doesn't fall for girl but needs a warm body while he's here. Girl gets knocked up. Boy's visa suddenly "expires," and he hightails it back to Egypt. Girl never sees boy again. Stuff of romance novels, right?

From what I've heard, my biological mother couldn't stand looking at me. With my thick dark hair and olive skin tone, I was a daily reminder of the love she lost. Auntie Lola cared for me well enough. My memories of her are hazy, but I remember her as being kind.

"Listen," Jenna continues. "I just want you to think about it, okay? Think of the real reason you're changing your name. Is it because you want to be Penelope Jackson, or is it because you want to forget Penelope Reza?"

"I...I got to go," I murmur, fisting the pillow in my hand. I glance down at my white knuckles, realizing my suffocating grip, but I don't relent. I feel like shredding the pillow with my bare hands. Jenna says something, but I'm already hanging up. I'll apologize tomorrow. Tonight, I can do nothing more than shut my eyes and scream into my pillow.

The bell rings and I'm transported back into the here and now. Kids return their dirty trays, sending them clattering onto the big silver cart at the head of the cafeteria. The janitor sweeps the floor with a wide broom, collecting candy wrappers and hair ties into neat little piles.

Carlos crushes his empty milk carton into a ball. "I got this," he tells Jenna as he collects her plate and heads toward the trash can. I give her a side-long glance. *How can she be so oblivious?* If a boy acted like that around me, I think I'd notice.

Jenna lifts her neon pink book bag from the floor and slips the straps over her shoulders. I unwrap the hair from around my finger and stand. Jenna lays a hand on my shoulder. "You'll figure this out."

I smile a little. "I hope so."

After a quick stop at our lockers, Jenna, Carlos, and I part ways. Carlos heads to the gym to change for Phys Ed. I am so glad I don't have P.E. first thing in the morning. Since I refuse to step foot in the gym showers, I'd be forced to remain sweat-stained the rest of the day. I'll never understand how boys can actually shower at school. I would just die if I had to. I wonder if it's awkward in there. You know, with all those naked bodies running around? I wrinkle my nose, imaging them doing typical "boy" things while butt-ass naked: burping, arm-wrestling, high-fiving…

Jenna disappears into her Spanish classroom, calling out *"hola"* to everyone. I filter slowly through the crowded hallway, my mind wandering aimlessly until it snags on Mr. Douglas, with his narrowed eyes and condescending tone, telling me, *"Jackson is a fine name." And Reza isn't?* I think with a frown.

I bump into somebody. Automatically, an apology spills from my lips. My head clears, taking Mr. Douglas with it, and I stare at the person before me. "Matt?"

"Hey," he says, his mouth curving into a slight smile. He turns so we are standing face to face. His hair, black as an oil slick, is combed neatly, as if he'd just come out of a shower. He smells like it too…like soap and aftershave.

"What are you doing here?" I ask him. I haven't seen

Matt since he withdrew from Reedmont our freshman year. His parents are divorced, and he wanted to try living with his dad in Sacramento. I'm guessing things didn't work out there.

"I moved back in with my mom," he says without much emotion. "Dad and I…we…"

I wait. Something passes over his face. He scrubs at the back of his neck, trying to find the words. The final bell rings and Matt seems relieved. *What was he going to say?*

I loop my thumbs through the straps of my book bag. "Well, I guess I'll see you around."

"Yeah. Maybe I'll see you in class."

I smile. "Yeah, maybe."

Matt steps aside, and I walk away. I chance a peek over my shoulder, surprised but excited to see him still standing where I left him. He's watching me. My cheeks ignite. I quickly turn my face, only to hide the fact that I'm blushing. Walking with my head down, I hurry to class. Matt still looks as good as I remember. Broad shoulders carved by wrestling and tanned skin that almost matches mine.

I round the classroom threshold. Mrs. Johnson is just about to shut the door, which means I was *almost* late to class. That never happens.

"Penelope," she greets. Mrs. Johnson is a petite, elf-like woman, with a milky white complexion, and deep-set eyes. I like her a lot. I consider her one of my all-time favorite teachers.

"Morning, Mrs. Johnson," I say as I slip past her. The door closes with a *click,* and I am forced to put Matt out of my mind. I slide into my usual seat in the front row and wriggle out of my book bag. I drag it across the desk and unzip it. I dig through the contents until I find the novel we've been studying, *Lord of the Flies*, and a spiral notebook. I drop the bag at my feet and spread the books in front of me.

Mrs. Johnson addresses the class. "Who can tell me what life on the island says about society?" She slowly paces the length of the room, patiently waiting for someone to raise their hand. No one does.

She keeps her unhurried speed, the quiet stretching on and on. She finally stops at my desk. I feel her eyes on me and I glance up.

She smiles down at me. "Penelope. Would you like to answer that?"

Mrs. Johnson tends to always call on me. And it's not just because I sit in the front row. I'm one of the few students in the class who actually read the books she assigns rather than downloading the cliff notes off the web. I shift uncomfortably in my seat. "Sure—"

A knock on the classroom door interrupts me. Mrs. Johnson goes to open it. All eyes are on the door and I'm sure the person on the other side can feel it too. The door swings open and in walks Matt.

Chapter 4

My mouth parts. Matt scans the classroom. He notices me and a grin breaks across his face.

"Do you have your schedule?" Mrs. Johnson questions. Matt hands her a slip of paper. She takes it, her eyes skimming quickly across the page. "English Lit. Room one eighteen. That's me. Take a seat anywhere, Mister…" She glances down at the paper again. "Garrison."

Matt strolls down my aisle and sits down at the desk directly behind me. I'm relieved. If Matt had sat anywhere in my direct line of vision, I don't think I'd be able to concentrate.

Mrs. Johnson opens her copy of *Lord of the Flies* again and picks up exactly where we left off. She turns to me. "Penelope, you were saying?"

I clear my throat. *What was the question again?*

Thankfully, she prompts me. "We were discussing life on the island compared to society."

Right. "It shows that it's human nature to crave companionship. That we build societies out of necessity and out of fear of being alone." I know that feeling all too well. Spending four years in foster care will do that. I was often lonely, though there were plenty of other kids around. The orphanage where I spent my time in between foster homes was always taking in as many kids as they placed. A steady influx and recession like the ocean. I learned quickly not to get attached to anyone because they never stayed. Except me. Looking back on it, I now know why.

Unfortunately for me, I was abandoned at the height of mass hysteria. 9/11 brought out fears and racism like never before. People with ebony hair and brown skin were not to be trusted. Even a little four-year-old girl, clinging to a tattered stuffed bunny was given side-eye glances and wide-berths whenever she passed by. It was clear then, just as it is now. No one wanted Penelope Reza.

"Good," Mrs. Johnson says. She picks up her slow pace again, drifting through the aisles as she explains how the characters use a conch shell as a structure of hierarchy and power. After a while, I tune her out, her voice becoming a drone in the background. My thoughts are too consumed by the boy sitting behind me. Matt and I were friendly freshman year. We met in Physical Ed, the only class we've ever shared. *Until now.*

Coach Bentley usually had us run the track to warm up, and because I only run when being chased, I was usually the last one on the track, lazily bringing up the rear. Matt would sometimes slow his pace just to keep me company. He was always easy to talk to, which I found pleasantly surprising. Since he was on the wrestling team, I figured him a meathead, only interested in locker room talk and game stats. I couldn't have been more wrong.

Matt taps me on the shoulder. I turn to find him leaning forward on his elbows, a pencil tucked behind his ear.

"You ever go to that festival?"

Festival? I tilt my head, confused.

"The book festival. What was it called again? Lit Fiesta?"

I laugh. "Lit Fest." I can't believe he remembers that. I recall our conversation from almost two years ago. It was a free day in P.E. meaning we could do whatever we wanted aside from burning down the gymnasium. Matt and a group of boys played basketball, their shoes squeaking on the polished floor as they ran back and forth, blocking shots and dribbling the ball. Some of the girls took up a game of volleyball. They obviously weren't keeping score. They were mostly chatting through the net instead of actually playing the game.

I decided to bounce a dodgeball against the wall to pass the time. I drew back and chucked the red ball at the concrete wall with all my might. It smacked the wall and careened back with unanticipated speed. I yelped and jumped back, letting the ball soar past me. It bounced a few times before rolling across the floor, right through the middle of the boys' basketball game.

I was mortified. Matt was the only one to break away. He bent to retrieve the ball, his eyes shifting around the gym until they landed on me. He squeezed the ball with both hands as he strolled toward me. I gulped as he approached, worried he was going to snap at me for interrupting their game.

"Lose something?" He held the ball out to me.

I took it, wishing my hands were a little steadier. "Thanks."

Somehow, we started chatting about nothing. I tossed the ball at the wall, and this time, Matt caught it. He smiled and lobbed it back. Our conversation came naturally. And before long, we settled into an easy rhythm, alternating throws, and catches.

"Got any plans for this weekend?" Matt asked between catches.

"Yeah," I said excitedly. "My friend Jenna and I are going to Lit Fest."

"Lit Fest?" he repeated, just before tossing the ball underhanded. "What's that?"

I caught the ball. "A book festival," I explained, holding the ball at chest level. "Lit Fest. Lit…literature, get it?"

He chuckled. "Yeah, I get it." He held out his hands, palms out, wanting me to toss him the ball. "That's your idea of fun, huh?"

I threw the ball a little high on purpose. He almost missed. With a laugh, he said, "Nice arm. All those books you carry must be paying off."

The class intercom crackles, and a voice calls out, "Ty Tillerson. Please report to the front office."

I blink away the memory. Matt is still waiting for an answer.

"Yeah. Plan on going this year, too."

"Cool." Matt leans back in his chair. "What class do you have after this?"

"Biology."

He picks up his schedule and scans it. "With Naylor?"

I shake my head. "No. With Rogers."

He quirks a brow. "AP Bio? Look at you, Miss Smarty Pants."

I cover my smile, ignoring the slow creep of heat climbing its way to my cheeks.

"Got any classes with me?" He hands me the paper. I read through the schedule. First period, English Lit with Johnson. Second period, Biology with Naylor. Third period, Economics with Durand. Second lunch—*same as me*—fourth period, Calculus with Spence, and finally World History with Jenkins.

I offer the slip of paper back. "No, just this one…and lunch."

"I guess I'll take what I can get." He stuffs the paper into his jacket pocket.

Why does it feel like a million butterflies just burst into flight inside me?

"Mr. Garrison," Mrs. Johnson says from the podium at the front of the classroom. Matt's gaze pulls away to look at her. There is something so casual about him, something so confident.

"Borrow someone's book and read the last paragraph of chapter four, please."

His eyes shift back to mine, his brows raised, waiting. *Oh right. My book.* I hand him the book, swinging my body sideways so I can watch him read out loud.

He finds the page and slips the pencil from his ear. I think he's going to use it to follow along with the words, but instead, he taps it lightly on the desk as he reads. His voice is gravelly and deep. It sounds more like a grown man's voice, rather than a teenager's. It's kind of…hot.

When he's through, he lifts his face from the pages. His eyes fall on Mrs. Johnson, who is still leaning over the podium. She removes her reading glasses and uses them to point at Matt. "Good reading, Mr. Garrison. Now tell me, there was an ominous tone to that paragraph. Why do you think that is?"

Matt's eyes shift to the book in his hand. His jaw clenches as he thinks. Finally, he says, "The kid is losing power over the group. He feels weak."

Mrs. Johnson's eyes tighten. "Have you read *Lord of the Flies* before?"

"No."

She seems impressed. "Well, for someone who has never read it, you clearly understand how the character is feeling."

Matt's eye twitches ever so subtly. The bell rings and the room flies into commotion. Books snap closed and book bags zip. Matt stretches out his hand, offering me the book back. "Thanks," he says.

"No problem." I stack it on top of my spiral notebook and shove them into my book bag. Students begin to file out of the classroom, drifting into the busy hallways. Matt stands up. He lingers, waiting for me. I climb to my feet and slide into my book bag.

He waves his hand out in front of him, signaling me to walk ahead of him. I do, but I'm self-conscious about it. I finger through my hair, taking a chunk of it and wrapping it around my thumb. Once I step out into the hall, Matt comes up beside me. We walk a slow pace, side by side, forcing kids to peel off around us when they grow impatient with our speed.

"Ever had Naylor before?" Matt questions.

"Yeah," I respond. "He's a good teacher. Offers plenty of extra credit if you need it."

"Hey, Penelope!" Carlos calls from across the crowded hall. He raises his hand high over his head in a wave. I wave back, watching him shoulder his way toward me. A boy in a white ball cap grabs his book bag and yanks him backward. Carlos stumbles but catches himself. The boy laughs, and Carlos scowls at him. "Derrick, you're such a dick."

Matt surveys the scene impassively. His hands

shoved deep into his pockets. Carlos glares at Derrick, who is too busy trying to kick the feet out of the girl in front of him to notice. Carlos adjusts the straps of his worn book bag. He walks up to me and Matt.

His face is flushed pink. I feel sorry for him. Derrick is not just the class clown, he's the class asshat. To his credit, he doesn't discriminate. He harasses everyone. Nerds, jocks, emo kids…anyone with a pulse, really. Carlos rakes his fingers through his hair, brushing it back over his forehead. He acknowledges Matt with a jerk of his chin. "Hey."

Matt doesn't reciprocate.

A flicker of question colors Carlos' face, but it passes quickly. He looks over at me. "I got after-school detention. Think you can hang out and wait for me?" Carlos usually rides the bus to school in the morning and then hitches a ride home with me in the afternoon. His neighborhood isn't far from mine, so I don't mind.

"Sure. I'll wait for you in the library." I can get a jumpstart on tonight's homework while I wait. "What did you do, anyway?"

"Towel fight in the locker room."

And I'm back to imaging boys doing stupid boy things while naked…

"Let me tell you, my ass cheeks are mad at me right now." He cranes his neck, looking forlornly at his backside. He winces for effect.

I giggle and shove him away. "Dummy."

The warning bell rings, and Carlos takes flight. "Gotta run. Thanks, Pen. I'll see you after school!" He sets off, his dark hair bobbing down the hallway as he jogs away.

Matt and I begin our leisurely pace again. We stroll

past a long set of windows that overlook the outside courtyard. A handful of kids are scattered about the open space. A few boys play hacky-sack while a group of girls wearing matching top-knot buns gossip nearby. Rays of sun stream in through the window, splashing puddles of sunlight on the hall's tile floor. "Is that your boyfriend?" Matt asks, looking straight ahead. I tug the hair around my finger even tighter.

"No," I say. "He's just a friend."

Matt looks over at me, his dark hair shining almost blue in the sunlight. With a crooked smile, he says, "Good."

My thumb goes numb.

Chapter 5

Algebra is a blur. I mean, it usually is with its mind-numbing fractions and obnoxious word problems, but today is different. Instead of deciphering why x equals y, I'm trying to figure out how a star player on the wrestling team equals *me*. A simple girl with simple interests. I read, watch too many 5 Minute Craft videos, and recycle like no other. But Matt is popular and excels in a sport that requires brute strength.

What do we possibly have in common? I think about his divorced parents and wonder how it affected him. *Does he miss his family being together? Does he blame himself?* Imagining him alone in his bedroom, reliving memories of when they all lived under one roof, I think, *maybe we have more in common than I think?*

Jenna is waiting for me when I come out of class. She's eating a gooey chocolate candy bar and points it at me when I walk up to her. "Bite?"

I take it, biting off a big chunk before handing it back to her. "Thanks," I say around the mouthful of chocolate.

We walk side by side, passing a series of posters splashed on the wall. TRINA EDWARDS FOR STUDENT BODY TREASURER! PRATT FOR PRESIDENT! I ignore them, letting my gaze drift along the row of grey lockers to my right.

"Heard you have to wait on Carlos today," Jenna

says. "What a dork." She rolls her eyes. "Can't believe he got detention for snapping towels. How lame."

I nod in agreement. But then again, everyone knows Reedmont has a zero-tolerance for bullying. Lately they've been cracking down on any form of violence...towel wars included, apparently.

"Wish I could hang around and keep you company, but my shift starts at three thirty." Jenna works part-time at Puffins, a locally owned snow cone shop that stays open year-round. I'll never understand the appeal of snow cones in thirty-degree weather, but since I drink hot cocoa in the summer, I'm in no position to judge.

Puffins is known for their flashy billboard signs with a cartoon puffin clad in beach attire, boasting over fifty unique flavors. I've only tried nine of them. Mint, bubble gum, pickle, ice cream, s'more, sour grape, mac n' cheese, chocolate popcorn, and cocoa flavored. Mac n' cheese is surprisingly delicious.

"No worries," I tell her, taking the candy bar out of her hand. "I have to read four chapters of *Lord of the Flies,* anyway." I break off a piece, the caramel stretching like taffy as I pull it free. I pop it into my mouth. The mention of the novel suddenly reminds me of Matt.

I swallow the candy, the caramel sticking to my teeth. "Do you remember Matt?" I scrape at the caramel with my tongue until it loosens. "He was here freshman year, then transferred out."

Jenna's brow furrows. "Matt who?" She reclaims her candy bar.

"Garrison. Dark hair. Tan. He was on the wrestling team." The sound of scuffing shoes echoes the hallway as kids tread their way to class around us. Occasionally, wafts of strong cologne or perfume suffocates me. *Why can't people learn that less is more?*

Dawning finally hits Jenna. "Oh yeah. Garrison. I remember him now. I had study hall with him. What about him?"

I didn't know they had study hall together. Why didn't she ever mention it? Probably because there wasn't a need to. I never told her about our conversations in P.E. because they were harmless. I knew he was out of my league, so I refused to get my hopes up. I figured he talked to me strictly out of pity. *But now?* Now it feels like pity has nothing to do with it.

"He's back," I tell her. "He's in my literature class."

Jenna looks indifferent. "I don't really know the kid. He didn't talk much in study hall." She finishes the candy bar and crumples the wrapper in her fist. The warning bell blares and it's off to biology.

****

Whoever made my class schedule is a sick son of a bitch. I stare down at the dead frog in front of me. *Who assigns biology right before lunch*? The strong smell of formaldehyde is enough to make my stomach turn, but coupled with the squishy, lifeless frog lying in a pan under my nose, it's enough to make me gag.

Mr. Rogers walks up and down the aisles of the science lab. He's handing out scalpels and forceps, the box of sharp utensils tinkling as he moves about the room. He gets to me and holds out the box. Mr. Rogers doesn't look like your typical science teacher. He's tall and brawny, with sandy-colored hair that is always unkempt. And he's not much older than us. Having graduated college only three years ago, Mr. Rogers looks more like a student of Reedmont High than a teacher.

I peer inside the box. Light reflects off the sharp scalpels and I select one. "Don't forget a pair of forceps," Mr. Rogers says, pulling out a pair for me. "You'll need that to pull apart the skin."

There's a tickle at the back of my throat and I realize it's bile. I bite it back. Mr. Rogers brushes past me and finishes passing out supplies. I stare down at the frog. It's lying on its back, its legs sprawled wide across the metal tray. It smells God-awful and I pray I don't have to touch it with my bare hands.

Mr. Rogers flips on a projector. An illustration of the frog's anatomy flashes up on the white screen at the head of the classroom. "Today we're going to learn to identify the internal organs of the *Lithobates catesbeianus*, or bullfrog. This image—" He points to the screen. "—is also in your textbook, so feel free to refer to it."

I glance down at the unmoving frog. *Because frog anatomy is something we all need to know.*

Mr. Rogers continues. "Use the scalpel to make a small incision starting at the throat and work your way down to its abdomen. Don't cut too deep. We want to keep the organs intact for identification."

Trina Edwards, a cheerleader, known for her…ah, let's say, experience with the male anatomy, raises her hand. She says the exact words that are running through my head. "Can we wear gloves?"

Mr. Rogers grins. "Where's the fun in that?"

Trina wrinkles her nose. "I'm not touching that thing without a glove."

I'm sure that's not the first time she's said those words. I hide my laugh behind my hand, trying to smother it before it goes too far. I have to remember to tell Jenna.

Mr. Rogers chuckles. "Okay, okay." He opens the cabinet on the wall behind him and shuffles through it. "Aha." He frees a box from the mountain of paper stacked inside and tosses it onto the lab table. It slides, coming to a stop right in front of me. "One size fits all...I hope."

It's a box of pop-up latex gloves similar to a tissue box. I tug two gloves from it and pass the box down. I slip a hand into one of the gloves, and of course, it's huge. I wriggle my fingers, trying to make it fit, but it's no use. I pick up the scalpel, anyway. *I look like Mickey Mouse*. My grip is awkward, but I wrap my fingers tight around the slender handle of the scalpel.

"Go ahead and make your incisions," Mr. Rogers says.

I lift the blade over the frog's throat and swallow. *Sorry, little guy.* Pressing down, I slit the amphibian's throat, easily slicing through its skin. My stomach sours. *Ugh.* I drag the blade down, parting the squishy abdomen. *There. I did it.* I set the scalpel down, glad to be rid of it.

Mr. Rogers is at my elbow. He takes the forceps. "Use the forceps to peel the skin back." He tries to demonstrate, but his big hands fumble with the tiny tool. He drops them and uses his fingers instead. He folds the skin back like a curtain, exposing the frog's innards. I stare down at the dull, minuscule organs. I suddenly wish I hadn't eaten Jenna's chocolate bar.

"Looks like you were a little heavy-handed with the scalpel," Mr. Rogers tells me with a laugh. "It's okay though. Everything is intact except the heart."

My eyes sweep across the frogs' tangle of organs.

The heart is sliced neatly in two. And just like that, me and the frog are one.

Chapter 6

I practically sprint out of biology. I feel like breaking my rule of not using the gym showers and washing from head to toe after dissecting that disgusting frog. The sight of its ramen-noodle-like intestines has completely ruined my appetite. *Take AP, they said. It will be fun, they said.* Fun, my ass.

The stench of formaldehyde is still burning my nose when I step into the cafeteria. I scan the tables, searching for Matt—I mean—Jenna. *Why would I be looking for Matt?* I clench my fists, irritated with myself. The cafeteria is in full swing. Kids crowd the lunch line and most of the tables are already claimed.

I keep to the far right of the room, letting my fingers drag across the navy-blue painted wall as I walk. The smell of pizza is strong, as that seems to be the food of choice today. Looking out at all the tables, pizzas far outnumber the hamburgers, which I guess is the other option on today's menu.

I spot Jenna. She's sitting at a booth with Rainey and Carlos. They have their lunches already, each with a tray in front of them. Jenna sees me coming and pats the empty spot beside her. Rainey, an exchange student from Sweden, is new to Reedmont High, and because Jenna loves to take in strays, Rainey's been a part of our little group ever since her first day here.

Don't get me wrong. I like Rainey. I especially like

her accent...it's *different*. In North Carolina, where southern accents reign, it's hard not to find her Swedish accent a good kind of different. However, the boys in school—aside from Carlos, who seems to only have eyes for Jenna—like more than just her accent. Rainey could easily be a supermodel, with her shockingly white-blonde hair and legs that are as long as I am.

Thomas Reese, quarterback for the football team, pulls a chair up to the table. He takes a seat and starts chatting to Rainey, completely ignoring Jenna and Carlos. I huff and shake my head. So far, no one has been able to snag a date with her. Whenever a boy sidles up to her, Rainey listens attentively as they rattle off their pickup line. She waits patiently until they're through, never looking away or acting annoyed or shy. Then, she hits them with it. The same reply she uses every single time. And I'm just in time to hear it again.

"Ah. So sweet. Not interested. Sorry."

Thomas jerks back, clearly surprised to be turned down. His cheeks flare red. The chair screeches across the floor tile as he scrambles to his feet. He lingers a moment, dumbfounded.

She points a slender finger at his crouch. "Lose the penis and we'll talk." She smiles sweetly at him.

Carlos bursts into laughter. Thomas' mouth pops open. He did not see that coming. He turns on his heel, and stalks away, like a dog with his tail between his legs. I slide into the booth, scooting close to Jenna. "Oh my God, Rainey! I can't believe you just said that!"

"Did you see his face?" Carlos asks, still laughing. "I thought he was going to cry!"

Rainey spreads her hands. "I thought gossip got around fast. Guess no one's got the memo yet." She looks at me and smiles. Straight teeth flash behind pencil-thin lips. Rainey isn't shy about her sexual orientation. I don't know whether it's because Sweden is more open and accepting than the United States, or Rainey is just that comfortable with who she is. She isn't into boys, and she isn't afraid to say so.

"I think you just fixed that problem," Jenna says giggling. She picks up a French fry from her tray. "Well done, Rainey. Well done." She dips the fry in some ketchup. A blob of it falls onto her hamburger bun, but she doesn't notice. She shoves the fry in her mouth and goes for another.

I glance at Thomas. He's sitting with his friends at a round table. His fallen face still the picture of disappointment. *I wish I had Rainey's confidence.* I shift my eyes back to Rainey and Carlos. She's scrolling through her phone, her pale face lit up by the screen's soft glow. Carlos picks at his pizza, tearing off pepperonis and stacking them in a neat pile on his tray. He lifts the wedge of pizza, the cheese oozing onto his fingers as he folds it in half and takes a bite.

"You hungry?" Jenna asks me. She's constantly trying to feed me. Jenna has a healthy appetite, though you wouldn't know by looking at her. Her size four frame is petite beside my hourglass figure. Looking at my backside in a full-length mirror often has me wondering how I got so much sand in the lower part of my hourglass. "Want some of my fries?" She slides the tray in front of me. The pile of grease-soaked fries makes my stomach turn.

"No thanks," I shove it back. "We dissected a frog in biology."

"Enough said," Jenna replies, wrapping her hands

around the burger and lifting it to her mouth. Mustard drips from it. "That's enough to ruin even my appetite." She sinks her teeth into the burger, tearing off a big bite. Her cheek swells as she chews. "Okay, Pen. We need to settle this once and for all. We only have four months, you know."

She's talking about Lit Fest. Jenna is a planner, and though it comes in handy a lot of the time, it can be annoying. She insists on deciding which authors to see, which discussion panels to attend, where to park, where to eat, and even what we're wearing *months* before the festival.

Jenna drops the burger back onto the tray and licks her fingers. "All right. I've narrowed it down to three authors." She turns to unzip her book bag. She withdraws a notebook and slaps on the table in between us. "Cami DeFord, Penbrook Powell, and—"

"Margaret Kenter." Our eyes meet. Jenna's mouth is a perfect "*o*" shape. "What? Am I right? I mean, you can't see Cami without Margaret."

Jenna looks at Carlos and Rainey. "You see? This is why we're friends." She nudges me in the ribs. "She totally gets me." She fishes her phone out of her pocket and opens up her trusty Lit Fest app. She scrolls through the day's schedule of events. "There's so much to do this year. I want to do it all!"

Rainey peers over her phone. "What is this…Lit Fest?"

Jenna's eyes light up. *Here we go.* Jenna embarks on the history of Lit Fest, practically giving a blow-by-blow account of its creation and development. I tune her out after a while. I've heard this all before. My eyes drift around the cafeteria.

Derrick is shaking salt into an unsuspecting girl's drink. *What a jerk.* Trina is sitting with the rest of the cheer squad, each more interested in their phone screens than each other. *Not that I blame them.* Then my gaze catches on a boy with tanned skin and slick black hair. *Matt.*

He's leaning against the wall at the far end of the cafeteria. A few boys I recognize from the wrestling team surround him. They seem to enjoy an easy conversation, probably talking about wrestling strategies or various ways to put someone in a headlock, no doubt. He senses my stare, finding me easily in the crowded room. Our eyes meet.

I reach for a strand of hair, but before I have time to twine it around my forefinger, Matt looks away. He says something to the redheaded boy beside him. They laugh together. I swing my gaze back to the table, staring at the words in Jenna's notebook. Her lists and schedules for Lit Fest blur as tears well in my eyes. I fight them away. *I was wrong about him. How could I be so stupid?* An evil voice whispers inside my head: *Matt Garrison doesn't want you. Nobody wants Penelope Reza.*

Chapter 7

The rest of my day sucked. Mrs. Henley gave us a pop quiz in World History, which I bombed, and Mr. Turnbell assigned a shit-ton of homework just for fun. *Great, just what I want to do all night—compare and contrast Europe and Asia's economic social classes.* I stalk the hallways, grumbling and kicking myself for agreeing to wait for Carlos. *I could head home right now. I wish I were there now.*

I want nothing more than to dive headfirst into bed and pull the covers up to my ears.

I wrench open the library doors and a rush of cold air fans across my face. I feel like I have a rain cloud hanging over my head, ready to let loose at any moment. *What is my problem?* I drop into a seat at an empty table. *Who am I kidding? I know what my problem is. His name is Matt Garrison.* How could I ever have thought he was interested in me?

I mean, what do I know about attraction? I've never had a real boyfriend before. *Crushes?* Now, I've had plenty of those. When I was nine, I mooned over Joey Leigh. He'd chase me during recess and pull my pigtails, but I didn't care. I thought he was so handsome with his long eyelashes and adorable laugh. Besides, he gave me a ring sucker. As soon as that giant cherry-flavored bobble slid onto my finger, I fell head over heels.

In fifth grade, I liked Bryce Potter. He was good at

soccer. He carried a soccer ball with him wherever he went. Bouncing it from one knee to the other while walking down the school hallways. He only liked girls who played sports, so Bryce overlooked me. In fact, I'm not even sure he knew I existed.

In middle school, I swore I loved Trevor Pollins. He was a friend of Trip's. I thought he was so mature, even though he had terrible taste in friends. I never understood why he put up with Trip. But, Trevor's mom was in the military, and they got orders to move to Hawaii not long after they settled in Charlotte. Long-distance love never works, so that ended that crush.

In ninth grade, I thought Dwight Danila was exotic, with his almond-shaped eyes and adorable accent. He was half Irish and half Filipino. I figured since I was bi-racial too, that we were destined to be together. We weren't. Once Dwight met Rhonda Grey, we were over before we ever started. They became the most popular couple in our grade and three years later, they are still going strong.

Last year, my heart belonged to the main character in an obscure crime-thriller series I was reading over summer break. That, by far, has been my favorite crush. Liking a fictional character is easier than liking a real boy.

Aside from Mrs. Arden, the school librarian, it's just me and three boys from chess club in the library. The boys are huddled around a small table. Two of them are actually playing chess, while the other plays coach, whispering and making hand gestures to them as they make their measured moves.

I pull out my economics book with a frown. I'm not looking forward to this assignment. It feels like busy work, and busy work always annoys me. It takes me close to a full hour to complete it. Massaging the cramp out of my hand, I glance up at the clock hanging over the door. Carlos will be done with detention soon.

I hear the library door click open. Mrs. Arden greets whoever it is, and the room is quiet again. I open *Lord of the Flies. Maybe I can read a chapter or two before Carlos gets here.* I settle in, completely absorbed by Ralph and Piggy and the rest of the boys deserted on the island. So much so that I don't hear someone approach until they thump the spine of the book, making it lurch forward. I nearly drop it in my lap.

"Son of a—" I stop in my tracks. I expect it to be Derrick the jerk, or even Carlos. I swallow. *It's Matt.*

He laughs. "Sorry, I thought you saw me coming."

I tuck a piece of hair behind my ear, wishing the sudden heat washing over me would go away. "I didn't, but it's okay," I say, righting the book in my hands. "What are you doing here?"

"Checking a couple things out. This." Matt raises a copy of *Lord of the Flies*. "And you."

Suddenly nervous, I shift my eyes to the table and keep them there. I used to think the old saying *hot under the collar* was a ridiculous term, but right now, it explains exactly what's happening to my body. "It's a little late, isn't it? Did you have detention too?"

Matt sits down. "Nah." He leans back in the chair. "Stayed back to talk to coach to see about getting back on the team."

I don't know what to say to that, but I have to fill the silence somehow. "So, um, is he going to make you try out all over again?"

"No, but I have to provide him the x-rays and

medical charts from my doctor in California before I can wrestle."

I give him a swift look. *X-rays?* Matt looks intact. In fact, he looks perfect. Broad chested, with muscular shoulders and strong thighs, like tree trunks. A wrestler's body. He's perfection on the outside, but something must be broken on the inside. "What happened?"

Matt spins his copy of *Lord of the Flies* on the table. It makes me dizzy to watch, so I watch him instead. I notice how his brows pinch a little and the corners of his mouth turn down before he answers. "A dude too big for my division roughed me up pretty bad last year. Broke my arm in three places. Asshole was eliminated after the match. His coach got fined for trying to slip him past the refs. And I was left with a fucked-up arm." He stops spinning the book.

"And you still want to wrestle after that?"

"It's the only way I can get into Ohio State. I'm depending on that scholarship."

I want to offer a retort, but I can't think of anything that sounds reasonable. College tuition is expensive, and if the only way Matt can go is through a wrestling scholarship, then I can't fault his reasons for sticking with the silly sport. I don't get wrestling…I mean, how can anyone find fun in watching two sweaty guys in tight trunks manhandle each other into submission?

"What about you?" he asks. "Miss Smarty Pants?" He smirks at me. "Where do you plan on going? Yale? Harvard?"

I get a lump in my throat. "UNC." I don't know why I'm embarrassed. The University of North Carolina is a great school.

"UNC? Or UNC Charlotte?"

"UNC Charlotte." I shift uncomfortably in my seat. *Why is he looking at me like I've just passed gas?* "What?" I demand. "It's a good school."

"I never said it wasn't."

"They offer Environmental Studies and English as Majors. I have the best of both worlds there." *Why am I explaining myself?* UNC Charlotte is perfect for me. Since I'm on the fence between Environmental Studies and English Literature, what better place to go, but to a college that offers both?

"Relax. You don't have to explain anything to me." Matt knocks my knee with his. "If you want to stay in this boring city forever, that's your decision."

I blink at him. "Huh?"

He lazily cocks his head to the side. "You have the chance to go *any*where you want. With your smarts, you could get into any university you want, and you choose to stay in Charlotte?" He shrugs. "Why?"

Mom pops into my head. Seven years with her is not enough. I'm not ready to be on my own again. I've been alone long enough. Of course, I don't tell him this. Instead, I cross my arms in front of me. "I happen to like Charlotte."

"I used to hate Charlotte." *How could he say that?* Charlotte is right smack dab between the mountains and the ocean. Where else can you make a split decision to hike Crowders Mountain one weekend, and then lounge on the sands of Wrightsville Beach the next? Seriously, how can anyone hate that? Matt stares at me, and I wonder what he's thinking. He knocks my knee with his again. "But…you're giving me reason to like it."

My mind goes nuclear.

Chapter 8

What kind of dangerous game am I playing here? Matt is on the wrestling team. He's popular and probably far more experienced with girls than I want to know. Me, on the other hand? I read too many books and have two spare fingers whenever I'm counting all my friends on one hand. There is him, and there is me. There is no us. But the way his deep voice reduces me to a panting lapdog, I am tempted to give *us* a shot. That is…if he is.

Matt's gaze moves past me. Instinctively, I look over my shoulder and see Carlos strolling in our direction. "Towel boy is here." Matt doesn't say it with malice, more like disappointment. Carlos stops at our table. "Hey," he says.

"Hey," I mirror.

Matt stands, lifting *Lord of the Flies* from the table. "Well, I guess I'll see you in class tomorrow."

I nod. "Yeah."

As soon as Matt walks away, Carlos takes his seat. "What's with him?"

I start packing my book bag. "What do you mean?"

"What do I mean? Don't you see how he totally ignores me?" He makes a *pfft* sound and glares in Matt's direction. "What did I ever do to him?"

I lift a shoulder. "He just doesn't know you, that's all," I reassure Carlos. If I'm going to go against my better judgment and test the waters with Matt, Carlos has to give him a chance. All I need is for Carlos to not like him, because then Jenna won't like him. And if my friends don't like him…then, how can I? I chance a peek back at Matt, but he's already gone.

Carlos grumbles something under his breath, but I ignore him. I zip up my book bag and sling it over my shoulder. "You ready?"

"I was ready an hour ago," Carlos says. "Detention sucks."

I roll my eyes. "It's supposed to." My cellphone beeps with an incoming text. I scramble to retrieve it. Mrs. Arden looks up from the computer and shoots me an annoyed glare. I mute the phone before it can beep again. "It's Jenna," I say. "She wants to know if we want to stop by Puffins."

Carlos brightens.

I type her a quick text in response. *—C-ya in a minute.—*

****

Carlos and I are at the ordering window at Puffins. No one else is here, which is no surprise. It's October. Who wants snow cones in October? We find Jenna scooping balls of shaved ice into tall paper cups. She slides the window open with an elbow. "Go sit down. I'll be out in a sec."

Carlos and I do as we're told. I let my eyes wander around the open-air parlor. Puffins has huge, gaping, glass-less windows. At night, they lower heavy bamboo curtains over them and latch them with heavy locks. I know because I've helped Jenna lock up countless times before.

Bubble gum pink tables and plastic barstools overwhelm the space. A gaudy fake palm tree strung with blinking holiday lights flourishes from the far corner. A sudden breeze blows through, and I pull the collar of my sweater higher, shielding my neck. Carlos doesn't seem to notice the temperature. He's too busy eyeing the menu.

A side door opens and Jenna flounces over to our table. She's carrying two cups filled to the brim with electric green snowballs. Plastic spoons stick out of them, and from here they look delicious. *Even if this is more like coffee weather, than snow cone.* She sets the cups down in front of us. I notice there's a tiny splash of blood-red liquid in the center.

I inspect it carefully. I have seen all of the snow cones Puffins has to offer, and this isn't one of them. "What is it?"

"Just try it," Jenna says, beaming. "It's my newest invention."

Carlos digs right in, fisting his spoon like a Neanderthal. I take a more delicate approach. I dip the spoon in carefully and put it to my lips. Something smells…spicy. I sniff again and then lick the shaved ice perched at the end of my spoon. As soon as I do—I regret it. My mouth burns and my eyes water.

"Sriracha!" I cry, shoving the snow cone away. My tongue wags like a dog, and I'm tempted to wipe it with my sweater. "Are you serious?" I jump up from the table and run to the bathroom. The door sticks a little, causing me to panic more.

I'm going to kill Jenna! Finally, it gives, and I dash to the sink. I jam my hands beneath the automatic facet. The water splashes into my cupped palms and I gulp swallow-full after swallow-full until the fire on my tongue extinguishes.

When I finally come back out of the bathroom, Jenna is sitting next to Carlos. I hold her gaze firm as I stalk toward her. She purses her lips. I don't say a word. I just glare at her darkly. She has the nerve to smile. I pinch her, right at the tender spot below the armpit. "Ow," she cries, swatting me away.

I laugh. "You're such a brat." I pick up the sriracha snow cone and head straight to the trashcan. "You could have warned me first." I drop it in, relishing the sound of it disappearing forever.

Jenna is all toothy smiles and twinkling eyes. "If I had, you wouldn't have eaten it."

I toss up my hands. "Exactly!"

Jenna makes a face at me. "So let's vote. Should I present it to Mr. Sullivan?"

Carlos says *yes,* at the same time as I say *no.*

Jenna divides a look between us.

"I liked it," Carlos says quickly. I roll my eyes. *Of course, you like it—Jenna made it. You'd eat a dirt snow cone if she made it.*

"Your vote doesn't count," I tell him. There's no way I'm letting Jenna present that. She'll be the laughingstock of Puffins. And how embarrassing would that be? Jenna's boss, Mr. Sullivan, told the staff that anyone who comes up with the next big flavor gets a dollar raise. Jenna's has been experimenting with flavors for weeks, trying to invent Puffins' newest flavor.

"What's wrong with normal ingredients?" I ask her. "Like cotton candy or gumdrops?"

Jenna puts her elbow on the table and props her chin up. "They've all been done before," she whines. "I need something different. Something Mr. Sullivan will love." Her bottom lip pokes out. "I'll never get that raise if I don't come up with something soon."

I lay a hand on the crown of her head. "Too bad you can't use wine, 'cause you sure got a lot of that going on right now." I give a good shake, mussing up her already messy bun.

Jenna sits up. "Wine. That's it!" She takes my face into her hands, squishing my cheeks so hard my lips pucker like a fish. "Penelope, you're a genius!" She giggles to herself and leaps up from the stool. I rub my cheeks, watching after her as she dashes through the side door and disappears.

"Wine snow cones?" Carlos asks. "She can't make those, can she? She's only sixteen." Before I can reply, my phone rings. I slip it from my pocket. It's Mom.

I answer it. "Hey, Mom."

"Hi, sweetheart. Where are you?" she questions.

"Puffins with Jenna and Carlos."

"Hello Mrs. Jackson," Carlos calls out in a sing-song voice.

"That was Carlos, by the way."

"I figured as much. Look, honey. I heard from Mr. Douglas today." Her tone is tight, like something is wrong.

I stiffen. "And?"

"And he was reminding us that the paperwork has already been dated." She pauses. "Penelope. He's giving us a deadline to sign the paperwork."

My throat threatens to close. "When?"

The line is quiet for a split second. "A week."

My temper flares. "A week! What kind of deadline is that?" *I can't be pushed into this! I won't!*

"He said if we don't have the paperwork back to him by then, he'll be forced to cancel the request and we'll have to re-file all over again."

A headache blooms across my skull as I recall all the exhaustive steps it took to file for my name change. And I'm not just talking about the legal stuff, such as petitioning the clerk of court and filing the paperwork with a lawyer.

I'm talking about the harsh realization that struck me like a blow to my gut during my freshman year. Equipped with a laptop and a search engine, I discovered that my parents could have easily changed my name when they adopted me. The screen before me was full of mostly jargon, but I understood enough to surmise that since my adoption was an open adoption, a name change would have been relatively simple.

An amended birth certificate, and a new social security card, bada bing bada boom. Done. With no biological relatives making things difficult for my adopted family, it could have been just that easy. Dejected, and empty inside, I wondered why they kept my last name. Why was I left to be the sole Reza in a houseful of Jacksons? Mom later explained that Wesley thought it best if they left the decision to me. Although reasonable, I couldn't help but feel betrayed. The sting of that discovery still hurts to this day.

Re-filing the name change paperwork will be simple now that all the hard work is done, but that's not the point. I don't want to be rushed, especially by musty, old Mr. Douglas. A ghost of his overpowering cologne wafts through the air around me, and I'm transported back inside his office. My hands grow clammy in my lap. I envision the lawyer standing over me, ten-foot-tall as he stares down his nose. I'm nothing more than a cockroach beneath his shoe.

I'm suddenly aware how chaotic I must seem to everyone around me. What seems to be a lifetime ago, I wanted so badly to be a Jackson, but Jenna took a dump on that dream when she said, "*But Reza is a part of who you are, Penelope. Are you ready to let that part go?*"

I squeeze my eyes shut, afraid to speak for what I might say. But it's hard to tamp down my anger. I curl my hands into fists. I'm not sure how long I can keep it at bay, because just like a sriracha snow cone...anger burns on my tongue.

Chapter 9

"Pen?" Carlos says at my shoulder. "You okay?"

I'm gripping the phone so tight I'm shaking. "I have to go," I tell Mom, hanging up before she has the chance to say anything else. My heart stings when I do it, but I go a step further, turning the phone off completely, not wanting her to call back. I'm done talking right now.

Carlos tries again. "Pen?"

I turn my face to his. "I'm ready to go, are you?"

He nods, his eyes searching mine. "Yeah," he answers softly. He goes to the ordering window and raps lightly on it. Jenna slides it open, her smile dropping when she notices me.

"What's wrong?"

I run my fingers through my hair, mindlessly wrapping the strands around my thumb. "The lawyer called Mom. He gave me a week to sign, or else we start the process all over again."

Jenna bites her bottom lip, worrying at it the same way I worry at the ends of my hair.

Carlos breaks the silence. "What are you going to do?"

I sigh, releasing my hair and swinging my arms out wide, holding them there, lost. "I...I don't know."

Jenna leans her body out of the window. She grabs me by the shoulders and pulls me in for a hug. It's awkward, with only half of her body hanging out of the small window hole, but it's a reassuring hug, nonetheless.

"You'll figure it out," she says against my ear. Jenna's athletic arms are strong around my shoulders, and I allow myself to be held. I need her support right now because inside, I feel weightless. "You're stronger than you think, Penelope Reza."

My eyes go wide at her words. We break apart, but our heads stay close. So close I can smell her shampoo. Jenna leans her forehead against mine. "Call me if you need me." She gives my arm a gentle squeeze, then wiggles back through the window.

Carlos calls, "Bye, Jenna." She waves at him, but her eyes flick right back to me. I throw my hand up to wave, but it's more like a motion of defeat.

****

I awake, disoriented and feverish. I had a nightmare. It's a suffocating nightmare where I feel stuck. There's nothing obvious holding me down: no quicksand, no chains, no hands. I'm just stuck. Frozen, completely unable to move, almost as if I'm scared motionless. The panic I felt in the nightmare was so real I wrap my arms around myself, trying to calm my trembling body.

The clock on my nightstand glows bright against the darkness. It's five AM. Have I really slept that long? After I dropped off Carlos, I went straight home. I remember dropping my book bag at the front door and kicking out of my sneakers. Mom was waiting for me when I got there, but I wasn't in the mood to talk.

She must have sensed that because she busied herself with ironing Trip's business suits instead of harassing me about the paperwork. I make myself a bowl of cereal and bring it to my bedroom. As soon as I shut my door, I heard Trip's voice booming from the living room. I lock it. I was not in the mood for his bullshit.

I climbed into bed fully clothed. I finished the bowl of cereal and placed the empty bowl on my nightstand. I wrapped myself in my fluffy comforter. *If only I can stay here forever,* I thought. *No paperwork, no Mr. Douglas.* A loud bang on my door made me jump.

"Nice to see you too, *Pee!*" Trip yelled from the other side of my bedroom door.

I rolled my eyes. I hate that name, and he knows it. Trip started calling me that about a year after I moved in. By then, we acted more like actual siblings than strangers. We fought like cats and dogs, but not because I wanted to. I was thrilled to have a brother. Trip, on the other hand, made my life hell. Forever taunting me.

Once, when he was thirteen, he stole an armload of my books and ripped out the last page of every single book. I cried for days. When he got older, he got crueler. Trip being three years old than me, forced us to share Reedmont for one grueling year. Mom made me ride with him on my first day.

Once we pulled up to the school, he blared the song, *Walk like an Egyptian* so loud, everyone turned to stare. I tried to slouch in the seat, but he opened the car door and shoved me out. It was humiliating. I remember running through the parking lot, the song chasing me the entire way. I never rode with him again.

He's never actually said it, but I know Trip wishes his parents never adopted me. He liked being the only child. When I came, he had to learn to share. Not just his toys, but his family. He blames me for ruining that. Trip's heavy footsteps faded down the hall and the front door opened and closed with a slam. After that, I pulled my phone out of my pocket and powered it back on. After watching crafting videos online for an hour or so, I finally grew tired and drifted off to sleep.

A long, restless sleep. I throw off the comforter and climb out of bed. My body is stiff from sleeping in jeans all night. I peel off my clothes and head to the shower. I make quick work of showering and toweling off. I don't get dressed in a hurry. Instead, I take my time deciding on what to wear.

Usually, I give little thought to clothes, but today I am careful with what I choose. I think of Matt and that rumbly voice of his. My heart swells a little and I lift my most flattering sweater from the hanger. It's a sleek navy-blue sweater with brown suede patches at the elbows. I pair it with a plaid cashmere scarf and soft blue jeans.

I scoop my thick hair high on my head and wrap it into a fat bun. I look around the floor for my sneakers, but then I remember I left them at the front door. I go to turn the knob on my door, but it's locked. *Oh, right. I locked it when Trip showed up.* I unlock it, and as soon as I pull the door open, I smell coffee and bacon. *My stomach growls.* The cereal I ate last night is long gone, and since I skipped lunch yesterday, my body is now fiercely protesting that decision.

I go into the kitchen. I find Mom standing over the stove. She's frying bacon. She notices me and smiles over her shoulder. "Morning," she greets. "I hope you're hungry."

I stand next to her, watching the bacon shrink and sizzle in the popping grease. "I am actually." I touch my rumbling stomach.

"Well, if you had eaten a real meal last night instead

of cold cereal…" She lets her words drift off and knocks me with her hip instead.

I cut my eyes at her. "I know, I know. Now hand over the bacon, lady, and no one gets hurt."

She laughs and jerks her head toward the kitchen table. I look over and see my place already set with a plate of scrambled eggs and a tall glass of orange juice. She even remembered the ketchup. I can practically taste the eggs already. I lunge for my chair, sliding into it like first base. I smother the eggs with ketchup and devour them in no time. Mom places three strips of bacon on my plate, and I devour those, too.

She sets a plate of bacon down on the table and turns to pour herself a cup of coffee. I steal three more pieces of bacon as soon as her back is turned. In the back of my mind, I think about my biological father. *What would he say about me eating bacon?* Isn't it sacrilegious to eat pork in his country? Or is that somewhere else? I grow sullen and snatch another piece. *Oh well. If you were around, I'd know these things…but since you're not, bring on the bacon, baby!*

Mom sits across from me, her hands wrapped around an oversized mug of coffee. It's the mug I bought her last year for Mother's Day. It's pink with a gold rim and handle. There's a unicorn reading a book on it. I got it for her because of our running joke about the uni-pen.

Mom doesn't say anything at first. She just watches me eat, occasionally lifting the mug to her lips. Steam wafts off the coffee, sweeping across her slender nose and cheeks.

I chug the orange juice, letting out a satisfied, "*Ahh*" when I'm through.

The corner of Mom's mouth lifts. "Was it good?"

"Delicious," I say. I glance at the clock. It's time for me to go, but Mom looks like she wants to talk. *She wants to know what I'm going to do about the paperwork.* My stomach knots, but I stay rooted to the chair.

She fidgets as she frames what she wants to say. I decide to just dive right in, rip the Band-Aid off all at once to get it over with.

"I need more time," I blurt out.

Mom's eyes grow round. Her hands tighten on the mug. So much so that I'm afraid she might shatter it. She swallows hard and says with a shaky voice, "What have I done to change your mind?"

My heart plummets. *Surely, she can't think this is her fault?* I shift from my chair to the chair directly beside her. I touch her shoulder. "Mom, no. It's nothing you did. I've just been thinking a lot lately and this name change thing…it's a big deal."

Those are Jenna's words. But she couldn't have been more right. Changing my name is a *huge* deal. I want to make sure I'm absolutely certain before I send Penelope Reza away forever.

Mom stares down at her cup of coffee and nods. "I'll let Frank know today." She sniffs and my heart feels as though it's being squeezed.

"Mom," I say. "I'm sorry."

She looks at me, her eyes awash with tears. "Don't be. I want you to be happy, Penelope. That's all I ever wanted. But, I thought being a Jackson is what you wanted."

"It was—is." I correct myself, but it's too late. Mom caught it and flinches as though I had ripped her heart out. I close my eyes. Even *I'm* frustrated by my own feelings. I used to want this more than anything, and now that it's within reach, I'm afraid to go through with it.

When I open my eyes, Mom is openly crying into her hands. I want to comfort her, but I know the only way to do that is to lie. To tell her I changed my mind. I'm ready to sign the paperwork. *One little lie will fix this,* I think. *One little lie will make all of this go away.*

I push myself to my feet. Mom lifts her face, her lips trembling, and her eyes rimmed red with tears. *Go ahead. Tell her.* I open my mouth, but the words do not come. I draw in a shaky breath and turn my back to her.

"I'm sorry, Mom." I leave her alone to cry.

Chapter 10

There's no time to meet Jenna and Carlos in the cafeteria. I head straight to English and take my usual seat in the front row. Mrs. Johnson is writing something on the board. Normally, I'd be reading over her shoulder, preparing myself for whatever work lies ahead, but not today.

I can't focus on much of anything. Even my nerves are jumpy. To be honest, I'm not sure if it's from Mom's breakdown this morning or because I know Matt is about to walk through the classroom door.

A dull ache blooms at my temples. *I've broken my mother's heart.* But, who knows, I may still sign the paperwork. I still want to be a Jackson; that never actually went away. Things just got too real, too fast. I need time to sort everything out.

I'm annoyed that my eyes keep darting to the door every time I sense movement. I grow even more annoyed each time it isn't Matt. I take out *Lord of the Flies* to busy myself and open it to the page written on the board. Mrs. Johnson takes her place at her podium. She's wearing a fuzzy striped sweater over a wool skirt. Her legs are clad in thick tights, and her feet are encased in thick-soled boots. She looks like she's ready to stomp through a snowstorm.

The final bell rings, and still no Matt. I watch the door expectedly. *Maybe he's sick?* I chew on my bottom lip. *Maybe he's changed classes?* Mrs. Johnson instructs the class to take out their books as she takes roll.

Matt strolls in just as she's calling his name. "Here," he says before casually dropping into the seat behind me. Mrs. Johnson gives him some serious side-eye but doesn't scold him for being late.

I glance over my shoulder at him. His head is down, flipping through the pages of *Lord of the Flies*. Suddenly, he stops and casts his eyes in my direction. I still, my gaze transfixed on him. His brows raise, and a slow smile creeps across his face.

"Hey," he whispers.

"Hey."

"Think I wasn't coming?"

I blush.

He chuckles and goes back to flipping through the pages. I wish I wasn't drawn to him. My book boyfriend won't hurt me. Matt is the kind of boy who will.

****

School cafeteria lunch lines are the worst. They are slow moving, and there is no reward for your patience. Like, take the fair, for instance. You could wait in line for the Ferris wheel for up to an hour or more. But patience pays off with a rad reward. An awesome, exhilarating experience awaits you at the end of the long, winding trail of people. Looking down at the slop they're serving at Reedmont, I can assure you—the school lunch is no Ferris wheel.

I'm standing in the lunch line behind Jenna. Carlos and Rainey are holding our table while we get our corn dogs and macaroni. I push my tray along the track, my eyes drifting along the food choices behind the glass. Dry hamburgers with dry buns. Fruit salad that should just be called…a bowl of *grapes*. And salad with browning lettuce. *Ew.*

"So I think I've perfected my wine snow cone," Jenna tells me. "I've even named it. *Mersno.*" She spreads her hands out like, *ta-da!* "What do you think?"

I snicker. "Mersno." Like Merlot. "Cute. But just how do you plan on getting your hands on some wine?" I bend and take a bowl of macaroni and cheese. Jenna goes ahead of me. I place it on my tray and slide it further down the line. Jenna's asking the lunch lady for two corn dogs when I come up behind her.

"That's easy," Jenna answers, setting her corn dogs down. She grabs a few packs of mustard from the condiments bar and tosses them on her tray. "I'll just raid my mom's stash."

"Jenna," I protest, taking my corn dog from the bar.

"I just need enough for one snow cone. She'll never miss it." She's paying the cashier now. I keep quiet until I'm done paying for mine. I don't need the lunch lady over hearing *this* conversation; underage teenagers stealing wine and making snow cones out of it.

After we've walked away, I ask, "What if Mr. Sullivan gets pissed you're presenting an alcoholic snow cone?"

She shrugs. "I don't know."

"What if he fires you?" I'm worried now because, in some weird roundabout way, Mersno was my idea. What if it gets Jenna fired? I'll feel so guilty if it does.

Jenna gives me a sharp look. "Did you know worrying causes wrinkles?"

I'm taken aback. "What?"

Jenna's face relaxes, and she laughs. "Lighten up, Penelope, or you're going to look like one of the Golden

Girls before you're twenty!" She flounces off and takes a seat beside Rainey. I shake my head at her and soon catch up, sliding my tray onto the table.

Rainey is eating her fruit salad—er grapes—and Carlos has already polished off his hamburger. He's working on his macaroni and cheese when I sit down next to him. Jenna is in front of me. I give her a look but don't say anything. She ignores me and starts squirting mustard onto her plate.

Rainey and Carlos start talking about some new meme they saw on the internet, but I zone out. My eyes are like magnets hunting for Matt. I don't see him, so I figure he's probably with his friends by the vending machines or something. I pick up the corn dog and take a huge bite.

Jenna's gaze is distracted. She's staring over my shoulder. "Um, Rainey? It looks like word still hasn't gotten around."

Carlos doesn't bother to look. He groans, "Another one? Damn. Does it ever get old?"

"No," Rainey answers simply. She sits up a little taller. "At least this one is cute."

When I turn around to see who they're talking about; I nearly choke on my corn dog. Matt is sauntering his way toward us. He's alone, none of his wrestling buddies with him.

He pauses at our table. "Hey," he says to me.

I swallow. The corn dog scratches its way down my throat. *Ouch.* "Hi," I say, brushing my fingers at the corners of my lips, hoping I don't have mustard smeared on my mouth.

"Mind if I sit with you?" He glances at everyone at the table. No one speaks. Carlos looks annoyed. Jenna's eyes are as wide and unblinking, like an owl. Rainey quietly sizes up Matt from behind her cellphone.

Matt takes a nearby chair, and drags it to the end of the table and plops down. His eyes are a little red, like he's sleepy. I wonder if that's why he was late this morning. *Did he oversleep?*

All of my friends' eyes shift to me and there's an uncomfortable silence hovering over our table. I clear my throat, wishing I could think of something clever to say. Actually, I wish I had a magical shawl that made me disappear. I'd wrap myself in it whenever I wanted to fade away…like right now.

Jenna doesn't need a magical shawl. She's brave, and independent, and always, *always* loses whenever dared to play the quiet game.

"Matt," she starts. I hold my breath, waiting for her say something embarrassing. Like how I don't know the words to any Rihanna songs, so I just hum to the beat. Or how I won't eat tuna salad sandwiches unless the crust has been cut off.

"Rumor has it you lived in Cali for a year. Did you see anyone famous?" She leans forward, eyes wide and hopeful.

"No."

She frowns. "Did you go to Hollywood?"

"No."

"Los Angeles?" My God, Jenna is relentless.

Matt lets out a huff that triggers a cough. He covers his mouth with a fist. *Is he okay?* He recovers quickly, clearing his throat before saying. "Sorry. No celebrity encounters in Sacramento." I don't understand why Carlos said what he said about Matt. He doesn't seem like he's ignoring anyone. He just seems shy, that's all.

Jenna sits back in her chair and crosses her arms in front of her. "Well, shoot. What fun is California if you don't go to Hollywood or LA?"

"Legal weed," Carlos responds, giving Matt a knowing nod. Matt looks at him like, *whatever,* and says to me, "Good news. Coach put me on the team." His smile is childlike. "My first match is match tonight. Want to come?"

I can feel six pairs of eyes boring holes in me. I gulp and squeak out a "Sure."

"Awesome. I'll see you then." Matt gets up and walks away, leaving the chair where it is. I glance at it, still reeling that Matt was just sitting there. Next to me. At our table.

"Oh my God," Jenna says. "I can't believe he came for *you*. I thought for sure he was coming for Rainey."

That stings. Though it shouldn't, because *every* boy that has ever approached our table is there for Rainey.

Chapter 11

It's after six o'clock and I'm still deciding what to wear. Matt's match starts at seven, and if I don't hurry, I'm going to be late. But, I'm torn between my Reedmont hoodie, to show support, of course, and a white, flirty blouse with billowy sleeves. I'm holding the blouse to my chest when Mom walks in. She does a double take.

"Are you going somewhere?"

"Wrestling match," I say, stepping up to my full-length mirror. "At school." It sounds silly saying it. Mom knows I have zero interest in wrestling. I bet she's wondering what bet I lost, since that's the only way I'd ever attend a match. *Until now.* I look at my reflection. The blouse is pretty, with corded burgundy rope along the neckline and at the wrists.

Mom crosses her arms over her sweater. It's knobby with wear, but she still wears it all the time. I remember being small and wrapping my arms around her waist. I'd press my cheek against her sweater, loving its softness on my skin. Mom saunters up to me. "Do you have a…*date?*" The way she draws out *date* makes me self-conscious. I ball up the blouse and toss it back on the bed. "No," I say sharply. I slip into my hoodie. Decision made. "A *friend* invited me."

Her brow arches high, and she gives me a look. She doesn't believe me. I drop to the edge of my bed to put my shoes on. Who cares if she doesn't believe me? It's the truth. Matt didn't ask me out. He simply asked if I wanted to see his match tonight. That's it. No big deal.

"Will you be home for dinner?"

I pull the laces of my sneaker. "Probably not." I tie them snugly and move on to the next. Things are still tense between me and Mom. This is the first I've seen her since I left her crying in the kitchen this morning. I'm not mad at her. There's no reason to be. She and I had this whole thing figured out. File the appropriate documents, sign them, and be on our merry little way. Then, I had to ruin things by overthinking.

"I'll leave soup on the stove for you. Make sure you have a bowl when you get home." She leaves and though I know I should stop her, I don't. She'll just bum me out. I'm actually looking forward to seeing Matt wrestle. I don't need her dampening that.

****

When I walk into the school's gymnasium, I'm surprised by how many people are here. The bleachers ripple Reedmont's colors, silver and blue. They're packed with students, parents, and even teachers. It's easy to spot the opposing team; Grainger High's green and yellow shirts stick out like a sore thumb. There's not many of them, and I can't help but wonder if they feel awkward, like strangers on enemy turf. I find an open seat on the end. It's near the exit so I can slip out whenever I want.

A referee walks into the middle of the gymnasium floor. The whistle around his neck flashes as he takes his place in the center of a big painted circle. With his two fingers, he gestures to someone.

I scan the sidelines and suck in a breath. It's Matt. My first instinct is to laugh. The blue singlet he wears is skin-tight, but when he turns his back to me, I suddenly don't find it funny anymore. In fact, I have to remind myself to blink.

Matt pulls at the strap under his chin, securing his headgear into place. He crosses the gymnasium floor. There's a purpose to his walk, an intimidating purpose. He stretches out the muscles in his arms, and shakes out his wrists, readying himself. Another boy, his opponent, steps out onto the floor. He's wearing a green singlet with a huge yellow "G" on the front. The two boys eye each other, sizing one another up. The referee says something to them, and they give a nod of understanding. They take their stances, each guarded and ready.

The referee blows a whistle and I'm expecting it to be a clash of the titans but instead the two boys stand poised, their arms extended and ready for the other to make the first move. Everyone in the gymnasium is quiet. It's as if we are all holding our breaths.

Grainger lunges and seizes Matt by the shoulders. He spins him around, so Matt's back is cradled against his chest. He holds Matt around the torso in a bear hug, all the while trying to lift him off his feet. Matt twists, and the boy's hold on him loosens just enough to allow Matt to swing an arm under his competitor, scooping him up almost effortlessly. He tosses him to the floor.

I wince when the boy's body hits the mat with an audible slap. Matt swoops right in, nearly sitting on the boy's back. He puts the boy in a gripping headlock. The boy struggles, trying to buck Matt off him like a bronco tries to unseat a cowboy. Matt doesn't budge. After a few unsuccessful attempts at freeing himself, the boy taps out.

There's a blast from the referees' whistle, and Matt

releases his hold and stands up. His mouth hangs open in a pant, his chest heaving under the thin straps of his singlet.

The referee takes him by the wrist and throws his hand in the air, announcing him winner. Matt's eyes glide across the bleachers. I sit straighter and wave, but he doesn't see me. He saunters away, leaving me with a view that is indescribable with words alone. It needs so much more, like an awesome soundtrack and starry-eyed emojis. With a heavy sigh, I quietly thank the wrestling gods for singlets…

Matt goes out the gym doors, likely heading for the locker room. Suddenly I feel alone. Like a fraud, in the midst of all of these people who actually know what a full nelson is. I watch two more matches, completely bored out of my mind. I think about leaving, but then the gymnasium doors swing open, and Matt walks in. He's changed into grey sweatpants and a zippered Reedmont hoodie. His hair looks wet and freshly combed. A sports bag hangs from his shoulder. He walks along the length of the front row. He pulls a phone out of the pocket of his hoodie. He looks to be making a call.

My cell phone beeps, startling me. I pull it out and look down at the screen. It's a text from Matt.

—*Hey. Are you here?*—

I text back. —*Yes. Near the far exit.*—

His chin raises, eyes scanning the still congested stands. I lift my hand in a wave. Our eyes crash over the din of the gymnasium. For a moment, it feels as if we are the only two people here. The only two people in the world.

He makes his way to me, and I grow more and more nervous the closer he gets. Why? It's just Matt. We hung out almost every day our freshman year. He's seen me in sweaty t-shirts and athletic shorts. *Oh God, I had forgotten. How could I have forgotten about that?*

He doesn't climb the bleachers, he stands at the foot of them, and with a quick jut of his chin, tells me, *"Let's get out of here."*

And like a hypnotized cobra, I stand and follow the simple command without hesitation.

****

Matt and I find ourselves back at the school's track field. I'd never seen it at night. Security lights flood blinding white light everywhere and the running tracks have been freshly re-painted. It even smells different, with the evening's dew already starting to settle.

Matt drops his gym bag to the ground. He says to me, "Shall we?"

My head bobs. "Sure."

We start our walk. It's slow, leisurely, and almost awkward. Almost.

"Like old times, right?" Matt says, putting his hands into the pockets of his hoodie.

"Yeah," I agree. "Except this time, I don't feel like a loser walking it."

"A loser?"

I finger the string of my hoodie. "Well, yeah. Everyone else ran the track. While I…well, I don't think you could call what I did, running." I think back to my meager attempts at running. Everyone seemed light-footed, with rod-straight backs. They looked so great running. Like professionals.

Me, on the other hand, I'd dash off, my feet slapping the ground like I was wearing clumsy clown shoes. My arms swung crazily, and after a few paces I'd have to stop to nurse the stabbing pains in my side and catch my breath. After that, I'd just give up and walk the rest of the way. Always the last one on the track. Except for the days Matt would walk with me.

Matt chuckles a little under his breath. "You had your own technique, that's for sure." He knocks me with an elbow, and I lose my footing, stumbling off the track. Matt catches my sleeve and pulls me back. He's laughing…not *at* me like most boys would, but genuinely laughing. I'm laughing now too, and I find myself noticing little things I've never noticed before. Like how Matt's eyes crinkle at the corners when he smiles, or how husky and low his laugh is.

We're not walking anymore. We're standing close. I can even smell the soap he used earlier. My heart feels like it's trying to claw its way out of my chest to see Matt for itself. If we were any closer, I think Matt would feel it, too.

He's not much taller than me, but still, I feel small, being this close to him. He's looking at me the same way he looked at me in the library. When he told me I was giving him reason to like Charlotte again.

Softly, he says, "Thanks for coming tonight."

I swallow, certain he's about to kiss me. Or at least I think he's about to kiss me. I mean, I've never actually been kissed before, so I'm not sure I'm reading the situation correctly. I don't say anything because I can't. I'm lucky to be breathing right now with him so close, invading my personal space like this.

"Do you…" Matt pauses, likes he's unsure if he wants to say it. "Do you want to go out sometime?"

Now my voice comes back with a rush, and before I can tamp it, my mouth spills, "Like a date?" Fire spreads across my cheeks. *Oh my God! Did I really just say that?*

Matt snickers, that husky laugh threatening to emerge. I wish it had. "Yeah. Like a date."

I can't keep a smile away. "Okay," I tell him.

The corners of his mouth turn upward, and we start our unhurried trek again. Every so often our elbows brush lightly against one another. We may not have kissed tonight, but this is just as good. I have a date. An *actual* date. A date with Matt Garrison. My eyes run over the length of track stretched out before us. I think back to our walks on it during gym. It always looked so endless back then. But, walking it with Matt at night like this…it doesn't look long enough.

Chapter 12

Every Saturday, I volunteer at Pointe Holden Hospital. I usually ride in with Mom. Her shifts are shorter on the weekends, so it works out nicely. As a volunteer, I'm responsible for delivering patients their flowers and get-well cards, directing visitors to their loved ones, and sometimes taking patients for walks, either up and down halls, or outside in the fresh air, if their illness allows it.

I didn't think I'd like it when I first started. I thought there would be too many people. Too many germs. Too much sickness and death. But, after a while, I grew to like it. The staff is friendly, and though that's a plus, that's not the reason I enjoy my time there. It's the patients. They are always so happy to get a delivery.

It's funny to think about, really. Cheap balloons and flowers that will soon wither bring so much joy to people. I think it's because it adds personality to their rooms. Think about it. Each room is a carbon copy of the next. There's nothing personal in them, nothing homey. But, when someone brings in a vase full of flowers that they hand-picked just for you, it suddenly brightens up the bleak room. It shows you that you are cared for, that you are loved, that you are wanted. That's all anyone really wants anyway…is to be wanted.

I put on my uniform and by uniform, I mean a crisp olive-green apron over my regular clothes. Thank God they no longer require the female volunteers to wear those old-fashioned red and white striped dresses. I shudder whenever I picture myself in one of those starched uniforms. A walking candy cane. Today, I'm extra comfy. Soft thermal shirt and my favorite jeans. The hospital is lenient on what you wear as long as it's tasteful.

However, they will send you home if you wear anything that promotes alcohol use or drug paraphilia. They consider that offensive. I never have to worry about that. I don't own anything offensive. Unless you count my t-shirt with the vulture eating roadkill on it. It says *"Nothing to see here. Carrion."* Get it? Carry on? Carrion? Sick but funny, right?

Mom pops the lock on her work room locker and shoves her purse inside. "Meet me in the cafeteria at noon?"

"Don't I always," I say.

The locker door slams shut. She gives me a wink and then we part ways. She heads to her office, which is located on the second floor, while I make a stop at the Hospital Gift Shop to see if anything needs to be delivered. No one other than Gina, the store clerk, is in the Gift Shop. Gina is in her late twenties. She's been working at the hospital for about a year now. Her blonde hair is woven into its usual thick braid, but today she's added a pretty silk headband that makes her look closer to my age.

Pointe Holden's Hospital Gift Shop is much like your usual hospital gift shop. Shelves overflow with various bouquets of flowers, Mylar balloons, and cuddly stuffed animals. It also sells candy and other snacks and soft drinks.

I pass the twirling racks of greeting cards. "Hi Gina," I call out.

"Penelope! Hello!" Gina is filling an orange latex balloon with helium. She secures it with a knot and ties curling ribbon to it. She lets it go, and the balloon soars to the ceiling, its ribbon within reach. "Can you deliver this when I'm done making it up? I just need to add three more."

"Of course," I say, leaning on the counter. She already has two balloons made. The orange one, and a silvery Mylar one with polka dots with *Get Well* across it.

She readies another latex balloon, fitting the mouth of it over the spout of the helium tank. She points over her shoulder. "That bouquet has to go too." It's a simple bouquet of yellow carnations, greenery, and baby's breath. The helium tank releases, and the balloon stretches and fills.

"I'll take care of it," I tell her, picking up the order pad from the counter. I rip off the tickets and put them in my apron pocket. I'll need them for the room numbers. I watch her finish the balloon arrangement, idly thinking about last night. I still can't believe it's real.

Matt Garrison asked me out on a date. *Me*. Penelope Reza. The girl who no one wants. I think about our freshman year, and wonder if Matt liked me back then. I doubt it. He was nice to me then, but it felt more like a brotherly affection, like he was looking out for me. Like he felt sorry for me.

The memory stings. I quickly shut it out, and relive our walk on the track. It was romantic with its moonlight and scent of dewy grass all around. Well, it was romantic to me at least.

Gina interrupts my thoughts. "Here you go," she says, holding out the balloons and carnations. I pull out the order form from my pocket and memorize the first room number before slipping it back. I take the tied balloons in one hand and the bouquet in the other.

I take the elevator to the third floor, greeting any nurses and doctors I pass along the way. Everyone knows me here. Not only am I Miranda Jackson's daughter, but I've volunteered here since I was twelve. Because of this, room 308 is easy to find. The door is open, so I go in. The bed is empty. There's a chart on the wall with the patient's information, so I know they haven't been discharged yet. Whoever it is, is either on a walk or perhaps in surgery or maybe away for some sort of testing.

I leave the bouquet of carnations on the table and set off to make my next delivery. I take the stairs to the fourth floor. This floor is quiet; the Pre-Op level, where patients go to get prepped for surgery. A couple of nurses flutter around the reception desk, too busy with their task at hand to notice me. This hallway has been recently cleaned. I can smell the disinfectant. The door to room 417 is ajar, and there are voices coming from inside. Raised voices. I hover at the door.

"I already told her no."

"I'd like to hear it for myself, if you don't mind, sir."

I grip the balloons tighter and peer around the corner. Nurse Ricter stands in the corner, small and unassuming, as if she were a bystander. She's shifting nervously on her feet, her hands worrying at the edge of the clipboard she has pressed to her chest.

Doctor Yassin is standing at the foot of the bed. He looks far more at ease. He's staring down at the man lying in the bed, overseeing him like the caretaker he is, with soft eyes and a tender smile. I like Dr. Yassin. He always smells of spearmint gum. And he's easy to talk to. I find myself taking advantage of that. I know it's silly, but sometimes, I wish Dr. Yassin was my biological father. How amazing would that be?

"What is it that worries you, exactly?" Dr. Yassin questions.

"To be frank…*you*," the man spits.

I suck in a breath of air. For a second, I'm worried they heard it. I step back a little, shame eating away at me. I shouldn't be eavesdropping.

"I am sorry you feel that way," Dr. Yassin tells him, his voice gentle. "But I haven't given you a reason to distrust me. I only want to help you."

The man scoffs. He's in his late fifties, maybe, it's hard to tell. He's a thick man all around. His hair is a bundle of thick, grey curls. His middle is thick, bulging under the thin hospital grade bed sheet. And his hospital gown isn't tied, so it hangs loose around his thick neck.

I lean around the corner again, watching with interest.

"I can refuse care. It's my right," the man says.

Dr. Yassin folds his arms. "Yes, I suppose you can. But Mr. Dodd, I assure you, I will give you the best care possible."

I watch, intrigued, my mind jumping to many conclusions. Why is he refusing care? Does he have cancer? Does he wish to live the rest of his life without chemo? Or maybe he has to have surgery of some sort? Perhaps he's had the surgery before, and would rather let nature take its due course rather than do it all again? My heart goes out to him.

"I don't want a Muslim opening me up. For all I know, you'll plant a bomb in me." The man is getting red in the face. My heart that once went out to him suddenly lurches into my stomach. "You will not touch me," he continues, his voice getting louder. "You understand?" He looks directly at Nurse Ricter. "Get me someone else." His gruff voice is so final.

Nurse Ricter looks at Dr. Yassin, who drops his arms, defeated, and says, "Very well."

The doctor is the picture of composure as he comes out of the room. Nurse Ricter hangs back to calm the patient, reassuring him she will find him an alternate surgeon.

Dr. Yassin's eyes widen just slightly when he notices me lurking by the door. "Penelope," he says, his voice surprised. "What are you doing here?"

I hold out the balloons in front of me. They bump into one another with a soft *bom bom* sound. "I have a delivery." I turn to the open door. "But I don't know if I want to go in there."

Dr. Yassin smiles at me ruefully. "How much did you hear?"

"All of it," I confess. The balloons slip a little in my grasp. I rub my sweaty palms on my apron. I shouldn't ask, but I can't help myself. "Did he really refuse to let you operate? Just because you're Muslim?"

Dr. Yassin purses his lips and lets out a long breath through his nose. Nurse Ricter slips past us. I see her cup Dr. Yassin's elbow as she does, a sort of *I'm so sorry* silent message. The doctor gives her grateful nod, then looks back at me. He cocks his head and gives me a sad, almost apologetic look. "Everyone is entitled to their feelings. For some, those feelings can't be reasoned with, no matter how hard you try."

"But…" I try to find the words, but they are getting swallowed by my hurt, by my anger. How can someone refuse surgery because of something as simple as skin color? As religion? It's absurd. It isn't hard to dredge up memories of my own. Prejudices hidden by naivety. Like when old ladies smile in my face, but ask me where my hijab is. Or pranks. Like Trip blasting, *Walk Like an Egyptian* from his car stereo.

"But he was rude to you, and you still wanted to help him." I stare at him incredulously. "How do you do it? How do you ignore it?" I'm on the verge of tears now, angry tears, but tears none-the-less.

Dr. Yassin must sense this because he lays a hand on my shoulder. The way he gazes down at me, his dark eyes kind and shining, like polished obsidian, is fatherly, and suddenly I feel a pang in my chest. *Is this what it would be like? To have a father? A father who looked like me?*

Dr. Yassin says to me, "There will always be people in this world who don't like me. Sometimes it's because of my personality. Other times, it's my humor. Once, it was even because of my laugh." His smile is genuine.

"And this time…it happens to be because of my religion. It may not be a good reason, or a just reason, but it's where we are. Not everyone will want me in their life, and that's okay. I know I'm wanted somewhere." He winks and walks away, his white lab coat swishing behind him like a flag in the wind as he hurries down the hallway to see his next patient.

Chapter 13

The rest of my shift consists of more deliveries, three walks, and I even got to hold a couple of babies in the NICU. They sometimes need cuddlers, as they call them, to snuggle with the preemies, providing the vital skin-to-skin contact they need to thrive. That's one of my favorite jobs. The babies remind me of porcelain dolls, fragile and small. I admit, they look alike to me, with their scrunched-up faces and tiny button noses. The only difference is their skin color and sometimes their hair…if they have any.

I'm spreading my lunch out in front of me as I wait for Mom. A Caesar salad with extra croutons, a turkey sandwich, a pickle, and a large sweet tea. I'm unwrapping the cellophane off the salad when Mom comes up. She sits down across from me and shrugs out of her sweater.

"Hey. How's your day going?" she asks, peeling the top off a strawberry yogurt. She drops the silver wrapping to the table.

"Okay," I hedge, debating whether I should mention what happened to Dr. Yassin.

She quirks a brow at me. "Okay? That's it?" She spoons some yogurt into her mouth. "Sounds about as uneventful as my day."

I pop a crouton in my mouth, crunching it between my teeth.

Mom keeps talking. "Oh. There was this one lady who told me her cat clawed up her bill." She takes another bite of yogurt. "That's not the first time I heard that one before. I wonder why dogs eat homework and cats shred bills?" Her laugh is timid. I laugh too, pleasantly surprised at her attempt to make a joke. Mom really does try. She may not always pull things off, but at least she makes an honest effort. I appreciate that.

I pick up my fork. "A man refused to let Dr. Yassin operate on him today." The words hang in the air, like wet laundry on a clothesline.

Mom's smile fades. "Really? Why?"

I pop another crouton. "Because he's Muslim." I say it so matter-of-factly it causes Mom to take pause, her spoon halfway to her mouth. Her eyes hold mine. She looks ill all of a sudden. I know she's processing what this means to me. *She wonders if I'm upset—if I'm thinking about my biological father…*

"I never knew someone's hate could be so strong, that they'd willingly risk their life for it." The words are heavy and painful to say out loud.

Mom sets the spoon and yogurt cup down. She's about to say something, but her cellphone rings. She rifles through her purse as it rings again. She finds it and answers it. "Hi Honey."

My stomach clenches. *Trip.*

"Yes, of course. That's no problem."

I've grown to hate that sickening sweet tone of hers. The tone she uses when she's talking to Trip. *Why does she put up with his crap? Because he's her son?* That's even more reason to not put up with it if you ask me. You expect strangers to treat you like garbage, not your own family.

83

"I won't be late." Mom's eyes shift to me. "No, you don't have to do that. I'll remember." She presses the phone tighter to her ear, trying to muffle Trip's voice. I can't make out what he's saying, but I am sure I can guess. He probably started off asking for a favor. Now, since Mom agreed, he's degrading her by insinuating she'll forget and botch everything up. My hands grip the seat beneath me. He is infuriating.

She hangs up and tries her best to avoid eye contact with me. She picks up her yogurt cup and starts scraping the bottom with her spoon. I watch her for a moment.

"What did he want?" I ask her.

She doesn't look up from the yogurt. "A ride to the airport next week."

I don't say anything. I've learned not to. It's a waste of time. Mom will never change. Trip will never change. There's no use trying. I only get frustrated when I do.

Mom and I eat the rest of our lunch in silence. The only time we speak is to bid each other goodbye as we head back to our respectful ends of the hospital. Mom to her office. Me to my deliveries.

****

I spend my Sunday scrolling through the Lit Fest schedule of events, trying to decide what's a priority and what's not. Jonathan Preston is a priority. In fact, he's my only priority. He's doing a book signing, and I am determined to get his autograph. He's my all-time favorite author. I've read everything he's ever published, and I follow him on social media. I browse the panels and other author book-signing schedules and after I'm satisfied with my itinerary, I call Jenna to give her my "must-do" list.

Jenna answers on the second ring. "Hey!"

"Hey. I have my list ready." I roll over onto my stomach, spreading my notes in front of me.

"Hold on," she says. "Let me get my notebook." I can hear shuffling in the background. No doubt she's collecting highlighters and her fancy set of felt-tipped markers. "Okay, let's hear it."

"First and most important, Jonathan Preston."

"Of course," Jenna says. I pause because I know she's writing it down. "That's at noon, so we have time to hit all the swag tents in the morning, then line up for Preston after that. What else?"

"Rouges and Redeemer's Panel. It's at two o'clock."

"I thought that sounded interesting, too. It was on my list."

"Soul sisters," I tell her, smiling. "Oh, and I'd like to watch the Keynote Discussion too."

"Definitely." She writes in her notebook. She's quiet for a moment, coming up with our game-day strategy. "Nothing overlaps this year. Awesome. Margaret Kenter and Cami DeFord are signing together again this year, so that will cut down on our wait time. And it looks like we can squeeze in lunch around eleven."

An hour later, Jenna and I have firmed up our hour-by-hour Lit Fest plan of events. Really, she plans most of it. This year, nothing matters to me except meeting Jonathan Preston. His books have been like friends to me. They've been there for me when I felt lonely and a comfortable place to go when I needed an escape from my own reality. I won't admit how often that was.

Chapter 14

I refuse to say how much time I spent getting ready for school on Monday morning. Let's just say I was late and wasn't able to meet up with Jenna for breakfast. She was annoyed with me for that. She wanted to give me my official Lit Fest schedule. A list she painstakingly types up each year on bright pink printer paper.

Mrs. Johnson shuts the classroom door. Matt isn't here yet. He must be running late again. I wonder how often he's late? Is this normal for him? Twenty minutes into class, I realize he's not coming. I'm disappointed. Tuning out Mrs. Johnson, I daydream about him. Wondering what his house looks like and what happened between his parents. It's silly, I know, but for some reason, I want to know everything about him. Even trivial things, like, what's his favorite animal?

Since Matt isn't at school, the day seems to drag on, unbearably boring. The highlight was the look Jenna gave me when I folded her Lit Fest schedule and shoved it into my back pocket. I thought she was going to strangle me. Carlos had to distract her with cookies to keep her from losing her mind in the hallway.

I wish Carlos would just come clean already. Jenna will never figure it out on her own. The girl is oblivious. She's so comfortable in their friendship that she doesn't notice the little things. Like how Carlos laughs at all of her corny puns. Or how he walks her to every class and patiently helps her with her Spanish homework. Why are things always unquestionably clear to everyone else, but not to the person directly involved? Seems like a cruel joke if you ask me.

****

I'm kicked back on the couch, reading *Lord of the Flies*, when there's a knock at the front door. *Who could that be?* I get up and go to the door. I take a quick glance through the peephole and see Mr. Bower. He's close to the door. His face is distorted, like a fun-house mirror and his nose filling up most of the pinhole. I open the door. "Hi Mr. Bower."

Mr. Bower is a slight man, with a curve to his back that makes him appear small and fragile. "Hi Penelope." A soft breeze catches his thin white hair, lifting it up and away from his scalp as if it's greeting me. I nearly chuckle. "Is your mom here?" I'm sure he already knows since her car isn't parked in the driveway.

"No. She's working the late shift tonight. Is there something you need?"

His hand flexes and re-grips the handle of his cane. He's about to ask me for a favor…I can tell. "I hate to ask you, but the pharmacy just called. Edith's prescription is ready. Do you think you can run to Sweetwater and pick it up?" He looks out across the sky. It's fading to a pretty pink. "Sun's going down. I don't think I can make it there and back before nightfall." He turns back to me, expectant. Again, he adjusts his grip on the cane. Must be his nervous tick. I think about my hair twirling. Everyone has one.

"Sure, Mr. Bower. No problem."

His dentures flash in the porch light. "Thanks, kid. I owe you." He reaches into his back pocket and takes out a battered wallet. He lifts out a twenty and hands it to me. "This will cover it. Whatever's left is yours."

I return his smile and take the money. "I'll bring it over as soon as I get back."

He waves me off. "No rush. Jeopardy is coming on. I'll be up."

Amused, I shake my head to myself as I watch him turn himself around and shuffle across the lawn. I wait until he's safely back at his front door before I slip back inside the house to grab my jacket and keys.

****

Sweetwater is the town's only family-owned pharmacy. Most of the city fills their prescriptions here instead of chain stores because of the cool vibe the pharmacy has. It used to be an old soda shoppe in the fifties, complete with funky bar stools and soda jerks. But, in the eighties, when business faded, the family who owns it revived it as a pharmacy. This was far more lucrative than the dying breed of soda shoppes, so the rest is history.

I push open the door, the bell above my head jingles. The pickup line is backed up with people. I take my place at the end and fish my phone out of my pocket to pass the time. I check my emails. They're mostly junk, so I dump them into the spam folder.

I move with the flow of the line, idly scrolling through my favorite mobile app, Gottaread. It's my go-to for all my book-nerd needs. They rate and review books, and always seem to be the first to know when a new novel drops. Shifting on my already tired feet, I read the synopses of a few YA books. I come across one that sounds good and move it to my "want to read" pile. I run my gaze along the length of the line, not really focusing on anything except how many people are ahead of me. Maybe about four? I go back to Gottaread.

The woman in front of me sighs dramatically. I ignore her, engrossed in a synopsis about a girl with a mechanical heart and a family she doesn't remember. *Interesting.*

"Oh, come on," the woman says with exasperation. I look up from my phone screen. She catches my eye, and tells me, "That guy up there is holding up the line."

I try to peer around her, but there are too many people crowded around the register to see who she's talking about. "Been up there for ten minutes. I got roast in the crock pot that's probably drying out." She huffs.

A woman with a baby carrier a few feet ahead peels off from the line. Guess she decided the wait wasn't worth it. We advance a couple of steps, bringing me closer to the pharmacy counter.

"Are you sure?" a deep voice growls. My ears prick with recognition. *I know that voice.* It's the same voice that has sent shivers down my spine the past two days. I lean around the woman in front of me, trying to catch a glimpse of him. *Maybe it's not him,* I think to myself. After all, I've only been dreaming of it incessantly the past couple of days.

"Yes," the pharmacist explains. "It's not here. I've checked twice. I'm sorry, sir."

"Well, can't you just fill it now?"

A big man in a baseball cap at the head of the line turns sideways, making it easier to see through the crowd. I see the pharmacist; she looks young, probably fresh out of college. She's petite, like Mom. But unlike Mom, she stands firm. "I am unable to fill your prescription." She shakes her head, sending her stick-straight, chin-length hair swinging. "You'll have to come back tomorrow and speak with the pharmacy manager."

That earns her a huff before the figure turns on his heel. It's Matt. His face is red and blotchy, like he's angry. He stomps away, his mouth a severe line. I swear, if a brick wall was suddenly in front of him, he'd blow right through it.

The woman in front of me breathes, "Finally", and takes a couple of steps forward. I don't move. I'm too wrapped up in staring at Matt. He's plowing past the people in line, his eyes are trained on the ground, but when I say, "Matt?" his whole demeanor changes. His eyes snap to mine, and his features go soft.

"Hey," he says, trying to sound casual. It doesn't work and I know he can tell. His brows pinch a little, but he tries to act natural.

"Are you okay?" I ask him.

He shoves his hands into his pockets. "Yeah." He tosses a dark glare over his shoulder at the pharmacist. "They won't fill my script. I don't know why."

I wonder what the prescription is for, but I don't ask. Somehow it seems rude. Intrusive.

"Hey, so." His face changes completely, arranging itself in a more animated way. "You still owe me a date, remember?"

I smile. "I know."

"How about tonight?"

Tonight?

I fumble with the tips of my hair, combing my fingers through it obsessively. I'm hesitating and I don't know why.

"Tell you what. Shoot me your address and I'll pick you up in an hour. Sound good?"

I swallow.

The man behind me clears his throat loudly and grumbles, "You're up."

Everyone in line shoots me dark looks. I redden.

"Text me," Matt says before strolling away.

****

Matt picks me up later that evening. After I delivered Mr. Bower's prescription, I stood at my closet for what seemed like hours, deciding what to wear. I finally decided on my usual jeans, an ivory blouse, and a cute corduroy jacket to pull it all together. Mom was still working, so I left a note telling her I'd be home no later than ten o'clock and locked the front door on my way out.

Sitting in the front seat of Matt's car, I feel oddly powerful. Important even. Wanted. I had seen girls at school riding shotgun with their boyfriends, windows down, with their hair whipping in the wind. They looked very much like couples in that way.

Do Matt and I look that way now? I hope so. The radio is turned low, but it's high enough to discern classic rock coming from the speakers. I don't know what I expected him to listen to, but classic rock wasn't it. The interior of his car is well kept. He probably details it weekly. Boys seem to like doing that sort of thing.

Matt smoothly slides the car into the fast lane. "Randolf's after the movie?" Matt questions. Randolf's is a quaint Italian restaurant in the center of town. It's known for its dim lighting and killer cannoli. Hmm. I can taste them already.

"Sure," I respond, shifting my eyes to the road ahead. We're roaring up on a silver truck. Matt hovers close to the truck's bumper until the driver finally changes lanes. My hands clamp down on the seat beneath me. I try to avoid eye contact with the truck driver. He's flipping us the bird.

Matt ignores it and coaxes the car even faster, the engine growling as we settle into a steady clip. My eyes flick to the speedometer. We're doing well over eighty. I can't help but wonder if we'll make it to the movie theater in one piece.

Matt's at ease behind the wheel. He sits languidly, legs spread wide. He's leaning back so far, he could probably see out the backseat window. The world outside flies past me in a whirl. Matt certainly has a lead foot.

I, on the other hand, am a sensible driver. I do the speed limit. I always use my blinkers, and I am courteous to a fault. I even stink at Mario Kart. I can't bring myself to toss bananas at the other players or shove cars off the road.

"So, where were you today?" I ask him.

His eyes are on the road. "Didn't feel like going."

Something feels off about that answer. "So you skipped?"

His hands tighten on the wheel. "I didn't skip. My mom knows I didn't go."

Oh. "Were you sick? Is that what the prescription was for?"

Matt's features tighten, making him unreadable. As the seconds stretch on, I start to feel small. Like he's measuring me, regretting he'd ever agreed to take me out. Like I'd said something wrong.

The movie theater parking lot is nearly empty when we pull in. It's odd to see it this way, but then again, it is Monday night. Jenna and I usually hit the movies on opening nights when the theater is packed with people.

We park, and he climbs out and slams the door shut. He waits for me to do the same. My heart deflates a little. *Did I make him mad?* I try to brush it off, but inside I'm disappointed. *Why?* Matt isn't my boyfriend. Besides, opening doors and pulling out chairs is only done in the movies. Guys don't really do that stuff.

I get out. The night air is brisk, but not too chilly. I stuff my hands into the pockets of my corduroy jacket and try to keep pace with Matt. The lights from the theater marquee light up the entire parking lot, and it's in those blaring lights I see his terse mouth and hard eyes.

Why is he so mad? I don't like how he's ignoring me, but I'm a little afraid to call him out on it.

A row of movie posters with blinking frames greets us as we make our way to the ticket booth. I'm prepared to pay my own way, but Matt holds up his hand as if saying *halt.* He pays for my ticket, and inside my chest, my deflated heart swells back into shape. Again, I'm washed with the feeling I had in his car. Of power and importance. Matt wants me here with him. Of all the girls in our school, he chose me. Penelope Reza.

Matt forgoes the concession stand, opting to head straight into the theater instead. There are a few people scattered in the seats, far from a packed house. I follow behind him, popcorn crunching underfoot as we walk. He picks the back row, which seems to be heavily shadowed and almost detached from the rest of the rows. My throat dries a little at the prospect of what could happen in the deserted, dark row.

Matt collapses into a chair, it squeaks under his weight. I settle into the seat next to him.

Matt leans in. "You've seen the first one, right?"

He's referring to the movie. It's probably something he should have asked me earlier, but I don't mind. I'd watch just about any movie he wanted me to, just to be with him.

"No," I say.

Matt's face falls. "Really?' He leans in closer. His cologne wafting dangerously near. I take it in greedily. He smells so good. "Everyone on the planet has seen it."

I shake my head. "I've read the book."

He fakes a groan. "Of course you have." A smile slips across his face and it melts me into the chair. There's no trace of the iciness he had in the car. Whatever it was has faded and the Matt I know is back.

The house lights dim, and Matt sits back in his chair. I watch him from the corner of my eye throughout the entire movie, from the previews to the credits, wishing he'd put his arm around me. I don't know why. I'm not sure what *this* really is. Matt called it a date, but that was only after I opened my big mouth and said it first. This could just be a friendly date. Two friends hanging out. Nothing more.

I'm so deep in my thoughts, I don't notice the movie has ended until Matt stands up. I rise and fumble out on the aisle. Matt comes up beside me and we walk out of the theater. We're both quiet until we're out into the parking lot.

"What did you think?" Matt asks.

"It was good," I say.

"But?" he prods, waiting for a car to back out of a parking spot. I linger beside him, watching the car pull away.

"But the book was better," I admit with a smile.

"There it is," he says, laughing. "I knew you were

going to say that." He takes my hand in his. Is it possible for your body to go rigid and languid all at once? Mine does. Surely, he feels my fingers, stiff in his, but how's he to know that *inside* I'm a gooey mess? I feel like one of those Tootsie Rolls Pops. A hard candy shell with a soft center.

He whispers, "Is this okay?"

I nod shyly, stealing a peek at our clasped hands. I had to see it with my own eyes, or I wouldn't have believed it. We're actually holding hands! I want to squeal with delight, but I purse my lips instead, relishing the feel of his warm palm against mine. By the time we reach his car, I'm flying. Perhaps this is a real date, after all?

Chapter 15

How did I get here? Is this real life? I'm standing on my front porch with Matt, looking into his dark eyes, scared but excited at the idea of a goodnight kiss. The porch light is on. Mom must have turned it on for me. I wonder what she thought when she read my note. I didn't mention Matt or a date. Does she think I'm with Jenna?

Moths fly drunkenly around the porch light. Some cling to the glass globe seeking warmth. I'm shifting on my feet, my nerves fraying like a stretched rope into my gut. The cannoli from Randolf's in my stomach suddenly feels heavy and I'm wishing I hadn't eaten it. Mom's car is in the driveway, but there's no movement from inside the house. She's in bed already or in the shower.

Matt casually lifts his right arm, and flattens his palm to the door frame above my shoulder. I suck in a breath, securely pinned between the front door and Matt's body. "I had a good time tonight," he says. "Did you?"

I can only manage a nod. This seems to amuse Matt. The corners of his mouth quirk up, and his eyes dance like the moths around the porch light.

"Good," he whispers. He leans forward and captures my lips with his. He tastes like Randolf's marinara sauce, but I don't mind. I kiss him back anyway. His eyes are closed, but mine remain open. I don't want to miss a single second of this. Matt smiles against my mouth, and

I jerk away, my gaze steadfast on his curved mouth.

"What?" I demand, suddenly embarrassed. *Does my breath smell like garlic?*

"You're better at that than I thought you'd be." He fingers the loose strands of hair over my shoulder, and tucks them behind my ear.

I should be insulted. Matt expected me to be reluctant, to be clumsy, to be awkward. And I was all of those things, but he just didn't notice. I shouldn't be surprised. I'm known for being shy. Why would he expect anything else from me?

"I hope we can do some more of that sometime," he says, unhitching himself from the door frame. "See you at school tomorrow?"

"Yeah," I murmur, wrapping myself in a hug to hide my shivering body. I watch him cover the front lawn and disappear into his car. He pulls away, leaving me alone on the front porch. Alone to reel. Alone to pinch myself, because this all can't be real. No, this certainly can't be real life. With the taste of his kiss still on my lips, I think, *or can it?*

When I push open the front door, the smell of coffee hits me like a splash of cold water. My dreamy haze awakens with a jolt. Mom's still up. I find her sitting at the kitchen table, nursing a mug of black coffee. Oh, no. *She's drinking the hard stuff. Something must be wrong.*

I slip into the chair opposite her. "Why are you still up?" I toss a nervous glace to the clock on the microwave. "I'm not late."

She looks at me with tired brown eyes. "I know."

It's then that I notice the stack of stapled paperwork in front of her. My stomach twists at the sight of them. She had slipped them out of the manila folder, and even had the Uni-Pen lying atop of them as if she was so sure I'd be signing them.

"Tomorrow is the deadline, Penelope and you haven't made any mention of it this entire week. You have to decide." She taps a slender finger on the stack. "Once and for all. Are you going to sign them or not?"

"You make it sound like this is it. If I don't sign them tonight, I'll never have the chance to again."

Her brows knit. "Why are you hesitating?"

"Why are you pressuring me?"

Mom's eyes snap open wide. "Pressuring you? I'm not pressuring you, Penelope. You're the one who pestered me to start this process, remember?"

She's right. I did bug her to go to Mr. Douglas all those months ago. I wanted so badly then to be a Jackson, but that seemed like a lifetime ago.

Calmly, I pick up the stack of documents, flicking my eyes across the typed text and jargon. Here it is. The thing that would legally make me Penelope Jackson. It seemed so harmless, and so incredibly easy. With one swipe of the Uni-Pen, I could erase Penelope Reza from existence. I reached for the manila envelope. Without another word, I slip the paperwork into the envelope and seal it shut, never once lifting the Uni-Pen from the table.

Chapter 16

Looking back, I can pinpoint the day our (our, meaning Matt and I) little routine began. It was the day after our first date. Our weekdays go like this: Matt meets me at my locker every morning. We walk to English together, spend much of the class whispering, stealing glances, and passing notes. Then, he walks me to Biology, where I squirm throughout the next fifty minutes, itching to be with him again. Then, the bell finally rings after what feels like eternity and it's time for lunch.

For the first two weeks or so, Matt sat with Jenna, Carlos, Rainey, and I at our usual booth, but then, he and I began drifting away from the others. We prefer to sit alone in the cafeteria or on a bench at the courtyard. Jenna has been giving me the cold shoulder since we started doing that. She says, "Matt's keeping you from me," which always instigates a fight between us.

She's not wrong, though. Ever since Matt and I started dating, I seem to have little time for her. But she should understand. Matt's my boyfriend. *Boyfriend.* I'm not sure I'll ever get used to calling him that. But that's exactly what he is. Somedays, it still doesn't seem real.

Mom and I haven't revisited the night in the kitchen, where I chose to put changing my name off for a while longer. I could tell it hurt her, but she just gave me a sad nod when I handed her the sealed envelope as my answer.

I never look back on that night. I made the right decision, and besides, it's not like I'm never going to sign them. I just need more time, that's all. I need to decide—am I Penelope Jackson, or am I Penelope Reza? Can I be both?

Halloween is less than a week away. For the past two years, my tradition has been pretty tame. I dress up as some sort of cutesy animal, and binge on chocolate while I pass out candy at home. This year though, Matt has other plans. Dylan, one of his friends from the wrestling team, is throwing a Halloween party, and against my better judgement, I've agreed to go.

Tonight, Matt and I are working on our costumes. Since Matt is only willing to wear all black and go as a shadow, that left me little to work with. The best I could come up with was Peter Pan. I'll of course be normal Peter, while Matt is Peter's lost shadow. *That's cute right?*

I'm hot gluing a long red feather to a green felt hat when Matt says, "Please tell me you're going to sex this up a little?" He picks up the green tunic I had slung over the kitchen chair. He holds it up in the air, scrutinizing it closely. It's boxy and unflattering, but once I cinch it with a leather belt, it will be fine.

"Don't be a prude, Peter Pan. A little cleavage never hurt anybody."

I give him a little shove. "Matt."

He chuckles and presses a kiss to my temple. I love when he does that.

I slip the hat onto my head. "What do you think?"

Matt nods appreciatively. "Cute. Think everyone will know who we are?"

Unplugging the glue gun, I say, "How could they not? Everyone knows who Peter Pan is." I take the costume from him and lay it back over the chair, smoothing it out so it doesn't wrinkle. "The scene where Wendy sews Peter's shadow back onto his feet is one of the most memorable parts of the book."

Matt cocks his head at me.

I feel his eyes on me. "What?"

"How did I end up with the hottest book nerd on earth?"

I blush. The way he's looking at me like I'm some sort of mythical creature has my stomach doing weird flips. I want to smother him with kisses, so I wrap my arms around his neck and do just that.

Chapter 17

It's the night of the Halloween party. I'm pacing the living room in my Peter Pan costume. My nerves starting to get the best of me. *Will people laugh at my costume?* Peter Pan isn't exactly sexy. I'm betting all the girls there will be some variation of sexy. Sexy librarian. Sexy devil. Sexy angel. I've even seen a sexy banana. Which is just plain weird.

I wasn't going for sexy per se, but I tried to rev it up just a little, for Matt. I've cinched the waist of the green tunic with a thick leather belt. The collar of the tunic was loose to begin with, so it naturally shows off my collarbone. I gathered my hair into a low bun at the nape of my neck and I opted for simple makeup. No foundation, no blush. Just lip gloss and a touch of glittery eyeshadow. I have on thick green tights, and Mom's borrowed ankle boots, which really pulls the look together.

I adjust my hat and start twirling a lock of loose hair. My costume isn't the only reason I'm nervous. I've never been to a real party before. I mean, I've been to plenty of birthday parties as a little kid, but I've never been to a *party* party. A high school party. Where there will be alcohol and making out.

I gulp. *Do people still play Spin the Bottle?* I pull apart the window curtains for the hundredth time. I'm just about to call Matt when his headlights swing into the driveway.

I straighten my felt hat, and out the door I go. As I open the passenger door, Matt says, "Damn. Peter Pan got legs for days!"

Rolling my eyes, I laugh. "Oh, stop."

His eyes drift down the length of me. "I'm not kidding, Pen." He lets out a low whistle. "You look amazing."

I get in and give him a quick peck on the cheek. "Thanks." I pull the seatbelt over me. "You look…" I squint my eyes, pretending to think long and hard. With a smile, I tell him, "Tall, dark and handsome."

****

The entire school is at this party. Music blares from a set of speakers at the fireplace. It pulses at my temples. The air is thick with a nauseating mixture of smoke, perfume, and sweat. The living room is choked full of people, making it hard to get anywhere. Matt takes my hand and leads me through it. With his broad shoulders, it's easy for him to plow through the crowd. We stop at a table where Matt gets a drink. He offers me one, but I decline.

Just as I've thought, all the girls there are dressed in risqué costumes. Compared to them, I feel stupid in mine. I self-consciously tug at the hem of the tunic.

Matt puts an arm around me. "Quit overthinking," he says. "Loosen up. Have a good time."

Dylan comes up. "Hey, Matt. You made it." They high-five each other.

Dylan gives me a measured look. "Peter Pan. I dig it." His eyes shift to Matt, who's wearing black jeans and a black hoodie. Matt pulls the hoodie up over his head, to give the full effect. "And you are…hold on. Let me think about it." Matt suddenly picks me up under the armpits, lifting me effortlessly into the air.

"Hey!" I protest, my feet dangling like I'm some sort of puppet. I start to thrash, but Matt is unfazed. He sets me in front of him, so that I am standing on his feet. "What are you doing—" It takes me a second, but then I realize he's making it look like he's my shadow. I stop squirming, but I worry that I'm hurting him. My boots have to be digging into his feet. Matt aligns his arms with mine.

Dawning hits Dylan's face. He snaps his fingers and says, "Peter Pan's shadow. Clever." Dylan looks at me. "Clearly you were the brains behind this."

I flush crimson.

Matt laughs. "Asshole," he says, playfully punching Dylan in the shoulder.

Across the room, Rainey catches my eye. Surprised to see her, I wave enthusiastically. I am so relieved she's here. To have a friendly face in this sea of popular kids. She makes her way through the room, politely prying herself from boys as she does. When she finally makes it to me, she hugs me.

"You look adorable!"

"Thanks." I step back to get a good look at her. She's dressed as a badass biker and she's killing it. Her normally white-blond hair is tucked away beneath a severe ebony wig, and her long legs are clad in black leather pants. She even has an unlit cigarette dangling between her lips. "Great costume, by the way."

She looks down at herself. "Eh. I threw it together at the last minute."

"You can't tell."

"Have you seen Jenna and Carlos?" Rainey takes the

cigarette from her mouth.

My heart squeezes. "I doubt they were invited." It hurts me to say that. Aside from Rainey, my friends and I don't get invited to parties like this. The only reason I'm here is because of Matt. I know that. Everyone knows that.

Rainey's blue eyes hold mine. "Matt invited them." She says it matter-of-factly. Like I should already know.

My mouth pops open. "What?" I turn to Matt. "You invited Jenna and Carlos?"

He smiles sheepishly. "Yeah. I figured you'd want them here."

I twine my arms around his waist, pressing my cheek against his chest. I can hear the steady beat of his heart through his thick hoodie. "Oh, thank you!"

As if on cue, Carlos emerges from the thick of the crowd. Jenna is at his side. "Pen," he calls over the noise. He's carrying some sort of box with him.

"Carlos!" I rush to meet them halfway. I divide a hug between them. "I'm so glad you guys are here." Jenna looks great as an elfin archer. Her makeup application is so immaculate, she looks as though she's stepped off a movie set. She even has the pointy latex elf ears and all. I tug at the braid hanging over her shoulder. "You need to wear this to Lit Fest."

"Not until I get a better bow." She shows me her mini bow and arrow. She must have borrowed it from her little brother. The arrows have suction cups at the tips.

I laugh and turn to Carlos. "So where's your costume?" He fits the box he's been holding over of his head. It's then that I realize it's a pixelated worm from his favorite video game, Slugs 'N Creepers. I groan. "Really?"

Carlos spreads his arms out. In a muffled voice he says, "Creepers gotta creep."

Matt comes up behind me, pressing a hand to the small of my back. "Want to dance?" he asks against my ear. I get all tingly inside. Will his voice ever stop doing that to me? I hope not.

"Sure," I say, allowing him to lead me away.

As we sway to the music, I look out at my friends. Jenna and Rainey are chatting about something, and as usual Jenna is unaware that Carlos is stealing glances at her. I make a mental note to probe Jenna to see if she feels anything for Carlos in return. I won't tell her he likes her. That's not for me to tell, but the least I can do is feel her out for him.

Matt's hands drift down to my waist. I lift my face so I can look into his eyes. "Thanks for inviting them," I say. "That was really sweet of you."

Matt bends and plants a kiss on my lips. "Anything for my girl."

I let out a satisfied sigh. *His girl*. Can this night be any more perfect? I'm at a real party. My friends are with me, and I'm slow dancing with Matt Garrison. And just like that, I know why Peter Pan didn't want to grow up. I too want to live in this very moment, forever.

Chapter 18

After Halloween, it always feels like you're on a fast track to Christmas. Stores start decorating, skipping right over Thanksgiving, which is fine by me. Thanksgiving has never been a favorite of mine. The Jacksons didn't have much of a tradition. Unless you count Mom fretting over an elaborate dinner that Wesley would tear down, and Trip would refuse to eat.

Mom always seemed to tread lightly on that day, so overtime, I've developed a real aversion to the holiday. Now, with Wesley gone, Mom and I all but avoid Thanksgiving. The first year after Wesley passed, Mom tried to keep the normalcy going by cooking a huge meal for me and Trip. The three of us sitting at the table felt forced and completely fake.

By that time, I had built an impenetrable wall between me and Trip. Just being in the same room with him made me cringe. I guess Mom and Trip felt it too, because the next year Trip spent the day at his girlfriend's house while Mom and I went to Granny's Kitchen, our town's favorite go-to spot for traditional southern food. The restaurant is chock-full of quaint rustic décor, and they offer outdoor seating with rocking chairs and corn-hole boards. The food is so delicious, you half expect Granny herself to be in the back, cooking your order on a potbelly stove.

That's been our tradition ever since. We eat sugar-cured ham, sweet potato casserole, cranberry relish, and corn muffins. When we're through we play a game of corn-hole on the patio. It's nice actually. Matt wanted to join us this year, but his mother insisted he go with her to Pittsboro, where her sisters live.

"I think I'm going to switch it up this year," I tell Mom as we pour over the Thanksgiving menu.

She arches a brow. "Really? How so?"

"I think I'm going to get the turkey n' dressing."

"What? No ham?" She covers her heart with her hand. "How dare you? Everyone knows you eat ham on Thanksgiving and turkey on Christmas."

"Then why is it on the menu?" I point to it.

She waves me off. "It's for the few who don't know any better."

I laugh and go back to studying the menu. A waitress soon flounces over. Her high pony swinging like a horse's tail swatting flies. "Happy Thanksgiving, y'all. My name is Megan. Can I get you something to drink?"

"Yes, but I think we're ready to order, actually." Mom's eyes slide to me. "Right?"

"Yeah," I agree, looking at Mom from over the top of the menu. "You go first."

Mom doesn't switch it up. She orders her usual and a diet soda. The waitress scribbles in her notepad, then looks to me.

"What about you, doll?" She snaps her bubble gum.

"Sweet tea." I pause, pondering over the photo of the moist sugar-cured ham. I can almost taste it falling apart in my mouth. "Um." Mom is watching me, expectant. I speak fast, ordering ham, cranberry relish, sweet potato casserole, and corn muffins. I close the menu and hand it back to the waitress. "And a side of dressing, please." That makes me feel triumphant. I know how to shake things up.

Mom and I share an easy conversation over dinner. The food is good, as it is every year, and we are happy to leave the dirty dishes behind. Another perk to eating out on Thanksgiving. No fuss, no muss. We take our pumpkin pie to the patio, setting our stuff down on the rocking chairs before we begin our game of corn-hole. In between bites, we toss our bean bags across the lawn, some sliding home with ease, while others tumble off the board completely. We laugh as we play, gently heckling one-another. Mom attempts to strategize, even though there really is none in the game of corn-hole. You just need decent aim.

It's my final turn, and when my bean bag doesn't hit home, I know the game's over. Mom's been a savage the entire game, hitting nearly every target. I sit down in the rocking chair and pull out my phone. I open it to find a text from Matt.

—I have a lot to be thankful for this year. Happy Thanksgiving babe.—

Mom finishes her turn and does a little happy dance over her win. Smiling, I feel like a winner too, I have a hot boyfriend and an awesome mom. What more do I need?

****

In our neighborhood, the day after Thanksgiving is a green light to go all out for Christmas. Mom and I usually wait until December first, but the turkey leftovers aren't even in the garbage can before our neighbors are already dragging out their decorations. We live in a cul-de-sac, so it's a bit of competition between all the neighbors on who can outdo who. Each year, we battle it out in what we've affectionately dubbed the Great Cul-de-sac Christmas Contest.

My strategy is to wait until everyone has their decorations up so I can do a little recon first. I scope out what everyone's theme is for the year before I give our great reveal. This year, I'm thinking about doing a rustic theme. Wooden snowmen, reindeer made of logs with branch antlers, tartan ribbons, and bows.

I've also agreed to help Mr. Bower with his decorations. He used to be a fierce competitor in the contest, but as he gets older, it's becoming harder for him to partake in the fun. His specialty was his decked-out roof. He'd write out things like *Santa Parking* or *Merry Christmas.*

That always impressed me. Lights can be super tricky. When one bulb goes out, they all go out. I tend to steer clear of them, opting for festive garlands and pretty wreaths instead.

I'm thoroughly tangled in a string of Mr. Bower's twinkle lights when Matt pulls up. He sees me struggling and jogs over to help.

"Oh good," I say with relief. I heave the bundle of lights into his arms. "You handle the lights while I inflate Santa Claus."

I unroll the deflated Santa on the lawn and fit the adapter into the small fan that comes with the inflatable. Matt frees the lights and climbs the ladder to hang them. I plug the fan into the extension cord, and it kicks on immediately, filling the inflatable within minutes. I stand back. *Wow!* Santa stands over seven feet high!

While Matt finishes stringing the lights, I arrange Mrs. Bower's plastic nativity scene in her flower garden. The set is so old, Mr. Bower has had to repaint baby

Jesus a few times, and one of the Wise Men has silver duct tape running along the length of his back.

The front door opens, and Mr. Bower comes out. He's carrying another inflatable. "Forgot about this fellow." He shakes it out, holding it up in the air. It's Snoopy wearing a Santa hat. I rise to my feet and take it from him.

"He's adorable. Where do you want him?"

Mr. Bower looks around his yard. "How about next to Santa? I've got another extension cord in the shed. Let me go get it for you." Carefully, he treads across the lawn and disappears behind the house. Matt climbs down the ladder and takes a step back to admire his work.

I wrap my arm around him. "Nice job. Think you can do my house next week?"

He gives me a sideways look. I can tell he doesn't want to, but he's having a hard time telling me so. That's what I love about him. Matt's always willing to do anything I ask. No matter what it is.

I kiss his cheek. "I'm kidding. We don't hang Christmas lights."

He looks relieved.

"But, I could use your help with the garland." I grin up at him.

He runs his hands through my hair, and says, "Just tell me when and I'll be there with bells on." He winks.

With the blowup Santa looming over us, and the cracked Wise Man smiling serenely in our direction, Matt and I share a sweet, but body-tingling kiss.

****

Christmas time at Pointe Holden Hospital is a little "extra" because of me. I decorate the break room, the Gift Shop, the cafeteria, and every nurse's station. I'm stringing a popcorn garland around a tree on the third floor when Dr. Yassin stops to help. "Did you make this?" he asks, taking up the loose end. He starts artfully arranging the garland on the branches. He's doing a pretty good job, so I leave him to it.

"Yes. It would have been longer if my boyfriend hadn't eaten half of the popcorn." I rifle through the storage box and find the tree skirt. I remove it and shake it out before I kneel and wrap it around the tree stand.

Dr. Yassin chuckles. "I don't blame him. I love popcorn myself. Your garland might not make it through my shift tonight." Dr. Yassin has a smile that changes his entire face.

He's a handsome man, but when he smiles, he looks younger, carefree. Dr. Yassin has never been married and doesn't have any children. He's probably not much older than my mom. It may just be the emptiness inside of me, but I can easily envision Dr. Yassin as family.

Mom has been widowed for over five years now and hasn't been on a single date. I should ask her about Dr. Yassin. Of course, he's completely opposite of Wesley Jackson. Where Wesley was abrasive, Dr. Yassin is soft-spoken. Where Wesley was selfish, Dr. Yassin is generous, but not overly so that it becomes a fault…like Mom.

I open a box of ornaments, and start hanging them. "What are your plans for Christmas this year, Dr. Yassin? Are you working?"

He plucks a shiny red ornament from the box. He holds it up to the tree, deciding where to place it. "I work the night shift on Christmas eve. My brother is having a drop-in on Christmas day, so I'll probably pop in for a visit." He finally settles on a spot.

A plan hatches in my head. I'm going to invite Dr. Yassin over for Christmas dinner. Mom won't mind. In fact, she'll think it's a good idea. She doesn't like for people to be alone on the holidays. I'll just conveniently leave out the part about his brother's drop-in. Easy peasy.

Dr. Yassin and I hang the last of the ornaments. He steps back and examines the tree. "What do you think?"

I hand him the star and say with a smile. "Almost perfect."

He stretches up on his tiptoes and slips the star into place. When he looks at me with that smile, he shines almost as bright as the star atop the tree.

"Now, it's perfect."

Chapter 19

Our three-month anniversary is nestled right into the heart of winter break. I still can't believe Matt and I have been together that long. I'm standing in the living room waiting for him. Impatiently, I might add. He gave me instructions to dress up and be ready by five. I chose a flattering mustard yellow shirt dress, my Peter Pan hunter green tights, and gold flats.

I even wore my prettiest bra and panty set. Teal lace with little velvet bows. My most expensive set yet. Even though I'm the only one who ever sees them, I feel sexy knowing they're under my clothes. It took me nearly an hour, but I tamed my hair into chunky curls, which was no easy task. Matt better appreciate all this hard work.

He pulls into my driveway just after five o'clock. I run out to meet him. Clicking the seatbelt into place, I look over at Matt. He's grinning.

"You look…"

I smooth my skirt over my knees.

"Hot," Matt finishes, giving me a low whistle. "I'll have to keep you close tonight or someone might try to steal you away."

I giggle. "Stop. No one is taking me away."

He takes my hand and presses a kiss to my palm. "They better not."

I smile at him. "So, where are we going?"

"Randolf's." He gives me a quick wink and looks

back at the road ahead.

"Our first date." I think back to that night. How nervous I was, and how it felt like I was in a dream. Someone else's dream. I gaze at Matt, my heart full and my body tingling with anticipation for tonight.

Matt's phone beeps. I let him slip his hand away to take out his phone. He glances at the screen. He purses his lips, then makes a sudden U-turn. I scramble to grab hold of the dash.

"What's wrong?"

Matt glimpses in the rearview mirror. "Nothing. I just need to make a quick stop somewhere."

"Where?"

"Don't worry about that. It will only take a few minutes."

"Is everything okay?"

He looks at me. "Yeah," he assures me. "I just need to meet up with a buddy of mine. He owes me money."

This feels thin. Like a lie, but I don't challenge him on it. I stay quiet as he drives us through a neighborhood with neat little houses and manicured lawns. We pull into a driveway of a cozy brick house. The porch light is on, casting a buttery yellow glow across the house's façade. The front door makes me smile. It's wrapped like a giant Christmas present.

"Stay here," Matt tells me. "I'll only be a minute." He gets out of the car and crosses the lawn to the front door. I watch as he raps on it a few times. The door opens and a boy, maybe in his early twenties, steps outside. Even though the air has a chill to it, he stands barefooted on the welcome mat.

There isn't much chatting. In fact, there's a brisk handoff and Matt is already on his way back to the car.

The boy disappears back inside, and the front porch light cuts out.

"See?" Matt says, pulling the seat belt over him. "I told you it would only take a minute." We back out of the driveway. Matt lays a hand on my knee, and just like that, I am floating.

****

Dinner is delicious. We start off with spinach-artichoke dip with pita chips. I eat over half and make a mental note to learn how to make it myself. I order rigatoni with meat sauce, with extra mozzarella cheese. Matt gets the shrimp scampi. He must have eaten too much spinach-artichoke dip because he hardly eats the scampi.

I'm surprised because I thought teenage boys had hearty appetites. Jenna can out-eat Matt any day. The best part of the meal is the dessert: coffee and tiramisu. This sounds silly, but I feel so grown up, talking over steaming cups of coffee. Laughing between bites of shared tiramisu. It feels like we're in Venice.

We go back to Matt's house. His mom is out with friends, so we have the place to ourselves. It's rare that we ever get time truly alone, so whenever we can, we take advantage of these scarce snatches of precious time. We watch Netflix on the sofa for a while, snuggling under a soft fleece blanket. It's sweet; like our very own rom-com, and I can't help but smiling to myself at the thought.

"Want something to drink?" Matt asks, pausing the show.

"Sure," I say, untangling myself from his arms.

He stands and goes to the kitchen. I hear him adding ice to a glass, and the pop of a soda can. Matt strolls back into the living room and offers me the glass. I take it, and drink. Matt is regarding me with soft eyes.

"What?"

"I got something for you."

"Really?" *I didn't get him anything! I didn't realize we were supposed to. We've only been together three months. Man, I really suck at being a girlfriend.*

"Be right back." He jogs away, and I hear the hall closet door open and then shut. Matt comes back holding his letterman jacket. He gestures for me to stand up. I oblige, and he drapes the coat over my shoulders.

I look down at the blue wool jacket. His name is embroidered in silver over my heart. I feel like crying. "Why are you giving me this?"

He grips the collar and pulls me close. "Because you're my girl. Wear this coat, and everyone will know it."

This is the best present I have ever received. Not just because it's from Matt, but because of what it means. It's a public announcement. Telling everyone, that Matt Garrison loves Penelope Reza.

"Wow," I breathe. "I love it. Thank you."

Matt smiles down at me, and I take in this moment. I am going to remember it always. Then, we are kissing. Not just sweet, tender kisses, but open-mouthed, sensual kisses. I wind my arms around his neck, pressing my body against his. Everything feels so good that I lose myself in this very moment, never wanting it to end. My heart speeds up and so does our kissing. Matt's hands slide down to my hips. I shiver.

"Let's go upstairs," Matt murmurs.

My heart leaps, and suddenly I'm nervous. "No," I stutter. "We shouldn't."

"My mom won't be home until after midnight." He takes my hand. "It's okay."

Reluctantly, I follow him up the stairs and into his bedroom. Discarded clothes, Maxim magazines, and empty water bottles litter the floor. It's not the first time I'd been in Matt's room. We've studied in it before, but always with his mom home. I've never been in his room alone.

Matt flips on the small lamp on his nightstand. It casts a golden glow across his bed. *Has his bed always been that big?* I gulp. "Come here," he urges. I step over his wrestling gear. Matt takes my face into his palms. "Stop overthinking." He kisses the tip of my nose. I relax marginally. He knows me so well. Of course, I'm overthinking. I overthink everything. But right now, the way my body is tingling from my toes to my ears from Matt's kisses, I can't think of anything beyond his lips.

I kiss him, eager to feel that way again. Between kisses, he sheds his shirt and drops it to the floor. His fingers move deftly at the buttons of my dress. A little moan escapes his lips when he sees my bra. "I like this." He bends and brushes kisses across my collarbone. *And I like this.* Matt wraps his strong arms around me, and we tumble into his bed. *This is it,* I think. *There's no going back from here.*

Where Matt is tender and patient, I am awkward and fumbly. But, somehow, it's enough for Matt. I am enough for Matt. And he is more than enough for me.

Chapter 20

True to tradition, Mom and I sleep in on Christmas morning. I laze around in my bed for a full hour before I finally climb out of it. I pad to the kitchen. Mom's still asleep, so I start brewing a pot of coffee and decide to prepare us breakfast. French toast with extra powdered sugar.

I'm just about to go wake her when I hear her coming down the hall. She's wrapped up tight in a knobby robe, mismatched socks on her feet.

"Morning sunshine," I say, with extra perk just to rub it in.

She groans like a zombie.

Laughing, I hand her a cup of coffee. She takes it appreciatively, wrapping her hands around the mug. She takes a long sip as she shuffles to the table.

I plop down and stab a piece of French toast. "Ready for tonight?"

With the mug still to her lips, I notice her take pause.

"Dr. Yassin is a good-looking guy." The mug almost slips from Mom's hands. Her eyes dart to me. She is clearly shaken, but I just grin and wag my brows for emphasis.

She gives me a look. I laugh and stuff a piece of toast in my mouth. I think I've said enough. For now.

****

Mom is bent at the oven, checking on the turkey for

the hundredth time. This is how I know she's nervous about Dr. Yassin coming over.

"Mom, let it cook," I tell her, pouring green olives into our crystal dish. She sticks her tongue out at me, then shuts the oven door. She takes up straightening the placemats on the table.

"Do you think it will be strange to have Dr. Yassin in our house?" Mom muses as she circles the kitchen table, adjusting the napkin rings.

"Not really," I say, carrying the olive dish to the table. "What will be strange will be seeing him without his lab coat." I screw the lid back onto the jar of olives and put it back into the refrigerator. "He's a really nice guy, don't you think?" Mom agrees, so I venture further. "I'm surprised he isn't married, aren't you?"

"Probably too busy for a social life. It's hard enough for doctors to find time for themselves."

I glance at the clock. It's almost five o'clock. He'll be here any minute. I cue up my phone and *Jingle Bells* starts playing. I look around the kitchen. I've set out our best dishes and silverware. I even folded the plaid napkins into fancy triangles. The centerpiece is an old string of fake holly that I fashioned artfully around a cluster of Balsam Fir and Cedar scented candles.

The doorbell rings.

"He's punctual too," I say.

Mom freezes. Popping an olive in my mouth, I run to the door and throw it open. It's Matt.

"Merry Christmas," I say with a smile.

He kisses me. "Merry Christmas, babe." As he makes his way to the living room, Matt sheds his jacket and dumps it on the armchair.

Mom comes in, stopping short when she sees Matt.

Her smile falls, but she quickly recovers. "Hello, Matt," she says, lifting a pillow from the couch. She fluffs it. I wish I could pinpoint why she's obsessing.

Absolutely, it's nerves because Dr. Yassin is coming over and she wants to make a good impression, but is it because she likes him, or because she's being...*Mom*? Meaning, she's eager to please him. Either way, she's extra anxious tonight, fretting over dinner, and obsessively tidying up the house.

Matt doesn't seem to notice, though. He plops down onto the couch and salutes Mom with two fingers. "Mrs. Jackson." A shadow of a wince passes over Mom's face. She must be thinking, *I just fluffed those pillows!*

There's a sharp knock on the front door. For a beat, I don't move, waiting to see if Mom wants to answer it. She just stands there, like a statue, so I go open it.

Dr. Yassin is standing there, holding a bottle of wine. There's a light dusting of snow on his coat. Like he's been sprinkled with powdered sugar, much like our French toast from this morning.

He smiles at me. "Merry Christmas, Penelope."

"Back at you, Dr. Yassin. Come in, come in."

He steps inside, his eyes washing over the living room in one big sweep. When he sees Mom, he walks over to her. "Merry Christmas, Miranda. This is for you."

She takes the wine bottle. "Thank you, but you didn't have to bring anything."

He waves her away. "Bah. Where would my manners be if I didn't?"

The corner of Mom's mouth lifts. *Are her cheeks pinker than normal?* Dr. Yassin unfastens his coat and slips it off. He holds it for an awkward beat, wondering what to do with it. I save him since Mom is too busy being awkward herself to be of any help. "Let me take that for you, Dr. Yassin."

"Ah, thank you," he says, handing me his coat. It's heavy wool and smells of him. I gently drape it over the back of the armchair, ignoring Matt's wadded up jacket. *Boys.*

Dr. Yassin turns, his eyes landing on Matt. He strolls closer, extending his arm for a handshake. Matt obliges, and I am happy to see them exchange a firm handshake. I hate weak, half-hearted handshakes. They feel like wet noodles slipping through your fingers. Shudder.

"Hello. Jamil Yassin."

"Matt," he replies simply. I give him a sidelong look. *Just Matt?*

"Dr. Yassin, this is my boyfriend." I can't squelch the smile saying "boyfriend" brings to my face.

Dr. Yassin notices this, and smiles back. "Ah, yes." His eyes shift back to Matt. "I've heard about you—all good, I assure you."

Matt grins at this. I don't want a lull in the conversation, so I quickly add, "I hope everyone's hungry, 'cause we have a great spread prepared."

Mom finally snaps to attention. She walks ahead of us into the kitchen and goes to pull the turkey from the oven. Dr. Yassin, being the nice guy that he is, goes to help her.

"Let me help you with that." He takes the oven mitts from her and slips them on. I giggle because I'm used to seeing him scrubbed up in latex gloves, not oversized oven mitts. He reaches into the oven and grips the pan solidly. "Where do you want it?"

"Center of the table is just fine," Mom answers.

Dr. Yassin slides the pan from the rack. We all give

him space so he can get the main course to the table without incident. The turkey is golden brown and smells like perfection. I hurry to set out the rest of the food.

I took care to make sure everything was prepared just right. Creamy mashed potatoes with gravy, sweet potato soufflé with caramelized brown sugar, wild rice, green bean casserole, and buttery croissants. And for dessert, chocolate silk pie with whipped cream, and gooey marshmallow crispy treats.

Mom gestures for everyone to sit, and we do. She goes around the table, filling everyone's glass with sparkling grape juice. As she fills Dr. Yassin's, he smiles at her from over his shoulder. It's so sweet to see them interact this way. Like two shy teenagers. With any luck, this is the beginning of something special. I can definitely see Dr. Yassin and Mom together. I hope she can see it too.

Mom takes up the carving knife.

"Matt. Penelope says you wrestle for Reedmont?" Dr. Yassin inquires.

With his elbows on the table, Matt nods. "Yep."

Pleased that Dr. Yassin remembers that about Matt, I lift the glass of sparkling grape juice to my lips and take a sip.

Dr. Yassin turns serious. "You use protection, I hope."

I choke on the juice. *What!* Sputtering, I try to catch my breath.

Matt looks concerned. He takes the glass from my hand. "Are you all right?"

Dr. Yassin jumps up and runs to me. He delivers three quick blows between my shoulder blades. Mom watches with panic-stricken eyes.

Wheezing, I say, "I'm okay. Just went down the wrong pipe." Dr. Yassin gives me a good once-over before going back to his seat. I cough into my fist one last time, and eventually collect myself. *Why would Dr. Yassin ask about our sex life?*

Matt addresses the doctor. "To your question."

I inhale sharply. *What is he doing?* I'm consumed with embarrassment. I need to steer this conversation in the opposite direction, and I need to do it now! Mom has taken up the carving knife again, portioning off thick sections of turkey. "Need any help with that, Mom?"

"No," she answers without looking up. "I've got it."

Matt doesn't notice me squirming in my seat. He's looking at Dr. Yassin. "Protection is required. The pads, the guards, the headgear. All of it."

Pads. Guards. Headgear? Relief seeps through my bones. Dr. Yassin's question was harmless. How could I ever have thought he'd ask about something so private?

Placing some turkey onto Matt's plate, Mom says, "I've heard of boys your age getting too many concussions during football, and it causing long-term medical issues for them."

"Yes," Dr. Yassin agrees. "There's research studying the head motion on young players during a collision. The neurocognitive findings will aid in training athletes on how to avoid head injuries while on the field." All of our eyes are on Dr. Yassin. He must feel it because he reddens. "Sorry. Research excites me."

Mom smiles fondly and loads his plate up with thick slices of juicy turkey.

Dr. Yassin regards Matt again. "You never compete outside your weight class, do you?'

Matt shifts in his seat, uncomfortable. "Try not to."

Dr. Yassin quirks a brow. "It's imperative that you don't. That's when injuries are sure to ensue." I swallow. If Dr. Yassin only knew. I steal a glimpse of Matt. His jaw is set tight. He must be thinking of the boy who broke his arm.

Dr. Yassin asks, "What's your team rank?"

"Reedmont is ranked fifth in the state."

"Impressive." Glancing down at his plate, Dr. Yassin says, "Speaking of impressive. Miranda, this looks amazing. If it tastes half as good as it smells, then we are all in for a treat."

Chapter 21

Christmas dinner with Dr. Yassin was such a success Mom invited him over for a New Year's Eve get-together. It will be a small gathering of people. Mom, Me, Matt, Jenna, Carlos, Dr. Yassin, and our neighbors, the Bowers. Even though they'll be gone way before midnight. Mom also invited Trip, but since he couldn't be bothered to visit her on Christmas, I doubt he'll show. *Thank God.*

The theme of the party is Shakespeare's Midsummer Night's Dream. I've re-purposed our Christmas garland and created whimsical topiaries with lavender peonies and baby's breath. I even hot glued some adorable fake birds with hot pink feathers onto them. They really make the pieces pop. I strung twinkling lights throughout the living room and dimmed all the lights, so everything is glowy and ethereal, like an actual moonlight night.

Matt has been at my house all day. He was supposed to be helping me decorate for the party, but he hasn't been doing much. Aside from catnapping on the couch, all he's done was offer to taste-test my red velvet cake. I scoffed at that. I don't need him to taste-test my prized red velvet cake.

I've made this cake a thousand times. It's actually one of my signature desserts, so to suggest it needed a taste tester was offensive. He gave me puppy dog eyes, though, so I let him lick the cream cheese frosting from the bowl and spatula.

Mom got home around seven, and has been in her room for almost an hour getting ready. The Bower's drifted in about ten minutes ago. They won't stay long. Mrs. Bower will need to take her medication soon, and Mr. Bower will want to watch the news, so they're just here for pleasantries and maybe some food.

Carrying out a cheeseball and cracker plate, I hear the front door open.

Jenna bursts in. "Hey, party people," she calls. "Carloco and Jen Jen are here! Let's get this party started!" Carlos trails close behind her, snickering all the way. I can feel my eyes bulge. Jenna has gone all out for this party.

She's dressed in a black and white off-the-shoulder maxi dress. Below the hips are layers and layers of loose ruffles that billow down to the floor. She has on a sparkly HAPPY NEW YEAR headband and crazy champagne bottle sunglasses.

Seems she's dressed Carlos, too. He's donning the champagne bottle sunglasses as well and is sporting a cool bowtie. When you're close enough, you can make out the little palm trees.

"I've brought enough for everybody," she says, holding up the sunglasses and headbands.

Matt groans, but I take a headband and slip it on. Jenna offers Mr. Bower a pair of sunglasses, and surprisingly, he puts them on. I laugh because he looks like some weird alien.

Jenna takes in the room. "Wow. This looks amazing, Pen!"

Carlos taps one of the fake birds in the topiary. "Nice touch."

I look around, pleased. "Thanks."

Mom finally comes out of her room. She definitely put thought into her outfit. She's wearing a delicate lace blouse with cap sleeves and slim slacks that make her look ten years younger. Her hair is down in loose beachy waves. Seeing her like this, there is no denying she likes Dr. Yassin.

"Mom," I say, going over to her. "You look great." I wrap my arms around her neck and give her a squeeze.

"Really? I wasn't sure about the pants."

I step back and take an appraising look at her. "Why? The fit is awesome."

She glances down at her legs. "You think so?"

"Absolutely. Dr. Yassin won't be able to take his eyes off you."

Mom hooks a loose strand of hair behind her ear. "Oh, stop that."

Jenna walks up. "She's right, Mrs. Jackson. You're one hot mama." She pokes Mom's shoulder and makes a hissing noise. "Ouch!" She shakes her hand out. "See?"

Mom laughs, but she's blushing from all the compliments. She's not used to them. Wesley's words were rarely sweet.

"Speaking of clothes." I look down at my stained sweatshirt and yoga pants. "I need to change real quick," I tell Jenna and Mom. "Be right back."

I run off to my room. I've been so wrapped up in preparing the house for the party that I forgot to prepare myself! I rifle through my closet, tossing out possibilities onto my bed. I holler for Jenna.

She comes in and plops down on my bed. "You rang?"

"Help me pick out something."

She inspects the pile of clothes on the bed, sorting them into two groups: maybe and heck no. By the time she's through, the maybe pile has only one option. A flouncy floral dress that falls just above my knees. I'm not entirely sold on it, but before I can say so, she's already digging out a pair of boots from under my bed.

"Just shut up and wear it," she says, breathlessly. She passes me the boots. "You'll thank me later." She swipes a finger across her upper lip. "Jesus, Pen. You have me sweating like a pig here…which is fitting since I had to root around under your bed for your shoes. It's a pigsty under there, seriously."

I roll my eyes. "Okay. Enough of the puns." I drop the boots onto the bed. "Go back out there and entertain everyone, will you?"

Jenna gives me a saucy look. "Of course, darling. Entertaining people is my specialty."

I shove her out into the hallway and shut the door. Turning back to the dress, I stare at it. It's cute, but it's one of those dresses I bought on a whim and never actually had the nerve to wear. I hold it up to me. It looked so cute on the rack, but once I got it home and tried it on, I felt it wasn't me. It was too trendy. Too cool. Too much like what all the popular girls at school would wear. I don't know why I never returned it. I frown at it.

It's flirty and feminine. Matt will like it—I know that. Wanting to please him, I decide to put it on. I examine myself in the mirror. My brown skin stands out against the soft peach fabric, and it makes for a pretty combination. I bundle my curls into a fat bun and pull a few tendrils down at my temples. I sweep on some shiny lip gloss and pull on the boots. With a deep breath in my lungs, I open my bedroom door.

****

Matt stares at me. Jenna grins at me. Carlos does a double take, and Mom and Dr. Yassin stop talking long enough to give me an appraising look. The Bowers are gone, so they must have gone home early like I figured they would. Mom smiles and goes back to her conversation. Dr. Yassin doesn't miss a beat, picking right back up where he left off.

I walk toward Matt, but he meets me halfway. "Wow," he breathes. "You look amazing."

"Thank you," I say, heat flooding my cheeks.

He rests his hands on my waist. "I'm looking forward to kissing you at midnight."

I flatten my palm against his chest, feeling his heartbeat. "Ditto."

He glances back at the clock on the end table. It's not even nine o'clock. "Oh, screw it. Why wait?" He presses a soft kiss to my lips. Maybe it's the swoon-worthy atmosphere, the fancy topiaries, and the dreamy lights, but I forget everyone else in the room. At this moment, there's just Matt and me. I become delirious with happiness and soon, I'm dizzy from his kisses. When we finally part, I feel drunk, silly, and light on my feet. If I can expect more of this at midnight, then the New Year is looking pretty good already.

****

In unison, we count down, "five, four, three…" All eyes are on the television as the ball slowly makes its descent in Time Square. I've never watched the ball drop before. It's actually more exciting than it sounds. Everyone on the street is festive, full of energy, and alight with hope the New Year is going to be better than the last. I'm not sure my year could get any better. I already have Matt. What more could I want?

When the ball finally drops, officially ringing in the New Year, Jenna and Carlos cheer. Matt and I share a quick kiss. Dr. Yassin takes Mom by the hands and brushes a chaste kiss on her cheek. I beam at her, though she doesn't see me. In fact, I don't think she sees anyone but Dr. Yassin right now. I'm glad for it. Mom deserves to be happy.

From the corner of my eye, I see Carlos hand Jenna a folded note. *Is that a love letter?* Suspicion clouds her face, but she opens the note, anyway. Carlos watches her expectantly. His leg bounces with nervous energy. Her eyes skip across the paper, then dart to Carlos. He smiles sheepishly at her.

"What's going on over there?" Matt whispers.

I shush him, staring at Jenna as I await her reaction.

"You are the biggest dork I know," Jenna says with a laugh. She catches my eye and holds the note up in the air. "Can we be season three Ross and Rachael?"

My mouth pops open. "What!" I run over to the couch to where Carlos and Jenna are sitting. I snatch the note from her hand and read it for myself. "This is actually really sweet." I hand it back to Jenna. She rereads it before carefully folding it and tucking it into her bra.

Carlos shrugs. "I've been season one Ross for years now. Thought it was time to take a chance." He glances at Jenna, uncertainty tightening his dark eyes. She reaches out and places a hand on his arm. Patting him gently, as if she's petting a timid dog, she says, "How about we start at season two, and see where that leads?"

A grin breaks across Carlos' face. "I'll take that." They share a sweet smile and for the first time ever...I see Jenna blush.

Chapter 22

Winter break is officially over. After the past two magical weeks I've had, I'm finding it hard to settle back into my normal routine. And who could blame me? My anniversary was something out of a rom-com. Mom and Dr. Yassin are nearly exclusive, and I think Carlos finally broke free from the friend zone. Love is definitely in the air, and it makes me excited to see what's in store for Valentine's Day. But that's still over a month away.

It's my turn to make dinner, so I'm preparing something simple. Spaghetti, salad, and garlic knots. Jenna's in charge of the garlic knots, and since she's staring at her phone screen, I'm wishing I gave her the task of making the salad. She can't burn salad.

I tiptoe over to her and loom above her shoulder. I clear my throat as loud as possible.

She startles, almost dropping her phone. "Hey!"

"You're going to burn the garlic knots," I scold her. "Pay attention to the oven, not your phone."

"I am."

I go to the oven and open it. The garlic knots aren't ruined, but the edges aren't golden anymore. They've darkened to a crispy brown. I take a pot holder and pull them out, showing them to Jenna. "Oh, really?"

She takes one, dropping it to the table with a hiss. "Shoot, they are hot."

"I just took them out the oven. What do you

expect?" I shake my head and go back to my pasta. The water is bubbling, so I shut off the stove. Jenna throws the garlic knots in a bowl, then covers them with a towel to keep them warm.

"Mom should be here any minute," I say.

"Good, 'cause I'm starving." Jenna pulls out her phone again. She starts talking about her coworkers at Puffins, and the different flavors everyone has been presenting her boss, Mr. Sullivan. So far, no one has produced the raise-worthy flavor.

I'm straining the pasta when Mom comes in from work.

"Hey, honey," she says, setting her purse down on the counter. "Hi, Jenna."

"Hi, Mrs. Jackson," Jenna greets back.

Mom has dark circles smudging her eyes, and her face is gaunt. Overtime is wearing on her. I decide to cook dinner tomorrow night too, even though it's Mom's turn. She deserves another night of rest.

"You're just in time," I tell Mom, returning the pasta to the pot. I open a can of marinara sauce and dump it over the pasta. "It's all done."

Mom pulls the bread bowl toward her and lifts a corner of the napkin. She inhales deeply. "Hmm. Smells delicious."

"Made them myself," Jenna says, grinning widely.

I place the pot of spaghetti in the center of the dining room table. "Which means she took them out of a box and stuck them in the oven."

Jenna sticks her tongue out at me.

We settle in at the table. Jenna takes an extra helping of salad, and piles a mountain of spaghetti on her plate. Mom doesn't even notice. She's used to the way Jenna eats.

"You girls all ready for Lit Fest?" Mom asks as she twirls her fork in her spaghetti, wrapping the strands of pasta around until she makes a neat little bundle. I envy that. I can never do it the way she can. I try, but it takes me twice as long to eat when I do, so I always end up cutting my spaghetti into diced-up chunks and eating it with a spoon.

"Oh yeah," Jenna says around a mouthful of garlic knot. "I'm counting down the days. Only six more to go."

"Six?" Mom asks.

Jenna nods, tearing off another chunk of bread.

Something changes in Mom. Her shoulders go stiff, and she sets down her fork abruptly. I watch her closely. Jenna's unaware of the change. She's too busy working on her salad, munching away like a happy rabbit.

"Mom?" I say.

"Be right back." Mom leaves and goes to her bedroom. The longer she's gone, the more I think I should follow her, to see if she's all right.

I'm about to do just that when she returns. Her face is brighter now, and she's smiling at me. She's holding something behind her back.

"I have something for you," she tells me. "I was saving it for when you…" She hesitates. "For when you signed the papers. To celebrate. But you can have it now."

She presents me with a book. It has a big red bow on it, but I easily recognize the cover. My heart skips a beat. *Stillborn*, Jonathan Preston's first book. The only book of his I don't own.

I take it from her greedily, hugging it to my chest.

"Oh, my God. Thank you, Mom. Thank you!"

"Open it." She gestures to the book. Her eyes are shining now. She looks younger when she's happy.

I pull my eyes from hers, and carefully lift the cover. I'm not sure what I'm looking for. *An inscription, perhaps?* I glance up at her in question.

"Look at the copyright page." She's grinning now, and it makes my lips curve wider in return.

My eyes scan the text. I feel my mouth drop open. "First edition?" I snatch my head up to look at her. "You found a first edition?"

Her pretty face is glowing. Radiating like the sun, and I have never been so grateful to be in her orbit. I get a warm feeling inside. Mom is my mom in all the ways that counts. She knows me like a book—pun intended. She likes to take care of me like a good mother should, and she always tries to make me happy—and when she succeeds—she takes delight in it.

I don't know what else to say, except, thank you. Having someone know you so well is an incredible high. In my foster homes, the families tried, but they knew we were only temporary. So they never got too close. They wouldn't attempt to get to know us. Not really, anyway. They knew our backstories, our sob stories, and our triggers if we had any. They never knew what cobwebs we had in our minds, and what holes we had in our hearts. And those can be the most important parts of a person.

Jenna comes up beside me. "That's so cool. Are you going to have him sign it?"

I blink. I hadn't thought of that, but yes, of course I will. A signed first edition? I'd be stupid to miss that opportunity.

My phone rings. I dart to the counter, still clinging to the book. It's Matt. I answer it, eager to tell him all about Mom's gift. He acts interested for my sake, and that makes me happy. He's considerate in that way.

"Can I come over?" he asks after I'm through gushing about the book.

"Sure," I say. "Want me to save you some spaghetti?" From the corner of my eye, I see Jenna's shoulders go rigid.

He tells me no, and then we hang up.

Jenna is gone by the time Matt shows up. I am pretty sure she did that on purpose. Mom takes her cup of coffee to her bedroom and leaves Matt and me alone in the living room.

Beaming, I show Matt the book. "It's a first edition." I open the cover and show him. "See?" I point to the copyright section.

His eyes skim the page. "Does that mean it's worth some money?"

"Yes, but there's no way I'd ever sell it." I close the book. "Especially once I get Preston to sign it." Excitement fills me. Soon, I'll own a signed first edition Preston. I can't believe it!

Matt looks far away. It's then I notice the gauntness in his face. It's nothing drastic, but there's more of a sharpness in his cheekbones than before. My stomach churns uncomfortably.

"Is something wrong?" I ask him. His eyes dart to mine. He steps away from me and strolls through the living room at a slow pace. *Something is definitely wrong.* He finally sinks down to the sofa. I put down the book and run to sit beside him. I place my hand on his knee. "Matt?" Waiting for him to answer is excruciating.

Is he about to break up with me?

He turns to me, sitting forward so our faces are close. Something is going on internally, but what, I am not sure. I can only hold my breath and wait. His brown eyes are searching when he says, "Penelope. I need you to do something for me."

"What is it?"

He hesitates.

I give his knee a reassuring squeeze. "Tell me." His face is pained. My heart crumbles at the sight. I've never seen him like this. So unsettled. So unsure.

"Can you lift a prescription pad?"

I stare at him. *Did I just hear him right?* "What?"

He glances around the room and swallows hard. "A prescription pad. Can you get one?"

I jerk my hand away from his knee. "You want me to steal a prescription pad? Are you crazy?"

He shushes me.

I jump to my feet. Sternly, I whisper, "You're asking me to steal! From a hospital! I'm pretty sure that's a crime."

He grabs my arm and pulls me back onto the sofa. "Stop. Just listen to me, all right?"

I yank out of his grip and glare at him. *I can't believe he asked me this. Is this a joke? It doesn't feel like a joke.*

"I need a prescription." His hand is twitching like he has pent-up energy, or he's hopped up on too much caffeine.

"What kind of prescription?" I think back to the night I saw him at Sweetwaters. He tried to get a prescription then, but the pharmacist wouldn't fill it. I never asked him about it. My stomach fists at the memory. *Maybe I should have.*

"Oxy. I just need one more bottle."

"Oxy?" I shake my head, confused. "What's that?"

His eyes shutter, and he takes in a deep breath. When he opens them again, he steels himself before saying. "OxyContin."

I blink. "Why can't you just get it from a doctor?"

"Because!" he blurts with frustration. I startle backward, scared of this new, unfamiliar version of Matt. I want the old Matt back. The kind Matt that hung back on the track for me. The charming Matt that kisses my temple. Where is he?

He must sense my apprehension because he softens his eyes. "They won't prescribe me anymore. They say, if they do, I'll become dependent." His knee bounces. "They say I'm healed, and that I don't need it. But they're wrong. I still need Oxy. I hurt without it." His face screws up tight. "Please, Pen. I just need one more bottle. It will be the last one. I swear."

My throat dries as things click into place. The mood swings, the loss of appetite, the bloodshot eyes. I stare at him, my heart crushing in my chest. He's addicted to OxyContin. I'm in love with an addict.

Chapter 23

"Quit looking at me like that," Matt snaps.

"Like what?"

"Like that!" He waves his hand at my face. "Like you're disgusted." His eyes tighten. "Like I'm a damn junkie or some shit."

I don't know what to say. This is all new to me. I've never even smoked a cigarette. What do I know about drugs? Is OxyContin even considered a drug? I mean, doctors prescribe it. Maybe I'm blowing this out of proportion.

I let out a deep sigh, gathering my thoughts. "What happens if you don't get any more?"

Matt wrings his hands. "I'll hurt." He grabs my hands, clinging to them as if he's about to be swept away. "I don't want to hurt."

He looks so vulnerable I want to squeeze him and take all his pain away.

"How did you get it in the first place?" I ask.

"Wrestling injury."

"When you broke your arm?" I remember him telling me about the wrestler who cheated, outweighing him in the match and breaking his arm in three places.

He nods. "The doctor prescribed them for me. So, it's legit."

"He didn't mean for you to keep taking them."

Matt lets go of me and slams his hand on the coffee

table. I jump at the sound. "That dumbass doctor is the reason I'm in this mess. If he didn't prescribe them in the first place, I wouldn't be dealing with this shit right now."

"You can't blame him. He didn't make you—"

"Make me what?" he interjects. His eyes narrow. "Make me an addict?"

I open my mouth to speak but think better of it.

"Just say it. You know you want to." He frowns.

Slowly, I shake my head no. This side of him scares me. And his eyes. They bore into me, yet they don't seem to see me at all. "I can't."

"Can't what? Call me an addict, or…"

"I can't take a prescription pad."

He pinches the bridge of his nose. "Please. Penelope." Seeing him like this simultaneously frightens me and crushes me. I place my hand on his back. Matt suddenly collapses, his head falling into my lap. He clings to me, weeping softly. I run my fingers through his hair, trying to soothe him the way my mom did when I was a child. She'd pet my hair, lulling me into sleep. Her sweet voice like velvet on my ears.

I gaze down at him, my heart aching for this broken boy in my lap. Love is a powerful thing. I know this because before I fell for Matt, I would have never agreed to such a request. But because I love him, I can't see him suffer this way. Because of love, I will do whatever he asks of me.

****

"Lit Fest, here we come!" shouts Jenna as she runs across the lawn, toward my car. She opens up the passenger door and tosses her book bag to the floorboard. It hits with a thud. She's got it stuffed so full of books it probably weighs more than she does. She gets in, practically vibrating with excitement. It's catching. I push away the stress of the other night, when Matt asked me to steal a prescription pad for him. I refuse to let it dampen my favorite day of the year, Lit Fest. Jenna and I squeal in unison. Then we are off for a full day of YA fiction and fun!

Jenna and I hit all the vendor booths early. We rack up plenty of free stuff. Pins, bookmarks, posters, shirts, and tote bags. It feels great being among *our* people. Fellow book lovers and fangirls. Fangirls are the greatest. I used to consider myself a fangirl, but my devotion is subpar when compared to true fangirls. They're not afraid to take it too far, to be extreme.

Tattoos, naming their firstborn after a book character, cosplaying. So far today, we've seen a girl who I think was supposed to be an extraterrestrial bounty hunter, another girl dressed in a dreamy steampunk gown, five woodland elves, and what looked like a giant fox with psychedelic fur.

Jenna and I happily sit through a discussion panel, which is interesting as well as entertaining. I learned that fiction often mimics the author's reality in some capacity. Whether it's a re-telling of an event they've experienced, or a character is loosely based on someone they know. Stories are not always just made-up events on a page. They can be so much more.

Now it's time to get in line for Preston. We take up the end of the line and settle in for the long wait. In front of us is a boy and a girl around our age. They're eagerly chatting away, the tips of their noses pink from the chilly air. A group of middle-school-age girls get in behind us. They're gushing about some author they just met, and I can't help but smile. Everyone's giddiness is contagious. The air around Lit Fest is always thrumming with excitement and sheer joy. It's a book lover's paradise.

"Oh, hey," Jenna says. "I forgot to tell you. I got a fifty-cent raise." Jenna reaches into her book bag and withdraws a granola bar.

"That's awesome."

She unwraps the granola bar and offers it to me.

I shake my head.

"Yeah." She bites off a chunk of granola bar. "Mr. Sullivan really liked my Mersno-cone."

"Wait. I thought the prize was a dollar raise."

"It is."

"But you got fifty cents."

"I never said I won." She takes another bite. "Marcy did. German chocolate snow cone. Go figure. Chocolate always wins." She rolls her eyes. "Mr. Sullivan said mine would have won if Puffins had a liquor license."

I laugh and congratulate her again. I'm happy she got a raise. She deserves it. She worked hard to win that contest, even if she got second place. The line moves, and I'm bouncing on the balls of my feet. "I can't wait to meet Jonathan Preston. Think he'll take a selfie with me?"

Jenna shrugs. "Won't know until you ask. I'll take some pics of you talking to him, just in case."

A Lit Fest volunteer is making her way down the line. She's telling everyone, "Have your books opened, and ready to the page you want autographed when you approach the table."

"Can you get my book out?" I ask Jenna, turning around. She unzips my book bag and digs through it. "Uh, Pen? It's not in here."

"What? Sure it is. I packed it two nights ago."

She sifts through my book bag again. "Nope. It's not here."

"That's impossible. I know I put it in there." I slip out of the bag and search for it myself. She's right. It's not here. I begin to panic. "Where could it be?" My voice comes out high and whiny.

"Calm down," Jenna says. "It's probably in your room."

"No. I know I put it in here."

"Call your mom. Have her look for it."

My eyes skim the line. We are halfway to Preston. "There's no time. What am I going to do?"

Jenna looks around. "I can run to the book tent really quick and buy one of his books. If I go now, I should be back in time."

I pull at the ends of my hair. "Okay," I stammer, tears building up behind my eyes.

Jenna runs off, calling, "I'll be right back," over her shoulder.

I replay the night I packed *Stillborn*. It was the same night Matt came over to ask me to take the prescription pad from the hospital. I embraced him for a long time. Then I got up and poured him a glass of sweet tea. While he drank, I rubbed his back until he was back to his old self again.

We talked about nothing as I packed my book bag for Lit Fest. I filled it with snacks, Preston's *Stillborn*, the official Lit Fest schedule of events, and a copy of Jenna's itinerary.

I know I packed it. What could have happened to it? I call Matt. He doesn't answer. I don't leave a voice mail. Instead, I text him: *—Call me.—*

I wrack my brain, trying to think of all the places it could be, but nothing makes sense. *I know I put it in my book bag.* My phone rings. Barely glimpsing the screen, I answer it. "Hey."

"What's up?" Matt asks. "How's your book thing going?"

"Fine." I touch my forehead. "But I can't find my book. The new one Mom got me. You saw me pack it, right?"

Silence.

I pull the phone from my ear and glance at the screen. The call didn't drop. I put it back to my ear. "Hello?"

"Yeah."

"I thought I lost you. Anyway, so did you? I remember doing it, but now I can't find it. I'm in Jonathan Preston's autograph line, and it's not in my book bag."

Again, a beat of silence.

"I don't know," he finally says shakily.

"You don't know? You were sitting right next to me as I packed my book bag."

"You think I was actually paying attention to what you were packing?" He sounds annoyed now. "What does it matter, anyway?"

"What does it matter? It matters a lot, actually. I wanted to have it signed, and now, since I can't find it, I can't."

"Have him sign something else."

I'm done talking to him. He doesn't get it. He doesn't understand how much that book, and how much Jonathan Preston himself, means to me.

"Never mind," I say with a sigh. "I'm going to go."

"It's just a book, Penelope. Don't let it ruin your big day. Besides, I'm sure it will turn up sooner or later."

"Yeah. You're right. Talk to you later, okay?"

We hang up, but I'm still unsettled. I know I packed the book. I *know* it. It couldn't have just disappeared.

Jenna is back. Out of breath, she says, "Got it." She glances up ahead. "And just in time, too. You're up."

I take the book from her, one I already own, and open it to the title page. Jenna gets her phone ready, snapping pictures of me walking up to the table. Jonathan Preston smiles warmly at me, a pen poised in his hand. My heart accelerates.

Meekly, I greet him. "Mr. Preston I am a huge fan of yours. Your books are my friends." Silently, I groan. *Did I really just say that?*

Taking the book from my hand, Jonathan Preston's eyes sparkle. "Friends, huh?"

I gulp. "Yes." *I might as well explain.* "They each have their own story, their own personality, and they are always there for me. I can turn to them whenever I'm having a bad day. So yeah. They're like friends."

Jonathan Preston scribbles an inscription, and hands me the book back. "Which makes us friends by proxy." He gives me a wink.

I beam, hugging the book to my chest as I walk away.

"You didn't ask him for a selfie," Jenna reminds me.

"I don't need one. I am never going to forget this day." Ever.

Chapter 24

I never found *Stillborn*. I haven't told Mom yet. I don't have the heart to. Not yet anyway. My signed Preston book is on the bookshelf beside a framed photo of me talking to Jonathan Preston at the table. I'm so glad Jenna snapped that picture. Not that I need it to remember that moment. It will be seared in my memory forever. Jonathan Preston said we were friends by proxy. *How awesome is that?*

I have to be at the hospital in an hour. To kill time, I pull up Google on my laptop. I punch in OxyContin in the search bar, and it pulls up dozens of links varying from Wikipedia to pharmaceutical sites, to opioid addiction helplines. Intrigued, I click on one of the opioid addiction websites.

I scan through the signs of addiction and the symptoms of withdrawal. Opioid addiction is not much different than any other drug addiction. Addicts will do almost anything to get their hands on it. I frown at myself. Even ask their goody-two-shoe girlfriend to break the law...

My stomach is in knots. I don't want to do this—I don't, but I feel as though there is no other way. I want to help Matt. Deep down, I know this is wrong. Not only is stealing a prescription pad a crime, but I'm abetting an addict. I cringe at the word, *addict*. No, that is not what Matt is. He just needs a little more time to heal. He'll wean himself off the medication and he'll be fine. I'll make sure of it.

My shift is almost over, so I head to Dr. Yassin's office, replaying my plan in my head. As I round the corner, I see that his office door is open, like it usually is. If I've planned this right, he should be at his desk, reviewing charts or something of the like. He's scheduled for an operation at five, so he'll be preparing for it.

I peek inside and sure enough, he's perched on the edge of his desk, poring over a medical chart. His eyes are laser focused. He doesn't hear me come in.

I clear my throat.

Dr. Yassin lifts his head. "Penelope." He's surprised to see me. He smiles and sets the chart down. "Nice to see you. Is there something I can help you with?"

I worry at a loose string on my apron. My head is screaming at me to end this. To walk away now and not go through with it, but I push on anyway. "I just wanted to talk about what happened before, with that patient."

His thick brows pinch. "Which patient?"

"The one who refused care. Remember him?"

He nods in recognition. "Ah. Yes, I do. What about him?"

"How do you not let it get to you? The hate, I mean."

Dr. Yassin's eyes are gentle when he says, "Hate is ignorance, plain and simple. When you start seeing hate as something as small as that, it doesn't hurt as much." He lifts the chart from the desk and stands. "I have to go scrub up for surgery, but if you want, we can talk about this later."

"No," I say. "That's all right."

"You know my door is always open. If you need to

talk."

I don't know exactly why I brought up that incident again. I suppose it was because it was safe. A neutral experience that we both shared, and was personally impacted by, even if Dr. Yassin seemed unfazed by it.

I could have asked him about Mom. About their relationship, and where it was headed, but it didn't feel right asking him about her now. It would be too weird, like she was in the room with us. And if she was in the room with us, then that means she'd see me steal. See me become someone I'm not. I swallow the guilt before I can change my mind.

"Thank you, Dr. Yassin." I watch him whisk away, waiting a few extra seconds before I turn to his desk. *I'm so sorry,* I think as I pull open his desk drawer. I glance up, making sure no one is coming, before plucking out a prescription pad. It's stamped at the top with the hospital's logo and beneath it is Dr. Yassin's name. Shame blooms in my gut. Slipping the pad into the pocket of my apron, I rush out of his office, my chest constricting with every step I take. My cheeks burn with disgrace, but I keep moving. The pad in my apron feels heavy, or maybe it's just my imagination.

****

When I get home, I hide the pad under my mattress. Shame festers inside of me, rendering me useless. I crawl into bed, fully clothed, and curl into my blanket. *Did I really just steal for Matt? What was I thinking? What if Dr. Yassin notices the pad is missing? Will he know it was me?* The hospital could fire me. They could press charges. My stomach twists at the thought.

I'm tempted to call Jenna. I need to tell someone what I've done. I need reassurance from some who won't judge me. But Jenna won't offer me any reassurance. She'll be disappointed. I know she will. Of course she will. I'm disappointed in myself.

Chapter 25

The gymnasium is packed. So much so that I have to remove my Reedmont hoodie because of all the body heat. Reedmont versus our rival, Valley Ford, brings people out in droves. Because of the occasion, I decided to show my school spirit by painting a silver and blue heart on my cheek. For Matt.

With a bag of popcorn held high in the air, Dr. Yassin side-steps through the row of seats and sits down next to Mom. He hands her the bag. "Have some," he urges her. Mom fingers a few pieces and pops them into her mouth. Dr. Yassin unzips his fleece jacket and shrugs out of it. He's as casual as I've ever seen him. Dark jeans and a grey pullover sweater. I'm growing used to seeing him this way.

"Are matches always like this?" he asks, taking back the bag of popcorn and looking out across the room.

I lean across Mom so he can hear me above the din of the crowd. "No. It's because we're up against Valley Ford." His eyes shift to the wrestlers donning the red and black singlets.

"Ah. I see. Nothing like some good old-fashioned rivalry." A mischievous smile crosses his face, his eyes glinting like stars. I catch Mom gazing at him, and it brings a small smile to my face. It's refreshing to see her carefree. Youthful. Piqued. I know she loved Wesley, but it seemed different. Like it was required. Obligated love.

That's what it seemed like. Like she had no choice but to stay and make the most of it while she did.

"There's Matt," Mom says, sitting up taller. I find him easily, as if my eyes are trained to hone in on him on cue. He's slipping on his headgear, strolling to the edge of the mat. Another boy, this one in a Valley Ford fire-engine red singlet, saunters across the gym floor. He looks solid, like every muscle is rock-hard. Shaking out his hands, the boy gets into position.

The referee stands in the center of the mat and readies to blow his whistle. Matt doesn't rush to form his stance, but when he does, he looks menacing, like a snake ready to strike. The whistle blows and the boys start the now familiar dance of bluffs and footwork.

Matt seems to sleepwalk through the match. *What's wrong with him?* They finally lock arms. Valley Ford grabs Matt's right knee and throws him off balance. Matt is slow on his feet, and the boy takes advantage of it, easily tossing him to the floor and pinning him. The match is called and Valley Ford wins.

Matt drags himself to a stand. I cover my mouth with my hand when I see him sway. *Is he okay?* My nerves thrum so hard I'm practically vibrating. The coach jogs over to him. He lays a hand on Matt's shoulder, bending to look closely into his face. Heated discussion ensues. I squint, trying to read their lips, but I can't make out anything. The referee glides over. He says something to the coach, crossing his arms firmly over his chest.

"What's going on?" Mom asks me.

"I don't know."

"Doesn't look like he's returning to the mat anytime soon," a man behind says. "Bet he got caught juicing or something."

Dr. Yassin's eyes switch between Matt and me, shrewd and all-seeing. *Can he tell Matt uses?*

Hot prickles of unease erupt across my skin. The coach is now pointing to the locker room. Matt shrugs out of his grip and stalks off.

I get up and hurry down the bleachers toward him. The set of his shoulders tells me he's angry. He doesn't hear me call after him. He disappears through the gymnasium doors. I follow behind him, yanking the door open in time to see him round the corner to the locker rooms.

"Matt," I shout, running after him. Again, he doesn't hear me. He must be in his head again. That's what I call it when he's wrapped up in his thoughts. When he's lost to me. I'm not sure what he's reliving whenever he gets that way, but whenever that dark cloud emerges, I tend keep quiet and stay out of his way.

With an angry thrust, he shoves the locker room door open with a bang. I consider going back out into the gymnasium. To leave him to sort his feelings out on his own, but I want to make sure he's okay first.

Placing my hand on the locker room door, I slowly push it aside. An endless wall of grey lockers stretches out before me. Other than Matt and me, it appears empty. "Matt?" He's at the far end of the room, facing an open locker. His singlet straps hang at his waist, his back completely bare.

"What?" he spits without turning around.

"You okay?" I walk in, letting the door sweep shut.

Hanging his head, he says, "I'm fine."

"Doesn't look like it," I hedge.

He slams the locker shut. I jump at the echoing sound.

"I just want to make sure you're all right. Things looked pretty tense between you and Coach."

"Son of a bitch benched me."

I'm so close now I can see the trail of perspiration trickling down his spine, and the red burn the mat left on his skin. "Why?"

He whirls around, his mouth screwed tight. His face is ashen and drawn. "Just leave me alone, Penelope. Please."

I take pause at his wild eyes. "Are you...high right now?"

He scoffs, but doesn't deny it.

I back away. "You are. That's why he benched you."

Matt glares at me.

"Why would you use before a match? You know Coach would notice something like that!"

As quick as lightning, Matt's fist snaps outward and smashes into the nearest locker. I flinch. "Get out," he grounds out.

The fire in his eyes scares me, so I scramble out of the locker room, and I don't look back.

****

I still haven't told Matt what I'd done. And after the other night, I don't think I want to. The prescription pad is still stuffed under my mattress, where it haunts me. It's like the story. You know the one, where the sound of a heartbeat from beneath a floorboard drives the narrator insane. Instead, this is a pad of paper.

I'm thinking about returning it, but I haven't come up with a way back into Dr. Yassin's office yet. Not a convincing way anyway. He told me the door was always open if I ever needed to talk. Maybe I could make up a story about how someone is discriminating against me because of my nationality? My stomach sours. *Lying and stealing? Who am I?*

This is all Matt's doing. After I ran out of the locker room, I had to lie to Mom and Dr. Yassin to cover for Matt. I told them he was sick, and that Coach sent him home. As the lie came out of my mouth, disgust seeped through me. This is not who I am. I don't lie, and I certainly don't steal. I stayed up most of the night beating myself up over allowing this new version of me to evolve. This shadow of myself not only repulses me, it scares me. *How did I lose myself along the way? Where is Penelope?*

I've ignored all of Matt's phone calls and texts. High or not, I don't like the way he talked to me. And I hate the person he's making me become.

I spend two hours at the library working on a research paper that's due next week. Then, I treat myself to a chocolate-dipped biscotti and hot cocoa at a nearby coffee shop. As I'm paying, my phone beeps with a text. I wait until I'm seated to read it. It's from Matt.

—I'm a dick. I'm sorry.—

I dunk the biscotti in the cocoa to soften it. My mind wanders to Matt. *Am I being too hard on him?* People with addiction problems need love and support. I bite off a chunk of the dripping biscotti. *Hmm. Yum.* I open up Google on my phone and type "OxyContin addiction support groups" into the search engine. Several pop up, dotting the Charlotte map on my screen. I find one in town, called "Opioid Crisis Help Center."

They meet weekly at the DHEC business office. I'll show this to Matt. I'll even offer to go with him. Together, we can overcome this. Matt just needs encouragement, and who better than his girlfriend to do it?

****

My head is already aching from the Matt drama, not to mention the lack of sleep, so you can imagine my irritation when I see Trip's SUV in our driveway. I consider going straight to Jenna's just to avoid him, but I don't. Mom's alone with him, and that is never a good thing.

I park, taking my time to stroll past his SUV so I can peer through his windows. The passenger seat is a mess. Strewn papers, Styrofoam coffee cups, and burger wrappers. As I draw closer to the front door, I can hear Trip's voice booming from the other side. The biscotti and cocoa in my stomach suddenly feel heavy.

Snatching open the door, I find Trip looming over Mom. She's sitting on the sofa, her neck craned so she can look up at him.

"You're paying the reconnection fee," Trip screams. "It's not my fault you can't remember shit."

"I told you I would," she says meekly.

"What's going on?" I interject, dropping my book bag to the floor.

Mom's head snaps to me, her eyes wide. Deep worry lines fan out at the corners of her eyes. Her face is ghost white. Usually, Mom just ignores Trip's bluster, but this time, she looks scared.

Trip gives me a look that says drop dead.

"Why don't you back off?" I say.

"Why don't you mind your own fucking business?"

I cross the room to stand at Mom's side. I notice the quake in her clenched hands. Red hot anger seeps into my bones. I narrow my eyes at Trip. "What's your problem?"

He stabs a finger in Mom's direction. "I asked her to do one simple thing for me. Take care of my bills while I was away, and she couldn't even do that. Because of her, they shut my fucking lights off on me."

"How is that Mom's fault? If they cut off your electricity, then that means you were already late to begin with," I argue.

He glares at me. "That's beside the point." He stares down at Mom with such loathing, she wilts into the sofa. My heart literally hurts for her.

He holds out his palm. "I want the money."

Mom stutters.

He bellows at her, "Now!" My breath catches as his hand balls into a fist.

My hands react before I can think better of it. I shove Trip as hard as I can. He loses his footing a little, but only because I caught him off guard—not because of my strength. Trip is easily a hundred pounds heavier than me, so my shove probably felt like a snowball hitting him in the chest.

Trip's eyes are hot coals, burning into me.

Mom stands, putting herself between us. She gives me a pleading look before she turns to Trip. "I'll write you a check right now. Just calm down."

"Calm down? That bitch shoved me!" He pushes Mom aside like she's a ragdoll. "I'm not the fucking one," he hisses. "I don't discriminate. I'll punch a girl."

"Go ahead," I taunt, getting in his face. "I'll call the cops so fast your head will spin."

"Penelope." Mom's soft voice tries to tamp down the tension, but it doesn't help. Not this time. I am livid and I refuse to back down like I always do. Like Mom always does. "Penelope," she tries again. "Don't. This is all my fault. I forgot to pay the bill. Trip has every right to be angry."

I snap my head to look at her. "What?"

Her big brown eyes remind me of a doe. A doe startled by an on-coming semi-truck. "Don't make excuses for him. He's out of line and you know it."

Trip balks. "No. She fucked me over. As usual, I can't depend on her."

"Excuse me? Mom does everything for you without so much as a thank you. Why don't you grow up and do things on your own?"

"I already told you, I don't have a problem laying you out." A muscle in his cheek flexes menacingly.

"I wish you would."

"What are you going to do? Hit me back?" He chuckles. "Yeah right." He acts as though I'm nothing but an annoying fly, pestering him while he eats. I hate that. It makes me feel insignificant.

"What are you waiting for?" he barks at Mom.

"Mom," I plead. *Please stand up for yourself.*

She just stares at me, blinking at me with blank, almost dead eyes. *Does she feel anything? Where's her self-respect?* She walks away and gets her checkbook from her purse. She makes out a check, and as she does, something inside me snuffs out. With sadness, I realize it's my respect for her.

How can I respect someone who thinks so little of themselves? How can I respect someone who doesn't stand up for themselves when they're being shoved around, literally, and figuratively? How can she allow herself to be used like this? Doesn't she see how he treats her? My thoughts come fast, pelting me like blows. With a gasp, it finally hits me. I am her, and she is me.

Chapter 26

I'm waiting for Matt at the track. I asked him to meet
me there so we can talk. This winter is sure to be a bitter
one. It's not even nightfall and already my breath is
coming out in puffs. I'm glad I remembered to bring
gloves with me, but now I regret leaving my thermos of
hot chocolate in the car. I slip my gloves on and cinch
the belt on my peacoat tighter.

I sense someone coming. It's a dark figure in the
distance, but I can tell it's Matt. It's funny how you can
come to know someone so well. You learn their likes and
dislikes, their mannerisms, and their bodies. I gulp,
thinking about Matt's body. The muscles in his back and
chest. I regret having sex with him. I was foolish enough
to think Matt and I would be together forever. But I was
wrong. Dead wrong.

I take in a deep breath when he walks up, steeling
myself for what I'm about to do.

"Hi," he says casually.

"Thanks for meeting me here," I tell him.

"No problem. What's up? Or are you just in the
mood for a late-night stroll?" He comes close, reaching
for my hand. I back away, sure that if I allow him to
touch me, I'll lose my nerve.

His brows knit. "What's wrong?"

"I did it."

"You did what?"

"I took a prescription pad."

His eyes brighten. "You did? Pen, thank you." He moves to embrace me, but I sidestep him. His arms drop; his eyes hurt. "What is wrong with you?"

My own eyes cloud with tears. "I can't do this anymore."

Matt frowns. "Do what?"

"Us," I say, my voice cracking. "I can't do...*us* anymore."

"What? Why? What did I do?"

I stare at him, wishing I could erase the last week. Why did he have to ask me to steal that prescription pad? Would that change things? Would I be able to stay with addict? Perhaps I could. Who knows?

"Did you know I volunteered at the hospital before we got together?"

Matt's mouth hangs open. "What the hell does that have to do with anything?"

"Answer the question."

"Yes, but so what?"

My heart becomes a boulder in my chest. *I knew it. I didn't want to admit it, but deep down, I knew it. He used me. Matt never liked me—not really. He just wanted the prescription pad. How could I be so stupid?*

"How did you know?"

Matt throws his hands out. "What is happening right now?"

"Did I tell you?"

Matt paces a small circle. "Yes. A long time ago. In gym."

My eyes close for a beat. *Right.* The conversation comes back to me. We were walking the track—of course—and I was gushing about being made a cuddler in the NICU. It was a big deal to me then. It meant I graduated from being a mere balloon deliverer to a full-fledged volunteer.

"I need to know something else," I hedge.

Matt stares at me, dark eyes credulous.

"Did you take my Preston book?"

He blinks at me but does not respond.

"Answer me," I say louder. "Did you take my first edition, Preston book?"

Matt takes a step toward me. "I can get it back."

My hands clench at my sides. *I knew it.* "What do you mean, you can get it back? Where is it?"

He licks his lips. "I pawned it."

"You what!" I want to strangle him. I want to scream. I want to turn around and run away and never look back, but my feet stubbornly stay grounded, refusing to budge. "How could you?"

"I needed the money. It's still at the pawnshop. I have two weeks before they sell it."

My head is ringing. I can't even hear Matt anymore. *How could I have been so stupid?* First, I allow him to talk me into stealing, and now this? He stole from *me*. Me. The person he supposedly loves. I almost laugh at the absurdity of it all, only I can't. This whole situation is making me sick. My knees go weak, threatening to give out at any moment.

Matt looks up at the sky, almost as if he's searching for a way out of all of this. Then, he has the nerve to heave an exasperated sigh, like I'm the one who did something wrong.

"On our anniversary, you said your friend owed you money. Did you use it to buy Oxy?"

Matt gazes down at the ground. I can tell he's

grinding his teeth by the way the muscles in his cheeks flex. I wait, watching him carefully for a sign of regret or remorse. There isn't any.

He toes the dirt and grounds out an angry, "No. That wasn't my friend. That was my supplier."

The world tilts. Remember when I thought dating Matt wasn't real life? Well now, this is the real deal. There is no way, THIS is my life. My boyfriend—ex-boyfriend—has a supplier. A drug supplier. For the first time, I'm disgusted by him. Before, I felt sorry for him, like his addiction was accidental, like catching a cold. That it would pass as quickly and as easily as it came.

But now, knowing he has a supplier, not to mention the lengths he'll go through to get Oxy, I know deep down in my heart this is all too much for me. I have no business pretending I understand because I don't. I've never been addicted to anything in my life. Except for the summer I was obsessed with Sour Patch Kids. I ate them until I was sick. I puked up so much neon, I vowed never to touch them again.

Matt is staring at me. I think back to our kisses and shared secrets. I think of the night in his room when I gave myself to him. And just like that, I break. I can't hold back the tears. They slip out, icy on my already cold cheeks. "I gave everything I had to you. And it's still not enough. Why? Why am I not enough?"

Matt reaches out for me, but I back away, avoiding his touch as though it were toxic. *It is,* I think sharply. *His touch is toxic. Look what he's doing to me.*

"Pen, don't do this. I need you."

I shake my head, disbelieving. "No, you don't. You need your precious *Oxy.* That's all you care about." I wipe the tears from my chin. "I deserve more than this,

Matt. I deserve to be first in your life. Right now, I'm second to a *drug*. Do you know how that makes me feel?"

He angrily rakes his fingers through his hair. "That's not true."

"It is true! You lied to me. You *stole* from me!" I stomp my foot, not caring how childish it may look. "I know my worth, and it's a hell of a lot more than some stupid drug." I straighten myself, squaring my shoulders when I look him in the eyes and say, "We're done." I walk away, sniffing, but determined to not look back.

Matt calls after me. His voice wounded, and weak. There was a time when that voice would have drawn me back in. When I would have run right back to him. But not anymore. Not ever again.

Chapter 27

I get to school early. I plan on sneaking Matt's letterman jacket into his locker before English. I could just hand it to him, but I'd rather do it this way. It will be easier. Looking him in the eyes as I return his jacket will be too hard. Too final. Tossing harried glances over my shoulder, it takes me three tries to get the combination right. I shove the jacket inside and slam the door shut. With misty eyes, I spin the dial and walk away.

****

"Damn," Carlos says, sliding in next to me. "I have detention *again*."

"What did you do this time?" Jenna questions, picking at her sloppy joe.

"Fart contest in Calculus."

Rainey shoots Carlos a disgusted look over the top of her phone. "How mature of you."

Carlos lifts his hands. "Hey, I wasn't a contestant. I was the judge." He tries to stifle a smile, but fails completely.

"Gross," Rainey says, shaking her head. She goes back to scrolling through her phone.

Jenna giggles.

Carlos looks over at me, his eyebrows raised expectedly.

I roll my eyes. "I'll wait on you."

He looks relieved. Smiling, he says, "You're the

best. Oh, and don't forget, I have that interview today at Mario Bros. You still willing to take me?"

"Do I really have a choice?"

Carlos just grins at me. I take a bite of my dry bologna sandwich. I curse myself for forgetting the mustard. I packed a lunch this morning. Bologna and cheese sandwich, chips, salted almonds, and a bottled water. I did it mainly so I wouldn't have to walk through the cafeteria. Ever since I broke it off with Matt, I've been avoiding him as much as possible.

I just keep my head down or my nose in a book to keep from making eye contact. It's strange to not talk to him. To know he's there, but he's not mine anymore. It hurts actually. I have to keep reminding myself that it was my decision to give him up.

****

While Carlos is doing his time in detention, I'm in the library, working on homework. A few kids loiter around, bent in whispered conversations, while the Chess Club kids are embattled yet again over a game. I'm poring over my *Lord of the Flies* study guide when Matt walks up to me. I try to ignore him, but it's hard when he's towering over me, his stare like needles in my skull. My eyes flick to the right. In his fist is the letterman jacket. *Gulp.*

"What the hell is this?" he asks in a hushed voice, bringing the jacket close to my face.

I swat it away. "Your jacket," I reply pointedly. "Duh."

"I know that," he says through clenched teeth. "Why was it in my locker?"

"Because I returned it." I know I'm being obstinate, but I really don't care. Matt doesn't deserve civility at this point.

"Why are you doing this?"

"Doing what?" I go back to my study guide.

"All of this." He's getting louder now. "Breaking up with me. Avoiding me. I called you ten times last night."

"Quiet," I tell him, looking around. "You're in a library."

"I don't give a fuck," he growls.

I glare at him.

"So?" he demands, scowling. "Are you going to answer me or not? I didn't do shit to you, you know."

My mouth hangs open. "Excuse me? You did a lot to me. If I have to explain that all again, then I'm shutting down this conversation right now."

"So I asked you to lift something for me. Big deal. It's not like you got caught."

"That doesn't matter! You put me in an uncomfortable situation. You never should have asked me to do that. Plus, you stole from me, remember?"

Matt rolls his eyes to the ceiling. "God. It's not that serious, Pen. It's just a stupid book. I told you, I'll get it back."

"A stupid book?" *How can he say that? He knows how much that book meant to me.* I have a chokehold on my poor pencil. Matt is lucky it's not his throat. Before I snap my pencil in two, I start packing my things. I need distance from Matt right now.

He just doesn't get it. He doesn't think stealing is a big deal, or that he has an addiction problem. But *I* do. And that's all that matters. My eyes are finally clear. I see Matt for who he is. An addict who chooses drugs over me. And because of that, I have to let him go. I am done being stepped on, under-loved, and used. I refuse to be like my mother.

"Pen—" Matt tries to take my book bag. "Wait."

I wag a finger in his face. "No, you wait. You need to take responsibility for what you did. You *stole* from me. How can I trust you after that?"

"So you're going to just walk away? You're not going to give me a chance to make it right? What a caring girlfriend you are."

"I am not your girlfriend," I hiss. "Not anymore."

His eyes narrow. "Maybe that's for the best. I need someone who will be there for me. Through the good and the bad. Looks like you only care about being there for the good."

I leap to my feet. *How dare he say that!* "Go to the hell."

Matt grabs my wrist. "Not that it matters, but I didn't use you."

His hold on me is firm, constricting, like a snake. "You're hurting me."

He doesn't relent. "I didn't use you," he repeats, pulling me closer. "How could you think that? I love you, Pen. Don't leave me. I need you."

I wrench out of his grip. "I can't. I can't be with someone who…"

"Who what?" he demands, his face screwed tight.

"Who uses the way you do. You're addicted, Matt. You need help."

He *huffs* and shoves me away.

"Is there a problem over there?" Mrs. Arden says. I turn to see her peering over her glasses at us. She's giving us a disapproving look.

Matt backs away from me. "No, ma'am."

I shake my head woodenly, heat clawing its way up

to my ears. I collect my things, and dart out of the library, away from Matt and away from Mrs. Arden's pitying, prying eyes.

I'm so flustered, I don't see Carlos heading straight toward me until I bump into his chest. My notebooks scatter across the floor.

"Whoa," he cries, staggering back. "Watch the shoes, man." He makes a show of checking his sneakers over for damage.

"Sorry." I flush hot and drop down to collect my notebooks.

He crouches down and helps me. "Damn. What's the rush, anyway, Reza?"

I nervously tuck my hair behind my ear. I haven't told anyone that I broke up with Matt yet. It's a secret that I wish to keep to myself. For now. "Nothing," I lie, clutching two notebooks to my chest. Impending tears start to well. I stand, averting my eyes from him.

Carlos stands, one brow cocked in question. He hands me a notebook. "You sure about that?"

I ignore him, taking the notebook and shoving it, along with the others, into my book bag. I zip it up with purpose, and say, "Ready for your interview?"

A smile breaks across Carlos' face. "You know it."

****

Forget TGIF. Thank God it's Saturday is more like it. I can sleep in, and since there is no school, there is no Matt. That's a win/win. After a half hour of scrolling through social media, an hour of playing games on my phone, and several wasted hours on mindless videos, I'm getting a severe case of cabin fever.

Buttoning myself into my favorite baby pink and purple plaid shirt, I tell myself that a few hours at the hospital will be good for me. *A distraction. That's what I need right now.*

I grab my keys off the kitchen table.

Mom is curled up on the couch, a fleece blanket draped across her lap. She looks up from her coffee cup. "Where are you headed?"

"Hospital. I need something to do, you know?"

She nods. She knows about the breakup now. I came clean to her and Jenna last night. Mom's been supportive, even though I know I've been distant. It's hard to face people. They look at you with those apologetic eyes and give you the same worn-out lines, like; *There are plenty of other fish in the sea* and *If you love something, let it go. If it returns, it's yours; if it doesn't, it wasn't meant to be.* Or something like that.

Breakups are hard. And complicated. Matt may have screwed up, and there is no way I'd ever take him back, but I do still care about him. I genuinely hope he gets the help he needs.

"Snuggle a few babies," she says. "That always makes the worst of days better."

I give her a weak smile and shut the door behind me.

Chapter 28

Mom is right. Snuggling babies is therapeutic. There's just something about the hypnotic rhythm of a rocking chair, and warm little body tucked in your arms to make all your worries wane away.

I leave the NICU feeling warm and fuzzy inside. I think about checking in at the Gift Shop to see if anything needs delivering, but I decide to head to the Emergency Room instead.

Sometimes things get so hectic there, staff relies on volunteers to help direct families to coffee stations and waiting rooms. The ER is high-paced, leaving little downtime. Which is exactly what I'm looking for. I need Matt out of my head space, and a busy shift in ER will surely do the trick.

It doesn't disappoint. Within an hour, there's already been two broken bones, a heart attack, a concussion, and a seizure. I'm refilling the coffee station with sugar packets and stirrers when the double doors of the ER room slide open. Curious, I peer around the corner. Paramedics hover around a stretcher, working swiftly as they roll the patient in.

They head in my direction, so I step back to get out of their way. As they rush past the coffee station, I catch a quick glimpse of the stretcher. I drop the box of creamers when my hands fly to my mouth, smothering a strangled gasp. *It's Matt.*

I chase after the paramedics. Matt is unconscious, that much I can tell. His skin is shockingly pale. His lips tinged an eerie blue. Immediately I think of hypothermia, but that can't be what's wrong. Matt's in basketball shorts and a tank top. If it was hypothermia, surely the paramedics would try to warm him up with blankets?

One of the paramedics, a woman with a cropped pixie cut, notices me keeping pace with them.

"What happened?" I ask her.

Her eyes quickly roam over my volunteer apron. "Overdose," she says. I stop in my tracks, watching as they wheel Matt into a room, drawing the privacy curtain closed behind them. *Overdose?* I feel like I'm about to throw up.

A doctor and several nurses duck behind the drawn curtain. Their voices are muffled, but before long, the paramedics emerge from behind the curtain and leave. Their work is done. It's up to the doctor and nurses now.

I stare unseeing at the curtain. Behind it, they're working on Matt, likely pumping his stomach. Around me, people dart to and fro. Other tragedies unfolding and fires being put out, but I'm too numb to move. *Matt overdosed. Was it intentional? Accidental?*

"Penelope?" I turn to find Matt's mom. She's in her yoga clothes, so she must have just come from a workout. Her eyes are panicky and weepy. The sight of them is like a stab in the gut.

"Mrs. Garrison."

"Where's Matt?" Her voice is strained with worry.

"There." I point to the room.

She follows my finger. "How is he?"

"I don't know," I confess. "The doctor hasn't come out yet."

She darts off, snatching the curtain back before she storms into the room. A stocky nurse in purple scrubs gently takes her by the shoulders and steers her away.

Digging her heels, Mrs. Garrison cries, "What's happening? Is he okay?" The nurse is ever the professional, politely guiding her away. In a reassuring voice, she says, "He's in stable condition."

Mrs. Garrison twists in the nurse's arms, looking back at Matt. "Let me see him!"

"You can see him soon. Just have a seat in the waiting room. Someone will be out soon to get you." The nurse catches me watching. She signals to me. "Can you take her to the waiting room?"

I nod. As soon as the nurse's back is turned, I touch Mrs. Garrison's elbow. "Come on, Mrs. Garrison. I'll sit with you."

We're forced to wait an excruciating hour before the doctor finally comes. "Mrs. Garrison?" The doctor's tone is clear but low. She reaches out and shakes Mrs. Garrison's hand. "I'm Shelia DeRand. I'm Matt's doctor." I've seen Dr. DeRand before but didn't know her name. She's known for her cold bedside manner, but from what I've heard, she's a damn good doctor.

"Is he all right?" Mrs. Garrison asks with hope in her eyes. "When can I see him?"

Dr. DeRand nods, "He's doing just fine. He's resting now, but you're welcome to visit with him."

Mrs. Garrison stands to go, but before she can, Dr. DeRand says, "Mrs. Garrison. Did you know your son had access to OxyContin?" She says it like she already knows the answer.

Mrs. Garrison's eyes widen. "Excuse me?"

"OxyContin," Dr. DeRand says again. "He was well

over the commonly prescribed dose, so that leads me to believe he's outsourcing it somehow."

"It's prescribed," Mrs. Garrison huffs. "He had a wrestling injury."

Dr. DeRand stares at her with shrewd eyes.

Mrs. Garrison juts out her chin stubbornly. "Call his doctor in California if you don't believe me. He'll attest to it." And with that, she turns on her heel and trots away.

Dr. DeRand looks at me. "Friend of his?"

"Something like that."

"Wait here," she says and goes behind the nurses' desk. She comes back with a pamphlet and hands it to me with a firm look. "Make sure he gets this."

A lump forms in my throat. The pamphlet is about opioid addiction.

****

I give Mrs. Garrison some time alone with Matt before I go in. I don't want to intrude on any tender moment she might have with him. When I finally decide to go in, I find her sitting beside the bed, clutching Matt's hand. Her eyes are wet with tears, but she doesn't pry them off her son.

"I knew about his problem," she says to me. "It's why his dad shipped his ass back to me. I just wasn't going to admit it to that know-it-all doctor." She pulls her gaze from Matt and looks pointedly at me. "Did you see the look she gave me? Like I'm a bad parent." She wipes her cheek with her free hand. "Who does she think she is?"

"She's just doing her job," I say in return. "After all, she saved Matt."

She balks, but when her eyes drift back to Matt, her lips press together. She doesn't say anything more. She knows I'm right.

On heavy feet, I walk closer so I can get a better look at Matt. His skin is still pale, but his lips are no longer that icy blue, which is a relief. He looks peaceful. If it weren't for all the wires, and the clicks and beeps of hospital equipment, I could trick myself into thinking he was merely sleeping.

"How about you, Penelope? Did you know?"

I look from Matt to Mrs. Garrison. She searches my eyes, waiting with bated breath for me to answer.

"Yes," I whisper.

She nods knowingly. "Matt never was good at keeping secrets."

Matt stirs. Mrs. Garrison and I whip our heads to watch him, eager for him to wake and talk to us. Eager to see with our own eyes that he's okay.

Matt's eyes flutter open. He sees his mom first. "Ma?"

Mrs. Garrison beams. "Oh, sweet boy. I'm here." Tears slip down her cheeks. Tears of relief, of joy, or maybe both. Probably both. I know what it's like to have conflicting emotions wrestling inside of you.

Matt's eyes lift, and though they are weak, they pin me into place. "Pen?"

I force a smile.

"Ma, can I talk to Pen…alone?"

Mrs. Garrison's smile slips. "I don't want to leave you."

"I'm all right," Matt assures her. "Could use a drink, though. Can you get me one?" He touches his throat. "I'm so thirsty."

"Of course." She kisses his knuckles and leaves.

"What are you doing here?" Matt questions as soon

as the curtain swings closed.

"I saw you come in." I drop into the chair beside the bed. "What happened?"

He rolls his head on the pillow, looking straight up at the ceiling. "What do you think happened?" His voice is oozing with venom.

"I know what happened. I just want to know *how* it happened."

He cuts his eyes to me. "Thought I was taking 40s. Ended up being 80s. Amateur mistake. Won't happen again."

My blood runs cold. "Won't happen again? What does that mean?"

"It means, it won't happen again. I'll be more careful next time."

Did I just hear him right? He just OD'd and still refuses to quit? My hands curl into the armrests. "Are you kidding? How can you be thinking of next time after what just happened? You almost died, Matt. This is serious. Besides, I thought you were going to stop. What about all that stuff you told me? That you were going to wean yourself off."

He scoffs. "What the hell do you care? You broke up with me, remember?"

"Is that why you did it?"

His brows lift high. "Wow." He barks a condescending laugh. "Do you actually think I'd kill myself over you? A little drastic, not to mention pathetic, don't you think?"

I'm comforted, knowing that I wasn't the cause of any of this, but Matt's attitude is grating on me. I stand. With the curtain in my hand, I turn one last time and say, "I'm glad you're okay. I wish you'd consider getting help, but that's for you to decide, not me. But just think about it, okay? For your mom. And for you." Then, I slip past the curtain, letting it swing back into place as I distance myself from Matt for the final time.

****

My footsteps are swift and determined. Thankfully, the office door is open because I swoop in like a hawk. Dr. Yassin is on the phone, sitting behind his desk. When he sees me, he holds up one finger, so I take a seat, picking at my cuticles as I wait. He wraps up the call, smiling at me as he sets the receiver back on the cradle. "Penelope. How are you?" My wide-eyed expression must say it all because he frowns. "Is something wrong?"

I bite my lower lip, deciding on how to frame my thoughts. "Dr. Yassin. I need to tell you something."

"Okay." His dark, deep-set eyes are questioning now.

My heart beats, rapid fire within my chest. This is harder than I thought. I lick my dry lips and say, "I took something that belongs to you." I dip my fingers into my apron pocket. I lay the prescription pad on his desk and push it toward him. "Every page is there. I swear."

Dr. Yassin eyes the pad. "I see."

Shame almost doubles me over. "I'm sorry." My eyes prick with tears.

He leans forward. "Falsifying a prescription is a federal crime."

There's no holding the tears back anymore. They run hot down my cheeks.

Dr. Yassin watches me thoughtfully.

"I'm so sorry," I tell him again, my voice coming out in hiccups. "Are you going to have me arrested?" Then, I really start to panic. "My mom. Are you going to

176

tell my mom?" I lean forward in my seat, pleading. "Please don't tell her."

He picks up a box of tissues from his desk, and offers it to me. I take one and wipe my nose.

"I won't," he says. "But only on one condition."

Sniffling, I look at him in wonder.

"That you get help." *Help?* My stomach sours. *He thinks I stole the pad for myself. He thinks I'm the addict.* "We have recovery specialists here, but I understand if you want to go elsewhere, for the sake of anonymity."

"No, Dr. Yassin. It isn't like that. I didn't take it for me. I took it for Matt." Rubbing the Kleenex between my fingers, I tell Dr. Yassin everything. From Matt asking me to steal, our breakup, and everything in between. When I'm through, he gets up out of his chair and walks over to where I'm sitting. He rests a hand on my shoulder. "My condition still stands."

I blink up at him. "I don't understand."

"Penelope, you may be what they call a co-addict. That's someone who enables an addict. There are support groups for that. They help identify why the behavior manifests within you and give you coping skills for future relationships."

Slowly, I nod. What else can I do but agree? Dr. Yassin is being generous. He could easily fire me, tell Mom, or even turn me in for theft.

I leave Dr. Yassin's office with a phone number for a co-addict support group that meets weekly at J. Murrey Atkins Library. I'm apprehensive about going to a support group, but given the alternative, I don't have much of a choice.

Chapter 29

Thank goodness Jenna isn't the "I told you so" type, though I know she's secretly thinking it. And who could blame her? She knew Matt wasn't right for me all along, but I wouldn't listen. Love really is blind. I never realized how true that old saying was until now. Others around you see them for who they really are, but you're too busy walking around with star-struck eyes. You never see what they see. Until it's too late.

Jenna and I fell right back into our old routine after the breakup. I'm glad for it. It's a nice distraction from thinking about Matt all the time. I may be mad at him for what he did, but I loved him. I can't just shut that off, though I really wish I could.

We're watching self-help TV and painting our toes when there's a knock at the front door. I screw the cap back onto my bottle of Chinaberry Red polish and stumble to the door on my heels to open it. It's Carlos. He holds a pizza box and a bottle of soda out toward me like an offering.

"You girls hungry?"

Before I can answer, Jenna hollers, "Carlos! Get your happy butt in here! And that pizza better have banana peppers on it."

I laugh and step aside so he can come in. Jenna must have texted him. I'm happy she did. I'm starving, not to mention stress-eating, so a slice of gooey Mario Bros pizza is just what I need right now.

Carlos sets the box on the coffee table and sits down on the floor. He glances down at Jenna's blue toes. She wiggles them at him. "What do you think? It's called 'Iced Princess.' "

He wrinkles his nose. "They look frostbitten."

Jenna grabs a pillow from the couch and throws it at his head.

I ignore them and flip open the lid of the pizza box. Half pepperoni, half banana peppers. I take out a slice. *Mmm.* The cheese melts in my mouth.

Jenna inspects the pizza and gives a nod of approval. "Well done, Rivera."

"Did you make this yourself?" I ask between bites. Carlos got the job at Mario Bros Pizzeria. He started a couple weeks ago. I drop him off at the pizzeria after school instead of his house now, which means he needs to stay out of detention, or he'll miss his shift. So far, he's been staying out of trouble, but knowing Carlos, it won't last long. He'll be involved in some sort of hijinks or disgusting body function contest and that will be it for him.

Carlos grins. "Yep." He laces his fingers and cracks them like he's about to do some hard labor. "Good, right?"

"I'll be the judge of that." Jenna snags a slice and stuffs it in her mouth. Her eyes light up, then she closes them as if in ecstasy.

"You like?" Carlos asks, amused. Jenna swallows and says, "Oh my god, Carlos. You. Are. A. Pizza wizard!"

We share an easy laugh, which is nice. And normal. It's almost as if the past five months haven't happened.

There was no Matt. No tension. No heartache.

****

The weekend went by too fast for my liking. Sleeping in and zoning out in front of my laptop has kept me from rehashing everything that happened between me and Matt. Being back in school, I'm forced to relive our time together. Our stolen moments in the hallway. Our relentless flirting in English class. Sitting side by side on a bench in the courtyard during lunch. I see Matt everywhere. There isn't an inch of this building that doesn't remind me of him.

Sitting in Mrs. Johnson's class, I find my gaze drifting to Matt's empty chair. He hasn't been back to school since his overdose. *I wonder what his coach will do once he finds out? Will they kick him off the team?*

Mrs. Johnson interrupts my thoughts. "Penelope. Can you read the last two paragraphs of the chapter out loud?"

I snap into focus. "Y-yes." I clear my throat and start reading. My voice cracks a little, but somehow, I make it through. In fact, I make it the rest of the day. I aced a pop quiz. I laughed with friends and actually stomached a little bit of food. It's a small victory, but given the cruddy way I've been feeling lately, it's a big win for me.

****

After school, I drop Carlos off at work and then head to the library. The support group doesn't meet until five, but I can work on homework while I wait. The library's parking lot is nearly full, so I'm forced to park pretty far away. I reach into the glove box and take out my wool beanie. I pull it over my ears and get out of the car. The wind is really cutting today. I hustle across the parking lot, cinching my coat tight, hoping to keep out some of the icy breeze.

Relief comes in the form of central heating as I push through the library doors. It's toasty inside, and the smell of the books is making me want to forget about homework and instead, settle into a comfy chair in the corner with a juicy page-turning novel.

I tug at the straps of my book bag, and it grounds me. I can't do that. I have a big biology test this week and I need to pull off at least a B if I want to maintain my average.

I decide to hit the restroom first. The last thing I need is to settle into some deep studying and then have to pee. Coming out of the stall, I catch a glimpse of myself in the mirror. My nose is bright pink from the cold. I touch my fingers to it. *Ugh.* I look like Rudolph's adopted sister. My cheeks are the same color, but it looks more like well-placed rouge.

My beanie, on the other hand, looks every inch of its second-hand store find. It's a royal blue knitted cap with curling edges. It used to have a fluffy pompom on the crown, but it tore off last winter when Jenna snatched the beanie off my head. I can still see her staring at the pompom in her fingers and saying, "Oh my God. I yanked your ball off." Carlos thought that was the funniest thing he'd ever heard. He literally collapsed to the floor with laughter.

I finish washing and drying my hands go to look for an empty table. I find one near the Xerox machines, which isn't ideal, but with the crowd in here today, there aren't many other options.

I drag out my biology book, the study guide Mr. Roger's gave us this morning, a green highlighter, and set forth to cram as much information about heredity and genetics into my brain as I can in two hours.

It's going well until I get a text from Matt.

—*They're releasing me today*—

I stare down at the lit screen. Should I respond? My initial reaction is relief that he's okay, and then elation that he is well enough to go home, then comes reality. Matt's not my boyfriend anymore, therefore he's not my concern. I'm about to tell him as much when the phone vibrates in my hand.

—*I still love you*—

My throat goes dry. I close my eyes for a beat, searching for strength. It feels so good to be loved. To be wanted. But I have to remember that Matt doesn't really love me. He doesn't even really *want* me. At least not as much as he wants Oxy, and for that, I have to move on. I deserve to be someone's first, not a runner-up to a drug.

When I open my eyes, I read the text one more time, and then I delete it.

Chapter 30

I'm so entrenched in studying, I nearly forget about the support group until I hear a group of people bustling in through the library doors. There are four of them, and they're exchanging pleasantries in hushed voices. They peel off, and go into the vacant meeting room of the library. I check my phone. It's just before five o'clock.

That must be the group. I gather my books from the table and slide them into my book bag. I stand up and walk to the room, but as I do, I'm suddenly stricken with nerves. I don't have a clue what to expect. Everything I know about support groups is from movies. Will they make me stand up and say something like, *"Hi. My name is Penelope, and I'm a co-addict."*

What a silly term anyway, *co-addict*. Couldn't they come up with something better? Something flashier? Something that reflects how I felt when I was with Matt? Desperate abettor. Lovesick accessory. Those are more realistic. When I stole that prescription pad for Matt, I honestly felt that I was helping him with his addiction.

It's ridiculous, I know, but I believed that with my help, he would wean himself off the Oxy. That my love and support would bring him safely out on the other side of addiction.

A gold plaque on the door reads: Joseph Salvador Meeting Room. The chairs are exactly how they are in the movies. I gulp. They're arranged in a circle, and the four people I saw earlier have already taken their seats. They watch me as I sit down. I pull my book bag across my knees and take in the room. Other than the gigantic whiteboard at the head of the room, and a few framed photos of exotic birds, the room is uninviting and severe.

A man, maybe in his mid-forties, enters the room.

"Good evening, all," he greets, smoothing his coppery wind-blown hair back into place. He unbuttons his navy-blue sports jacket, his eyes drifting over the room. When they land on me, a brief moment of surprise registers on his face. With purpose, he walks over to me and offers his hand.

"Dave Mathers."

I take it. It's like shaking hands with a snowball. "Penelope."

"Welcome to the group," he says. His cheeks are ruddy from the cold. I'm glad when he finally releases me. I draw my sleeves over my hands to warm them. "If there is anything I can do to make you comfortable during your visit with us, please ask."

"Oh, I am just here to listen, really."

"Of course." He gives me a meaningful smile. He checks his watch. "Time to get started." He turns and addresses the room. "Welcome everyone. And thank you for being here with me, yet again this week." Mr. Mathers' voice drones into white noise as my eyes touch on each person in the room.

A woman, probably in her thirties, sits perched in her chair directly across from me. She's slight, with hair that looks as though it has never been touched with scissors. She fusses with it, weaving the long strands into a never-ending braid. She's wearing a burgundy turtleneck and high-waisted jeans. Her face is just as simple as her wardrobe, save for her unkempt brows. They stand defiant against her pale skin.

A woman a few seats away from her idly twirls the ring on her finger. Her cotton-candy blue hair is a pretty contrast against her dark skin. She sways back and forth in her chair, humming to herself, every now and then shutting her eyes as if in prayer.

A man, older, perhaps in his sixties, glowers to himself, his arms crossed over his barrel chest. He doesn't look like he wants to be here anymore than I do. He feels me staring, and when our eyes meet, he cuts his away so fast I felt as though I've been nicked with a knife.

"Court ordered," says a gruff, but feminine voice to my left. I turn to find a woman settling herself into the chair beside me. She lets out a heavy sigh, as if she exhausted all her energy on the act of lowering herself into the seat. Her thin lips are painted red, and her brows are painted black.

"Excuse me?"

"Ernie." With a thrust of her rounded chin, she points at the old man. "Court ordered to be here. It's better than being behind bars, I suppose. He helped his daughter forge checks. Poor soul. He thought she was using the money to pay for his grandson's medical bills. Turns out she was spending the money on gambling and keeping the sharks off her tail." She *tsks*, shaking her head gravely. A tendril falls over her forehead. She pushes it back impatiently.

I swallow.

Her eyes slide to me. "What about you, dear? What brings you here?" She smiles warmly.

I grope for something to say, but I'm wordless.

Admitting that I stole a prescription pad for my boyfriend to this seemingly nice, old lady seems all wrong.

"That's all right," she says. "Our stories are all different here, but our endings are very much the same." She winks, and turns her attention to Mr. Mathers.

He opens his arms out wide. "Judith," he greets. "What say you? Feel like starting us off?"

"Sure, why not?" she answers. Her gaze sweeps across her attentive audience. "My son, Anthony, called me this week. As you know, he's been sober for six months." Everyone applauds. Judith nods her head graciously. "Thank you. I am proud of him, too. We had a wonderful chat. I did as Dave instructed me. I praised him for his accomplishment and did not feed into any negativity."

"Very good, Judith," Mr. Mathers says, clapping. "Well done."

The meeting room door opens and in walks a bearded man with raven hair. He's lean and long-legged. Very handsome for a middle-aged man. Behind him, a boy who looks to be copied and pasted from the same DNA wanders in. His dark chestnut hair is shaggy, but not from neglect, more like personal preference. Like the long wisps shield him from the world somehow. The boy looks downright bored, plopping down into the nearest empty seat. He takes out a pen from his jacket pocket and starts sketching something on his sneakers.

"I'm so sorry we're late, Dave," the man says in a rush. "Traffic was a nightmare coming come from work today." His eyes shift around the room. "Sorry for the interruption. It won't happen again."

"Sam," Mr. Mathers says patiently. "We were just

beginning our opening shares. Judith already told us she had a successful conversation with her son this week."

Sam looks at the old woman. "Congratulations."

"Would you like to go next, Sam?"

Sam reddens. "I have nothing of importance to share this week." He looks down at the floor. The boy scoffs, but doesn't offer much else. Sam lifts his gaze to the boy and purses his lips so tight they disappear into the thick of his beard.

"Chase?" Mr. Mathers says. "You're free to share if you'd like."

He shrugs. Sam and the boy exchange a heated look. Mr. Mathers waits, eyebrows lifted with curiosity. I lean forward, enraptured by the tension. Judith shifts in her seat. The woman with the unruly brows stifles a cough. Finally, Chase runs his fingers through his long bangs and shakes his head. Mr. Mathers continues, unfazed. "All right then. How about you, Mika? Care to share your week?"

The woman with blue hair sits up a little straighter. "Unfortunately, I had a backslide." She glances down at her fingers and takes up twirling the ring again. "Ray has a big competition this weekend and…" Her voice is brittle as a snowflake. "Swore that if he placed, it would be the last time he used."

Her eyes well, and soon she's unable to keep them at bay. "Lord, help me. I was so selfish." She breaks down, sobbing uncontrollably. Mr. Mathers goes to her and kneels, taking her hands in his. "The devil enticed me with the prize money. Greed blinded me." She collapses and wails into Mr. Mathers shoulder.

I stare, transfixed. This is not a game. People are struggling every day to keep their loved ones clean, and this woman admits she gave Ray, whoever that is, clearance to use so long as it benefited her. Ernie committed a crime for his daughter and almost had to do hard time. Then, I think about myself. How I stole for Matt. From Dr. Yassin—a man I respect. My stomach sours.

Mr. Mathers' and Mika's heads are bowed close in hushed conversation. Once he calms her, he rises and catches my eye. "As you can see, progress and regression are forever dueling. We take pride in admitting to enduring both. Once you can note your regression, true progression can emerge."

I have to remind myself to blink. The atmosphere in the room is as rigid as a fence post. Mr. Mathers drifts away from Mika, starting a slow procession around our circle. "Realizing your judgment has lapsed is a victory! You have learned to identify your weakness, even if you acted upon it. Some folks go months, years, even decades without noticing that they are cultivating a toxic relationship."

Mr. Mathers launches into a speech about self-confidence. I try to listen, but I'm distracted by Sam and the boy named Chase. They argue in hushed voices, and from the way everyone ignores them, I get the feeling they do this a lot. I study them. Sam is ruggedly handsome, with a greying beard and sideburns. Chase favors him in many ways.

Both have piercing blue eyes and crooked noses, but where Sam is broad-shouldered as an anchor, Chase is the rope, slender and lithe. Their muttering gets louder, but it's only when Chase lets out a sound of annoyance does it catch Mr. Mathers' attention.

"Everything all right?" he asks.

Abashed, Sam mumbles, "Fine. Please continue."

Chase runs his fingers through his hair. The long bangs sweep back over his crown, exposing his eyes better. They suddenly swing over to me, pinning me still. We stare at each other for a beat, but then he sharply averts his eyes back to his father. He glowers at him darkly.

Mr. Mathers eyes Sam for a moment. "We are here to support one another, Sam. Not for me to deliver lectures." He strolls over to him and places a hand on his shoulder. "If there is anything I can do to offer you, or your son support, please feel free to say so." Giving him a squeeze, he adds quietly, "We can talk privately, if you'd like."

Sam gives the smallest nod in return.

Mr. Mathers picks up where he left off, saying something about setting and achieving small goals to use as the foundation for positive self-esteem. My thoughts drift to Chase and Sam. I wonder, *what's their story*? As Judith put it, *our stories are all different here, but our endings are very much the same.* I consider asking Judith about them, but before I can, the session is adjourning.

I blink in surprise. *Has it been a full hour already?* Chase is the first one out. Sam lingers, waiting for Mr. Mathers. I'm still stuck to my chair, watching the people around me gather themselves. Mika hugs Mr. Mathers before she leaves. The other woman, whose name I still don't know, exits the room quietly. Judith heaves herself to her feet. She looks down at me.

"That wasn't so bad, was it?"

"No," I admit.

"So, does that mean we'll be seeing you next week?"

I nod.

Her red-stained lips spread into a smile. "Well, all right then. Perhaps you'll bless me with knowing your name." She winks, and then moves off, her gait heavy as if her feet are weighted.

I stand, slipping my book bag on as I head for the door. Sam and Mr. Mathers are in deep discussion, so I leave quietly. Judith's slow pace allows me time to jog ahead of her. I open the library doors for her, smiling as she walks past.

"Thank you, dear," she says.

"Penelope," I tell her. She pauses, her eyes meeting mine. "Ah. Penelope," she says with a smile. "Pretty name for a pretty girl." She clutches my hand. "I pray you find whatever it is you need here, dear."

When she walks away, I see Chase leaning against the brickwork of the library. His hands are stuffed into his jacket pockets, his long bangs blowing wildly in the wind. His eyes are downcast, so he doesn't see me watching him. He looks as though the weight of the world is resting on his slim shoulders. I allow my gaze to wander over him one more time, then I pull my hat snug over my ears, and head home.

Chapter 31

The week is almost over when Matt strolls back into Mrs. Johnson's class. He looks good. His skin is its usual tan, and his eyes are bright. He slides into his desk without acknowledging me.

"Today we are doing some silent reading," Mrs. Johnson announces. She peers at us over her hot-pink reading glasses. "If you've read ahead, then this is the perfect time to complete your study guides. You'll have a test on the material next week."

I haven't read ahead, in fact, I'm behind. I've been so uninspired to do much of anything that doesn't involve solitaire or old soap opera reruns. I open *Lord of the Flies* and begin to read. I'm halfway into the chapter when a folded piece of paper slides across my desk. I glance up. Matt gives me a weak smile, then turns his back to me. I take the note and slowly open it. In his familiar scrawl, it says, *I miss you.*

I crumple up the note and leave it balled in my fist. I go back to the book in my hand. Matt slips another note. *I'm sorry. Forgive me. I need you.* This note suffers the same fate as the last. Another sheet of paper skims across my desk. I snatch it up angrily. *I'll stop. For you. Promise.* This one makes me take pause. Would he do that? It's all I ever wanted.

Clean Matt is the ideal boyfriend. He's funny, charming, and sensitive. A thought stirs within me.

Matt's wrestling injury happened when he was in California. *Before* he came back to Reedmont. *Before* we reconnected. *Before* we started dating. He was using our entire relationship. Did I ever really know him at all? My head grows fuzzy.

My hand shoots up in the air. "Mrs. Johnson, may I be excused?" She looks up from the stack of tests in front of her, startled. I don't give her time to respond. "I think I need to see the nurse." I hastily shove my things into my backpack and sling it over my shoulder. Heat rushes to my cheeks when I feel the entire room's eyes on me. Even Matt is staring.

Mrs. Johnson stands, concern coloring her face. "Of course," she tells me, coming over to hand me a hall pass.

I take the hall pass and slip it into my pocket. "Thank you." Noticing Matt's last note is still on my desk, I reach out and snatch it up quickly. Keeping my head down, I dart out of the classroom. Once in the hallway, I'm finally able to breathe. Away from Matt. Away from his heavy stare. Away from his stupid notes.

I open my hand and look at the waded paper. Why can't he just leave me alone? Doesn't he realize how difficult he's making this? Since I broke things off with him, I've been in constant limbo. My brain knows breaking up with him was for the best, but my heart still needs convincing.

What if I tried harder? What if he tried harder? What if he loved me more than the Oxy? Again, the familiar frustration with Matt is back. Somehow, I always circle back to this thought. What if Matt chose me over the Oxy? I glare at his note, still bunched in my palm. But he didn't. He chose the drug. I fist the note, crushing his words and fake promises.

****

Mom and Dr. Yassin are on a date. A full-fledged, just the two of them, date. I'm wrapped in a fuzzy blanket on the couch, waiting for Mom to get back home and spill all the details. While I wait, I flip through the channels on the television, not really watching anything in particular.

For a Friday night, there's not much on. But to be fair, my attention is elsewhere. I keep thinking about Mom. This is the happiest I've ever seen her. She's still the same meek woman who never returns her food at a restaurant if it's prepared wrong, but the smile on her face is finally genuine, not the usual complacent curved lips she normally wears.

A knock on the door startles me. I shove off the blanket and go to the window. I slide the curtain aside, expecting to see Mr. Bower standing there but instead, I see Matt. My stomach clenches at the sight of him. His profile is well-defined in the moonlight.

I always liked his chin, especially when he'd let it stubble. I'd run my fingers along it like I was reading braille. I linger on the memory and almost smile. I force myself to tear my gaze away, letting the curtain fall back into place. I put my hand on the doorknob and take a deep, cleansing breath. *Be strong,* I tell myself, before opening the door.

Matt's standing with his hands jammed into his pockets. Despite the cold weather, he's only dressed in sweats and his Reedmont Wrestling hoodie.

"What are you doing here?" I demand.

His eyes, wide and hopeful, lock onto mine. "I wanted to see you."

"Well, you saw me." I go to close the door. Matt's

hand shoots out and stops the door from shutting in his face. Annoyed, I glare at him. "What are you doing?"

"Just talk to me."

"There's nothing left to say." I cross my arms over my chest, and the distant idea I'm somehow protecting my heart isn't lost on me. I should have protected it sooner, and none of this would have happened.

"There's always more to say," he argues. "And if you think I'm going to let you go this easily, you're crazy."

I grab my jacket from the coat rack and step outside. "Matt," I say, my breath coming out in puffs. "We are done. There is nothing you can say to change that."

"Not even, I quit?"

I feel my brows meet in confusion. He waits patiently for me to piece it all together. I feel lightheaded. I grope for the doorjamb to steady myself. "What are you saying?"

"I quit." His dark eyes hold firm. "I haven't touched Oxy in over a week. If quitting is what it will take to get you back, then I'll do it."

My heart becomes liquid, pooling into my gut, as I think back to freshman year, and the boy who walked the track with me. The boy who had yet to discover OxyContin.

"I...I don't know," I whisper. The wall I built around my heart since discovering his secret suddenly doesn't feel so impenetrable.

He must sense it, too. Emboldened, he closes the space between us with one quick stride. He takes hold of my waist. "I love you, Pen. Don't walk away when I need you the most." His eyes glint, searching mine for some understanding and maybe even weakness.

I try not to show him how much his words are affecting me, but it becomes too difficult. Emotions overwhelm me. My eyes mist, and soon I'm sobbing into his shoulder. He smells as if he's just come from practice. Coach must have allowed him to stay on the team. I'm glad for that. He may have lost me, but at least he still has wrestling. His only chance for a scholarship.

"What about all those things you said at the hospital?" I ask, sniffling.

"I was angry," he says. "I hated you for breaking up with me." He smooths my hair down my back. "I didn't mean what I said. I was an idiot, Pen. An idiot who was out of his mind with depression and withdrawals…"

He untangles himself from me. I wipe my eyes, catching a shaky breath. His hands move to my face, cupping my cheeks and bringing my nose to his. "I'm sorry, Pen. Please say you'll give me another chance." He presses his lips against mine. At first, I don't react. I'm limp in his arms. Then my body betrays me, giving in to the feel of his mouth against mine. I kiss him back. I know I shouldn't, but I do, and it feels good. His embrace is familiar; his taste missed.

Could I have the Matt I want? The one that doesn't come with baggage? The one without addiction? Or better yet, can I be the Penelope he needs?

Headlights swing into the driveway, breaking us apart. Dr. Yassin's Cadillac eases to a stop, and the engine cuts off. Dr. Yassin gets out of the car and opens the passenger door for Mom. She beams as she covers the lawn in hurried steps. Her tailored coat, cinched tight at her waist, accentuates her lean body.

Even in the darkness, her blonde hair shines like a halo. She's a vision of happiness. Dr. Yassin's expression is a contrast. His brows are pulled low across his eyes, and his mouth is grim. He slams the car door shut.

"Matt," Mom greets. "How are you?"

"Better now, Mrs. Jackson." Matt grins at me, his eyes twinkling like a little boy.

Dr. Yassin strolls up, his mouth set tight as he swings a cutting glace from me to Matt.

"Dr. Yassin," Matt says politely.

Dr. Yassin gives a courteous nod of acknowledgment but says nothing. My cheeks burn with shame. *He knows what I did for Matt.* Per our agreement, Dr. Yassin wanted me to break the cycle of co-addiction, and here I am, caught in Matt's arms.

"Where is your coat?" Mom asks Matt. "It's freezing out here." She shivers for effect.

"Not to me." Matt stuffs his hands into the pocket of his hoodie.

Dr. Yassin's brow arches just enough for me to notice.

"Must be that athlete's blood of yours," Mom says with a shake of her head. "Always runs hot." Her hair looks pretty tonight, curled into beachy waves down her back. "As for me," she adds, brushing past me. "I can't feel my toes, so I am going in. Good night, Matt."

"Good night, Mrs. Jackson."

Wordless, Dr. Yassin follows Mom inside the house.

"What's with him?" Matt asks me.

"What do you mean?"

"You didn't notice the stink eye he was giving me?"

"No," I lie.

Matt regards me for a moment. "Does he know

about…you know?"

My vision narrows. "About stealing from him? Yeah, he knows."

Matt winces. "Your mom?"

I shake my head. "No."

Matt gives a knowing nod. "That's good."

We stand silent for a few moments, neither knowing what to say next. Something flutters in the corner of my eye. The window curtain draws back, and Mom's face appears beyond the glass. Her wounded expression is a stark contrast to what it was just moments ago. *What's wrong?* A second later, the front door pulls open. Warm air rushes out, teasing me. I rub my frozen hands together. "Mom—"

"Please tell Matt goodnight and come inside." Her tone is clipped.

"Is everything okay?" I ask her.

She walks away from me, disappearing into the living room. She leaves the door open, expecting me to follow.

I turn to Matt. "I better go."

"Talk to you later?"

Before I can answer, he moves in to give me another kiss. I tuck my chin, letting his lips fall against my forehead. He takes it in stride, smiling at me when I lift my eyes.

"Are we good?" he asks.

I should be honest; I should say no. But the happiness in his eyes snatches the words from me. My smile is strained, but it's all I can offer him. He takes it gladly, grinning at me and saying, "I'll text you later." His steps are light as he crosses the lawn to his car. When he's in, he rolls down the window and calls out, "I love you!"

I stare blindly into the night, watching the taillights as his car drives away. Once they've faded from sight, I drag myself inside the house. I'm not ready to face Mom, or whatever she's about to tell me. I find her perched on the edge of the loveseat, her hands clutched in her lap. Whatever joy she felt earlier has diminished.

The high of her date with Dr. Yassin has worn off, and she's all harsh angles and shadows beneath the lamplight. Dreariness has seeped into Dr. Yassin too. He sits hunched, his elbows resting on his knees on the chair. His head is bowed, his eyes on his steepled fingers.

"Sit," Mom says quietly.

I do as I'm told. The tension in the room is stifling. "What's going on?" My voice sounds unfamiliar to my own ears. Small and breathy as anxiety stirs within my gut. *What's happened?*

"Penelope." Mom's tone is sharp. "How could you do such a thing?"

I look at her in question.

"Stealing from the hospital?" Her eyes cut like daggers. "From Jamil?"

My head swims. *She knows*. Feeling betrayed, I jerk my head to glare at Dr. Yassin. "You said you wouldn't tell her!"

Dr. Yassin's dark eyes rise, meeting mine. "That deal went null tonight." His words aren't dripping with anger. In fact, just the opposite. He sounds…hurt? No. I must be reading that all wrong.

I feel hot all over. I touch my temple in a meager attempt to ward off vertigo. "But I agreed to go to that stupid group."

"Yes," Dr. Yassin shoots back. "But what's the

point when you align yourself with the trigger?" His gaze is relentless, and I squirm under the weight of it.

I tug at my hair, mindlessly wrapping a strand around my index finger. "What do you mean?"

Dr. Yassin straightens his spine. "You know exactly what I mean."

I shiver, my eyes darting to Mom. Her brows are pinched, and her mouth is a hard line.

"Mom. I'm sorry," I murmur. "I don't know what I was thinking." I cast my eyes down in shame.

Mom is silent as stone.

Tears start building and the longer she's quiet, the harder it becomes to keep them at bay. I lift my quivering chin. "Mom. Say something."

Mom stands. "What's done is done. Go to bed now, Penelope. You have school in the morning." Dr. Yassin climbs to his feet and follows Mom into the kitchen. They talk in hushed voices, clearly done with me. I begin to sob. Somehow, I knew she wouldn't punish me. She never does.

Part of me wishes she would.

Chapter 32

I've never skipped school before, so I'm not exactly sure how to pull it off. I could drive straight past the school and take the nearest exit to the beach. No. It's the end of winter. I'll be a popsicle by the end of the day. I could drive to the library. No, that wouldn't work. The librarians would spot me, and call the cops. Wait. Are the cops even called when kids are found skipping school? I'm clearly no juvenile delinquent. Then, I remember Carlos. He didn't feel like catching the bus today, so I promised him a ride. Thanks Carlos, for dashing my dreams of skipping school.

That way, I could just go home and get back into bed. Of course, I can't do any of those things because of Carlos. He's waiting for me to pick up him, as usual, so if I don't go to school—he doesn't go to school. Not that he'd care. If I asked him to skip with me, he'd probably jump at the chance.

Mom finds me brooding over the toaster, waiting for my wheat toast to pop. "Morning," she murmurs, her slippers scuffing the floor as she shuffles through the kitchen. The toaster *clicks* and I pluck out two pieces of hot toast. I toss them onto the plate and blow on my smarting fingertips. When I look up, I notice her eyes are puffy, like she'd been crying.

"Mom? Are you all right?"

She nods woodenly and takes a mug from the

cupboard. I set my plate down and go to her. She puts on a pot of coffee. Her movements are automatic as she's done this morning dance, day after day, for years.

"Have you been crying?" I examine her face, noting the faraway look in her eyes as though her thoughts are a million miles from here. "Mom?"

Her eyes settle on mine. "Jamil and I are…" She inhales, and says in one long breath, "taking a little break."

"What?" I touch my heart. It hurts for my mom. Why would they need to take a break? Things have been going so well.

Mom hugs herself, her robe almost swallowing her whole. "I was the last to know what you did. Jamil should have come to me when it happened."

I stare, dumbfounded. *Now? Now she grows a spine?* "Mom. I am sorry for what I did. All of this is my fault, not Dr. Yassin's. I asked him not to tell you."

"That doesn't matter," she snaps. "I'm still your mother." For the first time, I see rage build within my mother. "I should have been told my daughter committed a felony." She wipes her eyes angrily.

That was a knife to the heart. "Mom," I plead.

"And then, that boy has the nerve to show his face here after that?" She scoffs. "Knowing what he made you do?"

"He didn't *make* me do anything," I interject, wincing.

The muscle in her jaw tightens. I've never seen this side of Mom, so I decide to stay silent, ready to weather whatever storm she brings. In fact, I welcome it. Let her unleash whatever anger she has inside. I deserve it.

Mom's gaze is heavy upon me, but as quick as the

storm came in, it recedes just as fast. She turns her back to me and says, "You're going to be late."

****

"What's your problem, Reza?" Carlos asks for the hundredth time since I picked him up.

"Nothing, okay?" I stare at the road ahead, scowling.

"Right, and I fart fairy dust."

This thaws me a little, and a giggle escapes me.

"There she is!" Carlos throws his hands in the air, raising the roof. "Whoop whoop. Finally!"

I shove him into the car door. He fakes an injury to his shoulder. "Geez girl, why you got to be so violent? I'm a delicate flower, you know."

Carlos can be juvenile and obnoxious at times…well, most of the time really, but he's also a wonderful distraction. I forget about my anxiety and it's not until we throw open the school doors do I remember why I wanted to skip in the first place.

Matt's in the foyer, talking to Dylan. My feet pause for a beat. He doesn't see me. His head is thrown back in laughter. Once upon a time, that laugh was infectious. Now, it's repulsive. How can he be so carefree? While I am upside down over what's happened between us. Does he not feel the push and pull that I feel? Plus, I blame him for Mom and Dr. Yassin's breakup.

Deep down, I know it was really all my fault, but I'm angry that Matt was the catalyst in everything that was going wrong in my life. Bitter, I shift my gaze off him and veer a hard left.

Carlos calls after me. "Where are you going? The cafeteria is this way."

I ignore him, hurrying through the halls toward my locker. My heart is pounding as I spin the combination.

It takes me a few tries, but I finally unlock it. I stare at the books inside, collecting my thoughts.

What am I going to do? My head's been a jumbled mess since Matt's surprise visit last night. He thinks we're back together, and I'm still reeling over our conversation. *Can he really quit just like that? He makes it sound so easy.*

My locker door slams, echoing through the empty halls. Knuckles rap against my skull. "Anybody home in there?"

I blink, bringing Jenna into focus. She stares at me, wide-eyed. Her hair is drawn into two low pigtails and she's wearing *my* yellow cardigan over a logoed J. Murrey Atkins Library t-shirt. A perk to being a volunteer page. She snaps in my face. "Hello? Are you sleepwalking or something?"

I shake myself. "Just lost in thought, I guess."

"She's been acting weird all morning," Carlos adds, bending down to spit-shine his sneakers. I kick him, causing him to topple over. Sprawled on the tile, he shouts, "Hey!" He frowns up at me. "What was that for? It's the truth." He climbs to his feet and slings his book bag over his shoulder. He looks to Jenna, gesturing at me with his hands with a face that says, "See?"

Jenna's face screws up like a fist. Her eyes all squinty as she surveys me from shoes to the shamefully messy top knot on my head. Finally, she says, "You look like hell. What's going on with you? Is it Matt?" I want to tell her, but the words are trapped in my throat.

Why can't I admit to my best friend what's really happening? That my head is so messed up right now that I can't think straight. I bite my lip to keep it from quivering. Who am I kidding? I know exactly why I can't tell her. I'm ashamed. I allowed myself to be manipulated once before and last night, I did it *again*.

I roll my eyes. "No. It's nothing, all right? God, would you two just get off my back?" I storm off and neither Carlos nor Jenna come after me. Thank God they have the good sense to leave me alone.

My stomach is in knots by the time Matt slips into the desk in front of me. "Hey," he says casually.

I stare at the desk. "Hey," I mumble.

His cologne wafts over me, and I do my best to ignore it.

"Can I come over after school?"

"I'm going to the hospital." It's a lie. The support group meets tonight. Though, I shouldn't go to it. I'm a fraud. There's got to be some sort of unspoken group rule against dating the very person who put you there. But then, I think of Ernie, who's there because of his daughter, and Judith, who's learning to tell her son Anthony, "no."

With sadness, I realize it's your loved ones who can hurt you the most. My thoughts drift to Mom and Wesley and Trip.

"The hospital? On a Friday?" Matt sounds doubtful.

I raise my head. "I don't only volunteer on Saturdays, you know."

He studies me. "Okay. What about tomorrow? Want to see a movie?"

"Look, Matt," I say. "I think we ought to take things slow. We can't just pick up where we left off."

"Why not?"

Impatience flares within me. "Because!" I open my mouth to say more, but Mrs. Johnson walks through the classroom door. The leather satchel slung over her shoulder almost outweighs her. "Clear your desks." She drops the bag on her desk and unzips it.

"This test is a conglomerate of multiple-choice, short answer, and true/false." She lifts out a stack of stapled tests and hands them out. "Good luck."

Thank God for Mrs. Johnson and her hour-long test. I was able to elude Matt right up until the bell rang for second period.

"How do you think you did?" Matt asks when we step out into the hallway.

"Good."

Matt regards me with a sidelong glance. "Everything okay?"

"Fine."

"Are you sure?"

"Yes."

"You don't seem okay."

My clipped answers aren't deterring him. I stop short. Something slams into me from behind, causing me to lurch forward. Matt catches me.

A boy, red-faced and startled, blinks at me. With cellphone in hand, he points to it as if it explains everything.

"Watch it," Matt snaps. His glare is daggers, and it scares me. I withdraw from him.

"I'm all right," I say, studying his eyes. They are blown wide, like the eyes of a trapped feral animal.

The boy mumbles an apology and quickly peels off and walks away in a hurry.

"It was an accident," I tell Matt.

"He shouldn't have been walking so close. Probably had his eyes on your ass the whole time."

"What?" I say incredulously. "Don't be ridiculous."

Matt scowls, his heated gaze trailing the boy as he fades down the hall.

Why is he so angry? A memory surfaces. His rage after Coach benched him was like a whip that night, quick and cutting. He was using then, which means he's using now. I collect a cleansing breath in my lungs. I hold my palms out. "Look, Matt. I think we need to talk."

His eyes swing to my face. "Later, okay?" he says, hooking a piece of hair behind my ear, noticeably tender now. I fight against the urge to shiver. "Coach wants me in his office, and I'm not about to piss him off any more than I already have. See you at lunch?"

I swallow.

He doesn't wait for me to answer. He retreats backward, grinning. "I got the best girl in Reedmont." Matt's sneakers squeak on the tile as he turns and jogs away.

I stand rooted. Students weave around me in the hallway as I stare after him. This is what I always wanted. It's what every girl wants. A hot, popular jock boyfriend. I think of his mood swings and how easily he asked me to steal. No, not this. *This* is tainted. *This* isn't love.

This is dependence. Desperation. Like the parasitic, symbiotic relationship, Mr. Rogers taught us in biology where two beings share a life, but only one benefits from the union. Matt is just that. A parasite that is sucking all the good, all the trust, and all the life right out of me.

I avoid everyone during lunch by going to the library. Mrs. Arden smiles at me when I push through the door. Her greying hair is styled into an exaggerated bouffant. I catch a whiff of her sweet perfume as I walk by. "Hi, Mrs. Arden," I whisper.

"Hola," she whispers back.

I find the farthest corner of the room and sit cross-legged on the floor. I press my back against one of the towering bookshelves and settle in. An ache nags at my brow, but I've grown used to it. I tend to keep a constant headache these days. I take out a bag of jelly beans from the pocket of my book bag and funnel a fist full into my mouth.

I think of Jenna, and how she picks through the bag, plucking out her favorites. Pink and red. She's probably wondering where I am right now. *I shouldn't withdraw from her*, I think with a frown. *But I just need time to think. Time to be alone.* I nearly scoff at the absurdity of it. Me—wanting to be alone. It's such a foreign feeling for me. I never want to be alone.

I'm thumbing through a magazine when my phone vibrates with a text message. It's Jenna.

—I know where you are, punk.—

I smile. Another text follows. This one is from Matt.

—Where the fuck are you?—

My body floods with adrenaline, like my fight-or-flight instincts are kicking in. A moment later, the library door clicks open, and dread creeps through my bones. I stiffen at the sound of footsteps drawing near. Matt appears at the end of the aisle. His stormy eyes glare down at me.

"Are you avoiding me?"

"No," I mutter, my blood rushing hotly to my cheeks.

He stalks toward me. "What happened to meeting me?"

"I never agreed to that." I crane my neck to look up at him.

Standing over me, he says, "I needed you."

My heart twists in my chest. "What?"

His hands ball into fists. "I needed you." He grimaces, his eyes shuttering for a quick beat. "And you weren't there," he snarls.

I clamber to my feet, relying on the bookshelf beside me to give me the support I need to stand.

"What happened?" I lay my hand on his arm. He snatches away from me. I recoil, shocked at his response to my touch.

"I got kicked off the team." Matt's eyes began to water. His mouth curls into a sneer as he fights back tears. "My life is ruined. No wrestling. No scholarship. No college."

I stare at this broken boy before me, who I once loved fiercely, yet I am unable to feel sorry for him. The mess he's in is his own doing. I tried to help him once, and he refused. He chose Oxy over me—hell, he chose Oxy over *himself*. I swallow back the lump in my throat. He's lost so much for that stupid drug. *Including me*.

Chapter 33

I am done. I know I've said that before, but whatever lingering softness I felt for Matt vanishes into thin air. I level a hard glare at him. "You did this," I say through clenched teeth. "Maybe now you'll see what that crap is doing to your life."

"I quit," he barks, his voice loud in the near silent library. He glances around him, but no one is nearby. It's just him and me amongst the towering bookshelves. His eyes are wild, but yet he splays his hands out in front of him as if I'm the feral one. "I told you I haven't touched it in over a week," he murmurs in a hushed voice.

I nearly laugh. Lying comes easily for him. Slowly, I shake my head, suddenly too exhausted to continue this conversation anymore. Ever again.

"Get some help, Matt." I push past him, but he grabs my wrist and yanks. I crash into his broad chest, my wrist smarting under the pressure of his grip.

He leans in close. "Don't do this," he growls, his heaving breathing fanning across my face.

I squirm under his viper-like hold. "You're hurting me."

He releases me. My breath catches as I rub my aching wrist. His dark eyes sweep around us. He sticks his hands in his pockets as if to hide them, but it's too late. They already did their damage. I bite back a sob before turning on my heel and running away.

****

Jenna finds me weeping in a stall in the girl's bathroom.

Through the crack of the door, she whispers, "Pen?"

"I'm fine," I say between sobs.

Her voice is tender when she says, "Can I come in?"

I unlock the door. She pushes in and shuts the door behind her. "What happened?" She pulls me into a tight embrace.

Squeezing my eyes tight, I say into her hair. "So much. So much has happened, Jenna."

"Tell me."

Some girls come in. They chat animatedly about nothing as they hover at the sinks, likely checking their makeup in the mirror. I sniff, trying to smother my cries in Jenna's shoulder. I wait until they leave before I say, "Matt uses. That's why we broke up."

She stills, but doesn't offer anything. She lets me talk, uninterrupted, stroking the length of my hair as I spill everything. The stealing, Matt's overdose, the support group, Mom and Dr. Yassin, Matt hurting me…

When I'm through, she leans back and takes in my face. "Ragamuffins after school. My treat."

My smile is weak, but damn it, it's still a smile. I will overcome this. I will welcome the pain and whatever else comes with it so long as I make it to the other side.

Chapter 34

For the second time today, skipping crosses my mind. I really don't think I can sit through the support group tonight. The wounds from Matt are too fresh, and knowing that I am there because of him will be too much to bear. But then, I think about Dr. Yassin. I have to uphold my end of our deal, even if he didn't.

I remove my coat, draping it over the back of the chair before taking a seat next to Judith, and we exchange polite nods. Mika is already here, as is the woman with the waist-length hair. Neither of them are speaking.

Mika looks battle ready, her features hard as steel. Her blue hair is in a thick braid trailing down her back. The other woman has somehow piled her never-ending hair into a French twist, and she's pinned it with a pretty barrette. She catches me looking. Her eyes touch on mine, then avert with all the nervousness of a frightened mouse.

Ernie bustles in with such over-the-top sullenness, I feel as though I'm watching a slap-stick comedy. He frowns at everyone, tightly crossing his arms over his chest with an audible harrumph. "He's late," he grouses sourly.

Judith checks her watch. "Your clock must be fast, Ernie. Mine says six o'clock on the dot."

Ernie casts his watery blue eyes around the room.

"He ain't here, so that means he's late."

Judith just purses her painted lips.

With that, Mr. Mathers blows into the room, much like he did last week. He seems to be perpetually animated, like one of those inflatable men with crazed arms at car dealerships. He takes in the room with a quick glance.

"We're just missing Sam and Chase."

Ernie grunts. "What else is new?"

Mr. Mathers eyes swing to Ernie, but they hold no irritation. In fact, he almost looks sad. "Quite right, Ernie." His gaze slides over to me. "Ah, Penelope, is it? Yes. I am so glad to see you've returned."

"She made it through the first meeting and actually returned," Judith says, elbowing me. "Means we got you on the hook." She lets loose a throaty laugh, which transforms into a phlegmy cough. She covers her mouth with a fist, straining to catch her breath. The coughing hurts, that much is plain on her face. As the fit stretches on and on, I grow worried. Mr. Mathers goes to her, touching her shoulder.

"Are you all right, Judith?"

"I can get her some water," Mika offers.

"That would be good," Mr. Mathers says to her, his face grim.

Judith is red-faced, and gasping for breath. I'm growing panicked. Judith looks to be struggling for air, her coughs wet and throaty. Mika returns with the water. Her eyes are round and worried. "Should we call 9-1-1?"

Judith shakes her head vehemently. She takes the paper cup from Mika and takes a swallow between gasps. The entire room is watching her. Mr. Mathers stays at her side, his hand never leaving her shoulder. "Do you need anything?" he asks.

"An inhaler maybe?" Mika offers.

Judith shakes her head, no. So, we wait on pins and needles, staring helplessly at the old woman. Soon, the coughing subsides. She wipes her eyes with her fingers and clears her throat. "Damn COPD," she murmurs. "Sometimes it flares up on me. I'm sorry to have frightened ya's." Her flattened palm rubs a circle over her heart.

I lean back in my seat, relieved.

"I'm just glad you're okay," Mr. Mathers says, giving her shoulder a squeeze. "You had me worried."

"I don't have any plans to kick the bucket just yet," she says with a tested laugh. "But when I do, it will be with these babies." She straightens a leg to show the room her blood-red, square-toed cowboy boots.

Laughter erupts and I find myself joining in.

From the corner of my eye, I see movement. I turn my head to see Sam and Chase coming through the meeting room doors. Sam finds a seat quickly, trying to fade into the faces before Mr. Mathers calls him out for being late. Chase, on the other hand, strides in without a trace of care.

Today he's wearing black-framed glasses that give him a sweet, scholarly look. He strips out of his jacket and drops it into a heap on the floor just before he flops into the empty chair beside me.

He unwraps a piece of gum and pops it into his mouth. He stretches out his long legs, crossing his blue Chucks at the ankles. I can't help but steal glances at him. He's lean, but not skinny. He keeps fidgeting with his glasses, adjusting them on his face over and over as if he just needs something to busy his hands.

I study him, curious about his story. Why is he here? Why is his dad here? When he shifts positions to lean forward in his seat, I can see the defined muscles work along his back and shoulders beneath the thin cotton fabric of his t-shirt. He catches me staring and I blush. His usual expression of sullen disinterest morphs into a crooked smile. Being this close, I notice just how beautiful his eyes are. They're twilight blue and as bottomless as the sky. I smile shyly back, averting my eyes to my lap.

Mr. Mathers is addressing the room, saying something about alcoholism. "For those of you with loved ones suffering from alcohol addiction, attending their AA meetings with them can be beneficial to both of you. But remember, as a co-addict, you need to be aware of your own afflictions. You know you. You know why you're here. You tend to fall in love with potential, not reality. Be supportive, but not so much that you don't recognize true commitment in your partners and family members."

Chase snorts and shakes his head. Straightening in his seat, he casually casts his gaze out to the room. His eyes flick to his father, who doesn't seem to notice. Chase's jawline works as he grinds his gum between his teeth.

"Chase," Mr. Mathers says, walking over to him. "It's been a while since you've shared. Care to share an update with the group?"

Chase's denim-blue eyes slowly roll to Mr. Mathers. He smirks, chewing his gum thoughtfully. I shift in my seat uncomfortably, the tension mounting as Chase gives Mr. Mathers a long, measured look. Finally, he says with a bored tone, "Sure. Why not?" "Excellent," Mr. Mathers says with a clap of his hands. Sam's face pales and I can see his throat working below this thick beard as he swallows tensely.

Chase stares at Mr. Mathers. "My update is…my mom is still an alcoholic. There. The end."

Mr. Mathers offers a kind smile. "I didn't ask for an update on your mother, Chase. I asked for an update on you."

Chase's eyes darken like a storm cloud. The muscles in his jaw flexing as his gum chewing grows aggressive. "Fine. You want an update? Mom hasn't been sober, not even once, in the past week. The only time she acknowledges me is when she needs help from the floor after she's passed out. Dad works all the time, but when he is home, I might as well be invisible." His eyes cut to his father. "He acts as though she's the only one who needs him."

Sam's eyebrows bunch over his eyes, his expression pained, flushed with embarrassment for being called out in front of the entire group.

Mr. Mathers speaks first. "Your feelings are valid, Chase. Often, co-addicts allow the addicts in their life to overtake all other relationships. The addicts are the priority, as in the eyes of the co-addicts, they are the ones in need. Everyone else is capable. Able to function day to day without their aid.

"Co-addicts focus on healing the addict, the damaged good, if you will. If they can fix them, then life will be perfect. They fail to realize that other lives, including their own, are impacted by their neglect."

Chase looks smug, as if vindicated by Mr. Mathers' words. Sam looks sick. A sheen of perspiration dots his hairline. His eyes, weak and misty, shift to Mr. Mathers.

"I'll do better."

Mr. Mathers gives him a tight smile. "Sam. It's not about you doing better. It's about self-realization. The atmosphere in your home is toxic for your son. We need to get you to the point of self-understanding. It's not about wearing yourself thin by being there for both, Chase and your wife. It's about being a stronger Sam."

Sam blinks, but is otherwise a human statue, motionless and expressionless. Chase seems annoyed by this. "Forget it. He's not going to change. Neither is my mom."

"Everyone is capable of change," Mr. Mathers says to Chase.

Chase folds his arms over his chest and frowns. "I'll believe it when I see it."

Mr. Mathers' voice is nothing more than white noise after that. I find myself drawn to Chase now that I know a little of his story. It's much more than I expected. His mother is an alcoholic and his dad is a co-addict, enabling her toxic behavior. I wonder why Chase attends the meetings at all. They must be boring for him.

Chase suddenly stands. His chair falls back, crashing to the floor. Judith noticeably startles. Mr. Mathers is taken aback. Chase strides out of the room, the glass doors banging open as he explodes through them. I glimpse Sam, his bulging eyes trailing Chase the entire time. Shocked still for a second, I look over at Mr. Mathers. He scrubs the back of his neck, a placid look of defeat washing over him. We lock eyes, and when he gives me a gentle nod, I realize what I must do.

I lift Chase's jacket from the floor and dash after him. I scan the library, but don't see him anywhere, just a couple librarians working and half a dozen people poring over books. With a few quick paces, I hurry through the sliding library doors and head outside. The early evening air is crisp, splintering into my lungs as I breathe it in.

I find Chase leaning against the building, much like he was a couple weeks ago. His face is turned upward to the sky. He looks fragile in the moonlight. Slowly, I walk up to him.

"My family is fucked up," he says without looking at me.

Sadness tugs at my heart. *Poor Chase.* It doesn't seem fair that he's been dealt this hand. I can't imagine how hard it must be to have an alcoholic mother. At one time, I may have had the fleeting thought of, "*at least he has a mother,*" but seeing his suffering in person instantly consumes that thought.

He rolls his head to the side to gaze at me. He pins me with those starry dark-blue eyes. His cheeks and chin look smooth as milk, a contrast to Matt's usual stubble. Why I think of that, I don't know. Perhaps it's because of how different the two boys are, and yet…

Okay, I'll just say it: Matt and Chase are hot, each in their own way. Wispy bangs fall into Chase's eyes, but he doesn't try to brush them away. "What about your family, kid? Must be fucked up for you to be here. Fucked up parents create fucked up families."

My mouth grows unbearably dry.

His gaze is pointed. I wilt like a flower beneath his shrewd eyes. The corner of his mouth quirks and he says, "Yeah, you're fucked up. I can tell." He goes back to staring at the sky overhead. Twinkling stars punctuate the blanket of dark blue above us. With the sun long set in the west, the evening sky matches his eyes.

Glaring at his profile, I wonder what it is he sees in me. Why would he assume that I'm messed up? Because I belong to a support group? Clutching his jacket, I frown. "Why would you say that?"

"Oh, don't get worked up over it," he tells me. "I didn't mean anything by it. I mean, everyone is fucked up in some way. Am I right? Just some more than others."

"Here's your coat." I hold it out to him.

"You need it more than I do." He's right. I'm shivering in my thin cotton shirt while my coat is still draped over the back of my chair in the meeting room. I slip into his jacket, catching the clean scent of detergent on the wool fabric.

"Thanks," I murmur, rubbing my hands together for warmth.

"So what was your name again?" He unhitches himself from the brickwork, shoving his hands into his pockets. His jeans are frayed at the knees and worn into loose threads at the ankles.

The siren of a passing ambulance screams in the distance. I let the siren slowly fade to silence before I say, "Penelope."

He smiles an easy smile. "I'm Chase. You weren't here the night Mr. Mathers made me introduce myself." He toes a pebble, kicking it into the road, his face suddenly boyish and shy. In a very monotone voice, he says, "Hi. My name is Chase and my dad's a co-addict." He laughs a little, though it seems forced.

"Why do you come to the meetings?" I ask, genuinely interested.

He lifts a shoulder. "Making sure my old man sticks to his word, really. Plus, I thought it would help me too.

You know? I wanted to know the signs of being a co-addict because I never want to be one. They suck. Nothing but spineless wimps—"

I wince at his words, and he notices. Hard, sapphire eyes drill into me and realization dawns on him. His lips twitch into a deep frown. "Oh. I see." He retreats a few steps backward as if I'm infectious.

I feel small where I stand. The distance between us a clear reminder that I am here because I am weak. I let someone have control over me. I let my standards sink to the point of no return. I essentially taught Matt how to treat me by tolerating things I never should have. Things I never would have, but I thought I was in love and love blinds sometimes.

The library doors slide with a whisk, and my fellow co-addicts spill out into the night. Ernie completely ignores us, head down in the chilly air, bustling himself into his old truck in a hurry. Mika casts a quick glance at us and offers a polite smile. Sam strolls toward us, his clunky boots chewing up the concrete with determined, sleek strides.

"What the hell was that all about?" Sam demands, more confused than angry.

Chase lazily drags his gaze to his father. "He asked me for an update. What did you want me to do? Lie?"

Sam expels a deep, exhausted sigh. "Chase. I'm trying here, damn it. Cut me some slack, will you?"

Aware that I'm intruding on a moment, I slip out of Chase's coat and hand it to him. "I'm going to go," I whisper to him.

He takes it, shifting his attention back to me. He just stares at me, unspoken words die in his throat, offering nothing more than just a wild searching of my eyes. I swallow thickly and turn away. Judith ambles out of the library, Mr. Mathers at her side. He's carrying my coat and book bag. I hurry over to retrieve my things.

"Thank you," I tell him, eagerly shrugging into my jacket.

"How is he?" Mr. Mathers questions, his eyes flickering to where Sam and Chase stand arguing.

I follow his gaze, frowning at the way Chase looks. So forlorn, so forgotten. Like even his screams fall silent at home. My heart clenches within my chest. All he wants is to feel loved. That's all anyone wants. I can't bring myself to say any of this, so instead, I lie. "He's okay."

Mr. Mathers studies me, his eyes tightening at the corners. "Thank you for keeping him company. I bet it meant a lot to him, even if he doesn't say so." His lips curve into a smile. "Have a good night, ladies. Be safe and see you next week." He peels off, his loafers clicking as he walks away.

I take Judith by the elbow to help her step down from the curb.

When her foot is solidly on the ground, she breathes a "Thanks, dearie."

"Are you all right, Judith?" I ask, regarding her round, rouge-red cheeks. "You really scared me earlier."

"Oh, I'm fine." The cold air has her wheezing. "My COPD acts up sometimes, that's all. It's as unruly as a herd of raccoons in a candy shop."

We walk a few steps in silence, Judith's steady shuffle setting the leisurely pace. "That poor boy needs someone to love him," she says suddenly.

"What?"

"Chase." Judith leads me to a lime-green hatchback.

"Sam loves him, of course, but he's so busy showering Belinda with attention, he forgets his boy has feelings, too." She presses her thumb to her key fob and the car doors unlock. "One day, I pray Sam will have his breakthrough, or Belinda will clean up, or heck, if the Lord will grant it, both. For the sake of Chase's heart."

We turn to watch Chase and Sam stomp away toward an SUV parked at the far end of the library's parking lot.

Judith *tsks* solemnly. "Bless his little heart."

Chapter 35

I forgo volunteering this weekend for fear of running into Dr. Yassin. Yes, I'm ducking him, and yes, it's childish, but I'm just not ready to face him. I'm responsible for his breakup with Mom and I know if I run into him at the hospital I'll probably curl up into myself like a hedgehog and cry myself into a puddle of guilt.

Instead, I opt to flip through hundreds of TV channels and eat my way through no less than two sleeves of cookies while doing so. I'm halfway through my first sleeve when I get a text from Matt.

—*Going to Cali for a while*—

I blink at the screen.

—*Thought you'd want to know*—

I want to scream. *Why would I want to know?*

I power off my phone and toss it onto the recliner. It bounces off the cushion and falls to the floor. I leave it there.

What is wrong with him? Why can't he see we are over? Though I'm angered by his text, I'm relieved to know he won't be at school tomorrow. I'd been dreading literature because I knew I'd have to see him, and there was a good chance he'd sit in front of me again. After this text, I know for a fact he'd plop right down in front of me, oblivious to the fact that I'd rather he sit anywhere else.

I settle into the couch, propping myself with a cushy pillow and for the next two hours, lose myself in back-to-back true crime documentaries. The lemonade I'd been sipping finally catches up with me, and I'm forced to hit pause on the remote and take a bathroom break. As I'm walking back to the living room, the doorbell rings. I pause in my footsteps. *No please,* I think. *Don't let it be him.*

Whoever it is grows impatient. They give a hurried knock on the door. I swallow down my fear and walk to the door. I reach a shaky hand to the doorknob and lean in close to the peephole.

"Reza!" Carlos hollers from the other side of the door. "Open up! I know you're in there!"

Relief floods through me. I yank open the door to find Carlos standing there, his smile as wide as I've ever seen it. A honk from an electric-yellow clunker in my driveway catches my attention. I see Jenna waving from the passenger seat.

I step outside, barefoot and shielding my eyes from the sun. "What the—"

"She's all mine," Carlos says with a stupid grin. "Been saving my paychecks, yo. What do you think?"

I pad across the lawn to give the car a closer inspection. It needs a lot of work. The windshield is cracked, it's missing a brake light, and one fender is crushed, like it had been pounded by an elephant on a rampage. Carlos is practically glowing beside me, so I don't say any of that. I peer inside the cab. Jenna is bouncing in her seat.

"Cute right?" She looks around herself at the tiny cab space and gives a little squeal of joy.

Carlos climbs in, slamming the door so hard I think

it might fall off. The roof is sagging so much it skims his hat and it smells of soured milk.

"Wanna go for a ride?" Carlos offers, revving the engine. The smile he shoots me is sly, then he wags his eyebrows, and I can't help but laugh. I look back at the house, weighing the options.

"Come on, Pen," Jenna begs. "It will be fun."

I heave a sigh and say, "Let me get my shoes."

Carlos whoops. Jenna claps her hands happily.

In the house, I find my house keys and step into my fleece-lined boots. As I stride through the living room, I glimpse my phone, still laying on the floor. I pick it up and slip it into my pocket without turning it on. Locking the front door behind me, I run out to Carlos' new car.

It's a two-door, so Jenna is already standing with the passenger door open, ready for me to get in. Even though it's Sunday, Mr. Bower is walking to his mailbox. He always does, even when the post office is closed, and no mail has been delivered. I think he just enjoys the walk. I wave to him and slide into the backseat, which is in desperate need of upholstering. It's cracked and worn with age and sun damage.

Jenna sinks into the front seat and draws the seat belt over her. Carlos backs up. The engine sounds as if a swarm of bees is trapped inside it. On the street, Carlos takes it slow, as if he's still getting used to the manual drive.

Eying the stick shift, I say, "You sure you know how to drive this thing?" His dark eyes lift to the rearview mirror. "You wound me, Reza. I'm a Rivera. We can drive anything." That I believe. His family owns a repair shop in town, and it has been his father's hope to hand the shop down to his sons, Hernando and Carlos, but so far, Hernando is the only one interested in pursuing the family business.

Carlos helps his dad every now and then but he's adamant that he doesn't want to be a mechanic. He wants to be a software engineer, whatever that is. The Riveras are good with their hands, it's just Carlos' fingers are better suited for a keyboard than the inside a car engine.

We putt past a neighbor of mine walking her dog. The brown spaniel cowers at the woman's heels when the car backfires and spits. Carlos shifts gears and applies more gas, jutting us forward in a series of bumpy jerks and shakes.

"She takes a minute to warm up," he explains. "She'll get there." He runs his palm over the steering wheel, petting it. "Come on, girl. You got this."

I lean back in my seat and watch the world go slowly by my window. Mr. Naylor is outside, raking leaves. He lifts his head from his work to watch us drive painfully slow past his house. We eventually settle into a faster pace and soon pull out of my neighborhood onto the main road.

Looking around the car, I ask Carlos, "So no more hitching a ride with me?"

"Nope," Carlos replies with a smile. "It's the end of an era, Reza."

"Thank God. If I had to wait on you through one more detention, I was going to snap."

Jenna tosses a glance over at her shoulder at me, laughing.

"Hey," Carlos retorts. "That was our thing, you and me. You're going to miss it, you wait." Our gaze meets in the rearview mirror. His eyes sparkle with humor.

I cross my arms and lean back. "Nah, I don't think

so."

Jenna reaches over and touches Carlos on the knee. "You can come see me at work now whenever you want."

He turns his head to look at her. "You gonna give me free snow cones?"

"Sure."

"I'll be there." He winks, then adds, "Whenever I'm not working, anyway."

"So that's how you paid for this, huh?" I ask. "Marios?"

"Yes ma'am. Been saving since I started. Course, she only cost me fifteen hundred, so it didn't take long to save."

That's a thousand too much, I think to myself. "When did you get it? Today?"

"He picked it up this morning," Jenna tells me. "We tried calling you, but you didn't answer. What were you doing, anyway?"

"My phone's off," I force out, looking out the window to avoid their eyes.

Jenna turns her body as much as the seat belt will allow in her seat. "Why?" she asks suspiciously.

I feel her gaze burning into me. I don't want to tell her, but she already knows. Carlos, too. They're not stupid.

"Matt texted me this morning. He told me he was going to California for a while."

Jenna frowns. "Why would he tell you that? Does he really think you care?"

I shrug. "I didn't answer. I just shut my phone off."

"Dude is delulu," Carlos says, easing the car to a stop. The car shudders, and threatens to shut off. Carlos pumps the pedal, and the car growls to life again and lurches forward. Thankfully, the light turns green. Carlos leans into the gas, and the car seems happy to be on the move again.

My mood dampens with the discussion of Matt and I'm ready to go back home. I don't want to ruin Carlos' fun, so I shut my mouth and pretend to be having a good time.

"Let's get some milkshakes," Jenna suggests, pointing to Rugger's Burger Joint.

Carlos pulls up and calls over the rumbling motor, "Two vanilla milkshakes and one strawberry milkshake, please."

"Repeat that," the speaker box crackles back.

Carlos tries again, hollering this time, "Two vanilla milkshakes and one strawberry milkshake!"

I guess the Rugger's employee understood because they shout back a total and tell Carlos to pull forward. Carlos pays for the milkshakes and passes them out. Vanilla for him and me, and strawberry for Jenna.

As we sip our milkshakes, our destination is literally nowhere. We cruise through town, wasting time and wasting gas, backfiring here and there as we go. After the sixth or eighth time, a giggle bubbles inside me.

Each time a driver or a pedestrian snaps their head toward the loud bang, I chuckle and soon I'm rolling in the backseat, wiping away tears of laughter from my eyes.

My afternoon of binge-watching true crime and sipping lemonade has been replaced with a-slow-as-a-tortoise clunker and an ice-cold milkshake. Looking between Jenna and Carlos as we all laugh and cut up, I realize it's a trade I'm happy to make.

Chapter 36

The past week at school without Matt was blissfully uneventful. And now that Carlos has his own car, I've been going right home after school and relaxing on the couch. I've been doing a lot of that lately, so much so that I think I might have a permanent butt print in the cushion. But, unfortunately, there's no relaxing in the forecast for me today.

It's Friday, which means it's co-addict support group night, but at least Mom's taking the Bowers to their beloved Bingo Night, so I don't have to worry about throwing together something for dinner. I go home long enough to grab a snack of string cheese and crackers and to tame my out-of-control hair.

I'm not sure why I care what my hair looks like, but I take the time to smooth avocado oil into it until it shines. I keep my school outfit of slim jeans and mock letterman jacket sweater on. It's cute and comfortable. I slick on some lip balm, then I'm out the door.

Inside the Joseph Salvador Meeting room, I find an empty seat beside Judith. Today, she's at her finest, probably trying to prove to us that last week's scare was just a fluke. She's in a pale pink, A-line dress that looks pretty against her complexation. Her neck is draped with fat pearls, a matching set to the oversized clip earrings she's wearing.

"Look at you," I say to her. "Pretty in pink."

She smiles wide, her perfect dentures flashing. "Why, thank you, dear. Thought I'd drag out my Sunday best."

"What's the occasion?"

Judith's eyes catch on someone coming through the door. I follow her gaze and see Ernie hustling in with his perpetually furrowed brow and stern mouth. *Oh. I see.*

Judith tracks him until he's seated. Her hand comes up and fluffs the tight curls at her nape. She feels me watching, turning her head to shoot me a sly smile. "How's your week been?" I think about Matt and his text message.

—Going to Cali for a week—

—Thought you'd want to know—

My smile drops. "Okay."

Her hooded eyes survey me intently. "Perhaps you should share with us tonight. It will do you good to unload that worry from your heart."

I can't dispute that. I've been carrying around anger, guilt, and embarrassment among a trove of other emotions for weeks now. I can't share these feelings with my mom. She shuts down and tries to change the subject each time I bring Matt up. Jenna is a good sounding board, but I know I've exhausted her with my problems, though she hasn't said as much.

"Maybe," I say slowly.

Mr. Mathers enters the room. Tonight he's swathed in a thick scarf and quilted jacket. Our eyes touch.

"Chilly out there tonight," he says, more to the room than to me. "Old man winter is not ready to let go of the evenings just yet, is he?"

"The bastard killed my persimmon," Ernie grumbles.

"Language, Ernie," Mr. Mathers scolds, scanning the room. "We're amongst ladies here."

"Bah," Ernie grouses, tucking his hands high into his armpits. His pudgy belly hangs over his belt buckle, but his snow-white hair is combed neatly behind his ears. What Judith sees in Ernie, I'll never know, but then again, I've learned just how blind love can be.

Mika walks in and strides to her usual chair. She greets Mr. Mathers with a tight-lipped smile.

"Evening, Mika," Mr. Mathers says pleasantly. His eyes swing to the door. "Evening Yvonne."

I turn to find the plain woman with unruly eyebrows coming into the room. *Yvonne. Finally, I know her name.*

"Good evening, Dave," Yvonne speaks so quietly her voice is barely above a whisper. She reminds me of a timid mouse, wary of everything around her for fear she'll be someone's lunch. She takes a seat next to Mika and the two exchange polite hellos.

Sam and Chase are the last to stroll in, which isn't surprising, but what is surprising is that they are actually on time for once. Chase's eyes drift around the room until he sees me. He veers away from his dad, and casually takes the seat beside me.

"Hey," he says with a jerk of his chin.

"Hey," I say back. Instinctually, I seek out a strand of hair and wrap it around my finger. I focus on his shoes, beat up blue Chucks with black doodles on the toes. I squint to make them out. Targets, arrows, and a drawn bow clutter the toe of one shoe, while the other is crammed full of comic book words like: BAM, KA-POW, and BANG.

Mr. Mathers paces our little circle. "Once again, welcome back. I am grateful that each of you took the time to attend tonight. It shows your commitment to understanding and dealing with co-addiction. Would anyone like to start us off with an update?"

Someone coughs, but no one offers an update.

"All right. Then, would anyone like to retell their story?" His eyes move over each of us, waiting.

Chase turns his head ever so slightly and looks at me from the corner of his eyes. Something in me breaks, like the strength of holding onto my story is too much to bear. I sit up straighter and unwind the strand of hair from my finger. Clearing my throat, I say to Mr. Mathers, "I'll go."

My head swims a little when all eyes jump to me. I curl my fingers around my chair, holding onto it for dear life, to keep from falling off it.

Mr. Mathers' face brightens. "Penelope, wonderful. Now everyone, let's give her the floor and be respectful as she speaks." He comes closer, speaking directly to me now. "Take your time and only share what you're comfortable sharing. We're here for you."

I nod and take a moment to gather my thoughts. *Where to begin?*

"My Mom's…boyfriend gave me an ultimatum. Come to group or he'd tell my mom what I'd done." My mouth is so dry my breath scrapes my throat. "I chose to come. Obviously."

"What did you do, dear?" Judith questions.

I'm flushed to the ears with humiliation. "I stole a prescription pad for my boyfriend."

Chase goes rigid in his seat.

"Ex-boyfriend," I blurt out. For some reason it's really important to me that Chase knows that. "I never gave it to him though. I realize it was a pretty stupid thing to do."

Judith takes my hand in hers. Surprisingly, her grip is solid, and it brings me some comfort. "You're amongst friends here, doll. We understand. No need to feel ashamed."

I glance around the room, taking in all the faces before me. They regard me with empathy, understanding, and warmth. Well, except for Ernie. He looks at me with contempt, but then, he looks at everyone that way.

Lastly, I turn my head to Chase, anxious to know what he's thinking. His face betrays nothing. He's unmoving, save for chewing at his bottom lip.

Mr. Mathers sinks into a crouch before me. "Thank you for sharing, Penelope." He lightly touches his fingertips to my knee. "That took a lot of courage. I want you to remember, admission is healing. And you just started mending." His smile is sincere and reassuring. He rises and addresses the room.

"Wow. What a great session, huh?" He spreads his hands out. "Each of you has now shared your stories openly, and now the true work begins. Coming to terms with the reason you are here tonight is step one. Step two is identifying the triggers and situations that make you vulnerable."

"That's an easy one," Judith says with a dry laugh. "Love."

Mr. Mathers nods enthusiastically, his auburn hair shaking loose. "That's right, Judith. Love. Love gets some of us in trouble, am I right?" He sweeps his hair back into place. "But why do we do it for love? Why do we do things we know aren't right for love? Love isn't compromising beliefs. Love isn't lowering standards.

Love isn't walking on eggshells or tossing away one's dignity or faith, or convictions."

Mr. Mathers picks up his usual pacing, his strides tight within our circle. "Love is…what?" His eyes hover over each of us for a beat. "Anyone care to finish that thought?"

"Love is patient," Yvonne offers shyly.

Mr. Mathers whirls to her voice. "Excellent." His eyes dart around the circle, eager for more.

"Laughter," Judith supplies with a hearty laugh of her own.

Mr. Mathers beams from the group participation tonight.

"Forgiveness," Sam says solemnly, his blue eyes drifting to his son. Chase doesn't take the bait. He sits stone-faced, crossing his arms tightly over his chest.

"Good one, Sam," Mr. Mathers says. "Anyone else?" He looks at me, eyes hopeful.

"Love is peaceful," I say wistfully. I shut my eyes for beat, wishing my time with Matt reflected that. It's how I always envisioned love to be, but it's far from what I got.

Chase adds to the discussion. "Love is more than just words." My eyes snap open. He's talking about his parents. My heart breaks a little for him. I know how it feels to feel unloved.

For years, I wondered why my father didn't love me enough to meet me. I wondered why my mother didn't love me enough to keep me. I wondered most of my adolescent years, why strangers didn't love me enough to adopt me. What was wrong with me? What was so wrong with Penelope Reza?

"Care to expand on that?" Mr. Mathers presses.

Chase shifts in his chair. "Love is making someone feel worthy. With actions, not with words. Hearts don't have ears. They can't hear love. They can only feel it."

"Amen," Mika mutters.

Mr. Mathers' gaze swings around the room. His gentle face is pleased with our progress tonight. "Who's up for a short session tonight? We're way ahead of time, but I think we ought to end things here." He pumps his fist in the air. "What an enlightening meeting tonight, am I right?" His lips stretch into a wide smile, crinkling his eyes at the corners. With his already ruddy cheeks flushed bright with adrenaline, he seems more suited for coaching than leading a support group.

Everyone murmurs an agreement as we rise to our feet.

"Nice job tonight!" Mr. Mathers brings his hands together in a loud clap. "See everyone next week!"

The small group filters out of the room. Chase keeps pace beside me, his hands in his pockets, head down. I think he wants to say something, but we move through the library in silence.

Outside, Sam walks up to Chase. "Ready?"

Chase's eyes float to me. "In a minute," he replies.

Sam focuses his steely eyes on me, his thin lips curving into a slight smile. "I'll wait in the car." He strolls away, but says over his shoulder. "Don't be long. We need to get home to Mom."

Chase gives a frustrated shake of his head, staring down at the pavement under his feet.

I hover, waiting, not sure what to do. The night sky over us is a streak of black. A dusting of dark clouds blots out the stars. Rain is coming. I shiver and fold my arms in front of me. "So," I test. "See you next week?"

"Yeah," he says with a sigh.

Something holds me there, not ready to leave just yet. Across the parking lot, I see Mr. Mathers escorting Judith to her car, keeping stride with her stunted shuffles. Ernie is long gone, having hopped into his truck, and tearing away in a hurry.

"How long have you been coming to the meetings?"

His blue eyes trace over my face, thinking. "A little over a year."

"Your mom?" I say. "Does she attend any meetings?" The question feels intrusive, and I wish I can take it back. Just snatch it from the air and swallow the words back down before he hears them.

Surprisingly, he doesn't seem bothered by it. He just snorts. "She used to. She said it was a waste of time. She didn't need help from a group. She could quit on her own." A mocking laugh escapes his lips. "Yeah right."

"I'm sorry, Chase." I don't know why I said it, but it just felt like the thing to say as I studied his pained face, hearing the resentment in his voice.

His features harden. "Don't." He turns his back to me. "I don't want you looking at me like that, okay?"

"Like what?"

"Like poor little Chase." He raises his voice an octave, clearly and annoyingly trying to mimic me. "His family is so screwed up. I feel so bad for him."

"I'm not looking at you like that. I'm looking at you like, 'poor Chase. I know exactly how he feels.' "

He turns his face, his profile silhouetted in the flood of harsh security lighting. "What?"

"My family is fucked up, too."

He laughs, remembering our conversation in this very spot last week. The one where he told me his family was fucked up, and that fucked up parents make fucked up families.

I don't believe that to be true. People can overcome. They can change…if they really want to. "One day we'll have to compare families," he says to me, turning around. "Winner owes the loser a movie."

It's my turn to laugh. "Is there really a winner in a battle of fucked up families?"

His face breaks into a grin. "You're right. We can both be losers together."

A car honks. Sam is leaning out of the driver's window. "Come on, Chase. We need to go."

"Okay, hold on."

"No. Now," Sam argues. "We need to pick up dinner and you still have lessons to finish."

Chase groans. Sam frowns and rolls the window back up.

"Lessons?" I ask, looking back to Chase.

"I'm homeschooled," he explains. "Well, more like, I'm homed, minus the schooling part."

I stare at him, questioning.

"My mom used to teach me. But now that she's…" He swallows thickly. "Well, now I'm on my own."

"How's that going?"

"Total fail," he says, trying to sound light.

"Why don't you go to regular school?"

"I thought about it, but if I'm not home during the day, who will watch my mom?"

My heart breaks within my chest. Chase is angry with Sam for enabling his mom, but he's doing it too by sacrificing his education for her. He just doesn't realize it.

I unfold my arms and step forward. "I could help."

He watches me, suspicious. "Help? How?"

"I could tutor you. We could meet here." I sweep my arm out toward the library.

He looks unsure, but intrigued. Slowly he starts to nod his head until they become more determined. "Okay, sure. I could use the help."

"Four o'clock, Friday. That should be enough time before the meeting starts."

"You got it." With a mischievous glint in his eye, he adds, "Teach."

"Okay. I'll see you then." I smile, and go to turn away.

Chase touches my elbow. "Wait."

I pause, my gaze sweeps upward to his sapphire-like eyes.

"Shouldn't I get your number, or something?" His cheeks grow pink, and it sends my heart soaring.

"Yeah, you probably should," I tell him.

He takes his phone from his pocket, punching in my number as I recite it. When he looks up, his face aglow from the screen of his phone, he smiles at me.

Sam honks the horn again, and I jump at the jarring sound. Chase's smile slips a little, but he holds my gaze. "I got to go." I watch his throat work as he swallows.

"I know," I whisper.

"See you later, Teach." He winks, and strides to the car where his father waits. I stand there a moment, watching the black SUV back out and pull away.

Chapter 37

I decide it's finally time to face Dr. Yassin. With my uniform apron tied snugly around my waist, I march straight to his office. The door is open, as I knew it would be. I find him seated with a chart, his fingers flipping through the paperwork. He's engrossed in it, so it must be the chart of his next surgery. I shouldn't bother him now, and yet, my feet keep moving. He lifts his head when he hears me enter.

"Penelope," he says with surprise. His discarded lab coat is draped over the back of his chair. His starched pin-striped shirt is rolled up past his elbows, an attempt at comfort as he studies patients' medical history.

"Hi, Dr. Yassin." I pull up a chair and sit before I lose my nerve. His office is warmer than the rest of the hospital, and typically I'd welcome it since they keep the hospital a cool sixty-six degrees, but right now it only feels stifling. I lick my dry lips and say, "I just wanted to say I'm sorry for what's happened with you and Mom."

Dr. Yassin lets the paper fall. The leather cushion of his chair squeaks as he leans back, regarding me thoughtfully. "I don't blame you, Penelope. I am the one who betrayed your mother."

"Because I asked you to," I add quickly. "I shouldn't have put you in the middle like that."

"And I could have refused," he reminds me. "I hurt your mother by withholding what I knew. She has every right to be angry with me."

I scowl. "Fine time for her to grow a backbone."

Dr. Yassin's eyes pinch. "What do you mean?"

"Mom's always been a doormat. Run over by Wesley. Trip." My ears burn with shame. "Me." Yes, even me. As a little kid, I knew how to manipulate her into getting what I wanted, but the longer I watched Trip and Wesley abuse her, I vowed to be different. I love my mom, and I refused to treat her that way.

Somehow, Dr. Yassin is smiling. A true smile that reaches his eyes and brightens his face. I watch him curiously. He pushes out of his chair, sending it rolling back. "She found her voice."

"What?"

He paces the length of his office. "Your mother." He rubs his smooth chin, thinking with a smile. "She finally found her voice."

My mind reacts, reaching and piecing things together. "It's you, isn't it? That's why she's changed."

"No." Dr. Yassin shakes his head. "Her change is all her. I don't deserve any credit."

"But it was you," I insist. "Wesley brought out her weakness, but you…you brought out her strength."

Dr. Yassin stops pacing. He looks at me, sure of his words, when he says, "That's what love is supposed to be, is it not?"

****

I'm at the end of my shift, so I meet Mom at her office. She's cleaning up her desk, ready to clock out for the day.

"Hey," I say hesitantly.

"Hi," she says, cleaning up her stacks of folders around me. I watch her for a few minutes, the quiet around us growing stifling by the second, until I can't take it any longer. I go to her and wrap my arms around her waist, pressing my face into the crook of her neck. She smells of sweet perfume, and I take it in. She stills under my embrace.

Mom and I haven't spoken much the past couple of weeks. She's been painfully distant, and it hurts. We've always been close. The first day I laid my eyes upon her, I was drawn to her kind smile and tender voice.

I clung to her skirt when the social worker got up to leave. I thought she was going to take me away from the nice lady with the friendly eyes. I clung to her then, much like I cling to her now.

"I'm sorry," I whisper.

She shushes me, her hand flattening on my back, rubbing a soothing track. "It's okay. It's okay," she reassures me.

All of my poor decisions rush back to me. Matt. Stealing from Dr. Yassin. Keeping it all a secret from Mom. That's when the sobbing begins. "I don't want you to hate me."

She pushes me back, looking me squarely in the eye. "Penelope," she scolds. "I don't hate you. Honey, I love you."

I wipe my eyes. "I disappointed you."

She blinks. "I was more disappointed in myself than in you. When I found out what you did…" She casts a hurried glance around the office. No one else is here. "I felt like I had let you down. I had no idea you were going through any of this. I was completely blindsided. I felt like a failure of a mother."

"Mom." I sniff. "You could never be a failure. You gave a strange kid a home. A family. That's far from a failure."

Now Mom is crying. Her face goes blotchy, and her mascara runs. I regret doing this here, but after patching things up with Dr. Yassin, I couldn't wait to fix things between me and Mom.

"Mom?" My tone sounds small and childlike. "I think I'm ready to be a Jackson." I don't know why I said it. I don't mean it. Seeing Mom wither before me had me scrabbling to do something—anything—no matter what the cost.

A flash of shock colors her face. "What?"

I just give a thin-lipped smile. She pulls me back into her, her grip around me as fierce as a mother lion.

We hug for a long while, but we're eventually interrupted by Michelle, Mom's coworker.

"Oh, I am so sorry," Michelle mumbles. "I didn't mean to intrude." She starts to back out of the office.

Mom and I break apart. "It's all right, Michelle. Come in."

"Is everything okay?" Michelle asks, taking in our swollen, red eyes and tear-streaked cheeks.

"Fine," Mom says, squeezing my hand firmly. "Just doing some mending, that's all." She looks over at me. "Come on. Let's go grab some dinner."

We head to the break room to get Mom's purse from her locker.

"Ragamuffins?" I ask as we walk through the hallways, arms linked.

"I said, dinner. Not dessert."

"Order a whole cheesecake and call it dinner."

She throws her head back and laughs. A free laugh that I haven't heard since she broke up with Dr. Yassin. A part of me remains hopeful that I can mend things between them. My relationship with Matt is shattered beyond repair, but Mom and Dr. Yassin's relationship isn't.

Chapter 38

My nerves are getting the best of me this morning. I woke up with a churning stomach and a splitting headache. It's no doubt from the guilt and regret that's devouring me from within. *Why did I say that to Mom?* I don't want to be a Jackson—not anymore, anyway. I only said it to make her happy, but at what cost? My own?

The unease eating at me is also from the prospect of seeing Matt again. I glance down at my left wrist. There's no mark, nothing visual anyway. But, for me, I can still see his fingers gripping, feel the strength and anger in them as they tightened. I swallow back a lump of emotion that threatens to choke me.

I dress slowly, picking plain jeans and a black sweater with a severely stretched-out neck. I don't care what I look like today. I'm barely functioning, so this is as good as it gets. I decide to leave my hair loose out of sheer laziness and when I catch a glimpse of myself in the mirror, I look exactly how I feel. Sullen.

Like a bloated storm cloud, ready to let loose a flood of tears at any moment. I don't really understand why I feel this way. I know it's mostly because of Matt, but I should feel good about yesterday. I apologized to Dr. Yassin and saw with my own eyes that his love for my mom remains. Mom and I are back to normal, which is a huge relief. It's been tense at home, and I hated feeling detached from Mom like I had. It was unnatural. And lonely.

Grabbing my book bag from my bed, I heave it over my shoulder and head to school, forgoing breakfast at home so I can eat with Jenna. I grab a chocolate chip granola bar from the pantry and I'm out the door. The morning air is chilly, and it snaps me fully awake. Mr. Bower is roaming his front lawn, checking on his creeping trumpet vines and cluster of rosebushes he keeps covered during the winter.

"Hi, Mr. Bower!" I call, waving.

The old man looks up from his roses and lifts his hand in greeting.

My breath comes out in puffs, a reminder that winter is not quite done with Charlotte just yet. I can't *wait* for summer. Jenna and I like to read in Cannon Park, a little forgotten park just outside of the city limits. We found it by accident about a year ago, when I first got my license and we were joyriding, just wasting gas, and hoping to be seen.

We drove here and there, down roads we never heard of, and through one intersection and then another. Eventually, we got lost, and I grew more nervous with each passing mile. My palms slick on the steering wheel when I finally pulled over to cry. Jenna spotted the park through her window as I sat in the driver's seat, nearly hyperventilating.

"Pen, look," she said, pointing. Through my blurry eyes, I saw it. The park, filled with huge oak trees and blooming dogwoods, lay sprawled over a rolling hill in the distance. Jenna insisted I dry my eyes, and go investigate the park. I did, of course, curious about what was inside the aged wrought iron fencing. It was beautiful. The towering oak trees wept Spanish moss, and old cobblestone paths cut through beds of brilliant purple wildflowers.

We were lost already, but within that park, we got lost all over again. We spent a full hour there before gathering our courage to find our way home. Which we did, of course, and somehow, we were even able to remember our way back to the park later that week, when we brought our books and a picnic basket full of snacks. It's been our summer tradition ever since.

I hurry to my car and start it up. I set the heater to full blast, listening to the motor whirl. Freezing, I rub my hands together to warm them as I watch the frost slowly melt away from the windshield.

I notice Mom's bedroom light click on, so I know she's up, moving about as she gets ready for work. I picture her running into Dr. Yassin and I wonder how hard it would be to arrange that. I'll have to work on a plan for that later. Today, I only have the interest and the energy to make it through the day. Nothing more.

****

I spot Jenna at a booth. She's holding out her phone in front of her. I don't see Carlos anywhere so that probably means he's standing in line for a tray already. I cross the cafeteria, weaving my way through the tables, and slide in beside her. I glance at her phone screen. Her face is haloed with animated red floating hearts. Her phone makes a *click* sound, and she swipes to the next filter.

"Morning, morning glory." She angles her head to the side and fluffs her hair. She takes a photo of herself with rainbows spilling from her mouth.

"Hi," I say, wriggling out of the straps of my book

bag. "Where's Carlos?"

"Getting food," she says, puckering at her phone screen. "Take a picture with me." She snuggles closer and holds the phone screen before us. We both have unicorn horns protruding from our foreheads, and white cartoon clouds fill the corners of the screen. I make a silly face and Jenna snaps the photo, giggling.

She sets her phone down on the table and turns to me. Her eyes squint appraisingly. "What's this?" Her hand waves over me. "What's going on here?"

I cast my gaze down at my worn sweater. I pull at the collar. "What?"

"This sad sweater," she continues with a huff. "Something going on with you I need to know about?" One eyebrow lifts high over her sharp, green eyes.

"No," I mutter, reaching for her carton of chocolate milk. I take a sip, wiping my mouth before I hand it back to her. Doubtfully, she eyes me, but she keeps her mouth pressed tight.

Carlos walks up to the table, two plates in hand. He sits one down in front of Jenna. Her eyes brighten, and she licks the cherry lip balm off her lips. Carlos scoots into the seat opposite us, sliding his plate with him. On each paper plate is a puddle of golden-brown pancakes and two sausage links.

"Hey! Reza!" Carlos says, dropping a few packets of butter and syrup onto the table.

"Hey," I say, unzipping my book bag to retrieve my granola bar.

Jenna plucks a butter packet from the pile and peels back the plastic. "She is in a mood," she warns Carlos.

Carlos leans back, as if to say, *whaaaat? "Again? What's going on with you, girl?"* He fists his fork and stabs the pancake whole, lifting it to his mouth. He nibbles off a piece with his teeth. Chewing, he says, "Is it that jackass, Matt?"

I unwrap my granola bar. "I don't know." I break it in half and take a bite. "I guess I'm just nervous about seeing him. I wish I could switch classes."

Jenna expels a breath. "But you love Mrs. Johnson."

"I know."

She frowns. "I hate seeing you like this, Pen."

My cellphone suddenly chimes with a text message. I look at Carlos and Jenna, the only two people who regularly text me other than Mom. *Oh no,* I think. *What's wrong?* I drop my granola bar and scramble for my phone. Before I check the screen, my stomach dips with dread.

What if it's Matt? I push that thought away in a hurry. *What if it's Mom, and something's wrong?* When I check, it's a text from a number I don't recognize.

—*Hi-ya, Teach. Learn a lot today so you can share all that brain power with me.*—

I smile at the phone, my heart fluttering up to my throat.

Jenna takes notice right away. "*Who* was that?"

Carlos slaps his palm to his forehead. "Please don't say Matt."

Somehow, I'm not annoyed by the comment. Instead, I stare, grinning like an idiot at the screen.

Jenna looks over my shoulder. "Well?"

Blushing, I tuck my hair behind my ear. "A boy from my support group."

Jenna's face breaks into a knowing smirk. "Really? What's his name?"

"Chase." I lift my fingers to my cheek, feeling it

redden.

Jenna blinks at me with doe-like eyes. "Remember when I said I hate seeing you like this?" She leans closer and rests her chin on my shoulder.

"Yeah."

"Well, this…" She gestures to the grin plastered on my face. "This I like."

Me too, I think happily.

****

Rainey finds me at my lockers. Her white-blonde hair is yanked up tight at the crown of her head, and a sleek ponytail cascades down her back. I envy the way her hair falls naturally stick-straight. I'm willing to bet she put it up on her way to school, too. Without blow-drying it, without hair gel, mousse, hair spray, or bobby pins. I hate people with cooperative, easy hair.

Rainey barely acknowledges Carlos and Jenna. Her blue eyes fixate on me, singular, as if she's trying to read my mind. "Did you hear?"

"Hear what?" I shove my math book into my locker.

She moves closer. "About Matt?"

My gut takes a blow. *What about him? What's happened?* I shrug, trying to pretend I don't care.

Carlos pipes up. "She don't care about that fool."

Rainey ignores him. "Word around school is…" She lowers her voice to a whisper. "He's a druggie. Got sent to rehab somewhere." She snaps her gum, brows almost meeting her hairline as she waits for my reaction. I don't give her one. I shut my locker door with a clang and turn my back to it. "Good for him," I say. Rainey blinks in surprise.

"Where did you hear that?" Jenna asks.

"Dylan".

Dylan? He's Matt's friend. Why would he say that? Because it's true, I remind myself glumly.

"Did you already know?" Rainey questions.

"Well, she was his girlfriend," Jenna says in her best 'duh' voice.

"I didn't know about rehab," I admit. So that's where he is. He's not in California with his dad. He's locked up somewhere, withdrawing. I wince at the thought of him desperate, and sweating, and cursing in pain. I chew my bottom lip. "Did he say when Matt will be back to school?"

Rainey shakes her head, her hair swishing gently behind her. A small part of me welcomes the distance between us. Matt needs to focus on himself right now, not me, not us. There is no us to worry about anymore.

The bell trills overhead, and we all set begrudgingly off for our classrooms. Jenna lingers by my side.

"You okay?"

"Yeah," I lie. She doesn't believe me, I know it, but she lets the lie slide, anyway.

"This is good for him," she says matter-of-factly, stepping out of the way of a couple of boys shoving each other down the hall.

"Yeah," I say again. We don't speak again until we're at the door to Mrs. Johnson's class.

"See you after class, Pen." She hugs my neck. "And don't worry about Matt. He's where he needs to be." She lets go and saunters away to her Spanish class.

My eyes land on Matt's empty seat. In my heart, I know she's right. Matt is exactly where he needs to be. Drawing in a deep breath, I go to take my seat behind Matt's empty desk.

Chapter 39

When the final bell rings, I merge with the flow of kids all headed for the school exits. Carlos managed to stay out of trouble today, so he's likely already on his way to Mario Bros, and Jenna is off to Puffins. I almost asked Rainey if she wanted to hang out after school, but I decided I'd much rather dive head-first into my bed and eat peanut butter out of the jar all afternoon.

Of course, I wouldn't admit that to Rainey, who's willowy as a wheat stalk thanks to healthy eating and yoga. She'd probably hassle me if she knew what I planned to do.

Before I crank up my car, I fish my phone out of my book bag and open up the text message from Chase. Tapping the keys in rapid-fire, I finally text back:

—*School's over for me. How about you?*—

He texts back almost immediately. —*Haven't even started. Too busy playing Dark Tenets.*—

I smile at the screen. —*And you wonder why you're failing.*—

—*It's how I socialize. Keeps me from being a homeschooler weirdo.*—

I snort with laughter. —*Too late for that. Besides, is it really socializing when you do it from behind a screen?*—

My phone dings. —*Yes. My Dark Tenets team has been on the same mission for two weeks. They're like family.—*

—Really? What's their names?—

—Green_Gobbler,   *Booknerdbabe055,*
BloodXBroX—

—Not what I meant, but OK. I think it's time you make friends with someone more...3D—

—Does VR count?—

—VR?—

—Virtual reality—

—No—

Long pause.

—Will you be my 3D friend?—

I smile and type back: *—Sure.—*

Smiley face emoji.

I look up and notice the student parking lot is nearly empty. I blink in surprise. I start the engine, but before I can shift the car into drive, Chase texts me again.

—I know it's not Friday, but do you wanna to meet at the library, my 3D friend?—

Before I can reply, Chase texts again.

—Meet me @ 4?—

Forgetting all about my date with a jar of peanut butter, I reply simply, *—K—*

I glance over at the clock. I won't have time to swing home before I meet Chase, so I head for the next best thing.

****

Jenna dumps the contents of her purse on Puffin's pink tabletop. Her uniform is covered with bright splashes of yellow, neon green, and red from the snow cones she's been making all afternoon. "I'm sure I have something you can use," she says, spreading everything out.

I pluck out a bottle of scented lotion and a pack of gum. I pop a piece of cinnamon gum into my mouth and slather on the vanilla lotion up to my elbow.

Jenna chuckles into her hand.

"What?"

"You," she says. "You're a mess."

"Gee, thanks."

"No, I don't mean it like that. I mean…a mess when it comes to this Chase guy. Look at you." She gestures at me. "Using lotion as perfume and gum as mouthwash."

A bubble of laughter escapes me. "Shut up and help me."

Jenna rifles through the pile. "Wish I had a shirt in here," she says, cutting her eyes to my worn sweater.

I stick my tongue out at her.

"Here," she offers me a mascara wand and a mirror.

I sweep on the mascara, blinking at my reflection in the compact mirror. *I wish I had time for a shower and blow-dry.* I hand Jenna back the wand and find a pretty barrette with sparkling rhinestones amongst the scattered items. I part my hair on the side and tuck the barrette in above my ear. "Good?"

She surveys me carefully, green eyes roaming over me slowly. "Yeah. You look cute."

I take my own lip balm from my pocket and smear some on. I press my lips together a few times and say, "You and the bottomless pit you call a purse are a lifesaver."

Jenna scoops everything up and dumps it back into her purse. "Forever a girl scout. I'm always ready for anything."

I help her clean up, tossing in her hairbrush, and a rolled-up pair of ankle socks.

"Want a snow cone for the road?"

"Sure," I say, throwing a crushed packet of crackers into her purse.

Jenna zips up her bag and taps me on the nose. "Be right back."

She comes back carrying a watermelon snow cone. Light on the ice, heavy on the flavoring, just the way I like it. I spit my gum into a napkin, just before she sticks a straw in the ice and hands it to me. "Here you go."

I take it, the cup cold in my hands. "Thanks!" I draw a long pull from the straw. It's sugary sweet, with just a touch of tart. "Yum!" I lick my lips with my icy tongue.

Jenna smiles and playfully slaps my arm. "Now get outta here. I got work to do. Shoo."

Grinning, I push my chair out and stand. "I'll call you later," I promise.

"You better."

I hurry to my car and drop the snow cone into the cup holder. It's almost four, so I check the mirror one more time. I look somewhat put together. My brown eyes pop from the mascara, and thanks to my lip balm, my lips look moist and supple. I turn my head slightly, smiling at the sparkling barrette holding the bulk of my heavy curls back. I touch the neckline of my sweater. It's spread wide, revealing my collarbone. But with the right attitude, maybe I can pull it off as a fashion statement. I put my car into gear and head to the library to meet Chase.

****

Chase is seated at a small round table near the Children's section of the library. He's flipping through a magazine and doesn't see me walk up. His head is hanging low, and his back is curved as he pores over the magazine. I watch him as he taps his middle finger on the table as he reads, absorbed in some article.

When I pull back the chair across from him, Chase's head snaps up. His usual brooding features brighten.

"Teach!"

I plunk myself down in the chair. "Hi." What I thought was a magazine is actually a comic book. "Fan of the classics, I see."

His mouth quirks. "Actually, yes." He closes the comic book and turns it around so I can read the title: Double Dimension. "This is a total classic."

I arch a brow, unconvinced. "No. War and Peace is a classic." I slide the comic book closer, inspecting the cover. I recognize the character, Teleporter, with his midnight black suit, and shiny fallen star insignias over his ears. "Comic books are nothing more than picture books."

Chase covers his heart, feigning to be deeply wounded. "How dare you? Comic books are more than just pictures. They're layered storylines and complex characters."

I stare at him blankly.

Chase's lips curve. "You were supposed to tutor me, but it looks like I'm going to have to school you on comics." He presses a finger to the cover. "Felix Yeager."

"Who?"

Chase rolls his eyes. "The Teleporter—when he's not the Teleporter."

"Ah. The Teleporter is Felix's alter ego. Like Clark Kent when he's not Superman?"

"Yeah." Chase seems pleased that I knew that. "So he's in this alternate reality without his speedster ability and to regain it, he has to—"

I hold up a hand. "Okay, slow down there, Teleporter. Why don't we start with *your* tutoring? Not mine."

Chase's smile holds my attention like no book ever has. It's inviting, like a siren song calling me closer and closer. It's a feeling similar to when I'm sitting in Cannon Park. Secluded in a beautiful space that is mine, and mine alone.

"So, where should we start?"

I blink to attention. "Huh?"

"What should we start with? You're the tutor, you tell me."

I'm a little shaken. "Um." I grasp for words. "How about math? What are you working on?"

"Polynomials."

"Okay. Do you have a workbook?"

He bends to rummage through a ratty book bag. It's an old Army issued bag, covered in patches and pins. One pin says, *Nirvana*. Another says, *Duffy's Comics*.

He slaps a worn workbook with curling corners onto the table. He flips through it, bookmarking it with a pencil. He shoves the workbook toward me. I study the problems on the paper, refreshing my memory of how to solve polynomials. "All right," I say, scooting to the edge of my seat. "To solve these, you first need to set the equation to zero."

Chase's brows are furrowed with concentration. I take the pencil into my hand and start sketching out the problem, walking through each step slowly until it's finally solved.

Together, we work through the next problem. Chase rubs his forehead as if it hurts to think.

"How about you do the next one?" I offer him the pencil. I hold my breath, waiting for him to take it from me. When he does, the touch is fleeting, but it does something to my insides. I become all gooey and warm. It's distracting, but it feels nice.

He glares down at the workbook, his eyes running back and forth across the page as he reads the problem. He bites his lower lip, thinking.

"Remember to set it to zero," I say.

He presses his pencil to the paper, scribbling out the solution. I wait patiently for him to finish, spending that time studying him. I'm drawn to a freckle on his left cheek, right where a dimple would be if he had one. His dark brows are thick, but one has a razor-thin slash through it from an old scar. I wonder how it got there.

He throws the pencil down. "Done." He rumbles his hair, mussing it to something that resembles bedhead. That move is almost my undoing. I swallow on a dry throat and try to focus on the numbers on the page.

"That's right," I tell him.

He blows out a relieved breath. "Thank God. Can we talk comics now?"

"Not so fast, Teleporter. Get the next three problems correct, and *then*, we can talk comics."

He gives me a long, searching look. "Whatever you say, *Teach*." He sets to work. His pencil scratching across the paper until he flips it around to grind his eraser into it, cursing under his breath. It takes the better part of twenty minutes before he's satisfied. He slides his pencil behind his ear and thrusts the workbook toward me.

I scan the answers, mentally solving each problem, and each problem is correct. I raise my eyes to find him watching me, thick eyebrows lifted high.

"Well?"

"So, tell me more about Double Dimension."

Chase grins and tells me all about Felix Yeager, Chuck West, Sinner Block, and more. So many that I can't remember them all. Our discussion flows easily, changing subjects so many times I lost all track of time until the library flickers its lights in its ten-minute closing warning.

"Oh!" I say, surprised. "Wow. They're closing already?"

"You don't charge by the hour, do you?"

"Nah. Just a flat rate."

Chase gives me an amused smile. "A flat rate of what?"

My eyes drift to the comic book on the table. "You let me borrow Double Dimension."

His dark-blue eyes widen, but he recovers smoothly. "Deal." He hands me the comic book. I take it and slide it safely into my book bag. A librarian with tight grey curls walks up to our table. "We're closing soon. If you have anything that needs to be checked out, now is the time to do so."

"Oh, no, thank you. We were just studying," I say to her. She smiles graciously and walks away. Chase and I stand, swinging our book bags over our shoulders.

"Same time tomorrow?" Chase asks, his eyes hopeful.

My face flushes. "Sure."

Together, we walk out of the library. He holds the door open for me and I scoot past him, reaching up to finger a strand of my hair.

We hesitate by the library's brick column. Chase regards me quietly, like I'm the lesson he needs to learn.

I fidget a little under his intrusive watch.

"Well," I say. "I'm going to go. I have a lot of reading to get done."

"Oh right. Double Dimension. Let me know what you think."

"I will." I retreat a few steps. "See you tomorrow."

When I turn my back to him and walk several paces, he calls out, "Hey Teach. I don't even know your last name."

I pause and turn on my heel. "Reza."

"Penelope Reza," he says, tasting my name. I have to admit, my name sounds strong on his lips. "That's a great name." He flashes that sexy, yet innocent, smile that sends tingles to my toes. Our gazes hold firm and everything else falls back.

With my heart swelling ten times its size in my chest, I breathe, "It is. Isn't it?"

Chapter 40

As soon as I get home, I shed my shoes at the door and pop a mini pizza in the microwave. Mom is still at work, and I don't expect her home until after ten. The microwave beeps and I don't even bother slinging the pizza onto a plate and sitting down. Instead, I slide it out its cardboard sleeve and eat it on the way to my room.

I'm starving. I usually eat dinner around six, but the hours with Chase blurred together, and I didn't notice how late it was until I stepped out of the library and into the dark of the evening.

Swallowing the last bite, I double back to the living room to grab my book bag. I spent all afternoon tutoring Chase, but I still need to do my homework. I have some scientific names to memorize for biology and I have until Thursday to read the last few chapters of the Lord of Flies and summarize them.

I dump my book bag out on the bed and shuffle through the books, looking for Lord of my book. My fingers brush along the smooth cover of Double Dimension. My lips draw into a smile. Taking the comic book into my hand, I plop down onto the mattress, crossing my legs at the ankles. I open it, my eyes falling on the vibrant colors of the page. I flip through the pages, absorbed in the story.

There's a knock at my opened door, and I startle upright.

"Mom," I breathe, my heart in my throat. *Is it after ten already?* "I didn't hear you come in."

"Sorry, honey. I didn't mean to scare you." She wanders over, her gaze casting down at the book in my lap. "What are you reading?"

I close the comic book and lay it beside me on the bedspread. "A comic book," I admit sheepishly.

Her brow lifts high. "Really?"

"Chase let me borrow it."

"Chase?" Mom perches on the edge of my bed. She takes up the comic book and flips through the pages.

"A boy from support group."

A wave of emotion ghosts over Mom's face. I'm not sure what she's thinking or feeling, but whatever it is, it passes just as quickly as it came.

"Well, it's getting late," she says, handing Double Dimension to me. "I still need to eat a quick snack. Unless you cooked tonight?" Her big brown eyes look hopeful.

"No, sorry. I was tutoring Chase."

She gives me a searching look. I can tell she wants to ask about Chase, to learn more about him and figure out what's really going on between us, but that's not her style. She'll patiently wait me out, then listen stoically as stone as I unload on her.

One day it may play out just like that, but not today. I'm suddenly drained and ready for sleep. Mom must sense this because she stands and goes to my bedroom door. She pauses there, throwing a tender look over her shoulder. "Good night, sweetie."

"Good night, Mom."

She shuts off the bedroom light and I listen to her footsteps fade down the hall. When I settle back into my pillow, I can't stop thinking about Chase. Of course, I can't get his deep-blue eyes and quirky smile out of my head, but what really sticks is the way he said my name.

It's silly, but it was as if my name finally took on a meaning. Like it truly meant something other than a name that has always haunted me like a ghost all these years. When I finally give in to sleep, I know what I have to do. And it's probably going to kill my mother...

****

School drags more than normal. I know it because I am anxious to make the call to Mr. Douglas, and yet I find myself ready to get it over with. When the final bell calls, I bid farewell to my friends and run to my car. Fisting my phone, I take a deep breath. My gut tells me I'm doing the right thing. *So why is it so hard?*

With my stomach churning, I make the call.

Lisa answers. "Good afternoon, Douglas Law Firm."

"Hi, Lisa. This is Penelope Reza. I think my mom called a few days ago requesting Mr. Douglas reopen the name change paperwork."

"Oh yes. Miranda Jackson's daughter, right?"

"That's right."

There's a shuffling of paperwork. "Hold on a second for me, hon?" The line switches to classical music. I grow restless as I wait, tapping on the steering wheel with my finger.

The line clicks, and Lisa is back. "Hey, Penelope? I can't find any updated paperwork anywhere, and I asked Mr. Douglas about it, and he said he hasn't heard from your mother."

Mom never called? Relieved, I lean back into the headrest. "Oh, okay," I say. "Thank you anyway."

"No problem. Have a nice day."

"You, too. Bye." I hang up, a little bewildered. Mom knew I wasn't ready to change my name. She knew I only said that to make her happy. She knew I didn't mean it, which probably hurt her. My heart crumbles, knowing I caused her pain. It's the exact opposite of what I was trying to do.

I feel compelled to see her. To explain myself and make sure she's okay. But I don't have time. I have to meet Chase. I glance down at my outfit, and am satisfied. I took care dressing this morning, knowing I was meeting him after school. I chose a burgundy wool pleated skirt over thick black tights and a cute black and white horizontal striped shirt. Black ballet flats and a gold headband make the outfit complete.

Turning the key, I start up the car and click the radio on. My earlier grey mood lightens, almost matching the sunny February day. Singing along to every song, I drive straight to the library. Mom works late again tonight, so don't need to worry about being home to make dinner. I'll wait up for her so we can talk. I whip into a parking slot and kill the engine with a smile.

I walk into the library, expecting to wait on Chase, but there he is, sitting at the same table near the Children's section. Again, he's hunched over a comic book, oblivious that I'm here until I pull out the chair across from him.

"Hey," he greets with a sleepy smile. He raises his arms over his head, stretching like an old tomcat.

"You up to this today?" I ask, dropping into the chair.

Nodding, he yawns. His blue eyes dulled by the dark rings circling them.

"Stay up all night playing Dark Tenets?" I kid.

"I wish," he replies, shoving the comic book away from him. "Mom binged last night. Wouldn't let me or Dad get any sleep. She kept banging on my door, wanting me to stay up and talk to her. She even kicked in her bedroom door when Dad finally locked her out of it."

He leans heavily on his elbows, and it's then I notice just how disheveled he really looks. His flannel shirt is wrinkly, like he just picked it up from his bedroom floor. His tired eyes are hooded as if he could fall asleep at any moment.

Looking around the quiet atmosphere of the library, I realize this is the last place he needs to be right now.

I give him a wicked smile. "Let's forget the tutoring today. Want to get out of here?"

Chase brightens. "What you got in mind?"

"You'll see." I stand and walk away with him close on my heels. I lead him to my car, where he gets in wordlessly. I drive us to Ragamuffins, where Chase can get enough caffeine and sugar his eyelids will retreat into his skull for a full two days.

He eyes the wooden cupcake-shaped sign with cutesy teal font hanging over the door. "A dessert café? You badass you." His sarcastic smirk sends tingles to my toes.

Instead of acting on the impulse to kiss him, I shove him through the door. Ragamuffins' owner, Mr. Fritz, is stocking the display case with powdered donuts and slices of custard pie. He smiles at us in greeting but keeps to his task.

Ragamuffins is a quaint café in the center of town. It sits between a locally owned boutique and a ballet studio. In its previous life, the spot was a nightclub, dimly lit with shiplap boards from floor to ceiling. When Ragamuffins took over, they gutted everything except the bar. Now, the long strip of bar is lined with whimsical barstools, each painted a different color.

The glass dessert display case greets customers at the door. It's always filled with delicious cakes of all varieties, truffles with vanilla swirls, sugar-coated pastries, chocolate-dipped strawberries, and oranges sprinkled with sea salt, and more.

"Ever been here?" I ask Chase as we settle into the tall barstools. With his long, lean legs, he has an easier time than I do. I struggle to climb onto mine, and then I have to arrange my curvy bottom comfortably on the seat.

"No," he says, watching me with amusement. When I've finally settled myself onto the barstool, he hides a smile with his hand.

"Don't laugh at me," I scold him playfully.

Ragamuffins is pretty quiet this time of day. There's only a handful of people scattered amongst the bistro tables and bar. The sweet smell of candied apples and chocolate chip cookies sets my stomach to rumbling. I catch the eye of a waitress, and she flounces over, ponytail swinging behind her. She hands us a Ragamuffins menu to share.

"Afternoon, ya'll. Can I start you off with a drink?"

"Sweet tea for me," I tell her.

Chase is already nose-deep in the menu. "Root beer," he says without looking up.

"Okay," the waitress says pleasantly. "I'll be back in a few minutes to take your sugary sweet order."

Chase peers over the menu. "Sugary sweet order?"

I smile. "They always say that."

He snorts and dives back into the menu. "How do they expect you to pick from this? Everything sounds good."

"In that case," I say, leaning so close our shoulders touch. "Pick this." I point to the sampler dish called, "This and That."

He squints at the description. "Why choose one when you can choose them all? Ladyfingers doused with local organic honey, red-velvet cake with light cream cheese frosting, vanilla mousse whipped to perfection, lemon bar sprinkled with powdered sugar, and a bite-sized square of milk chocolate fudge."

He scrunches up his face. "There's no way anyone could eat that and still have their own teeth!"

I give him a broad grin, showing off my very intact teeth.

"No way!" He shakes his head, laughing. "The title of badass remains yours."

"Thank you," I say, puffing up my chest with exaggerated pride.

Turning back to the menu, he asks, "So, what do you usually get? And please don't say the 'This and That.' "

"No. I've only had that once. I usually get strawberry cheesecake."

His eyes dart back and forth over the cheesecake description and then skim over the photo of a Boston cream pie. The way his gaze lingers there, I know he made his choice.

The waitress comes back and sets our drinks down on the bar. "You guys ready?"

I look at Chase. He hands her back the menu. "Yep. Boston cream pie," he says with certainty.

"Strawberry cheesecake," I tell the waitress, reaching for my glass of sweet tea.

"Coming right up," she says before whirling away toward the display case.

"So." I take a quick sip of sweet tea. "I read Double Dimension."

His eyes and smile widen in adorable unison. He looks like a little boy. "You did? What do you think?"

"I have to admit. I liked it."

His smile creeps even wider. "See? I told you. Still think comics are nothing but *picture* books?"

I hold my hands up in surrender. "I was wrong. I should have never judged them so harshly."

He gives a knowing *humph*.

The waitress returns with our order. My mouth waters at the sight of my cheesecake, dripping with strawberries and sitting in a pool of red syrup. She sets the desserts down in front of us.

"If this tastes half as good as it looks, then oh, boy…" Chase picks up his fork and slices into his pie.

I slide my fork into the soft cheesecake and lift a chunk to my mouth. It tastes heavenly. "Why the Teleporter?"

Chewing, he replies, "What do you mean?"

"Out of all the superheroes? Night Ninja, Battle Axe, the Screamin' Vermin—"

He visibly winces. "Wrong universe."

"What?"

"The Screamin' Vermin. He's from 'X' League, not the DU. Dark Universe is a completely different publishing company. Not to mention multiverse."

"Okay, whatever. But you get what I'm asking. Why him?"

Chase puts his fork down. "Because Felix Yeager can run away." He looks directly at me. "Sometimes, I wish I was him." His chin trembles. "I'd run far away and never look back." He looks distant, as if picturing himself already there.

I'm curious now. "Where would you go?"

His shoulder lifts. "Anywhere. Anywhere but home."

I swallow thickly. As an orphan, a home is all I ever dreamed of and here Chase wants nothing to do with it. Ordinarily, I'd grow angry and think of him as ungrateful and stupid, but knowing his home-life, who could blame him for wanting to run away?

"How long has this been going on? Your mom, I mean?"

"Most of my life." He forks a chunk of pie and stuffs it into his mouth. He chews for a moment, thoughtful. "The worst of it has been the past, oh…" He pauses, calculating. "Four years or so? Back when my aunt Sarah died. She had pancreatic cancer. She and Mom were tight. Mom totally lost it when she passed."

He continues to eat as he talks, as if the tale he's telling is as normal as reciting a grocery list. "Mom has always been a drinker. White Russians were her favorite. She'd have one or two a night. I even learned how much milk to splash in her glass just so I could help her fix them." The slightest hint of a smile traces his lips. He finishes the last of his pie. I shove my own plate away, no longer hungry.

Like an approaching storm, his face grows darker. "After Aunt Sarah died, the White Russians were forgotten. They took preparation. She needed something stronger, without the fuss, you know? So she took up whiskey. Doesn't even bother pouring it anymore. Drinks it straight from the bottle." He looks down at his empty plate. "When Aunt Sarah's life ended. So did my mom's."

Chapter 41

All last night, I tossed and turned in my bed, obsessing over Chase. Compelled to help him, but not knowing how. He and I are surprisingly not that different. We both want a family. A family to love, and who loves us in return. For years, I never had a family, and for years, neither has Chase. Sure, he's had one by all outward appearances, but behind closed doors his family is shattered.

When the alarm blares, I'm already awake, staring up at the still dark ceiling. I slap at it, quietening the noise. I sit up and rub my tired eyes. It's Friday, and the most unfortunate of all days, Valentine's Day. Frowning, I swing my legs over the edge of the bed and slip my feet into my fuzzy purple slippers.

All day, there will be deliveries being made to classrooms of single long-stemmed roses to girls—and a few surprised boys. For two bucks, you can purchase a rose from the Rotary Club and have it delivered to your special someone in class. In front of everyone.

You can choose to sign it or send it anonymously. It's dumb if you ask me. There's always one or two cheerleaders that walk around with an armload of stupid roses, gushing over how many secret admirers they have. *Blech.* I pretend to hate the Rotary Club rose tradition because I've never gotten one myself. Maybe I'm a little bitter, but this year things could have been different.

Matt would've bought me one and had it delivered with a sweet note. But that's all dashed into dust now. He's in rehab somewhere, probably feigning for Oxy.

I wrestle my bedhead into something that resembles more of a French baguette than a French braid and slide on a leather headband for good measure. I dress in a robin's-egg blue cable sweater and khakis. I plop back onto the bed to pull on my pair of comfy boots.

There's a gentle knock on my door.

"Come in," I say, standing.

The door opens, and a heart-shaped box of candy peers around it. A grin pulls at my lips.

"Happy Valentine's Day." Mom steps inside my room, smiling. She's already dressed for work: a pale pink sweater paired with slim-fitting grey slacks. Her brown hair is curled in loose ringlets, which makes her look ten years younger.

She hands me the box, and I pull it to my chest. "Thanks, Mom." When I hug her, the red cellophane wrapper crinkles between us. Her perfume wafts gently around me, surrounding me like an embrace, much like it did in my youth. "Mom," I say with trepidation as we part. "I know about the paperwork. Why didn't you have Mr. Douglas reopen the file?"

Mom smiles a bittersweet smile. "Oh, sweetie. I know you're not ready to sign it." She cups my cheek, her palm warm against my skin. "And to be honest, I'm not ready either. You need to find out who you are before you go changing things about yourself. You are Penelope Reza. My daughter, whether we share the same last name or not." Tears cloud my vision, but before I can say anything, Mom presses a kiss to my nose.

"Remember, I'm working Michelle's shift for her,"

she says as she pulls away. "You going to be okay on your own?"

"Oh yeah," I tell her, blinking back tears as I slip the box of Valentine's candy into my book bag. "I'm tutoring Chase tonight, anyway. Want me to have dinner ready for you when you get home?"

"Nah. I'll probably just swing through a drive-through. I can pick you up something if you want. Chocolate shake, maybe?"

I grin. "You know me so well." I tug the book bag zipper closed before wiggling into the straps.

She follows me to the kitchen, chatting about nothing really as I pluck a granola bar from the pantry and snag a bottle of soda from the refrigerator. I check the clock on the microwave.

"I better get going," I tell her. "Happy Valentine's Day, Mom."

"Happy Valentine's Day, Sweetie."

****

I was wrong. Remember when I said one or two cheerleaders end up with loads of roses on Valentine's Day? Well, this year the entire squad ended up with so many Rotary Club roses that the Rotary Club president had to make an emergency run to a florist to fulfill their orders.

Every time there is a knock on the classroom door, I glare sourly at it. My jealousy flaring as I watch the kid deliver his roses around the room. *Please,* I think. *Can the day just end already?*

The third period bell rings, so I force myself to trudge past the squealing girls in the hallway, ignoring their beautiful bouquets as I head to the cafeteria. Rainey is already at our booth when I get there. Lying on the table in front of her are three long-stemmed roses. I sit down beside her.

I motion to the roses. "Got yourself a fan club there."

She barely glances at them. "I guess."

"Who are they from?"

"No one worth mentioning." She scrolls through her phone, bored.

"Well, all right." I spot Carlos and Jenna weaving their way through the crowded cafeteria. Jenna is holding a single red rose. I smile despite the fact that I hate the stupid Rotary Club and their stupid Valentine's Day roses.

Jenna and Carlos sit opposite me and Rainey. Carlos' chest is swelled with pride of a job well done and Jenna is almost glowing. There's a different vibe coming from them now. Gone are the days of one-sided admiration, where Carlos gazes at an oblivious Jenna like a love-sick puppy. By the smile on Jenna's face, the feeling is definitely mutual.

"Look what Carlos sent me in Spanish." She crams the rose into my nose, forcing me to inhale. I nearly choke on the sweet scent. "Ugh!" I shove it back at her. "You didn't have to ram it up my nose. I feel like I have rose petals stuck inside my nostrils."

"Sorry," Jenna says, bringing the rose to her nose. She smiles to herself.

"Nice job," I say to Carlos.

His cheeks flush pink, but I can tell he's pleased with himself.

"So, what are your plans after school?" I ask them.

"Taking her somewhere nice, I hope," Rainey questions from behind her phone screen.

"As a matter of fact, I am." Carlos' face breaks into a huge grin. "Julios. Unlimited chips and salsa, yo."

"And guac," Jenna adds. "Don't forget the unlimited guac."

Rainey rolls her eyes. "You two were made for each other."

If Carlos smiles any bigger, his cheeks will crack.

Jenna's face stills with worry. "What about you guys?"

Rainey lowers her phone to her lap. "Shopping and pedicures with Christina. I can't wait." Christina and Dennis Cooper are the couple hosting Rainey during her foreign exchange program. Christina is the wealthy wife of Dennis, some big-shot investor or something. She and Rainey blow his money all the time on shopping trips, lunch dates, and manicures, so of course, Valentine's Day would be no different.

Jenna's eyes drift over to me, holding me in a gaze that hints at pity. I swallow my aggravation and say, "I'm tutoring Chase tonight," as if that explains everything.

Everyone is quiet, and the silence becomes unbearably awkward. I have to address the lonely elephant in the room.

"Guys. I'm fine. Really."

Jenna's eyes are soft as she takes me. Measuring my tone and my expression to determine if I'm lying or not.

Surprisingly, I'm not. I am okay. Sure, it would be nice to have a boyfriend on Valentine's Day, but I've been in this boat for one for as long as I can remember, so why should this Valentine's Day be any different?

"You sure?" Jenna asks hesitantly. "This whole thing with Matt has been rough."

"I'm fine." It comes out sharper than I meant it to,

but really. Do we have to keep dragging this whole Matt thing out? We are over. The end. Roll the credits. Done.

For a moment in time, there was the making of a sequel, but that shattered for good that afternoon in the library. I should have known better than to try again, but my heart was more forgiving than my brain. From now on, I follow my head, not my heart.

Besides, everyone knows sequels suck.

Chapter 42

Everyone except Matt, apparently. He's standing beside my car waiting for me after school.

I see him from afar and my feet still. *What is he doing here? How is he already out of rehab?*

Anxiety wells up in me, suffocating me. I think about turning around and dashing back into school, but Rainey steps up beside me.

Her blue eyes follow my trail of vision. "Oh shit. What's he doing here?"

"I have no idea," I say, swallowing on a dry, parched throat.

"What a creep," Rainey says, disgusted. "He just won't take no for an answer, will he?"

"What should I do?"

"If I were you, I'd march right over there and kick him in the balls."

"Rainey…"

She shrugs. "You asked. That's exactly what I'd do."

I bite my lip, glancing back to the school doors.

Rainey notices. "Don't let him do this, Penelope. Go tell him, once and for all to fuck off."

I hesitate.

"I'll go with you."

I nod, forcing myself to ignore the fear that's prickling along my skin. It feels strange to be afraid of

Matt, but here I am, walking on shaky legs as I draw closer to him. A phantom ache blooms along my wrist where he grabbed me.

He's holding a bouquet of red roses in his fist, and for the first time ever, I don't find the flowers to be beautiful. They make me sick to my stomach. Even after being jealous of everyone receiving them today at school, I am not flattered by his offer. I do not want them. With the memory of his vice-grip still fresh, I'm repulsed by him, and the flowers he's holding.

When Matt sees me, he smiles. He actually looks, well. His tanned skin clear and his eyes bright. I hate to admit it, I really do, but sobriety looks good on him. *Why wasn't I enough to get sober for?*

Fear gives to anger. I glare at him with all the heat I can manage. "What the hell are you doing here?"

"I wanted to see you." He offers me the bouquet. "Happy Valentine's Day." He lifts the bouquet toward me, a peace offering. I don't make a move to take them.

Rainey, however, does. She shoves them away, practically knocking them from Matt's hand. "She doesn't want them. Why can't you take a hint? Been hit too many times in the head?"

Matt's eyes darken and dart to her. "Fuck off."

Rainey crosses her thin arms. "No."

I touch her arm, signaling to her I can handle this on my own. She purses her lips tight but keeps quiet. "You told me you were going to your dad's."

Matt's lips grow thin. "I did. But we realized we get along better when there's a few states between us."

"You lied to me. You made it sound like you were just going out to visit him. You never mentioned rehab."

"I wanted to surprise you. I thought once I was

sober, I'd come back, and things would go back to…you know…normal."

Rainey lets out an exhausted breath. He cuts a grim look at her.

I take a step closer to him, shielding Rainey from the wrath that is brewing within him. "Matt. We are over, remember?"

"I know," he says, the threatening expression in his eyes vanishing when he looks to me. "I just wanted to wish you a Happy Valentine's Day. What's wrong with that?"

I feel like I'm on a hamster wheel. This endless cycle Matt and I are on seems never-ending, and it's making me dizzy. "We aren't together anymore."

He grinds his teeth. "I know! Damn! You keep saying that like I don't know! Penelope, I know I screwed up. I'm getting clean—"

"Why aren't you in rehab now?" I counter.

"I…I snuck out." He digs his toe at a hole in the parking lot. The soles of his sneakers grinding across some loose rocks.

My cheeks burn hot. "You what?"

He kicks a loose stone. It pings off the hubcap of a nearby truck. "It's no big deal. I'll go back. I just wanted to see you today. And give you these." He holds the bouquet out once more. "To let you know I still love you."

I snatch the bouquet from him. "You need to love yourself right now, Matt. When are you going to see that everything you love is gone because of Oxy? Wrestling? Me? Where is rock bottom for you?"

He glares at me, but his eyes are almost blank, as if my words are adrift in the wind before they ever reach his ears. I sigh, resigned to the fact that nothing I say will ever sink in. He has to do this on his own. "Go get yourself clean, Matt." I step around him and unlock my car.

Rainey comes with me, tossing her hair sassily as she passes Matt. We get inside and lock the doors. My hands are trembling so bad I can't even get the key into the ignition. Rainey is quick to help me, covering my hand with hers, steadying me.

"It's okay," she whispers. "You were awesome."

The engine starts with a rumble, and I take in a deep breath, too scared to look outside my window. Matt is still standing there, watching. I can feel him.

Rainey lets my hand go and sits back in her seat. "He's so damn creepy. Look at the way he's staring at you." She leans across me and yells, "Asshole!" The bouquet in my lap crinkles and crunches from her weight.

"Rainey!" I push her back to her seat. "Don't do that! He's not…stable." My wrist flares, reminding me of what Matt's capable of. Fear grips me once more, suffocating me. I slam my foot on the gas, backing out in a hurry. Matt slams a fist on the trunk.

I hit the brakes, gritting my teeth against the sound of tires squealing on the asphalt. Matt rears up on my window like a looming shadow, banging on the window so hard I fear he might bust it in. Against my better judgment, I roll the window down.

His face is twisted in agony as if I had just hit him with my car. "I don't know how to live without you, Penelope."

Pity is all I feel. I give him the slightest of smiles, and tell him delicately, "You'll learn to. I promise." I hand him the bouquet of roses and roll the window up. He stands unmoving, staring at me. I pull away, feeling ten feet tall. Before, I would have melted at the sight of a dozen roses from Matt, but I know there is no future with him, even if he sobers up.

He proved time and time again that I wasn't worth more than Oxy. Before, I may have lived with that, but not anymore. I know my worth and someday someone out there will know it, too. I won't have to prove it, or beg for them to see it. They'll already know.

Chapter 43

After I drop Rainey off at home, I head to the library. When I stroll inside, I notice it's busier than usual. Groups of homeschoolers occupy most of the tables. Varying in ages from kindergarten to middle school. They're chatting quietly amongst themselves, with books spread across the tables.

I scan the room but don't see Chase anywhere. I walk through the maze of bookshelves, searching for him. Surely, he's here already. He's always here before me. I touch my hair, wishing I had taken the time to smooth the flyaways before I came in.

I find him sitting on the floor near the graphic novel section, his long legs sprawled out in front of him. He senses me and looks up from the book in his hands. He greets me with that signature crooked smile of his, and it takes all of my concentration not to melt right here.

Today, he's dressed in a loose red and black checkered long-sleeved shirt over a black t-shirt with an anime character I don't recognize splashed across the chest. His jeans are nearly white at the knees from wear and fraying.

"Hey," I say as I settle onto the floor beside him. "What's with all the people here today?"

"Homeschool kids," he explains. "The moms meet here each week trying to socialize their kids." He shakes his head. "Again with the 3D friends."

"3D friends aren't all that bad." I knock his shoulder with mine. "Are we?"

"Nah. You're tolerable."

I laugh. "Thanks." I look at the toes of his sneakers, smiling at the doodles. "Nice drawings."

He follows my gaze. "Masterpieces, right?"

"Heck yeah. True works of art," I tease. "What are they exactly?" I squint at them, making out the bow and arrow again. I saw them during our group meeting once.

"It's all my favorite things," he says, drawing his knees up. He points to the toe with the words BAM, KA-POW, BANG. "Comics, obviously." His lips curve into a youthful smile. His blue eyes trail over the other toe, where the bow, target, and arrow are. "Archery. When I'm not playing Dark Tenets—" he breaks off to shoot me a sly grin and sarcastic roll of the eye. "I'm actually outdoorsy."

"You shoot?"

"Yeah." He straightens his legs, crossing them at the ankles.

"I've always wanted to learn."

"Really?" His tone lifts with excitement. "I could teach you. I'm a regular Robin Hood."

"Or Nocked Blade," I add. A smile of satisfaction pulls at my lips at my newfound knowledge of comic book heroes. He doesn't know I've been studying up on them. I'd hoped to impress him with it, and by the size of his smile, I think it worked.

His thick brows lift. "Whoa. Look at you busting out the DU knowledge!"

I chuckle and glance around the aisle. We're alone and with the towering bookshelves around us, it's like we're trapped in our own little world right here.

"How was school?" Chase questions, closing the cover to the graphic novel he was reading.

"Fine," I say with a heavy sigh, reluctant to recall Matt and his surprise visit. "How was home?"

"Fine," he mimics with the same weary sigh. I look at him sideways, studying his features, wondering what that means. With what's going on with his mom, there's no telling. He doesn't offer anything else, so I don't pry.

He lays the book on the floor between us. "I have something for you." He digs through his book bag and draws out a thin brown paper bag. It's covered in black sharpie drawings. He hands it to me, a shy smile on his face.

The bag crinkles softly in my hands. The drawings are cartoonish but really good. He is a fantastic artist, especially compared to the stick people I draw. I hold the bag in both hands. There's a sketch of me on it with big, exaggerated eyes. I'm balancing a stack of books, all classics. There's a bubble over my head saying, "Stay classy."

Behind me, zooming away in a cloud of dust, is Chase dressed as the Teleporter. He's the size of a dime in the distance, as if he's running away from me and my offer of classic novels. I try to suppress a laugh by covering my mouth with my hand, but it's no use. A bark of laughter escapes me, ringing off the quiet air of the library.

He looks pleased. "Happy Valentine's Day, Penelope."

My heart suddenly feels heavy within my chest. *He got me something for Valentine's Day?* I'm shocked still for a moment.

"Open it," he urges.

I reach into the bag. My fingers brush against a glossy cover of a book. I slide it out. It's a comic book: Double Dimension #2. The Teleporter is encircled by a dozen or more identically cloaked figures menacingly advancing toward him. Somehow this is better than a single Rotary Club rose. Hell. It's even better than a dozen roses.

With Chase this close to me, and with his denim blue eyes holding me like a tender embrace, I forget all about my earlier jealousy of the cheerleaders. I forget all about Matt and his attempt to lure me back into his web. I had every reason to think this is the worst Valentine's Day in history, but it's as if those things never happened.

Gazing at Chase, with his long bangs swept into his eyes and holding the comic book between my fingers, my heart beats in a frenzy. Dreamily, I think to myself, *this is the best Valentine's Day ever.*

We forget all about tutoring. Instead, we talk. We talk about this, and that, and everything in between. After a while, I get the urge to tell Chase about Matt. I gaze at him, framing how to start.

Chase gives me a funny look. "What?" He rubs a finger under his nose. "Do I have a hitchhiker?"

"No," I say with a roll of my eyes. I reach up and thread a strand of hair around my finger. "I want to tell you something."

He sits up straighter, his face serious. "What is it?"

"The reason I'm in group."

He clears his throat, clearly uncomfortable. "I know why you're there. I was there the night you shared, remember?"

"Yeah." I look down at the comic book in my lap, talking more to it than Chase. "But there's more. That I didn't share. Matt—my ex-boyfriend—he is…hard to shake."

His brows furrow. "What do you mean?"

"He won't give up on us. No matter what I do. He's in rehab—for OxyContin—and he snuck out today to see me. He showed up at school and tried to give me flowers." I glance up at him. "I didn't take them."

His face stills.

"I've made it very clear that I want nothing to do with him, but he keeps trying. I don't know what else to do."

"When you first found out about him using. How did you react?"

I frown as I think back. "Well, at first, I was angry. And disappointed."

"And then?"

My cheeks flush with shame. "Then I felt bad for him. I thought I could help him. Hell, I even stole the prescription pad for him. But then, he stole from me." For the first time, my eyes grow moist as I recount how Matt stole my beloved Preston book and how it's rotting away at some pawn shop somewhere. I even tell him about Matt grabbing me by the wrist, hurting me physically for the first and last time.

Chase is quiet through it all. Only his hands move as I speak, clenching and unclenching in his lap. When I'm through, I wipe away the tears from my eyes and sniff.

He lays a hand on my knee. "You showed him kindness, Penelope. Compassion. That's why he won't give you up. When someone empathizes with you, you remember that you're human. And you're the only person who makes him feel worthy, so he's hanging onto that. You make him remember who he is—without the drugs."

He makes sense. "I tried so hard to get Matt the help he needed. I tried offering to go to therapy with him. I gave him a dose of tough love. I tried to love him through it, but I wasn't enough."

"You are enough," he says vehemently. "You, Penelope, are more than enough. Matt wasn't able to see that." He takes a calming breath, but refuses to unlock his fierce gaze. "But you want to know what I see?" His eyes bore into me, and I stare back at him, too dumbstruck to talk.

"I see a girl who gave her love to the wrong guy. I see a girl who needs someone worthy of her. Someone who will worship the ground she walks on and who would trap the very air she breathes if it were possible. Someone who won't just say I love you, but will make her feel it. Every single day."

My mouth opens to respond, but I'm speechless. My eyes skim the bookshelf, reaching up and up to the tiptop. Vertigo threatens to overwhelm me, but I close to my eyes to ward it off. My heart has worked itself up to my throat, and every part of me is vibrating as if I'm electrified.

His voice is dull when he asks, "Do you love him?"

My eyes snap open. He regards me thoughtfully, waiting for an answer.

"No." It came out so easy, so sure. "I mean, I did," I quickly add. "Or at least, I thought I did. But now, I know it wasn't real."

The tension in him wears off. "How do you know that?"

"Because he never made me feel any of those things you just said." I lean closer to him, my gaze falling onto his lips. I've never wanted anything so much. Before I lose the courage, I swoop in and press my mouth to his.

He kisses me back, and in no time, I'm floating up and up until I'm on cloud nine. His kiss is sweet and tender, and he tastes like bubble gum. When we break apart, I smile at him, suddenly shy.

"Wow," he says. "That was unexpected."

"Was it?" I reach for my braid, mindlessly twirling it in my fingers.

"Yeah. Normally, in the comics, the kiss comes after a fight scene or a harrowing rescue."

I flick my eyes at the comic book. The Teleporter is struggling in what looks to be a very climactic scene. "Who says neither of those didn't happen?" I raise my eyes to his. "After what I've been through with Matt, I'd call this my harrowing rescue."

Chase cups my chin. "Yes. But in this story…you, Penelope Reza, rescued yourself."

Chapter 44

Jenna and I are perusing our favorite book sale at the library. It's held twice a year, and we usually make an entire day of it. We fill our canvas tote bags with books, then fill our stomachs cheesecake from Ragamuffins.

The books are all used—donated by the public or retired from the library's inventory. Everything is pretty cheap, so Jenna and I usually walk away with bulging tote bags and armloads of books by the time we're done.

Today is no different. Jenna is struggling with her heavy tote bag, exchanging it from one weary shoulder to the other. She catches me watching.

"I swear to Tolkien, I am going to bring wheeled luggage next time…"

I let out a breath of laughter. The air smells of old, long-forgotten books, and perfume. The elderly lady near me reeks of something musky, yet floral. I feel as though I may choke on it. Backing away from her, I wander to the sci-fi section.

The book sale is held in the Joseph Salvador Meeting room. The same room where my co-addict support group meets. This isn't new; the book sale is always held here, but now the room takes on a new meaning. I feel uneasy, and watched in this room. Like it's harboring my secret, and at any moment it's going to do a grand reveal to everyone here. It also makes me think about Chase.

I think about what he's doing, whether he's alone or watching his mother drink herself into a drunken stupor. I think about his eyes, those deep as the ocean eyes, and my heart skips a beat. I still can't believe I kissed him. And he kissed me back. My insides grow hot just thinking about it.

"How about this one?" Jenna holds up a thin romance novel with a severely battered cover. "It sounds interesting." She flips through it. "It's a standalone, so that's good. No long-term commitment." She looks up at me and grins, waiting for me to give her the green light to add the book to her already bulging bag.

I give a little shake of my head. "Nah." I pick through the stacks, brushing my fingers along the spines as I read. Nothing catches my eye. I notice a volunteer straightening up the books. "Do you have any graphic novels? Or comic books?" The woman thinks a moment, her eyes skimming across the room at the hundreds of books around us. Finally she says, "No, I'm sorry. I don't think we do."

I frown. "Okay, thanks anyway."

Jenna comes up to me. "Are you seriously not going to buy *anything*?"

I lift a shoulder with indifference. She touches the back of her hand to my forehead. "Are you ill?"

I swat her away. "Remind me again why I keep you around?"

She leans in close with the biggest, cheesiest smile plastered across her face. "Because you love me." She bats her eyes dramatically.

Chuckling, I say, "You're lucky I do, or I would have kicked you to the curb a long time ago."

She *tsks*. "Right. Let's not forget who rescued who."

She gives me a pointed look.

She's right. If it wasn't for her, I'd probably be eating my lunches alone every day. The Jacksons had just moved to Charlotte from Concord, forcing me to change school districts. When I arrived at Reedmont, I didn't know a single person.

I remember standing on quaking legs, watching the rush of students go by. I had no idea what to do first. Find my locker? Find my classroom? Run to the nearest bathroom and cry? That seemed like the clear choice, but I must have looked completely lost because it wasn't long before Jenna walked up to me with an armload of textbooks.

She had on a sweet seersucker dress with a keyhole collar. Her beat-up beige sneakers were fraying at the toe. Her hair was swept into a high ponytail with a handful of pencils sticking out of it like a pincushion.

"Hi," she said, cocking her head to the side. "New here?"

"Yes," I stammered.

She shifted her stack of books to her hip, her emerald eyes raking over me. I stared back at her, too nervous to speak. Finally, she said, "Come on" before whirling around and walking away. She didn't have to tell me twice. I kept pace with her, and the rest is history.

"Well," Jenna says to me, fumbling with the straps of her tote bag. "If you're not going to get anything, then let's roll. I'm starving." She hobbles to the checkout, clutching her lumpy bag close.

I wait for her outside. March afternoons are such a tease of springtime yet to come. The temperatures warm to a pleasant degree and robins are returning from their migration. The sun is blazing overhead. I can almost shed my corduroy jacket, but not just yet.

My eyes are drawn to the brickwork of the library building, recalling Chase and the way he casually leaned against it. *Why do I keep thinking about him?* I tell myself it's because I'm at the library, where his ghost is everywhere.

Jenna emerges from the library, lugging her bag as if it weighs more than she does. I go to help her, plucking a few books from the tote bag to lighten the load some.

"Thanks," she puffs.

"No problem," I tell her. "Ragamuffin time?"

"Ragamuffin time," she mirrors with a grin.

****

We're finishing the last bites of our desserts; cherry cheesecake for me, tiramisu for Jenna, when Carlos comes through the door. His sneakers squeak on Ragamuffins' polished wood floor as he makes his way toward our table. Surprised, I put my fork down. "Carlos is here," I say to Jenna.

"I know," she replies around a mouthful of tiramisu. "I texted him." She doesn't even bother to turn around. She squirms in her seat. "God! This tiramisu is to die for!"

Carlos drops into a seat at our table. "What's up? How was the book sale?"

"Scored big," Jenna tells him, her eyes alight with her usual glee for books. She pushes her plate away and takes a long swig of her vanilla latte. When she sets her glass back down, she has a white frothy mustache from the latte's cinnamon foam.

"Cool," he says with a bob of his head. He takes a napkin and gently dabs Jenna's upper lip. They are so adorable together that I'm tempted to swoop them into a group hug.

His eyes slide to me. "What about you, Reza?" Carlos always reminds me of who I am. There's no denying my name when he's around. I used to hate that he called me by my last name. I'd cringe at the reminder that I wasn't a Jackson, like Mom or like Trip. A lone Reza in a house of Jacksons. But now, I'm growing more and more comfortable with it. Being Penelope Reza is not *that* bad.

"Came up empty," I grouse, picking at the remaining crust of my cheesecake.

"Which is so not like her," Jenna chimes in, setting her elbows on the tabletop. She gives me a long, appraising look. "What's going on with you, Pen?"

I drag my fork into lazy loops around the plate, unable to look her in the eye as I say, "Matt."

Silence hovers over our table.

I glance up to find Carlos and Jenna exchanging a harried look. *They think I miss Matt.*

My cheeks flood with heat. "It's not like that," I mumble, dropping my fork with a clatter.

Jenna spares a pitying look. "You sure about that?"

Shoving my plate away, I spat, "Yes! We are over. There's no going back from what he did to me."

"Rainey told us what happened." Carlos cracks his knuckles. "Boy better stay away from you or he's asking for a beatdown."

Jenna cuts her eyes to Carlos. "From who?"

"Me," Carlos retorts with a click of his tongue.

Jenna scrunches up her face. "You remember he's on the wrestling team, right?"

"Was," I correct. "Was on the wrestling team."

Carlos continues as if I never spoke. "Who cares?

That just means he knows some fancy wrestling moves. Doesn't mean he can actually fight. Especially the way I tangle."

"Tangle?" Jenna all but laughs in Carlos' face. If I wasn't convinced Matt would stomp Carlos into the ground, I'd laugh too, but since I've seen his rages firsthand, I know what he's capable of.

"There aren't going to be any beatdowns," I say, trying to change the direction of the conversation. "Matt knows better than to try anything again. I made it clear that we were over."

Jenna looks doubtful. "You made it clear *before*."

That stings a little, but she isn't wrong. I learned the hard way that you can't change anyone. You can influence them. You can direct them. You can cheer them on. But you cannot change them. They have to do that for themselves.

"This time is different," I mutter stubbornly.

She gazes at me like, *sure,* but only lifts her latte to her lips.

"I'm serious." I'm practically pleading for them to believe me, but to be fair, my track record isn't that great. I swore after he asked me to steal for him, after he broke my heart and walked away for Oxy that I was done. That I wouldn't allow him to hurt me again.

Jenna cocks her head, her dark eyes taking me with quiet measure.

"You got to believe me," I say, imploring. "I've grown a backbone."

Her brow arches high. "Have you?"

I swallow, thinking back to Trip standing over Mom. How small she looked, cowering beneath him. The white-hot anger that burned through me, and how my reserve seemed to harden. I knew then how much like her I truly was, and how badly I wished to change that.

"You'll see," I say to her and Carlos. They'll see. They'll see a new Penelope Reza.

"I believe you," Carlos says, adjusting his ball cap. He flattens the bill, pushing it high on his forehead. "But I'll still tangle with him if he tries anything funny." He puts his fists to his temples, index fingers pointed up. "Dude, don't want this bull's horns."

That brings a giggle to my lips, and suddenly the air around us shifts into something lighter. Jenna laughs and swats at him playfully. "You are so ridiculous." She checks her watch. "Oh shoot. I got to go work." She turns to Carlos. "Take me to Puffins?"

Chapter 45

I'm meeting Chase at his place today after school. He's finally going to teach me how to shoot a bow. I'm surprised at how excited I am. I've never been athletic, but ever since I discovered Artemis as a child, I've been eager to learn how to wield a bow like the Greek Goddess herself.

This morning, I took the time to weave my thick hair into a side braid. I paired olive-colored leggings with leather boots to complete the Goddess look. I'm hoping the effort isn't lost on Chase. I doubt he's read any Greek mythology, but maybe he's at least seen her in a few movies.

I leap from my desk the moment the final bell rings. As soon as I can break off from the crowded halls, I dart through the EXIT doors. The glare of the sun blinds me momentarily. I squint against it and take a second to adjust to the bright light. My book bag slaps hard against my back as I pump my legs into a run.

Jenna and Carlos know about my archery lesson, so they don't bother looking for me in the parking lot. I see Carlos' bright yellow car way off in the distance, shining like a tiny sun gleaming amongst the parked cars. I don't see Carlos, though. He probably has detention for leading the class in a belched version of the alphabet song or whispering one too many "that's what she said" in biology again.

Students are trickling out into the parking lot, but I'm way ahead of most. With excitement fueling me, I could almost put the track team to shame. I have to ask myself, is it the archery lesson I'm excited for, or is the opportunity to spend time with Chase?

As soon as I pull into Chase's driveway, the familiar sensation of jittery butterflies taking flight in my stomach tells me the answer. It's Chase. It was always Chase, and it will *always* be Chase. He must have been waiting by the window because he's already striding across the yard toward me.

His t-shirt of choice today looks to be from a gaming store bargain bin. A blinding neon cotton tee with giant overlapping pixelated dinosaur heads. I kill the engine and step out of the car, shading my eyes. "My eyes! Oh, my eyes!" I grope the air around me. "Chase? Is that you?"

"Such a comedian," he laughs, grabbing my outstretched hands and giving them a gentle squeeze. His gaze sweeps down my body, and I notice a hint of a smile playing on his lips.

"What?" I demand playfully. "Is it too much?"

"No," he says, shaking his head and hiding a grin.

"Do you even know who I am?"

"That chick from the hemorrhoid commercial?

I gape at him. "I should punch you."

He openly laughs now. I love his laugh. It's one of those laughs that has a lot of *tsks* in it, which makes it not only irresistible but also contagious. When his laugh finally tapers off, he looks at me with a mischievous twinkle gleaming in his deep blue eyes.

Still holding my hands, he grows more serious and says, "I'm kidding," he says, giving a wink that makes me grow weak in the knees. "I know a Greek Goddess when I see one."

He knows Greek mythology. There's a warmth in my tummy and it's oddly distracting.

I blush and pull my fingers away. He frowns a little, but doesn't say anything. I peer around him to look at his house. "Is anyone home?"

"My mom, but she's asleep." He strides across the lawn. "Come on." I follow him inside, where we pause long enough for him to turn off the television. The living room is cozy, with its dark brown walls and rich-colored furniture.

There's even a brick fireplace with a beautiful wrought iron screen pulled across it. Chase says they haven't lit a fire in years for fear that his mom will burn the house down.

He leads me through the kitchen, and out a sliding glass door that opens out to a big backyard encapsulated by a towering ten-foot privacy fence. The grass is well manicured, but worn in the center where he obviously does most of his practicing. A big circular target sits at least twenty paces from the worn sport. A pair of bows and two quivers lie across a patio table.

"I found my old bow." He lifts the smaller of the two bows from the table and tries to hand it to me. I don't make a move. It's black, with a neon orange grip. "I used it when I was a kid, so you should be able to draw it back."

"A kid bow?" I balk. "Do you think I'm weak?"

His brow arches. "Okay, Goddess. See if you can draw this one back." He grabs the other bow and passes it to me. It looks nothing like the tiny one he tried to offer me. It's wooden, without the fancy wheels and contraptions of the other, and it stands almost as tall as I do.

The bow is solid in my hand, but it's only when I raise it in the air do I feel its true weight. My arm shakes a little as I hold it. Chase smirks at me, crossing his arms over his chest, watching and waiting. I curl my fingers around the string and pull. It doesn't move.

I pull harder, my muscles burning with effort. I try to sound indifferent when I say, "I'll take the kid one." I offer him the bow back. He only chuckles, exchanging the heavy bow for the smaller one.

"This is a long bow," he tells me, gesturing to it. "Yours is a compact bow. See the gears here?" He points to what looks like a metal wheel or pulley on either end of the bow. "They're called cams, and they help you draw back the bow smoothly. Go ahead and give it a try."

I lift the compact bow, relieved to find it light and easier to grip. I wrap my fingers around the string and pull back. Although it's not as tough as the longbow, I'm still surprised by how much effort I have to put into it.

"Whatever you do, do not let go of the string. Just hold it there. Feel the tension of the string." He steps closer. "Now, slowly release the tension. Good. Now, let's nock an arrow and let one fly." He picks up a quiver of arrows and plucks one out. He runs his fingers over the feathered wings.

"These are called fletchings. And see this notch?" He taps at the center of the fletchings. "It's the nock, and that's where it will attach to the string. Here, give it a try."

I fumble with it at first. Readying a bow is not as easy as others make it look. I finally settle on a comfortable position, and carefully fit the string into the nock.

He scrutinizes my work. "Make sure you feel it click into place." He comes up behind me. My body responds by going all tingly. "Now, let's draw it back."

I raise the bow, holding the arrow between my fingers as I draw the string. He reaches around me and gently guides my arms into position. His touch weakens me, and I fear I might launch the arrow by accident. I swallow and focus on the target ahead.

"Look down the arrow and aim it just over the bullseye. When you're ready, just let go. It's that easy."

"Just let go," I repeat, peering down the shaft of the arrow. It looks just about dead on, so I take a breath before releasing my grip on the string. The arrow lets loose and soars like a miniature rocket through the air. It sinks into the target. Nowhere near the bullseye, but who cares! At least it hit the target! I shriek in delight.

"Good job!" He scoops me into a hug. His cheek brushes against mine. "You're a natural."

"Again," I say. He puts me down, and I snatch another arrow from the quiver. He smiles at me indulgently. I end up sending half a dozen arrows soaring over the target, two straight into the grass in front of me, and somehow land two into the target. By the time I nock the last arrow, my arms feel like mushy pudding.

"Final arrow. This one is going into the bullseye."

I lift the bow. My muscles scream in protest, but I ignore it. I sight in the bullseye and take in a deep breath. *Channel your inner Artemis.* I let the arrow fly. A second later, the arrow sinks deep into the outer edge of the bullseye. Not dead-on, but I'll take it!

He kisses my forehead. "Well done, Grasshopper."

"That was amazing! If my arms weren't Jell-O right

now, I'd keep shooting."

"No time. We got to get going. We don't want to miss group." He takes the bow from me and puts it on the table with his longbow.

Oh, right. Group. "Do you think I still need group?" I toe at the grass. "I mean, I think I'm good now. Besides, Matt's the reason I had to go in the first place."

He turns away from me. He doesn't say anything in reply, so I feel obligated to fill the silence. "I mean. If I hadn't dated him in the first place, I wouldn't have stolen that prescription pad, and I wouldn't have been forced to attend group therapy."

The tension in his shoulders is visible. "Matt. Me. Joe Blow, it doesn't matter." He finally faces me. "You have a co-addict personality, Penelope. It's *your* flaw, not whoever you're dating's flaw. Just because I don't ask you to do the things Matt did doesn't make you less of a co-addict."

My neck flushes. I don't like where this is going. He notices and puts his arms around me. "I just don't want you to get caught up in another situation like you did with Matt."

"But you won't ask me to do what he did," I say into his chest. "You're different."

Chase pulls back. We're staring at one another. His blue eyes hard and intense. My gaze is searching and blurring with tears. "No. I wouldn't. But if I did, I would want you to tell me to fuck off."

We stay locked in an exchange that doesn't need words. He isn't going to let me miss group. He thinks I'm the problem. He thinks I'm weak. My eyes drift to the longbow lying on the table. How hard it was to pull it back, no matter how hard I tried. No matter how badly

I want that string to bend to my will, I was not enough to do it. My thoughts wander to Matt. I wasn't enough for him either. He was just like the bow. Strong, unyielding, and unwilling to bend, Matt will have to fight his battle alone. I rub my eyes. "Let's go to group."

Chapter 46

I'm glad Chase persuaded me to go to group last night. Judith shared that her son is about to hit his one-year anniversary of sobriety. She's planning to take him to Oko's Hibachi House to celebrate. She even bought a new dress to wear. If people could really burst from pride, she would have been confetti. She had the biggest smile on her face all night.

Of course, Sam was late again. He apologized as he always does, complaining that work kept him late. Chase told me his dad wasn't really a flake. Whenever his boss asks him to stay late, or pick up someone else's shift, he does it without hesitation. Some of it has to do with his timid nature, but it's mostly because he wants the overtime. Being the sole provider, he is always trying to bring home more money for his family.

Chase shared last night as well. He shared he was worried he was going to either become an addict, or a co-addict.

"Either way, I'm doomed," he said.

"You can't dwell on that thinking," Mr. Mathers told him. "Everyone has a family member with less-than-ideal habits or behaviors. If everyone obsessed on what they *might* be, they miss out on who they *are*."

I think about that as I drive to Chase's house. People are easily influenced. I've lived with Miranda for ten years, and in that time, I've learned to mimic her co-addict nature. But what about the rest of me? Where did that come from? Is that truly me, Penelope, or is that a remnant of my biological mother? Or what about my father? A man I never knew, and doesn't even have a first name, but who is he? What's he like? Am I anything like him?

Before I can overthink anything of this, I pull into Chase's driveway. He isn't waiting outside for me today. I walk up to the front door and ring the doorbell. No one answers. I take out my phone and text him.

As I wait, I look around. The porch is a shadow of a once homey area. Dozens of old terracotta pots sit filled with dried dirt. The flowers that were once within them long gone. At least someone took the time to remove them, rather than leaving them withered in the pot. A wooden swing sways sadly in the breeze. The white paint peeling off the armrests. The cushions sun-faded and beginning to spot from mildew. No one has sat there in ages.

I ring the doorbell again, taking a step back to peer into the window. The curtain is drawn, so I can't see inside. The front door knob suddenly turns, and Chase cracks open the door. His mouth is screwed tight, and his downcast eyes are ringed with dark circles. He's wearing a black Teleporter zippered hoodie over an "X" League t-shirt.

"Hey." He steps outside and shuts the door behind him.

"Everything okay?"

"Bad day."

"Has to be for you to commit such a sin." I'm trying my best to take his mind off whatever just happened inside. It works for a split second. Chase's eyes swing to mine, the look of alarm coloring his sweet face.

"What?"

I motion to his clothes. " 'X' League and DU? Don't you know those two clash?" I cluck my tongue. "What a fashion faux pas."

He smirks and zips his hoodie up to his chin. "My apologies. I forgot I'm dating a comic expert."

"I prefer, com-oisseur." He blows out a great laugh, briefly turning his dull, tired eyes into the piercing, bright eyes I know. I watch him as he idly wanders the porch. He is restless with energy. "What's going on?"

He pauses, hanging his head. "March eighteenth. That's what."

"That's tomorrow," I say. "What about it?"

He leans his back against the porch's wooden post and stuffs his hands into his pockets. "Anniversary of my aunt's death. Mom used to only get this way on the eighteenth. Guess she's getting a head start this year." He lifts his face. I have never seen him look so defeated. "I shouldn't have let you come today, but I didn't expect her to be like this. Not today."

I move to be near him. "Do you want me to go?"

"No," he whispers. I slip my arms around him, linking my hands around his neck. The wind blows through a wind chime, sending it tinkling sweetly in the air. I shiver against him, wishing I was wearing my peacoat instead of a flimsy sweater.

He unzips his hoodie and opens it wide. I nuzzle in it as far as I can, tucking my arms against his chest. His body heat soon warms me like Mom's homemade chicken noodle soup. Our foreheads touch.

"Then I won't." We stay like that for a while, just breathing each other in, lost in our small, self-made cocoon. We're interrupted when the front door suddenly jerks open. Chase's mom stands in the doorway, swaying like the wind chimes over our heads, only she isn't making sweet music. She's thundering, red-faced, and slurring.

"Mom," Chase stammers, unlocking his arms from around my waist.

She blinks, trying to place me. With her inebriated state, she probably wouldn't recognize me even if we had met before.

"Hello, Mrs. Monroe. It's nice to meet you."

She squints so hard she looks like she's staring directly into the sun. "Who are you?"

"Mom, this is Penelope."

She fumbles for the doorjamb, gripping it to remain upright. "You his girlfriend?"

I blush.

"Mom, go back inside." He steps around me and gently takes her by the arm. She yanks free.

"No. I've been inside all day. I want some fresh air." She stumbles onto the porch, lurching for the porch swing. Chase is quick to help her. She falls heavily onto it. The swing creaks like the bones of an old man. I think of Mr. Bower and how he complains of knee and hip pain, especially before a rainstorm.

Mrs. Monroe is petite, probably no more than five feet tall. Her hair is piled into a messy top knot. Long bangs are held back with a white elastic headband, accentuating her deep-set brown eyes.

"It's too cold to be out here without a coat," Chase scolds.

She only swings. Pacing herself into a hypnotizing repetition. Back and forth. The swing creaking with each movement. Back and forth. Creak. Creak.

He gives up. "I'll go get it." He disappears inside the house, leaving me alone with her.

"You go to school?"

"Yes ma'am. Reedmont High."

She nods exaggeratedly. "Good school. Good school. Do you cheer?"

I balk. "No."

Distantly, she says, "I did. It was so fun." She smiles faintly. "I was a flyer. Know what that is?"

"Is that the girl that they toss in the air?"

"You got that right, sister." She tries to get to her feet, but the momentum of the swing makes her unsteady. When she collects herself into somewhat of a standing position, she breaks into a slow-motion cheer routine. "P-I-N-E-Y Piney Pirates gonna make you cry." She sways on her feet, giggling like she's back in school again. When our eyes meet, she turns serious. "Piney Ridge High. We were undefeated." She lets out a whoop.

Chase returns, holding a white cardigan. He wraps it around her shoulders. His gaze jumps to me, a nervous twitch in them that makes my heart squeeze with sympathy. He's on edge around her, scared of what she may say or do next. I felt that way around Matt when I knew he was using Oxy. It would make him unpredictable, volatile even.

"Mom, why don't you go inside? It's cold out here. I'll make you some tea." It's sweet how tender he is with her. I know he's angry with her, disappointed in what she's become, but he's careful not to show it. She lets him guide her to the door, but before she retreats inside, she turns to me.

"Night, Penny."

Chase is quick to correct her. "That's Penelope."

"Close enough," I say with a smile. "Good night, Mrs. Monroe."

"Call me Grace." She grins crookedly, her eyelids more weighted than before. She gives me a parting sloppy wave and staggers inside.

"Be right back," Chase says to me.

I nod and take a seat on the porch swing. I watch the wind chimes clatter, enjoying their pretty song. Chase is gone just long enough for my mind to wander to Matt. *Is he clean yet?* I used to think I didn't care if he ever got clean, but the truth is, I do.

Sober Matt is an awesome person, and as toxic as we are together, I hope he finds himself again. He deserves to be happy. And so do I. And Chase makes me happy. Happier than I ever was with Matt.

The front door closes and Chase steps onto the porch. "Sorry about that."

"It's all right. She was nice." I slide over so he can sit beside me. He takes the invitation, stretching out his long legs in front of him. I notice his shoes have some new art. I point to them. "What's that?"

The corner of his mouth tugs into a smile. "Remember when I said they were my favorite things?" He pulls his foot out of his shoe, and holds it up.

The word POW had been altered, the letters re-formed to spell REZA. Tiny black hearts surround it. My eyes lift to meet Chase's. We both smile. My heart feels too big for my chest.

"I'm touched," I say, glancing back down at the name I'd been hating for so many years. The way he wrote it, like beautiful graffiti, made me see it differently. Made me see for what it is. It is me. Reza is who I am. "I'm immortalized forever."

"All hail the mighty Sharpie," he says, slipping the shoe back on his foot. "For they wield all the power!"

We laugh as the swing lulls us into a steady motion. He drapes an arm around me. We forget all about archery. We forget all about group. We just swing in silence, enjoying the moment of us, being *us*. Chase Monroe and Penelope Reza.

Chapter 47

Chase promised me an extra archery lesson this week, so I take my time dressing for school this morning. I settle on a heavy wool sweater and brown knit leggings tucked into fuzzy warm boots. I layer thermal underwear beneath my clothes to starve off any shivers the crisp evening air might bring. My stomach is giddy with excitement for the lesson.

Archery is so much fun, and it's a good upper-body workout too. I never realized how much strength you had to have just to draw back a bow. Mom was suspicious at first, thinking I was only interested in it because of Chase.

No, I remember thinking. *I'm not you. I don't mold myself into others.* I remember when Wesley took up golf. It was a short-lived hobby, thank goodness. Mom swore she enjoyed it, but I could tell how miserable she was whenever he made her go with him. Once, she asked me, "Why does golf have eighteen holes? Isn't eight enough?"

I have some time to kill before class starts, so I slip out my phone and text Chase.

—*How's your mom?*— The little dots indicating he's responding appear.

—*Passed out after you left. Was down for the count all night.*—

—*That's good. Right?*—

Dots.

Dots.

—The early bird gets the worm. The tequila worm in this case.—

I groan. Poor Chase. Today is the anniversary of his aunt's death, which means Grace is drinking more heavily today, trying to numb her ongoing depression. I think about that. For Grace, losing her sister was too much for her to bear.

Grief is consuming, overwhelming, and insistent. The only way she knows how to escape its chokehold is to self-medicate with alcohol. And today, she'll drink until she blacks out. Every year, Chase and his dad prepare for this day.

They hover over her, watching and waiting for the moment they have to catch her before she falls. So they can carry her to bed and tuck her in, praying she sleeps it off by morning. I chew my lip, staring at the phone screen, wishing I could be next to him right now.

I type, *—I'm sorry—*

—Me 2—

—See u later?—

—It's a date.—

I put my phone on silent and bend to slip it back into my book bag. Someone plunks down on the desk in front of me. When I sit back up, my jaw drops.

"Matt. You're back." He looks more like the Matt I remembered. Gone are the gaunt, sharp-lined cheeks. Gone are the bloodshot eyes. Gone is the pale, sickly skin. Today he's clean-shaven, his dark hair slick as oil grease neatly combed back.

He holds my gaze, a feeble smile on his lips. "They let me out on good behavior."

"Really?"

"No," he huffs. "God, Penelope. You're so fucking gullible." I take notice of his leg shaking with nervous energy.

I swallow a thick lump in my throat. Part of me wants to change seats, or even shove myself backward an extra foot or two, just to put space between us. But I don't do either. I sit rooted, conflicting thoughts silently screaming inside my head. *This is the boy who hurt you. He's changed. He's trying. Give him a chance.*

"My stint at rehab is done as long as I agree to attend weekly therapy, monthly meetings with my case manager, and random drug tests at the request of my asshole father." His thick brows furrow menacingly.

"He just wants you to get better," I offer meekly, running my sweaty palms over my leggings.

He shoots me a disgusted look. "Bullshit. If he cared so much, he would have visited me. I never saw the prick." His eyes wash over me, hard and probing as if he was trying to read me. "Never saw *you* either."

"Matt."

He lifts a hand. "Save it. I know we're not together anymore. But you could have come. As a friend."

I chew on that. I suppose I could have, but Matt wasn't the only addict in the relationship. I was addicted to Matt—no—I was addicted to the relationship. I was addicted to the high of being part of a couple.

The consuming feeling that someone *wanted* me. I needed to quit Matt—cold turkey. He put me through too much not to. How could he think we could be friends after what he did?

"We're not friends right now, Matt." Everything is still too raw. With the memory of our rocky past haunting me, I decide it is finally time to lay my relationship with Matt to rest. I couldn't ignore him forever, nor did I want to. I want him to get the help he needs. I want the old Matt back. Not for me, but for himself. "I'm proud of you for going to rehab. It shows how strong you really are." I hesitate, unsure of what to say next. Matt stares at me—his eyes almost hollow—lifeless.

I swallow, and continue, desperate to get everything out—to purge myself of the poison that had once been our relationship. "You were an important chapter of my life. A main character even, but instead of being the antagonist in my story, I want you to become the hero in your own." The weight of this pending discussion has felt like a chain around my ankle, and I carried it around for far too long. With it finally done, I felt liberated. Free of the Penelope of the past. That painfully chapter of my life is officially over. The end. I purse my lips to keep from saying anything else.

His dark eyes smolder, the rage inside him brewing like an incoming storm. I hold my ground, staring back at him firmly. He turns his back to me, and for the first time ever, I'm okay with that.

When I pull into Chase's driveway, I'm surprised to see his dad's SUV there. He usually works well into the evening, getting as much overtime as his company will allow, so I hardly ever see him. Chase's mom is of course home, but she always home. Cooped up inside her bedroom, nursing her bottle of Vodka. I knock on the front door, surprised when it creaks open under my knuckles. *Weird.* I peek inside. The house is still.

"Hello? Chase?"

There's commotion upstairs. Heavy footfalls

pounding away overhead. Panic runs through me. It's March eighteenth. Dear God, what did Grace do? I step into the entryway and peer into the living room. It's empty. I close the door behind me, and stand at the foot of the staircase.

"Chase," I call. A sudden thundering of footsteps storm down the stairwell. It's Sam. Grace is folded like a broken doll in his arms. Her head lolls fluidly, and it's then I realize she's unconscious. My hand flies to my mouth. *Oh god! What's happened?* Chase is close on his dad's heels, his face stark white with worry. An ambulance siren blares in the distance, coming closer and closer until it's so loud I press my palms to my ears.

I scramble to get out of their way. "What happened?"

"Alcohol poisoning," Sam says, pausing to let Chase pass. Chase throws open the front door and Sam bursts out of the house, dashing toward the road. Chase runs along beside him. Grace's small body sways back and forth in Sam's arms. I hurry to keep pace with them.

The ambulance swerves into the driveway and stops short. EMS workers pour out, and meet us halfway. A stout man with a shaved head makes quick work of putting together a gurney. "Lay her down," he instructs. Sam gently lays Grace down on the gurney, taking care to smooth the hair from her face. A woman with a cool, koi tattoo on her wrist gets right to work, priming an IV as the man slides the gurney into the ambulance.

Sam climbs in after her. "I'll meet you at the hospital."

Chase nods, his eyes blown wide with fear. The ambulance door closes with a clang, stealing our view. The woman moves about, her head passing the small back window as she works to save Grace's life. The ambulance speeds away, sirens blaring.

Chase wrings his hands, watching after the ambulance.

"Come on," I say. "I'll drive you."

****

It takes three hours to stabilize Grace. The doctors had to perform what they called a hemodialysis. They explained it as sort of a fish tank filter system for Grace's blood. It will filter out the toxins and pump clean blood back into her body. Though they removed the alcohol, she still needs some TLC.

She'll stay overnight, hooked up to an IV and oxygen. Sam keeps vigilant at her bedside. Chase spent most of the time pacing the hospital hallways. He visited his mom once, but didn't linger. He couldn't stomach seeing his mom lying there, comatose in a hospital bed. Her skin had a sickly, yellow tinge to it, and it looked as brittle as parchment paper.

I was relieved when Chase told his dad that he was hungry, just so we could have an excuse to get out of there. Seeing his mom in that state reminded me of Matt when he OD'd. We head to the vending machines to get a bag chips, though I know neither of us plan to eat it.

I miss dinner, but Mom is quick to forgive me when she hears my reason why.

"Of all the nights for me to be off," she says. "Do you want me to come up there?"

"No," I answer with a yawn. "I'm good. She's doing better, so I think I might be heading home soon."

"Okay then. Well, you drive safe, and I'll see you soon. Love you, Honey."

"Love you too, Mom."

I hang up and look over at Chase, who has his head in his hands. I pat him on the back, wishing I could take away his pain. This is his worst nightmare coming true. He once confided in me that he felt alcohol was going to someday kill his mother. No doubt he felt that today was that day.

Grace is discharged two days later. Chase calls me during lunch with the good news. With his mom being sent home today, I can bank on Chase not questioning my cancelling of archery practice. I have an important errand to run after school. His birthday is next week, so I'm dragging Jenna and Carlos to the mall so I can shop for him.

****

"So, what does he like?" Jenna asks, running her hands along a rack of clothes. We're in a thrift store, just aimlessly browsing, hoping something pops out at me. "We hardly know this kid."

"Comic books. Archery. Nineties grunge."

Carlos rifles through a shelf of leather wallets. "Dude got a job?"

"No."

He abruptly stops looking. "Well, he won't be needing one of these then."

"He has to stay home to watch his mom," I explain. "His dad doesn't like her to be home alone."

Jenna crosses her arms. "What's with his mom anyway? Is she sick or something?"

Something like that, I think. I chew my lip, trying to think how I'll frame this. *My ex is an addict and now my new boyfriend's mom is an addict. At least he's not the addict, right?* My stomach twists. I haven't told Jenna about Grace. She knows I met Chase at group, but she has no clue that his mother is an alcoholic. I guess I haven't wanted to look her in the eye and see her disappointment.

Out of the fire, and into the pot, she'd say. Or something close to it. Jenna tends to be a bit judgmental, but she means well. She only wants what's best for me, and sometimes that more than I can say about myself.

"She…" I swallow on a dry throat. I lick my lips to try to moisten them. Every part of me feels brittle, like I'm about to crack. "She's an alcoholic."

Jenna's eyes grow round. "An alcoholic?" Carlos whistles low. "Pen. Do you really think that's a good idea? You know, being around *another* addict?"

"Chase isn't the addict."

"But his mom is. That's close enough."

Carlos drifts off, not wanting to be around for our tiff.

"He's not his mom," I counter. "It's unfair to compare them."

"I'm not comparing them. I'm just worried about you being mixed up with another messed up kid." Jenna is now talking with her hands, which means all hell is going to break loose.

I scowl. "Chase isn't messed up."

Jenna rolls her eyes. "He goes to group therapy doesn't he?"

My vision narrows, and I feel the anger rising in my gut. "I go to group therapy!"

Taken aback, Jenna blinks furiously. "Well. I didn't say you're messed up for crying out loud."

"You might as well have." I shoulder past her, my hands balled into clenched fists at my sides.

"Penelope, wait." She catches up to me and grabs

me by the arm. "I said wait."

I stop short. "What?"

"I'm sorry. I didn't mean that."

"Yes, you did. You think I'm a hot mess, don't you?" Feeling betrayed, my eyes well with tears.

"No, I don't," she says calmly. "I think Matt is a hot mess, and he just happened to drag you into it." I've heard enough. I start to walk away, but Jenna stops me.

"But I also know you're a fighter, Penelope. You're strong, and you're smart." She takes my hand, and holds it firmly. "Matt was just one chapter in your life and now you're on to the next. I want this chapter to be better than the last."

"It will. Chase is different."

"I'll be the judge of that. When can I meet him?"

Shrugging, I say, "I don't know. Whenever you want, I guess."

"The sooner the better. It's weird that I don't know my own best friend's boyfriend."

Carlos finds us again, grabbing a pocket-sized fart machine from the shelf. He mashes the buttons, simulating crude noises between his hysterical laughter.

"I'm buying this," he declares, wiping tears from his eyes.

Jenna plucks a pleated purple turban off the hat rack. It has a billowy peacock feather pinned to the front. She settles it onto her head, looking much like an eccentric carnival fortune teller. She presses her fingertips to her temples. "I foresee detention in the very near future."

****

After wandering the thrift store for another hour, we decide to go to Ragamuffins. As we wait for our order, I hit up my favorite on-line shopping site. I type *The*

Teleporter into the search bar. After scrolling through a dozen pages or so, I settle on a really cool Teleporter shirt for Chase and a butter-yellow Chuck West tee for me. Kind of cheesy, I know, but I think Chase will get a kick out of it. Chuck West is sort of the Teleporter's sidekick, so it's a silly interpretation of our comic book venture together. Never had I considered reading a comic book before Chase. I like that he pushes me out of my comfort zone.

Before I check out, I decide to one-click a copy of *Journey to the Center of the Earth*, by Jules Verne. The book practically invented the science fiction genre. I'm hoping Chase likes it.

I'm on my last bite of cheesecake when I get a call from Mom. She's hysterical on the other end, sobbing and gasping for air so terribly I can't make out a thing she's saying.

"Mom?" Terror floods through me, my head swimming drunkenly because of it. "Mom, calm down. I can't understand you. What's happened?"

Jenna and Carlos exchange glances. I jump to my feet. Jenna calls out, "Call me!" as I dash out of Ragamuffins, the phone pressed to my ear.

I sink into the seat of my car, my heart twisting as I listen to Mom cry on the other end of the line. "Where are you?" Between sobs, the words, "the hospital" finally eke out. My blood runs cold. *The hospital?* "I'm on my way!" I hang up and floor it.

I don't remember stopping at any stoplights, or even turning into the hospital parking lot, but I must have done all those things cause I'm running as fast as I can across the asphalt. I burst through the hospital doors, panting and frantic. I skid to a stop in front of the help desk.

"Have you seen my mom?" I ask Dorothy, the gray-haired volunteer at the desk. She looks up at me, her eyes big and glassy as marbles.

She shakes her head. "No, I'm sorry. Is something wrong?"

"I don't know. I…I have to find her." I whirl around and fling myself toward the elevators. I pound the first button I reach. "Come on!" It feels like hours before the shiny doors part with a ding, but in reality, it was probably only a few seconds. I hurl myself inside, nearly colliding with Nurse Ricter.

"Whoa," she says, blinking back at me.

I grab her by the arms, relieved I didn't knock her over, considering she barely stands five-foot tall. "I'm so sorry." Her sky-blue scrubs are a pretty compliment to her sun-kissed skin. Her thick brown hair is swept into a neat ponytail.

"Have you seen my mom?" I ask her.

Nurse Ricter's face falls, and I can tell she has bad news. "Third floor."

Third floor? That's where emergency surgeries are performed. Why is she there?

"Is she okay? I was just on the phone with her," I stammer.

Nurse Ricter lays her fingers on my elbow. A light touch, like a butterfly landing. "She's fine." Her eyes grow pitying. "It's Trip."

"Trip? What's happened? Is he all right?"

She swallows. "You need to go."

I follow her instructions, stepping into the elevator and gripping the handrails for support. Nurse Ricter walks away, and the elevator doors slide shut. *What's wrong with Trip?* I wonder, watching the floor numbers climb to the third floor.

When I emerge into the hallway, I glance both ways, searching for Mom. One hallway is empty, save for a nurse making her rounds. The other hallway is bustling with movement. Several nurses donned in surgical scrubs dart in and out of the farthest room. My chest burns, wondering if Trip is in there. *What's happened to him? Is he okay?*

Ahead of me is a waiting room. Mom is likely there, in pieces and sobbing. With feet like anchors, I push through the door, and I find her quickly. She's pacing the length of the room, hugging herself as if to keep herself from falling apart. Her face is blotchy, and her eyes swollen from tears.

I embrace her, pulling her close. Her slight shoulders shake as she wails into my neck. I hold her, letting her cry openly. It's only when she releases me to dab her eyes that I ask her what happened.

"Car accident." She pinches her eyes tight. "He hit a guard rail. They're telling me it's an act of road rage."

My hand goes to my mouth. You hear about road rage all the time, but to know someone who's actually been affected by it is sobering.

A couple of police officers shoulder into the waiting room. They make for an intimidating sight, with their crisp uniforms and biting handcuffs hanging from their hips. A broad-chested officer with thick arms and his partner, a tall man with cropped auburn hair, stride in toward us, their shiny badges wink from their chests.

"Mrs. Jackson?" The barrel-chested one greets somberly.

Mom wipes her nose. "Yes?"

The officers exchange a look. Something in the pit

of my stomach curdles like old milk.

The lean one takes out a notepad. "I'm Officer Childs and this is Officer Ray. We need to ask you a few questions."

Mom's watery eyes blink innocently. "Of course."

"Does your son have anger management issues?"

Mom looks aghast. "Excuse me?" She clutches her sweater to her throat.

"As you know, your son was involved in a road rage incident."

Mom swallows thickly, and nods. Understanding slams into me. Trip was the one with road rage, not the other way around. This makes more sense. Though, I wouldn't admit that to the officers. It's not my place.

I will Mom to say it. To admit to the officers what kind of person Trip is. How he berates and belittles her. How he tortured me throughout childhood, calling me names and degrading my nationality.

Mom's gaze shifts to me. I purse my lips, silently encouraging her to do the right thing.

The officer tries a different approach. "Bystanders report he side-swiped the other individual involved. Tossing obscenities out the window and driving recklessly. He lost control of his car and hit the guardrail."

Officer Ray cuts in. "We have a video taken from a witness. Do you wish to see it?"

Her sad brown eyes go steely. "No." She looks directly, almost defiantly, at Officer Childs. "My son is a good person."

I groan inwardly. *No, Mom, please. Don't do this. For once, face reality.*

Mom's voice breaks. "A good person lost, anyway."

She blows her nose. "But he does have a problem controlling his anger."

"Has he ever been to anger management?"

"No."

The tall officer scribbles something into his notepad. The waiting room door clicks open and in walks a weeping woman. Her blond hair looks unkempt, like she left the house in a hurry. She sinks into the nearest seat, crying into her palms.

"Excuse me," Officer Childs says before taking his leave. He heads to the woman. Their exchange is hushed, and I can't make out anything they're saying. It's obvious she's here for the victim.

Officer Ray furrows bushy eyebrows. "Mrs. Jackson, we will have to charge your son with assault and battery, and reckless driving. I suggest you pray the man he hit survives, or he'll be facing manslaughter charges, too." He stalks away, leaving me and Mom to digest his words.

Manslaughter? I regard the woman again. Her thin face is wet with tears, and her heart is clearly broken as she sits in the hospital waiting room, waiting. Waiting for news on her who? Her sister? Brother? Father?

I pull Mom down into a chair and put my arm around her. She's shivering like a wet cat. "Want some coffee?" I offer.

She doesn't answer me.

I squeeze her tighter. "Everything is going to be okay."

She pats my hand weakly. "I know."

I stand and leave to get her a hot cup of coffee. As I draw closer to the woman, I notice she's young, maybe early twenties. Her sweats are stylish, like the kind that have words like Diva or Princess across the butt. She looks worn and wrung out, so I know whoever she's here for is someone she deeply cares about.

I slip out of the waiting room and make my way to the complimentary coffee bar. I pour a cup, watching the steam swirl as I stir in two cups of creamer. The door to the surgery room clicks open. From the end of the hall, I stand rooted, watching Dr. Yassin step out, stripping out of his surgery scrubs.

He shoves them into the metal biohazard bin. He slams the lid shut. The force sends a resounding *clang* through the hall. He leans upon the lid for support, and it's then I know something bad has happened. Dr. Yassin hangs his head, defeated.

A fellow doctor walks by, pausing a moment to squeeze Dr. Yassin's shoulder in solidarity. I choke back a welling lump in my throat. *Something's wrong. Very wrong.* The fair-haired doctor slips away quietly, leaving Dr. Yassin alone.

Without thinking, my feet are on the move, slowly drawing me closer to him. He hears my footsteps and glances up, his dark eyes widening when he sees me.

"Penelope," he says, his voice raspy with anguish.

"Trip's gone, isn't he?"

He grimaces.

Tears pool at my eyes, and I sniff. "What happened?"

"Most of his internal organs were severed from the windshield. I couldn't save him. I tried." He dabs his eyes. "I tried. For him, for you, for your mother. I tried."

I throw an arm around him, pressing my cheek against his shoulder. "I know," I tell him through my sobs. "I know." He stands and we embrace. His arms a comfort around me. My soul sad for my mom. She's going to be devastated. First Wesley, now Trip. I'm all she has left.

"I have to tell Miranda," he says as we break apart. He scrubs a hand down his face. I've never seen him look so drawn. I can't help but think of all the people he's given bad news to. Terminal diagnoses, unsuccessful surgeries, and death. He likely handled them all professionally, with dignity, with respect and grace. But now, now he has to tell Mom—the woman he loves. It's obviously tearing him apart.

"I'll go with you," I tell him, taking him by the hand.

I hold my breath as Dr. Yassin pushes open the waiting room door. Mom's gaze jumps to us and she grips the armrests, her knuckles turning white.

Together, Dr. Yassin and I make our way toward her. With each step, my heart shatters more, until it's nothing more than powder. I'm hiccupping with strangled gasps by the time we're standing in front of her. Dr. Yassin drops to his knees before her.

"Miranda, I'm so sorry."

Mom lets out a tortured wail. "No!" He takes her hands, kissing her fingers and palm. "I'm so sorry. I tried." He collapses into her lap, wrapping his arms around her waist. She folds into him, and together they weep, a ball of tangled bodies and tears.

Behind me, the doors click open again, and in walks Dr. Ramone. She's a robust woman, with a blunt tongue and sassy attitude. She glimpses Dr. Yassin, her face colored with surprise. I'm sure it is a shock to see Dr. Yassin undone like this.

Dr. Ramone quickly composes herself and turns her attention to the other woman in the waiting room. They exchange words, and visible relief washes over the young woman. Her shoulders sag beneath her oversized sweatshirt, and she clasps her hands in a thankful prayer.

To my right is a woman relieved and given a second chance with her loved one. To my left is a woman grieving. A mother who will never see her son again. A wife who lost her husband. A woman who has unconditional love from an adopted daughter and an ex-boyfriend who still cares.

I pray to God it's enough.

Chapter 48

Alone, I go back downstairs and head outside. I need to get away from the hospital for a while. Away from the white walls, and sterile smell. Away from all the sickness, injuries, and sadness.

The sky is a slash of copper as dusk settles in. I stroll along the sidewalk mindlessly before drifting toward a patch of lawn that runs along the length of the hospital. It's landscaped prettily, with pansies and primrose. If you squint, and ignore the sirens from ambulances bustling back and forth, you could almost forget you were at a hospital.

I pull out my phone and call Chase. He answers with a chipper, "Hi-ya, Teach."

For a split second, I forget why I called. His voice brought a sudden smile to my face. I open my mouth to answer, and my happiness fades in an eye-blink. I remember why I called, and it's hard to say out loud. I clear my throat. Gripping the phone, I say, "Something bad happened."

"What?"

Before I can answer, he adds in a panicked tone, "Are you okay?"

"I'm fine." I frown at myself. *Am I fine?* I'm really not sure. Part of me is mourning for Trip, the other half isn't. The half that's mourning him hates the other for its indifference.

It's my brother, for God's sake. I should be torn up over his loss, but I can't find it in myself to do that. Trip hated me. He made my life hell for years. Not to mention how he treated Mom. He was downright nasty to her after Wesley died. "It's my brother, Trip. He was in an accident."

"Oh man. Is he all right?"

The lump in my throat grows, choking me.

"Penelope?" His voice is strained with worry.

"He's dead," I manage to say, pinching my eyes tight.

There's a beat of silence. "Oh, Penelope. I'm sorry. I'm coming. Just tell me where you are."

"Pointe Holden."

"I'm on my way." The phone goes dead, and I'm left standing listening to the silence.

****

Chase finds me in the waiting room with Mom. It takes her over an hour to even realize he's there. When her brown eyes register that Chase and I are sitting together—talking—she adjusts the collar of her sweater, and gives him a polite smile.

Chase looks at her sheepishly. "I'm sorry for your loss, Mrs. Reza."

Mom blinks at him with wide, glossy eyes.

"Oh, no," I tell Chase. "Reza is my last name. I'm…I'm adopted." I squirm in my seat, flustered to my ears with uncomfortable heat. Chase is shocked. His lips mouth an inaudible *whoa* as his cerulean eyes swing between Mom and me. Clearly, he sees the difference. Mom with her alabaster skin, and mousey brown hair and me with my dark skin, and thick ebony mane.

"It's okay," Mom says. "Reza, Jackson. Tomato

tamato. What difference does a last name make?" She tries to smile, but it's lost in her grief. She sniffs and brings a tissue to her nose.

My fingers entwine with his. Looking down into my lap, I murmur, "I'm sorry."

"For what?"

"You have your own stuff going on. I shouldn't have bothered you with mine."

He turns in his chair and cups my cheek in his palm. "Your stuff is my stuff now. You understand that?"

I nod pathetically. Tears threaten to let loose, but I hold them back. "How's your mom?"

Chase's hand slips away. "She's okay." Hope fills his eyes. "I think it might actually happen this time. She might actually quit."

"Really?"

"This scared her. She keeps telling me and Dad, she loves us and promises to change. She says she'll go to AA and everything. I've never seen her this way before. This might sound crazy, but I'm kind of glad it happened."

Dr. Yassin comes back and tells us it's time to go. Trip's body has been moved to the morgue and will soon be transported to Dirken's funeral home. Mom is again inconsolable. Dr. Yassin supports her weight as we make our way to the parking lot. Mom is clearly in no condition to drive, so we collectively decide to leave her car behind and have Dr. Yassin drive her home.

Chase offers to drive me, but it isn't necessary. I decline, telling him thanks, but I'll be all right. Chase walks me to my car, and though we stroll through the park lot at an achingly slow pace, we end up at my car sooner than I hoped.

We linger, both lost in our thoughts. What will Mom and I do now? The Jackson family is dwindling. Wesley's parents are long dead, and Mom's parents are in Utah.

Chase is the first to break the silence. "I didn't know."

I stare at him, unsure what he means.

"About you being adopted?" he prompts, shoving his hands into his pockets.

Oh, that. "Well, I never told you, so how could you?" He looks unsure of everything, like learning I'm adopted was an unexpected blow to him. I've gotten used to that look. I get it a lot from pure-blood kids. That's what I call biological kids. Kids whose DNA matches their families. When they learn I'm adopted, they look at me first with curiosity and then pity.

On rare occasions, I get a smart-ass who thinks it's funny to call me an orphan, but I can deal with those people. It's the people that stare at me with pity in their eyes I bristle under that stare. Just like I'm bristling under Chase's.

"I'm such a jerk," he says, pulling his hands free. He sits on the hood of my car, staring down at his hands.

"Why? Cause you didn't figure out that my porcelain *white* mom doesn't look like me?" I push up my sleeve. "If you haven't noticed, I'm not white."

He shoots me an annoyed look. "No. Because I used to wish I was adopted. I was always so angry with my parents a part of me hoped I was. That I had parents out there who loved me more. Parents who were sober, and there for me in ways my mom and dad weren't. Parents who were...I don't know..." He gives a half-hearted shrug. "Better than what I got, I guess."

I watch him struggle with himself, wanting to put my arms around him and hug him tight. When his blue eyes latch onto mine, I do just that. He lets me, and before long, his lean arms snake around my waist and pull me into him. I inhale his soapy scent, and allow his arms to be a comfort to me just as much as I hope mine are to him. We both need healing. We both need love. We both want to be wanted.

****

The rest of the weekend is a blur. Mom is a mess, not to mention drowning in funeral details, as well as wrapping up police reports with Officer Ray and Officer Childs. If Trip had survived, he would face assault and battery and reckless driving charges. According to the report, Tim Evans was driving on the interstate when Trip was merging on. Tim maintained his speed, which prohibited Trip from being able to merge onto the highway.

Trip sped up and used the shoulder to force his way over, directly in front of Tim. He faked braked several times, then swung into the middle lane, and attempted to side-swipe Tim. He rolled his window down and shouted vulgar obscenities. At this point, he lost control of his car and crashed into Tim, careening them both off the road and into the guardrails. Tim survived. Trip didn't.

Dr. Yassin has spent most of the weekend with Mom. Her anger long forgotten, she's been leaning on him since the moment he laid his head in her lap at the hospital. Isn't funny how tragedy brings people together? I haven't cried in days, and I hate myself for it.

Sure, Trip and I were never on friendly terms, but we grew up in the same house. I should feel *something*. Well, I take that back. I do feel something. My heart aches for Mom. The world keeps taking from her and I'm not sure why. She's the kindest, most generous person I've ever met. Why is God being so cruel to her?

"You don't have to go, you know?" Mom says to me. She's hovering over a steaming cup of coffee. Her eyes are puffy and red, like she's having a bad allergic reaction to something.

"I know," I tell her gently. "But I want to go. School will be a good distraction." That's not entirely true. Mom thinks I need a distraction from my grief, but what I need distraction from is *her* grief. Seeing her like this breaks my heart into pieces and knowing there's nothing I can do to fix it, pounds those bits into powdery dust.

Mom gives me an understanding nod. I hate the way her hand trembles on the handle of her mug. And how frail she looks. Have her cheekbones always protruded out like that? I scrutinize her further, noticing for the first time how unkempt her hair looks. Its usual shine and softness gone. Replaced with unwashed tangles. Her pretty face is dulled by frown lines and downcast eyes. In a matter of days, Mom looks to have aged an entire decade.

I vow to make dinner tonight and see that she showers and combs her hair. I'll brush it for her if I have to.

"Is Dr. Yassin coming over today?"

Again she nods, as if it hurts too much to speak.

"Good. He's good company for you." I kiss her on the temple. "I'll see you later."

****

School feels oddly surreal today. I don't even remember getting dressed this morning. By the look of me, I didn't put a lick of thought into it. Wrinkled jeans lifted out of the hamper and my faithful Reedmont hoodie. I'm here, walking among the school walls, but my mind is elsewhere. It's on Mom and Trip.

What an idiot. I wish I could say I'm surprised his temper killed him, but I'm not. His rage always boiled over, even over the smallest things. It was only a matter of time before someone got hurt. Because of his anger, he managed to not only injure an innocent stranger, but he thoroughly tore Mom's heart out. And for that, I hate him.

Jenna and Carlos already know what happened. I called them both later that night. Jenna was comforting, and Carlos was uncharacteristically quiet. I find them both in the cafeteria. Jenna's drowning her scrambled eggs in ketchup and Carlos is shaking up his carton of chocolate milk. He stops mid-motion when he sees me.

"Hey," I greet them, trying to act normal.

"Hi," Jenna says, scooting over to give me room. I slip in beside her and lay my head on her shoulder. "You okay?"

"Yeah," I sigh. "It's Mom I worry about. She's taking this so hard."

Jenna trails her fingers through my hair. The strokes calming and reassuring. "She's stronger than she looks, Pen. She'll get through it. Just be patient with her."

"Yeah," Carlos adds, opening his milk and taking a swallow. "She's the lone Jackson now. He wipes away his milk mustache with the back of his hand.

I straighten and snag Jenna's blueberry muffin off her plate. I cram it in my mouth, considering his words. The lone Jackson. He's right. Mom still has me, but I'm a Reza.

Chewing, I think back to how happy Mom was the

day of the signing. Back when she thought I was officially changing my name. The muffin turns dry in my mouth when I recall how hurt she looked when I decided not to. I hand Jenna the muffin, unable to eat anymore.

"When is the funeral?" Jenna asks me, her face solemn.

"Wednesday." I stare down at the table. "After school."

Jenna wraps an arm around me. "I'll be there."

I give her a tight-lipped smile cause that's all I can muster.

****

School wasn't as much of a distraction as I hoped. Mrs. Johnson, bless her heart, made a fuss about me being at school rather than at home grieving. After I politely declined an early sign-out, she doted on me throughout the entire class. I know she meant well, but it was a constant reminder of Trip. Matt ignored me in class, and bless him for that. I am in no mood to deal with him.

Even biology wasn't an escape. We started studying genetics and heredity, so I started dissecting Trip's DNA, piecing together Mom and Wesley's genes to see how he was Wesley's son in every way save for his deep brown eyes that were all Mom.

Lunch was an awkward conversation of tests, homework, and Rainey's recent date with Emily, the editor of our school paper. My interest waned, overshadowed by thoughts of Mom and Trip, but from the bits and pieces I heard, the date went well, and they have already agreed to a second one. The tone of the table talk was hushed, like the delicate whisperings around a baking soufflé. Only I'm the soufflé.

Why am I thinking about soufflé? I stare down at my cheese crackers, suddenly craving Ragamuffins. They mean well, but I'm annoyed by the way my friends act as though any moment I'm going to cave in. No matter how many times I say I'm fine. I'm okay, really. Trip's death embolden me. It made me realize that life is fragile and fleeting. There's no time to waffle between decisions. You either do or you don't. And it's time that I finally decide. I either become Penelope Jackson. Or I don't.

****

It's Tuesday, March 28th, Chase's seventeenth birthday. I made sure I got to the library before Chase today. I wanted to be there early to set up his birthday surprise. I sprinkle sparkly silver and garnet confetti on the table and arrange his wrapped presents artfully in the center. Last night, I baked a dozen chocolate chip cookies. They came out gooey and perfect. I packed them in pretty cellophane and tied it off with a red bow. I lay out two polka-dot party hats and wait, twirling my hair anxiously.

When I see him walk through the doors, my heart catapults into my throat. *God, he's adorable.* His jeans ride low on his hips, his svelte frame willowy like a reed. He looks great in his beat-up army jacket. When he sees the table, he laughs, shaking his head as he strolls toward me.

"What's this?"

"Happy birthday!" I don a party hat, snapping the strap under my chin with a flinch. He laughs again, and I hand him his. He takes one quick, sweeping look around the library, then slips it on. His long bangs get swept back by the elastic strap. He looks different without his hair brushing his eyes. More grown up. He pulls up a seat. I lean over to pinch his cheeks. "You're so cute! I could just dip you sprinkles and eat you with ice cream!"

A kid with a head full of cowlicks walks past the table. He gapes at us as though I've been belting out Happy Birthday at the top of my lungs.

Chase fusses with the strap of his party hat. "This thing is choking me."

"Me too." We drop our hats onto the table. "I made you cookies." I hand him the bag.

"Can I eat one now?"

"Go for it." I love to see him happy. A drastic contrast to the brooding boy I met in group so long ago.

He grins and yanks off the bow. The cellophane crinkles so loudly he gets shushed by a librarian.

"Here, this should be quieter." I slide the presents to him.

Resigned, he says, "You didn't have to get me anything."

I shove the presents closer. "Shut up and open them."

He carefully peels apart the tape and slips the box out of the wrapping paper quietly, keeping a watchful eye on the librarian. When he opens it, he lifts the shirt high into the air, admiring it. "Awesome! A Teleporter shirt!"

I lean back in my chair and unbutton my cardigan. "There's more."

His eyebrows disappear into his bangs. "Oh, really?" He rubs his hands together hungrily. "Well, as the saying goes: 'The Teleporter is…quick as a flash!' " He exaggerates the word "flash" wriggling his eyebrows at me.

I roll my eyes and flip open my cardigan. Chase's goofy expression changes in an instant. His face brightens, and he lets out a bark of a laugh. The librarian glares at us. I slap my hands over his mouth, shushing him. "You're going to get us kicked out." He mumbles something under my palms, but I ignore it. "Do you like it?"

He nods. I take my hands from his mouth. He's grinning wildly. "Sorry, but you were the one who decided to throw a party in the library, remember?" He gently pushes me back in my seat, eyes on my chest. "Chuck West." There's the Chase chuckle I love so much. "That is...so awesome." He shakes out his Teleporter shirt. "We make the perfect pair, you and me."

My cheeks flare with heat. *Will they ever stop doing that?* I secretly hope not. "One more to go." I nudge the other gift toward him, and again he opens it as quietly as possible. His eyes brush across the book cover, then up to me.

"What's this?"

"Think of it as a comic book. Without the pictures, and with more words."

After I explain how *Journey of the Center of the Earth* is considered the birth of Science Fiction, he seems touched by the gift.

"I'll start it tonight."

"You promise?"

He crosses his heart with his finger. "Promise."

Can I get him to promise to stay mine forever?

Chapter 49

Why are funerals so boring? No one wants to be there in the first place, so why torture them more by making them unbearably dull? I don't want a funeral. I want my friends to go camping. Slip my urn into their backpack and go on a hike, reminiscing about me the whole way. I want them to pitch tents, tell ghost stories around a fire, and roast gooey s'mores.

Under the blanket of stars, they'll pour out a hot chocolate for me, and if I planned it just right, they'll forget to miss me. They'll have so much fun that they'll never shed a single tear. It won't be like this. I look over my shoulder at the room behind me. The funeral home provides a pretty stale room for services.

Wall-to-wall panels of deep navy velvet fabric make for a dreary setting, and it's yet another reason I refuse to have a traditional funeral. The gaudy floor lamps and golden wall sconces make me want to gag, but at least they cast a gentle glow to the room.

People are slowly filing into the room, many of whom I don't know. With their black clothes and long faces, they look solemn as tombstones they shuffle in and take their seats. Mr. Douglas and his wife walk into the room. He's wearing a cheap black suit. A slash of red from his tie the only color on him, aside from his pink face. He ushers his wife, a small woman with a shock of bottle blonde curls, to a seat. He doesn't see me, thank

God, but it won't be long until he does. I'm not hard to miss sitting next to Mom.

She's working through her second box of tissues, openly crying. Dr. Yassin has his arm wrapped around her protectively, his fingers clamped on her shoulder like he needs her support as much as she needs his. I invited Chase, but I doubt he'll show.

I won't blame him if he doesn't. He has enough of his own problems going on at home. His mother nearly died of alcohol poisoning. I'm sure the last place he wants to be is a funeral.

Mom suddenly stands. "I need to look at his face. One more time."

Dr. Yassin gets to his feet. "I'll go with you." He glances at me, but I shake my head, not wanting to go. I watch them edge themselves toward the shiny casket. Mom's shoulders tremble and she hangs her head.

Dr. Yassin looks on stoically, and I'm suddenly grateful to him. His presence has been good for Mom— a rock whom she can depend on. Me, on the other hand, have been nothing short of a ghost. A quiet being moving through the halls, almost undetected save for the occasional creaking floor underfoot, or slamming of a door when I need to be alone.

Mom touches Trip's face. I watch her mourn from afar, my heart ceasing within my chest when there's a gentle pressure on my shoulder. I turn to find Jenna and Carlos. I'm disappointed it's not Chase, but I smile anyway. Jenna's wearing an olive-green shirtdress, which I'm betting belongs to her mom and my ankle boots she borrowed three months ago and never returned.

"Nice shoes," I say, standing to give her a hug.

"Thanks. Got them from a chic boutique called

Reza's."

A chuckle builds within me, but I swallow it.

"How you holding up?" Jenna asks.

I put both hands on her shoulders, and assure her firmly, "I'm fine." I look directly at Carlos. "Really."

Carlos offers me a sympathetic smile. "Would you tell us if you weren't?"

I blow out a frustrated sigh. "Yes."

A woman in simple clothes, to match her equally simple face, emerges from a side door and settles herself at the organ. She shifts through some sheet music and prepares herself to play. Heavy, forlorn notes fill the air.

Jenna takes Carlos by the hand, and they shuffle to the row behind me, and take a seat.

Jenna leans forward in her chair and whispers, "This place gives me the creeps." Carlos nods in agreement, looking uncomfortable in his starched collared shirt and black slacks.

The song slowly tapers off, and a tense hush envelopes the room. The service is about to begin.

I turn my back on Jenna and Carlos. Dr. Yassin gently pries Mom from Trip's casket. She collapses into his arms, and he enfolds her in a fierce embrace. She buries her face into his chest, weeping and grieving openly.

With superhero-like abilities, my senses tingle. *He's here.* I glimpse behind me. My senses are spot-on. Chase is gliding through the room. My breath catches at the sight of him. *He came. He actually came.* Our eyes meet.

I shouldn't notice how adorable he looks, but I do. He obviously took care in how he dressed, opting to forgo his usual t-shirt for a sophisticated polka dot button-up shirt. His dark denim jeans look brand new.

Even his hair is meticulously combed and gelled.

I find myself relieved to see he's wearing his graffiti-filled sneakers. Those shoes are Chase. Without them, I'm not sure I'd recognize him. When he comes closer, I notice the polka dots on his shirt are actually tiny tigers. I nearly laugh. Never mind, I'd definitely recognize him.

He sits beside me, and I'm transported to that day in group when I finally shared my story. How rigid he became when I mentioned Matt. How embarrassed I was finally admitting out loud that I enabled Matt by stealing that prescription pad. The freeing relief that came when I was through. No matter how humiliated I felt.

Dr. Yassin settles himself and Mom into the chairs at my left. Mom slumps into him, whimpering like a lost puppy. Heavy tears well in my eyes. Jenna leaps up and wraps Mom in a hug from behind. Dr. Yassin shoots me a floundering look. It's tearing him apart to see Mom like this.

A clergyman approaches the podium, and the room settles into silence, save for Mom's sobs and moans.

The service is much like any other. The dearly departed is in a better place, yada yada yada. A few scriptures. Don't mourn the dead, but celebrate their life, blah blah blah. My mind wanders to my own funeral again. Who will I be then? Will everyone be mourning Penelope Reza or Penelope Jackson? I close my eyes to better envision it, hoping whatever I see in my mind's eye will help me decide what to do. Once and for all.

"Are you sleeping?" Chase whispers close to my ear. My eyes snap open to find him gazing down at me. Those blue eyes are unwavering and unrelenting.

"No," I murmur. "Just thinking."

Chase slides his hand over and threads his fingers through mine. He gives me a little squeeze and I melt into the touch. Who knew the sullen boy from group could bring me so much comfort? That just his nearness could center me, steady me, upend me, and overwhelm me all at once. I never felt this way with Matt.

The service finally ends. Several people come over to Mom and me, offering condolences before they leave, but I barely register their empty words. From the way the room clears, it looks as though the only people attending Trip's burial are Dr. Yassin, Mom, Mr. Douglas, his tiny wife, me, Jenna, Carlos…and Chase.

The drive to the cemetery is quiet, with everyone lost in their thoughts or grief. I keep my gaze set outside the window, watching the world go by as we drive through town. It is odd the way the traffic parted for the funeral home's sleek, black sedan.

The sun shines like a coin in the sky, but the air is winter's frozen breath across the cemetery lawn. I pull my scarf to my chin with a shiver. Chase stands beside me, offering solidarity and support. He's trying to stay stoic, but I can tell he's uncomfortable by the way the muscles in his jaw tick as he grinds his teeth.

His eyes sweep across the ground as we walk in silence to the gravesite. Rows and rows of headstones fill the manicured lawn. Flowers of every shade and every variety offer a touch of spring to the gloomy landscape. I ignore that most are fake, opting to appreciate the tiny bursts of color among the grey-scape around us.

Someone from the funeral home has already been here. The flower arrangements from Trip's service are at the site, and it's an odd clash of color against the red-clay dirt of the opened hole in the earth. My throat dries at the sight of it.

Mr. Douglas and his wife come by to offer their sympathy.

"I'm terribly sorry for your loss, dear," Mrs. Douglas says, clutching her leather purse to her chest. She looks up at Mr. Douglas, unsure on what else to offer. *Yawn.* Typical funeral talk. Condolences. Pitiful looks. Empty words. I hate it all.

Mr. Douglas's brows furrow tight over his eyes. His jowly face pinches as if he's weighing the right words to say. He scrubs at his chin. *Just say it already*, I think to myself. Looking me dead in the eye, he says, "The good Lord is trying to tell you something."

I blink at him. "Excuse me?"

Mr. Douglas shifts on his feet. "The Jackson name. Your mother shouldn't be the only one to have it."

My temper flares. "You think God killed Trip, so I'd change my name?"

Mrs. Douglas lays a hand on her husband to either silently offer her support or quietly warn him. I'm not sure which.

"Don't be selfish, Penelope. Your mom needs a family. Why begrudge her one when it's as simple as a little ink on paper?"

Through clenched teeth, I say, "We can be a family without it."

He grunts. "You know it ain't the same. Besides, with the way the world is right now, you'd be doing yourself a favor by ridding yourself of the name." His lip curls. "Reza." He says it as though it leaves a bitter taste on his tongue.

I see red. Truly. I've read that expression a million times in books, but I never thought it was true, until now.

My hand shakes with the urge to slap him.

He glowers at me sourly. "You want to be stopped by the TSA every single time you step foot in an airport, then by all means, keep the name."

"Hey," Chase barks. "That's enough."

Everyone turns to stare at us.

Mr. Douglas smiles thinly, and lays a hand on his wife's back. "Let's go give our regards to Miranda, shall we?" They walk away, but as they do, Mr. Douglas shoots me a glare from over his shoulder. "Take my advice and bury Reza with Trip. You'll thank me later."

I fight the urge to flip him off. Frowning at the back of his retreating, balding head, his words come back to me. *You'd be doing yourself a favor by ridding yourself of the name Reza.*

I whirl to look at Chase. "Can you believe that guy?"

"Who is he?" Chase's eyes are nothing short of a storm.

"My mom's lawyer. He was helping me legally change my last name to Jackson."

"What?"

I wave it off. "That was before."

"You were going to change your name?"

"Well, I mean, I *am* adopted. I thought I wanted to share their last name. You know, to fit in. To be a family."

Jenna and Carlos come up, their eyes pinging from me, to Chase, to Mr. Douglas. "What just happened?"

"Nothing," I assure them. I cross my arms, trying to hide my trembling. Jenna eyes me suspiciously. She's ready to call bullshit, but the clergyman is making his way to our small gathering. His shoes pad softly over the grass, his long black robe fluttering in the gentle wind.

He greets us again, and then leads us in a short prayer as Trip's casket is lowered into the hard, North Carolina dirt.

Dr. Yassin holds tight to Mom's waist. I step closer to them, slipping my hand into Mom's. She clamps her fingers desperately around mine, and I help to keep her on her feet. The coffin lowers deeper and deeper and then disappears entirely. It's then that it finally sinks in, like Trip's body into the earth, that there is one less Jackson in the world.

Chapter 50

It's been three weeks since Trip's funeral, and things are slowly returning to normal. Well, for me anyway. Mom is still struggling with Trip's loss, and I suspect she always will. He was her only pure-blood kid. That's a bond she and I will never have, and it stings.

Mom finally exhausted her FMLA leave, so she trudged back to work today. Lately, all her motions seemed to be robotic. When Wesley died, Mom didn't have time to grieve. Trip and I were just kids when it happened, so she was too busy to mourn properly.

Now, I give her the space she needs. Keeping my distance when I sense she needs it, and wrapping my arms around her in quiet solidarity when I think she needs a hug. Dr. Yassin has been an unyielding force behind her, providing quiet strength and support.

Tonight he's taking her out to dinner, just the two of them. Mom needs some distraction right about now, and hopefully, a ten-hour workday and a dinner date will do it.

Chase asked me to meet him at the library after school today for some tutoring. I think back to the first day I met him there, finding him sitting in the children's section, reading a comic book. It seems like an eternity ago. When I walk in, he's not at any of the tables, so I figure he's sitting on the floor in some aisle somewhere.

I glance down several rows—all empty—so I keep

walking. A few librarians lurk about, but for the most part, the research section is empty as usual. Chase is sprawled on the floor with a stack of books beside him. He senses me and looks up. Our eyes meet and our smiles widen in tandem.

"What are you reading?" I ask, sitting down cross-legged beside him.

"Comic book history." He shows me an open book. "And a little who's who in the DU."

"Of course," I say. "What else?"

He flashes a boyish smile and looks back down at the book in his hand. "I read *Journey to the Center of the Earth*." He mutters it so nonchalantly, I almost don't register it.

My heart swells. "You did?" My cheeks actually hurt from grinning so hard.

"Yeah, I actually did." His eyes swing to mine. "But don't go getting any crazy ideas. I'm not giving up my comics for classics." He winks. "Oh, speaking of classics. Close your eyes."

I watch him suspiciously. "Why?"

"Just do it."

I do, hesitantly.

"Hold out your hands."

I do as I'm told. *What is he up to?*

There's some rustling, and then something weighted is laid on my open palms. It's a book, that much I can tell.

"Okay. You can open your eyes."

My breath hitches. I can't believe it. Jonathan Preston's *Stillborn*. Tears build, blurring everything, then run down my cheeks with abandon.

"Open it," Chase encourages, shifting closer. Our

legs are touching. Normally that would be distracting, but I'm dumbstruck at the moment. He lifts the cover and points to the copyright page. My heart lays one-two punches in rapid fire succession to my chest. I inhale a sharp, surprised breath.

"First edition," he whispers.

Tears drip from my chin, splashing onto the page. Chase runs his knuckles along my jaw. "Don't do that. You'll smudge the ink."

I hug the book to my chest. "Chase. I don't know what to say."

"Don't say anything. Just…be happy. You are happy, right?" His eyes search my face.

"Totally." I lean forward and press my lips to his. A librarian passes by and clears her throat sharply. We break apart, blushing.

"I wanted to give you back what Matt took from you."

My eyes drop to the book. "You've given me back so much already. My trust in people. My confidence. My laughter. My heart." I put my hand on his knee. The touch is igniting, and it emboldens me. Without hesitation—or a second thought—the words, "I think I love you, Chase," tumble out of my mouth and into the air between us. They hover there, like thought bubbles in a comic strip.

Chase's blue eyes grow wide.

A flare of panic washes over me. "Is that okay?"

A hint of laughter escapes him. "Better than okay. I don't think I love you, Penelope. I *know* I do."

My insides warm and I can't hold back a smile.

"Before you, my best moments only came while I slept." He tucks a curl behind my ear. "Now, I dream with my eyes open."

I literally feel my heart smiling, too. *A quote from A Journey to the Center of the Earth.* "Quoting classics now?"

"A girl I know digs it." He knocks his shoulder into mine. "She's kind of a book nerd."

I knock his shoulder with a mock punch before leaning in close. "Where you go, I go. Forever." A quote from Felix Yeager's long-time love interest, Lilly Lyle.

Taken aback, Chase blinks his sapphire eyes at me before saying, "Oh, yeah. There's no doubt. I love you."

We sneak a quick kiss before the librarian can catch us, then fall back into the bliss of sitting side-by-side amongst a floor of comic books and classics.

Chapter 51

Dr. Yassin's dinner date was just what the, ahem, doctor ordered. Mom is in better spirits this morning. The blue-black circles under her eyes are there, but faded, and for the first time in weeks, she isn't clutching a tissue.

I'm not naïve enough to believe that she's done grieving. She'll never stop grieving Trip. Or Wesley. But maybe she will someday move on. Maybe someday she will finally be happy. Truly happy. Not content, like I believe she was in her marriage to Wesley, but genuinely happy. Like she deserves to be.

From what I can tell, Dr. Yassin makes her happy. He loves her differently than Wesley did. Wesley loved her like he owned her. Like she was a pretty piece of artwork to show off and admire.

Dr. Yassin loves her like she's the artist that made that pretty piece of artwork. Like she paints the sky and arranges the stars by hand. Like she deserves to be heard, cherished, and respected.

Mom's sitting at the kitchen table, her fingers wrapped around a mug of coffee. The steam reaches for her face as she lifts it to her lips. I pour some cereal into a bowl and sit down. Mom glances at me, surprised I'm taking the time to eat at home rather than grabbing my usual granola bar and heading out the door. Her brow arches.

"Cereal?"

I shrug. "Got some extra time this morning."

She sets her mug down and stares into it.

"Mom," I start, hesitating. "Can I ask you something?"

Her brows knit with concern. "Of course."

"Are you upset I didn't sign the paperwork?"

She looks up from her coffee, considering her words for a moment.

"No," she says softly. "Because I knew, deep down, you weren't ready to take that step. Like always, you were trying to make me happy." She gets up and rounds the table, her slippers scuffing softly on the tile. She presses her lips to my forehead. "You're a great daughter, Penelope. With or without the Jackson name."

I push back the chair with a scrape, wrap my arms around her, and hug her tight. "Thanks, Mom. I love you."

"I love you too, Honey."

****

I draw back the bow and aim for the bullseye. The summer sun is high in sky as I point the arrowhead over the bullseye. Chase's hands find my hips, and for a moment I'm distracted by his touch. I center myself, holding my breath before I let the arrow fly. It hits home, sinking into the target with a *thunk.*

"Great shot," he exclaims from behind me.

"No thanks to you," I say teasingly, giving him a playful shove.

He spreads his hands out. "What? I was just checking your form!"

"Yeah right!" I counter with a giggle.

He swoops me into an embrace. "Your form is

perfect, by the way." He plants a kiss under my earlobe.

The back door slides open, and Sam and Grace come out. It's the perfect day for a cookout. The cloudless sky seems endless above us, and the grass underfoot is lush and sprawling. Though I prefer my fall wardrobe over my summer one, I feel flirty in my seersucker romper.

Grace has a plate full of hamburger patties. Sam goes to the grill and fires it up. Grace is wearing a cute tank top and fraying jean shorts. She's been sober for nearly five months. Her figure is fuller these days, a body changed by a better diet and exercise.

She's kept her word to detox her body of alcohol, and faithfully attends weekly therapy sessions and Alcoholics Anonymous meetings. The tone of the entire family has changed. Chase is carefree, like a teenager should be. Sam's face doesn't hold the tension like it used to. It's like time reversed for him, softening his features, and adding a newfound sparkle to his eyes.

Grace sets the plate down. "Hi, Penelope. Do you work today?" I got a part-time job as a library page for the summer. I absolutely love it. The library has become a special place for me. It cultivated my and Chase's relationship. From the group therapy session where we met, to the children's section where I tutored him, to the research aisles where we basically fell in love.

I squirm out of Chase's arms. "No, ma'am."

"Good. Then you can join us for burgers."

"That sounds great." The patties sizzle as Sam flips them. They smell delicious, filling the air with that good old cookout scent that everyone knows. The one that makes you jealous if you're not invited.

Grace smiles. "I'm going to get us all lemonade." She goes back inside, shutting the sliding glass door behind her.

"She's a completely different person," Chase states. I nod in agreement. I think of all the changes—no, not changes per se, but progression—everyone in my life has made in the past year.

Mom found her strength. Matt hit rock bottom and is slowly clawing his way out through recovery. Chase has gone from a surly, forgotten boy to a young man with an infectious laugh who is now the most important person in my life.

"There's something I want to do," I say to Chase, pulling out my phone.

"Invite Jenna and Carlos over?"

"No." I scroll through my list of contacts. Chase looks over at the screen.

"I'm going to settle something, once and for all." I curl a strand of hair around my finger.

Lisa answers on the third ring. "Good afternoon, Douglas Law Firm."

"Hi, Lisa. It's Penelope Reza, Miranda's daughter."

"Oh, right. Hello again, Penelope. Shall I tell Mr. Douglas you're ready to sign?"

My eyes flutter close. "No. I…I've decided not to sign. He can discard the paperwork." I chew my lip.

I can tell Lisa is taking notes. "I see. Would you like him to file them away should you change your mind?"

"No. I won't be changing my mind." I look over at Chase. "Or my name." This feels right. I know within my heart I am making the right decision. I'll never be a Jackson, not legally anyway, but I'll be one by proxy in all the ways that count. Miranda loves me like a pure-blood daughter, and that's enough for me. I hang up the phone and Chase kisses my temple. "I love you,

Penelope Reza." With a smile on my lips, I think, *I love her, too.*

A word about the author…

I work full-time as a zoo curator, so when I'm not running a zoo, I'm trying to tame the one I live in! I have two kids, and a husband who sometimes acts their age.

I can usually be found jamming to Elvis Presley tunes, or diligently chipping away at my never-ending 'to be read' pile.

I tend to gravitate toward anything paranormal. I love creatures who fly and characters who sprout fur or fangs. Sprinkle some romance and magic into the mix, and I'm a happy girl!

Thank you for purchasing
this publication of The Wild Rose Press, Inc.

For questions or more information
contact us at
info@thewildrosepress.com.

The Wild Rose Press, Inc.
www.thewildrosepress.com